D. H Stoever

The life of Sir Charles Linnæus

D. H Stoever

The life of Sir Charles Linnæus

ISBN/EAN: 9783742887153

Manufactured in Europe, USA, Canada, Australia, Japa

Cover: Foto ©Raphael Reischuk / pixelio.de

Manufactured and distributed by brebook publishing software
(www.brebook.com)

D. H Stoever

The life of Sir Charles Linnæus

THE LIFE

OF

SIR CHARLES LINNÆUS,

KNIGHT OF THE SWEDISH ORDER OF THE POLAR STAR, &c. &c.

TO WHICH IS ADDED,

A COPIOUS LIST OF HIS WORKS, AND A BIOGRAPHICAL SKETCH
OF THE LIFE OF HIS SON:

BY

D. H. STOEVER, PH. D.

TRANSLATED FROM THE ORIGINAL GERMAN

BY JOSEPH TRAPP, A. M.

LONDON:

Printed by C. Mobson, Bell-Yard,

FOR B. AND J. WHITE, FLEET-STREET.

1794.

TO

THE LINNEAN SOCIETY OF LONDON,

THIS

TRANSLATION

OF THE

BIOGRAPHY OF LINNÆUS

IS

MOST RESPECTFULLY DEDICATED,

BY

THEIR MOST HUMBLE,

MOST SINCERELY

DEVOTED SERVANT,

JOSEPH TRAPP.

TO THE PUBLIC.

THE great approbation which Dr. STOEVER'S Biography of LINNÆUS has met with in *Sweden*, and in almost every country of *Europe*, became my motive for undertaking this Translation. The original has been read on the Continent with an avidity bordering upon enthusiasm. Every impartial and well-informed person will readily allow, that no complete LIFE of LINNÆUS, except the present, has ever yet made it's appearance. As the fruit of the most indefatigable literary diligence, this work can also boast the distinction of containing a great number of novel and valuable facts and documents, communicated to the author by such persons as are surviving pupils,

pupils and friends of LINNÆUS, or otherwise eminent characters in the literary world.

Under these favourable circumstances I present
it to the Public, and shall be ever grateful and happy
if they deem it a performance worthy their enlightened taste and patronage.

It is generally a matter of regret, that into productions of such extent typographical errors and
inaccuracies will imperceptibly find their way ; but
I trust, that the indulgent liberality of those of my
readers, whose attention may be attracted by similar
imperfections in the present work, will kindly excuse
them wherever they occur.

THE TRANSLATOR.

PREFACE OF THE AUTHOR.

LINNÆUS, if we consider the extent of his scientific fame, and its influence over the empire of learning and knowledge, holds, doubtless, the first rank among the geniuses *Sweden* could ever boast of. He belongs to that small number of lumiries, who made a fresh epoch in the annals of literary greatness, raised their merit beyond the limits of their age, and rendered imperishable the splendor of their name. But as universal as the fame of LINNÆUS is acknowledged to be, as unknown are, upon the whole, the thorny and difficult paths on which he reached the pinnacle of his eminence. Needless would it be to mention to the learned any thing respecting that barrenness and biographical want, which the modern history of literature exhibits, with regard to him. How voluminous are not the writings on the learned of our age, whether great or little, and how small and disproportionate is the measure of every thing modern and essential relative to LINNÆUS! —Yet the life of this great man was superlatively rich in merits,

merits, abounding with singular and remarkable incidents, and most celebrated for wonderful vicissitudes and personal achievements.

Biographical essays and tracts on LINNÆUS, we certainly are not deficient in. The subjoined LIST contains a review of all those which I could procure knowledge of. A variety of authentic and valuable information has not yet been noticed by the literary world. Of this description are the accounts published at *Hamburgh*, those contained in the letters to Baron HALLER, &c. No collection of facts had ever been made, because no plan for a perfect and complete biography had till now been projected. The richness of those merely nominal biographical tracts, is therefore reduced to a small number of materials of real intrinsic value, consisting of fragments and sketches, the purport of which is a mere repetition, or a copy of two original portraits in miniature. These have, however, been so much mutilated and disfigured by false features and imperfect skill in foreign countries, that the original touches of the pencil of truth scarcely remain distinguishable. False statements are always the more prejudicial to genuine fact, if time has so strongly stamped them with credit, that they ultimately convert history into fiction.

But in this work a favourable circumstance intervenes— the surviving friends, pupils and evidences of LINNÆUS. I
had

had the good fortune to collect many valuable facts, which would, in all probability, have otherwise been totally los' I feel also great pleasure to premise here, that even in *Sweden* my design has given birth to an enterprise, which will reflect fresh honour on the memory of LINNÆUS.

That a detailed portraiture of that great luminary was no trifling labour, needs, from what has already been alledged, neither mention nor proof. As a friend to the history of lite-rature, as an admirer of literary merit which it is destined to record, I took upon me to draw this picture, with the humble, modest wish, that a better one may start *. The resources which I used in the performance of this arduous task, were documents in different languages, partly printed, partly in ma-nuscript. I collated and profited by them with critical keen-ness, and chose Truth to be my guide. Through many tortu-rous windings was I obliged to seek her; yet I found my industry truly rewarded. Some generous men, friends of truth, and privy to many minute circumstances relative to LINNÆUS, offered me with pleasure an helping hand, for which I thus publicly acknowledge my warmest and most heartfelt gratitude. I farther confidently declare, that the Public, in whose esteem they have long held a distinguished rank, will think themselves more obliged by their combined

---

* *Salvo meliori.*

assistance

assistance than by my own feeble exertions. In justice to them, I find it incumbent on me to name here the following conspicuous perfons:

The Chevalier THUNBERG, of *Upsal,* successor of LINNÆUS in his academical dignity.

Doftor A. O. KNOES, of the same University, who communicated to me the rare and valuable apology of LINNÆUS, and his letter to the Academy of Sciences at *Paris.*

JAMES EDWARD SMITH, M. D. and F. R. S. proprietor of the LINNEAN Colleftions, and President of the LINNEAN Society of *London.*

CHARLES NIEBUHR, Counsellor Justiciary of his Danish Majesty, and travelling companion of the celebrated FORSKAL.

P. D. GIESEKE, Doftor and Professor at *Hamburgh.*

FRANCIS EHRHART, Botanist, at *Herrenhausen,* near *Hanover.*

NEMNICH, L.L. D. of *Hamburgh,* Editor of the Catholicon or the Encyclopedic Diftionary in all the European languages, who has communicated to me several fafts in the Spanish and Portuguese tongues.

Doftor E. C. SCHULTZ, of the same place.

Doftor S. ... R at *H—.*

To these are to be added two friends at *Stockholm,* and two eminent German literati, who would not leave to gratitude the

2   satisfaftion

satisfaction of giving them this public testimony of their kind favours.

In some of the first sections, on the journey through *Dale-carlia*, &c. I must beg the reader to compare the annexed Supplements and Notes. Two of them I received at so late a period as to have found it impossible to insert them with my own text. Upon the whole, their authenticity entitled them to a plain and literal communication. In other respects, it would be an important and meritorious undertaking for any naturalist to bestow farther labours on the materials which contain a full explanation of the hypotheses of LINNÆUS, on the subsequent elucidations which either refuted or confirmed them, on the whole and separate parts of his reform, and the progress made after him. The result of such an undertaking would offer an interesting view and comprehensive account of the formation and improvement of natural science since the epoch of our great luminary.

With regard the annexed list of the writings of LINNÆUS, I have neither spared labour nor trouble to render it it as complete and as satisfactory as possible. In point of the academical treatises, I have mentioned those only which have received translations or commentaries. The motto beneath the portrait of LINNÆUS, which has been drawn from a most striking impression in plaster of *Paris*, will not, it is humbly presumed, offend the religious opinions of any reader. It originates with

a man

a man who has lived many years in the closest ties of intimacy
with the deceased, who combines with the rarest qualities of
the heart, an universal scientific renown.

I hope the addition of the following observations will not be
deemed extraneous to my subject.

It is well known, that the works of LINNÆUS are characterized with his religious sentiments. Nevertheless, they had
the misfortune of being considered at *Rome* as heretical and
materialistic productions. In 1758 they were inserted in the
catalogue of forbidden books. No one durst either print or
sell them, under pain of having every copy confiscated or publicly burnt; this proceeding was opposed by a fine contrast
during the reign of the excellent and truly enlightened GAN-
GANELLI, or Pope CLEMENT XIV. LINNÆUS himself mentions this occurrence in a letter to the Chevalier THUNBERG,
in the following words : " The Pope, who fifteen years ago
" ordered those of my works that should be imported into his
" his dominions to be burnt, has dismissed the professor of bo-
" tany who did not understand my system, and put another in
" his place, who is to give public lectures according to my
" method and theory *"

---

* Pafven, som för 15 ar sedan befalt, at, om mina böker dit komma, skulle de
brännas, har afsat Professor Botanices, some ej förstod min method, och tillsatt en
annor some skall läsa publice min method och theorie.—See *Collectio Epistolarum*
CAR. A LINNE, &c. edid. D. H. STOEVER, *Hamb.* 1792, octavo.

What

What Baron HALLER's opinion was of LINNÆUS, after their friendship had been cooled by the assertions made by the latter in his *Flora Suecica*, will appear from the following extract of a letter, never printed before, and written by HALLER from *Goettingen*, to his friend NILS ROSEN DE ROSENSTEIN, dean of the college of physicians at *Upsal*:

" The inclosed letter I beg you will deliver to LINNÆUS.
" Should he not return to more friendly sentiments, it may
" be the last I shall write to him. He has lately apolo-
" gized to me in a letter, but in such a manner, that I had
" rather been without his apology. I have, in many in-
" stances, shewn myself his friend, indulged his failings, con-
" tributed to his reputation ; but do not find that return for
" my kindness which I had a right to expect. I shall hereafter
" publish a *Prodromus Floræ Germanicæ*, in which I will treat
" LINNÆUS in such a manner as he shall then have merited on
" my account. The man is active I cannot deny, and a zea-
" lous lover of nature, for which I love him ; but his character
" has for me a something—I know not what to call it, of aspe-
" rity, fickleness and unevenness."

† LINNÆO nuper per litteras se purganti, sed ita, ut mallem, abstineret purgatione, has litteras trades, forte, nisi ad amiciorem sensum redibit, ultimas. Multum ipsi tribui, peperci erroribus, famam auxi: non invenio eum meæ comitatis fructum, quem sperare poteram.—Edam deinde Germanicæ Floræ Prodromum, in quo de LINNÆO ita agetur, ut interim de me merebitur. Laboriosus certe homo est et Naturæ cupidus, hinc mihi carus, sed cujus mores mecum nescio quid inæquabile habent et inconstans et asperum.—(Communicated from *Stockholm*).

1   The

The botanical gardens in *France, England, Spain*, &c. are all arranged according to the directions pointed out in the LIN-NÆAN method. The two keepers of that of *Madrid* have published after it the following work : *Curso elemental de Botanica, theorico y prattico, dispuesto para la ensenanza del Real Jardin Botanico de Madrid, de orden del Rey, nuestro senor, por e* DR. D. CASIMIRO GOMEZ DE ORTEGA *y* D. ADTONIO PALAU *y* VERDERA *Catedraticos primero y segundo del mismo Jardin.* Madrid, *en la imprenta Real,* 1785. *II. tom.* 8 *maj.* The *Termini Botanici* of Dr. GIESEKE, at *Hamburgh,* have likewise been used with advantage in the above work. A similar course of lectures, according to the LINNEAN method, has since appeared at *Parma*, and is the production of Dr. GIOVAN BAPT. CNATTERI.

The LINNEAN Society at *Leipsig* was founded by Professor LUDWIG on the 31st of January, 1789. The Literary Journal of that city, written in German by Professor ECK, and published in 1792, gives farther particulars respecting the constitutions of that society.

LIST

[xv]

A

L I S T

OF

BIOGRAPHICAL WRITINGS ON LINNÆUS.

———◆———

I.

HAMBURGISCHE Berichten von gelehrten Sachen, or the Hamburgh Literary Miscellany, *8vo. published by* Dr. J. P. KOEHL. *The three first years of this periodical work, from* 1732 *to* 1735, *contain also the first biographical accounts of* LINNÆUS, *whose authenticity is the greater as they came from himself. These accounts are communicated at large in the supplements, with a few relevant observations.*

II.

Orbis Eruditi Judicium de CAROLI LINNÆI, M. D. Scriptis; *or the Opinion of the Learned World on the works of* CHARLES LINNÆUS, M. D. Upsal, 1741, *only one sheet in small* 8vo.. *This as the rarest among all the biographical writings on* LINNÆUS, *deserves to be mentioned here, since it contains not only the panegyrics, but also the principal biographical particulars of his life..*

III. FRE-

III.

FREDERICK BOERNER's *account of the lives and writings of the celebrated German and Foreign Naturalists; in German.* Wolfenbuttel, 1749, 8vo. *part* 1st. *from page eigty-five to ninety eight.*

IV.

English Originals *in prose and verse, collected by* J. L. SCHULTZE. Halle, 1760 *and* 1766, 8vo.—*contains a short biographical essay.*

V.

MOEHSEN's *description of a collection of Medals at* Berlin, *mostly consisting of those which have been struck to honour the memory of celebrated Physicians; German.* Berlin, 1 *vol.* 1773.

VI.

Epistolæ ab eruditis Viris, ad ALB. HALLERUM Scriptæ, *or, Letters from the Learned to* BARON ALBERT HALLER. *Berlin,* 1773 *to* 1775, *six vols. large* 8vo. *The three first contain the Letters of* LINNÆUS, *from* 1737 *to* 1749, *making altogether twenty-five in number. These biographical literary articles called Letters, which* LINNÆUS *probably never expected would be made public, are truly valuable for the air of confidence with which they seem to have been communicated, and for their authenticity.*

VII.

Amminelse Tal öfver Hr. Arch. och Riddar CARL. VON LINNÉ, &c. *by* ABRAHAM BÄCK; *or Commemorative Speech on Sir* CHARLES LINNÆUS, *delivered in presence of the late King of Sweden, in the Academy of Sciences of Stockholm, on the* 5th *of December,* 1778, *by the Chevalier* ABRAHAM BÄCK, *Dean of the Royal College of Physicians: published*

at

at Stockholm *and* Upsal, *in the year* 1779, *in* 12*mo. one hundred and fifty-eight pages. An excellent though little performance, by the Chevalier* BÄCK, *who was one of the oldest and most intimate friends of* LINNÆUS.

VIII.

J. A. MURRAY's Pra&ical Medical Library, 1780, *vol.* iii. *in small* 8*vo.* German—*contains from page one hundred and fifty-eight, to six hundred and sixty-five, a short account of the death of* LINNÆUS, *and several tributes paid to his memory at* Stockholm and Paris. *The Author who is since dead, had it in his power to have said much more of his former Professor.*

IX.

More minute particulars of the Life of Sir CHARLES LINNÆUS, *by* JOHN CHRISTIAN FABRICIUS, *Professor at* Kiel, *in the German Museum;* Leipsic, 1780.—German; *No.* 5, *from page four hundred and thirty-one to four hundred and forty-one; and No.* 7, *from page thirty-nine to forty eight. These are the only particulars published in* Germany, *by a disciple of* LINNÆUS. *This biographical contour is short but valuable on account of the anecdotes annexed to it.*

X.

Eloge de M. de LINNÉ, par M. Le Marquis de Condorcet, * *in his History of the Academy of Sciences of* Paris, 1778, *avec les Memoires de Mathematique, et de Physique pour la même année, à* Paris, 1781, 4*to, sixty-eight pages.*

* The same who was one of the Leading Members in the French National Convention.

c   *Reprinted*

Reprinted in the Journal de Physique, *par* M. Rozier, *vol.* xiv. *page* 1. Linnæus *sent himself, a few years before his death, the biographical materials for this panegyric to the Academy. The whole is more an oratorical and scientific statement than a biographical account.—It only contains common places, and erroneous denominations and false assertions. For instance, page sixty-seven,* Condorcet *calls* Linnæus *while he was* Rudbeck's *substitute, le Professeur, qui quitta bientot* Upsal, *mais en conservant sa chaire. Il avoit fait un marriage heureux, qui lui a donné trois filles et un fils ;* Linné *mourut vers la fin mois de Janvier,* 1778, *&c. &c.*

XI.

Eloge de M. *de* Linné, *par* M. Felix Vicq d'Azyr—*in the second part of Histoire de la Société de Médécine ; à* Paris, 1780, 4*to.*

The unjust and false assertions in this panegyric, are refuted by M. C. M. Blom, M. D. *in the Swedish Journal, entituled* Samling *of* Rön och Uptäkter uti Physique, *&c.* Gothenburgh, 1781, 8*vo. and by* M. Hedin, *in his dissertation :* Quid Linnæo Patri debeat Medicina.

XII.

A short view of the Life and memorable adventures of Linnæus; German, *in* Schroeder's Physical Journal, *published at* Weimar, 1780, see vol. vi. *page five hundred and fifty-five to five hundred and sixty-nine—a mere extract from the Commemorative Speech of the Chevalier* A. Bäck.

XIII.

XIII.

A Biography *of* LINNÆUS, *taken from some English writers, and translated into German ; see No.* 3 *of the* OLLA PODRIDA, 1780. *The whole takes up but five pages, and is full of false names.*

XIV.

A Biographical Sketch, with a Genealogical Table, published likewise in English, inserted in the Hanoverian Magazine ; published at Hanover, 1782, *from page one thousand two hundred and twenty-two, to one thousand two hundred and thirty-two.*

XV.

Some short accounts of LINNÆUS *in* SCHLOETZER'S *Correspondence : in German, No.* xii. *page three hundred and thirty-five ; No.* xiii. *page forty-seven ; No.* xl. *page two hundred and fifty-two ; and his Genealogy in No.* xix. Goettingen, 1779.

XVI.

General View *of the* Writings *of* LINNÆUS, *by* DR. RICHARD PULTENY, M. D. *and* F. R. S.—London, 1781, 8vo. *This work begins with a general biographical sketch ; in the list of the works of our Great Botanist, the anonymous Apology of* LINNÆUS : *Orbis eruditi judicium de* CAROLI LINNÆI *scriptis, is, among many others not mentioned ; it is in several other respects imperfect and deficient. The learned Author ought to have had recourse to* BARON HALLER's *Bibliotheca Botanica, tom.* ii. *What follows is a translation of this work.*

c 2   XVII.

XVII.

Revue Générale des Ecrits de LINNÉ; *Ouvrage dans lequel on trouve les Anecdotes les plus interessantes de sa vie privée, un abrégé de ses systemes et de ses ouvrages, &c. par* R. PULTENEY, *traduit de l'Anglois par* L. A. MILLIN *de* GRANDMAISON; *avec des notes et des additions du Traducteur; à* LONDRES *et à* Paris, 1789, *Vol.* i. *three hundred and eighty-six pages; Vol.* ii. *four hundred pages, small* 8vo. *The most interesting Anecdotes from his private Life, mentioned in the title, it would be in vain for us to look after in the present work, unless we choose to take for such those given by Professor* FABRICIUS, *which the Translator has partly copied in the Second Volume, from page one hundred and seventy-six to page one hundred and eighty-three, from another French work entitled* Melanges de la Litterature Etrangére. *The original and translation might both have been very successful, had the Swedish Commemoration Speech and the German Authors been consulted. The Supplements of* M. de GRANDMAISON, *to the Second Volume of his work, from page one hundred and seven to two hundred and sixteen, are valuable as Botanical and Literary documents, but replete with errors and false chronological dates. To the Extract made by* DR. PULTENEY *from the seven volumes of* Amoenitat. Academ. *the French Translator has added the substance of* Tom. viii. and ix. *published by the Aulic Counsellor* SCHREBER. *It is asserted that* DR SMITH *of London, has communicated several Anecdotes to the Editor, but this assertion, I am authorised to assure my Readers, is totally unfounded.*

XVIII.

J. BJÖRNSTAHL Resa til Frankrike, Italien, Tyskland, &c. Stockhom, 1784, *contains a few original Annecdotes of* LINNÆUS *in the* i. iii. *and* v. *part.*

XIX.

Œconomical and Physical Library; *German, by* BECKMANN, *vol.* xii.—Goettingen, 1783, *page five hundred and ninety-three.*

XX.

Travels into Poland, Russia, Sweden and Denmark, *by* WM. COXE, A.M.F.R.S. *Three Vols.* London, 1782—*contains a biographical sketch of* LINNÆUS, *besides a few additions from* BÄCK *and* FABRICIUS.

The Author who is in other respects an excellent traveller, and was at Upsal in 1779, might, if a Biographical Essay had at first been his design, have obtained more ample and better information.

XXI.

The above work was translated with some additions, par M. WILLEMET LE FILS, *who went to the* East-Indies *in 1788, as Physician to* TIPPOO SAIB, *and inserted in the* Melanges de Litterature, ETRANGÈRE *tom.* ii.

XXII.

For an abridged copy of Mr. COXE's *account, see the* Historical Magazine *for Nov.* 1790. London, *from page four hundred and seven, to four hundred and nine, with erroneous names, as in the greatest part of the English and French accounts.*

XXIII.

Biographical Sketch of LINNÆUS; *in English. The author is anonymous, the work equally deficient.*—Berlin, 1783.

XXIV.

XXIV.

Dissertatio : *Quid* LINNÆO *patri debeat Medicina, dissertatione Academicâ breviter adumbratum, quam veniâ ordinis experientissimi Med. Upsal. publicæ proponit ventilationi* SUENO ANDREAS HEDIN, *Assessor Reg. Colleg. Med. Holmensis et ad Aulam regiam Medico Prim. Reg. Societ. Medicæ Hafniensis Membr. Respondente,* C. CARLANDER ; *in Academ. Gustav. Audit. Maj. die* 14°. *April.* 1784. Upsaliæ *typis,* J. EDMANN ; *twenty-six pages, in* 4*to.*

XXV.

Observationes Botanicæ circa Systema Vegetabilium Divi a LINNÉ, Gottingæ, 1784, *editum ; quibus accedit justæ in Manes Linnæanos Pietatis specimen, Auctore* ANDREA DAHL, *Westgcthiæ—Sueco.* Havniæ, 1787, *in* 4*to.* The *Dissertation of Inauguration of the Author, who was five years a disciple of* LINNÆUS *and of his Son.* The *conclusion contains an animated apology against the critique of the Supplementum Plantarum, in the* Commentaria de rebus in Scientiâ Naturali et medicinâ gestis, *Vol. xxv.* Lipsiæ.

XXVI.

A Biographical Sketch in the introduction to the edition of the Fundamenta Botanica; Lyons, 1788, 8*vo.—Extracted and inserted in the* Journal Encyclopedique. June, 1788, *Vol. iv. page two hundred and twenty-three.*

XXVII.

CAROL. LINNÆI Philosophia Botanica et Critica Botanica ; Colon. Allobrog, 1788—*Edit. a* J. E. GILIBERT.

2   XXVIII.

XXVIII.

The present Age; *or a Review of its most interesting Events and Occurrences, with an account of the greatest men it has produced ;* German, *by* D. H. STOEVER—Altona, 1791, *Vol.* i. *contains a concise character of* LINNÆUS, *from page four hundred and eighty-five, to five hundred and four.*

XXIX.

Separate accounts extracted from the Works of LINNÆUS, *especially from the* Amoenitat. Academ.—*in the Prefaces,* &c. German.

XXX.

Separate particulars in the Literary Notices ; German—Goettingen, 1758, *page six hundred and eighty-seven ;* 1779, *page three hundred and thirty-four.*—*In the Almänna Tidningar ;* Swedish, *by* ASSESSOR GJOERWELL.—*Others in the Archives of Swedish Literature by* DR. LUDEKE.—*A particular Anecdote in the Magazine of the Arts ;* German, *by* MEUZEL LEIPSIC, 1781 *; refuted by* DR. BALDINGER.

XXXI.

VIDA DE LINNEO, *traduzida da que em Latino corre impressa na* Philosophia Botanica, *dada a Luz no anno de* 1787, *em* Genova, *por* ALCINO SINCERO LUSITANO; *in the* Jornal Encyclopedico, *&c. destinado para instruacção general, &c. Abril,* 1789; Lisboa. *Portuguese.*

XXXII.

XXXII.

Floræ Lusitanicæ et Brasiliensis Specimen, et Epistolæ ab eruditis viris, CAROLO A LINNÉ *Antonio da* HAEN, *&c. ad* DOMINICUM VANDELLI *Scriptæ.* COIMBRA in Portugal, 1788, *in 4to.*

XXXIII.

Collecion de Cartas de D. GREGORIO MAYANS *Siscar* R. P. F. MARTIN *Sarmento,* D. ANDRES MAJORAL, *Arzobispo de Valencia el Senor* PLUER. DOCT. JOSEF FINISTRES; *el major juris Consulto de Europa, i los Senores:* SCHEIDENBURG, VERGER, VISENE, GOESSEL, HOPE, BARON DE HALLER, LINNEO, BERGIN, DE MURR, SCHREBER, BAIER, *&c.* A CAPDEVILA, *Professor Real de Botanica, Socio de la Real Sociedad de las Sciencias de Gottingen, &c. y de este à aquellos :* En Madrid, 177.—Spanish

XXXIV.

Collectio Epistolarum, quas ad viros Illustres et Clarissimos scripsit CAROLUS À LINNÉ. *Accedunt opuscula, pro et contra virum immortalem scripta, extra Sueciam rarissima. Edidit* DOCT. D. H. STOEVER, HAMBURGI, *apud* B. G. HOFFMANN, 8vo. *This work contains the Letters of* LINNÆUS *to* HALLER, *to the* Chevalier E. P. THUNBERG, *Professor* GIESEKE, *the Academy of Sciences at* Paris, *&c.—also* JOH. GOTSCH WALLERII *Decades binæ Thesium medicarum (against* LINNÆUS.) Upsal, 1741. *The Defence of* LINNÆUS, *under the title :* Orbis eruditi judicium de Car. LINNÆI, M. D. *Scriptis.*—Upsal, 1741. *Quid* LINNÆO *Patri debeat Medicina, Dissertatio Auctore,* S. A. HEDIN, *&c.*

ON

ON

PROFESSOR LINNÆUS JUNIOR.

———

PRISTE Tal öfver Herr. CARL. VON LINNÉ, M. D. *Prof. Medicin. och Botanik vid Kongl Akademien i Upsala, &c.* Swedish.—Upsala, 1784, 8*vo. or, A Speech in Memory of the Noble* CHARLES DE LIN-NÆUS, *Doctor and Professor of Physic ; Professor of Botany at the University of* Upsal, *delivered in the Cathedral at* Upsal, *Nov.* 30*th,* 1783, *by* C. H. REICHEL, *thirty-eight pages.*

THE

THE

CONTENTS.

————————◆————————

SECTION I.

SECTION II.

life

SECTION III.

SECTION

SECTION IV.

SECTION V.

2   reform

SECTION VI.

SECTION X.

REMARKABLE OCCURRENCES CONCERNING THE LIFE OF LINNÆUS,
FROM THE YEAR 1560, TO HIS DEATH ON THE 10th OF JANUARY,
1578.

Merits of *Linnæus* in the medical science—His various medical writings—
Anecdotes—Unfair criticism of *M. Vicq d'Azyr*—Refutation—Apology of
Assessor *Hedin*—Meritorious efforts of *Linnæus* in the Natural History of
the Animal Reign—His Classification of Minerals—His last Learned Labours—*Linnæus* was a member of twenty Academies of Sciences—His works
serve as the elementary basis of the Science of Natural History even at the
Universities of Spain and Portugal—Extraordinary present made him by
Lord *Baltimore*—Other presents—His good circumstances—His pension—
Honorary bestowed on him for his works—His Rural Estates—Respectful
homage rendered to him by several Sovereigns and Monarchs—Veneration
manifested by the French Philosopher *J. J. Rousseau*——*Linnæus* is
elected a member of the Swedish Bible Commission—His extensive correspondence—

e

A

LIST OF SUBSCRIBERS.

[N.B. *The Initials* F. L. S. *denote Fellow of the* LINNÆAN *Society.*]

A

ABBOT, Charles, Rev. M. A. F. L. S. Bedford.
Allen, Joseph, M. D. Dulwich.

B

Baker, Sir George, Bart. M. D. F. R. S. President of the Royal College of Physicians, Physician to their Majesties, Jermyn-street.
Blackburne, John, Esq. M. P. Park-street, Westminster.
Bourne, Ebenezer, Mr. Anderson's Buildings, Holborn.
Bourne, F. Esq. Lombard-street.
Burnham, T. Mr. Bookseller, Northampton.

C

Chesterman, William, Mr. Man-midwife, Streatham.
Coyte, William, M. D. F. L. S. Ipswich.
Craufurd, Patrick, George, Esq. F. R. S. F. L. S. Soho-square.
Cullum, Sir Thomas Gery, Bart. F. R. S. F. L. S. Bury.

D

Daval, Edmund, Esq. F. L. S. Orbe, Switzerland.
Dickson, James, Mr. Covent Garden.

E

D'Engeström, Lawrence, his Excellency, Chancellor of the Court of the King of Sweden, and his Envoy Extraordinary and Minister Plenipotentiary to his Britannic Majesty.
Ewer, Samuel, Esq. F. L. S. Hackney.

F

Favell, Charles, Rev. M. A. F. L. S. Brington, Huntingdonshire.
Forster, J. F. jun. Esq.
Freeling, Francis, Esq. General Post Office. Two copies.

G

Gisborne, John, Esq. F. L. S. Wooton, near Ashbourne, Derby. Two copies.

H

Hanbury, William, Esq. F. L. S. Kilmarsh, Northampton.
Harbridge, Thomas, Mr. General Post Office.
Hawkesbury, the Right Honourable Lord.
Heriot, John, Esq. Catherine-street. Six copies.
Hodson, James, M. D. Hatton-Garden.
Howard, Samuel, F. R. S. Southampton-street.
Hoy, James, Mr. F. L. S. Gordon Castle, Scotland.
Hoy, Thomas, Mr. F. L. S. Sion-House.

J

A LIST OF SUBSCRIBERS. xxxvii

J

Johnes, Thomas, Esq. M. P. Princess-street, Westminster.

L

Lambert, Aylmer Bourke, Esq. F. R. S. F. L. S. Lower Grosvenor-street.

Lettsom, John Coakley, M. D. F. R. S. Basinghall-street.

Lewisham, George, Viscount, F. R. S. F. L. S. Hayes, Herts.

M

March, Thomas Orlebar, Rev. F. L. S. Bedford.

Marsham, Thomas, Esq. F. L. S. Upper Berkeley-street.

Maskelyn, George, Esq. General Post-office.

Mather, John, Esq. Shefford, near Biggleswade.

Mathew, William, Esq. F. L. S. St. Edmund's-Bury, Suffolk.

Maule, Captain Alexander, British Head Quarters, Flanders.

Miller, Miss Sarah Amy, Bedford.

P

Plymouth, the Right Honourable the Earl of.

Pultney, Richard, M. D. F. R. SS. Lond. & Endinb. Honorary Member of the Medical Society of Edinburgh, and of the Philosophical Society of Bath, and F. L. S. Blandford.

R

Rivers, Lord.

S

Smith, James Edward, M. D. F. R. S. President of the LINNÆAN Society of London, Great Marlborough-street.

2   Sowerby,

Sowerby, James, Mr. F. L. S. Mead's Place, Lambeth.
Spry, Digory, Esq. Surgeon of Plymouth Dock.
Spry Edward, M. D. L.L. D. Plymouth.
Stafford, William, Esq.
Swainson, Isaac, Esq. Frith-street, Soho.
Symmons, J. Esq. Paddington House.

T

Taylor, John, Esq. Oculist to the King, Hatton-Garden.

V

Vaughan, Walter, M. D. Rochester.

W

Warren, Richard, M. D. F. R. S. Physician to the King and to the Prince of Wales, Sackville-street.
Watkins, Mr. Samuel, Surgeon and Man-midwife, Drury-lane.
Williams, David, Rev. Great Russel-street, Bloomsbury.
Williams, Thomas Amphlett, Esq. Surgeon.
Woodward, Thomas Jenkinson, Esq. F. L. S. Bungay, Suffolk.

Y

Young, Mr. Thomas, F. L. S. Little Queen-street, Westminster.
Younge, William, M. D. F. L. S. Sheffield.

Z

Zouch, Thomas, Rev. A. M. F. L. S. Wychcliffe, Yorkshire.

THE

L I F E

OF

SIR CHARLES LINNÆUS, KNIGHT.

SECTION I.

BIRTH, DESCENT AND NAME OF LINNÆUS.—HIS EARLY LOVE OF NATURE.—SIN-
GULAR INDUCEMENTS TO THAT EXTRAORDINARY PASSION.—HIS DOMESTIC
EDUCATION.—IS DESTINED FOR THE PULPIT.—GOES TO THE SCHOOL AT WEXI-
COE.—GATHERS FLOWERS INSTEAD OF LEARNING HIS PHRASEOLOGY.—IS RE-
CEIVED INTO THE COLLEGE AT WEXICOE.—COMPLAINTS OF HIS PROFESSORS.—
DOCTOR ROTHMANN SAVES HIS GENIUS, AND PREVAILS ON HIS FATHER TO
LET HIM STUDY BOTANY.—THE DOCTOR MEETS WITH OBJECTIONS ESPECIAL-
LY ON THE PART OF THE MOTHER OF LINNÆUS, WHO FEELS AVERSE TO HIS
DESIGN.—ANECDOTE OF THE BROTHER OF LINNÆUS.—LINNÆUS IS RECEIVED
INTO ROTHMANN'S HOUSE.—GETS ACQUAINTED WITH THE WRITINGS OF
TOURNEFORT.—LAYS THE FOUNDATION OF HIS SUBSEQUENT GREATNESS.

THE Northern part of Europe stands, originally, and in a great
measure, indebted to the Southern for the present culture of science.
From the latter, the Muses transmigrated into the former. All the principal revolutions in the fields of knowledge took birth there, and were
transplanted and fostered here. No genius of the North—excepting

B

the

the original and more Southern Empire of the BRITONS, and the most penetrating of their philosophers, SIR ISAAC NEWTON,—had as yet, reared his head in the learned world, as a new legislator and universal reformer of any one science. The discoveries and merits of a TYCHO BRAHE, whose country borders so nearly on that of LINNÆUS, will not stand a comparison here. The age we live in, is the first that made a new epoch in the course of national learning. Among the great apparitions, which the literary heavens have exhibited and rendered eternal, a star from the North has shone forth, the brightest and most illumining. Without comparing here LEIBNITZ, who run the best part of his immortal career in the last century, *Switzerland* found in HALLER, the greatest and most solid universalist; *Holland*, in BOERHAAVE, the greatest physician; *France*, in VOLTAIRE, the greatest wit and first favourite of the literary graces; but *Sweden*, the most *systematical* genius of the age, the most intimate and scrutinizing minion that ever graced the bosom of Nature; who rendered her knowledge the most regular and the most cultivated, and became her teacher in all parts of the world. Never was the name of any Literatus of his nation, or of Northern Europe at large spread so far, honoured so devoutly, and rendered so immortal as his. However distinguished and uncommon his merits were, as extraordinary and memorable became the vicissitudes of his fate, and as rugged and thorny the paths on which he attained the climax of his greatness.

CHARLES LINNÆUS was born on the third of May, 1707, at *Rashult*, a village in the province of *Smaland*. NILS, or NICHOLAS LINNÆUS, his father, who took birth in the year 1674, held the sacred function of pastor of the village, two years previous to that event. He was joined

in

in the banns of wedlock with CHRISTINA BRODERSON, the daughter of his predecessor in office. His ancestors were peasants. Several of his relatives, who had quitted the plough for the Muses, in the last century, changed their family name with their profession, and borrowed the names of LINDELIUS, or TILIANDER, *(Linden-tree-man)* of a lofty Linden-tree, which still stood in our time, in the vicinity of their native place, between *Tomsboda* and *Linnhult*; a custom not unfrequent in *Sweden*, to take fresh appellations from natural objects. The father of LINNÆUS, as the first learned man of his family, could not withstand following the example which his kindred had set before him. He likewise borrowed of the same tree a name which his son rendered afterwards famous and immortal in every quarter of the globe.

Our CHARLES was the first pledge of the young couple's mutual love. He was destined for the pulpit; a destination which his parents considered as the happiest, and through which they flattered themselves their son would one day become the prop of their old age. But, fortunately for science, this plan was overturned, even by those who felt its execution nearest to their hearts;—they themselves sowed, as it were, in the cradle, a seed in the infant's breast, which, in process of time, yielded the finest fruits.

The father was a singular lover of gardening. The smallness of his income, obliged him, at the same time, to make the best of husbandry. Flowers were the first things they gave the smiling babe, and it seemed to take a natural delight in the variety of their colours. The fragrant play-things thus instilled in the infant's breast an early passion for the beauties of Nature, which a concurrence of favourable circumstances , fostered and increased during the subsequent stages of his infancy. In

the

the year 1708 he obtained the living of *Stenbrohult*, a benefice rather more lucrative than that which he enjoyed before, and in which he continued until his death. The greatest pleasure annexed to his new tenement, was a good, extensive garden, in which he used to spend his leisure hours. He was a professed lover of flowers, and when a few years had elapsed, rendered his garden the finest and most variegated in the whole district. It contained upwards of four hundred species of flowers*, many of which were of foreign growth.

This darling passion of the parent, became transcendent in the son. The latter, in want of play-mates, made the garden the circle of his juvenile diversions. Whenever the father planted and cultivated the gay parterre, he was sure of finding CHARLEY skipping by his side, to share the pleasant toil, and to water the beds. The parent to reward and encourage the fondness and care of our infant florist, assigned to him, when he reached the eighth year, a separate spot in the garden; which, in honour of his son, was called CHARLES's GARDEN. This landed property strengthened the love and inclination of the young free-holder. Resolved to make his as diversified and copious as possible, he made little excursions in the neighbouring fields and woods, to collect flowers and plants to enrich it ' He carried this collection so far as to gather all kind of weeds and wild herbs,—a treasure which his father found afterwards a painful job to eradicate. The active youngster brought even wild bees and wasps in the garden, who by their hostile demeanour began to desolate the paternal hives. Some severe reprimands deterred

* LINNÆUS himself says of his father, in a letter to BARON HALLER, dated May 28, r· :?, in which he announces his death: " Fuit summus æstimator plantarum rariorum, et " semper habuit selectum hortum plantarum non vulgarium." He was an uncommon lover of rare plants, and had a select garden of several rare species.

him

him from farther attempts of this sort, which his innocent simplicity had
induced him to consider as an act free from mischief. Meanwhile his
collections and excursions increased his little stores of knowledge, and
roused in him that love of Nature, which at his farther advance into
life, derived additional energy as he gradually became more acquainted
with her beauties. Thus minute and accidental circumstances have
frequently become the sources of great results!

The father was the more willing to indulge his son in those botanical occupations and wanderings, since they constituted the most innocent and best of diversions, became serviceable to his health, and did
not interfere with his diligence in receiving instruction. He initiated
him in the elements of the Latin tongue, religion, geography, &c. All
this was done to qualify him for the pulpit; and in order to conduct his
studies more systematically, and to foster his love and desire of science,
he resolved to send his CHARLES to the Latin school in the adjacent
town of Wexicoe, in the province of Smaland.

At the epoch of this determination LINNÆUS had seen his second
lustre. He arrived at Wexicoe in 1717. The love and pursuit of his
favourite occupation did not quit him on his journey thither. He
spent in it every moment which respited him from h.   udies. On
holidays no pupil was so little found at home as LINNÆUS. The boy
took more delight in gathering plants, and examining them, than in
learning his phraseology, or writing out his themes. Had he remained under the immediate direction of his father, his zeal for the
science of which he was once to shine the luminary, would have much
suffered by lessons of divinity; but it fortunately so happened, that
the rector of the school at Wexicoe, whose name was LANAERIUS,
                                                            was

was also a lover of botany. He grew fond of a youth who at so early an age displayed the most extraordinary talents; he formed a proper judgment of his genius and application, while CHARLES's school-fellows considered him as a vagabond truant, who wasted his time in useless pursuits and running about. Upon the whole, LINNÆUS was much behind in the different instructions which were to qualify him for his future clerical avocation.

This backwardness manifested itself in a particular manner, when after having been in the grammar-school during seven years, he was received in the superior college at *Wexicoe*, in 1724. Dogmatical acquirements, the Hebrew language, and the more solid branches of scholastic science had been forgotten amidst the allurements of the goddess Flora, and still continued to enjoy their usual share of oblivion. All admonitions to a closer application to the studies of theology, were bestowed in vain. The passion strongly ingrafted by Nature combated against them, and proved victorious. The slowness of his progress induced at last some of the professors and lecturers of the college to complain to his father, and furnish him with bad testimonials. This his parents took much to heart, as they foresaw only a prospect of having their fondest hopes undermined. LINNÆUS stood bordering on the brink of the decision of his destiny. With filial obedience he avowed his readiness to study divinity; but owned at the same time, his want of inclination, and his great aversion to that sacred pursuit. His father, therefore, resolved to make his son take absolute leave of the Muses, and to bind him apprentice to an honest shoe-maker and cobler.

The

The case of LINNÆUS, whose parents had resolved to make him embrace a calling quite opposite to that prescribed to him by nature and genius, has likewise been that of no small number of other men, who have afterwards raised their name to immortality. LUTHER was intended for a lawyer, and became the reformer of the church. TYCHO BRAHE, was to have studied politics, and by his own inclination acquired the celebrity of one of the first astronomers of his time. SHAKESPEARE was to have wielded the yard-measure of a linen-draper, which his father had wielded before him; but his unrivalled parts rendered him the first pattern of tragical poësy: In short, to recur to the moderns, VOLTAIRE was to have been a barrister and counsellor of parliament; but instead of the pandects he studied the writings of the *beaux esprits*, and became himself the first of the age he lived in. TOURNEFORT and BOERHAAVE were destined to wear the cassock, but the former rose to be the greatest botanist of the last, and the latter the greatest physician of the present century.

The resolution of the parent of young LINNÆUS, who preferred binding his son an apprentice to a shoemaker to letting him become a botanist, sprung at least, considering a man of his circumstances, from a pure sentiment of parental fondness. What prospect of a solid income could he flatter himself for his son, if the latter applied to botanical study?—What reason had he to think that his son would once shine as the first connoisseur and reformer of that science? And had he adopted medical pursuits as an additional exertion of his mental faculties, how much more arduous and uncertain must have proved a career in which he would have erred unsupported by fortune?—To acquire eminence in those sciences a proper competence was absolutely re-

requisite—and this competence he could not expect from a father, whose circumstances bordered more on penury than opulence. His father was also destitute of that interest and those favourable connections which could hold forth the gilded prospects of preferment in the church.

These considerations and scruples could not therefore be deemed quite unworthy of paternal foresight. Fortunately, however, those objections were all done away. A physician arrogated to himself the merit of first forming the genius who afterwards raised himself the pride of Sweden and the boast of the learned world. The name of this man ought never to be forgotten in the history of his pupil. It was JOHN ROTHMANN, physician at *Wexicoe*, a man of consummate skill, who gained celebrity among his countrymen by divers learned productions. He was also professor of medicine in the college of that city. Here he took notice of the genius of LINNÆUS, of that spirit of penetration and knowledge so unusual to the youths of his age. He got intelligence of his father's design of removing him from college—a flower which was on the point of yielding the most luxuriant blossom was to be cropt by the profane and rustic hands of those who could not foresee its future utility. Such an event could never be indifferent to the fond sensations of a professor of science.

ROTHMANN applied to the father of LINNÆUS, described the diligence of his son, his peculiar endowments for his favourite studies, and conjured him, by the most persuasive and the most urgent reasons, to let him study physic and botany, since his inclination and genius promised, that he would once become eminent in those professions. Encomiums, so new, so well founded, mixed the joyful transport of the father with regret and gloomy irresolution. Had the Doctor sent him

tes-

testimonials, purporting that his son analyzed Hebrew better than his fellow-students, that he excelled them in his theological progress, he would have been far better pleased than with his improvement in botany.

Young Linnæus was not remiss in joining his intreaties to the kind intercession of his protector. His eagerness, his enthusiastic zeal for his favourite studies, had shut his eyes against the painful prospects of futurity. Many times had he heard his father say, that a young man ought to learn that which he felt the greatest inclination for, because the natural propensity of a person always advanced him most in point of perfection; Linnæus therefore supplicated his father to extend this lesson, this pattern of Nature to himself, since he felt but little inclination for all other studies, but the greatest propensity to the exclusive study of Nature.

The peculiar fondness and benevolent disposition of Rothmann, at last struck the balance in the struggle between the opposite wishes and designs of the father and son. The good natured Doctor promised to take Linnæus. into his own family during the rest of his scholastic term, to find him in every necessary; and that he might make a more rapid improvement in physic, to initiate him himself in the elements of medicine.

The parents of Linnæus yielded to these kind propositions, though with reluctance and little satisfaction. The mother especially, felt herself much hurt to give up the hopes of once seeing her darling son in a pulpit. The discontent of both remained manifest a great while after. In the year 1718, their family was increased by the birth of a second son, Samuel Linnæus, who was the only brother our

hero

ever had. As her CHARLES had renounced the cassock, she hoped at least to have the pleasure of seeing it one day on SAMMY's shoulders. But this stripling began likewise to imitate his brother's example, and to love flowers better than books of divinity. His mother, to suppress this rising inclination, forbade him most carefully the garden and the gathering of flowers. Her prohibition, however, would but little avail with SAMUEL to root out the impulse to the knowledge of Nature, which he afterwards made his favourite study, besides husbandry. He shone as one of the most eminent connoisseurs and authors in one of the branches of natural science. In the year 1768 he published a work on the breeding of bees, which met with so favourable a reception, that they gave the author the name of *King* of the Bees *(Bi Kung)*. The spiritual wishes of the mother were, however, ultimately accomplished in her second son. He became a preacher in the year 1741, and seven years after, on his father's demise, succeeded him in the rectory of *Stenbrohult*.

Meanwhile our LINNÆUS entered with freedom the career, in which he could thus far advance only by secret and interrupted steps. The certainty and limitation of a settled plan of pursuits doubled his zeal and spirit, which were under a sure and direct guidance. ROTHMANN became his leader. He gave him private instruction in the elements of physic, a circumstance particularly advantageous, and soon attended with happy consequences. LINNÆUS found in ROTHMANN's library the first resources, that procured to him erudition and elucidations in the science, which he had till then studied without a plan, or any scientific insight. Among these resources was the principal work of TOURNEFORT, entitled, " *Elements of Botany (Institutiones Rei Herbe-*
riæ,

riæ, Paris. 1700.*)"* This book became the torch which illuminated the path of the youth, and opened new prospects to his eager views; it was at the same time the source of the purer and greater light which he afterwards himself diffused. He now contemplated Nature, and that part of her creation which he loved so much, in a quite different point of view than he had done before! How little could ROTHMANN imagine that the young pupil then under his auspices, would one day be greater than the greatest botanist of his time—greater than even TOURNEFORT himself! The more LINNÆUS began diving into the wonders of Nature, the more extensive became his admiration and love of her study. As in his father's house, so he now continued at *Wexicoe,* to make the collecting of flowers, plants, insects, &c. the chief aim and result of his rural excursions. By which means he soon gained a considerable pre-eminence in botany over his fellow-students.

After having frequented college three years, and completed the twentieth year of his age, he prepared himself to go to the university; to that career which became so rough and thorny in the beginning, but so honourable and grateful at its conclusion.

SECTION II.

———

O F the two universities in the kingdom of Sweden, narrow-ness of family circumstances constrained LINNÆUS to fix his choice on that of *Lund*, situate in the province of *Schonen*. A certain pro-fessor HUMÆRUS, was his relative there, and had promised to support him. Under such auspices LINNÆUS set out for *Lund* in 1727, with the most pleasant prospects before him. But these all at once vanished. He scarcely had arrived there, and prepared himself to wait on HU-MÆRUS, when he was informed that the last duty had just been paid to

the

the lifeless remains of his protector and friend. Thus all his hopes were lost—but fortune soon compensated for this unmerited event.

KILIAN STOBÆUS, professor of physic and botany, and afterwards one of the physicians to the royal family of *Sweden*, who was then one of the most celebrated and eminent professors of that university, became the oracle of LINNÆUS. The lectures of this learned man enriched and rendered more exact the scientific knowledge of our young student, and procured him the first systematical acquirements, the principles of which he had began to cultivate. Among all his pupils LINNÆUS displayed the greatest diligence, the utmost attention to his professor, and a judgment in botany rare and egregious in a beginner. .

These qualities endeared him to STOBÆUS. He was apprised of and saw his indigent condition, and animated by the same generous and beneficent motives as ROTHMANN, resolved to afford him accommodation free from all expence in his own family.

In so good a situation LINNÆUS found fully fostered his love of science, the only object of his desire. Here he met, for the first time, with a well arranged collection of natural history, got acquainted with curiosities he had never seen before, and began to keep a regular herbal himself. This, though a small matter of itself, proved to him an object of great importance. It gave him an opportunity of observing plants more closely, of collecting them more diligently, of examining more carefully their internal structure, distinctive marks and properties, of giving short descriptions, and comparing them with those of TOURNE-FORT, whom his ambition made already his pattern, and of having more frequent occasions to make new observations by his penetrating genius. To enrich his herbal he took excursions into all the neighbouring

bouring districts, and explored not only the vegetable, but also the animal reign, especially the lower classes of the latter, which had already been an object of his attention during his residence at *Wexicoe*.

He had once like to have fallen a victim to his curiosity. An excursion hurried him on to the very brink of the grave. He was stung by a venomous worm, not rare in *Sweden*, and to which he afterwards gave the name of *Furia infernalis* (the Hell-fury) in his system of Nature*, No. 353. The poison circulated the faster, as he had gone farther into the country, where it was impossible for him to obtain speedy medical relief. He was obliged to keep his bed, and all hopes of his recovery were finally given up. The skill of STOBÆUS, however, saved him. This perilous accident, which might have terrified him for ever, only served to increase his courage and curiosity to get nearer acquainted with the inferior classes of the creation; and the success which attended his studious perseverance, is universally known.

The vegetable reign remained above all his favourite pursuit. His experimental knowledge, drawn from Nature, was rendered regular, exact, and more extensive, by that obtained from books. The library of STOBÆUS contained the most valuable works on botany. LINNÆUS procured them secretly, and impelled by his desire of learning novelties, he read and studied to the last glimpse of the midnight lamp.

---

* LINNÆUS in his *System of Nature*, edit. xii. p. 1325, gives the following account of this worm: " *Habitat in Bothniæ, Sueciæ Septentrionalis vastis paludibus conspicuis; ex æthere decidua sæpe in corpora hominum animaliumque momento citus penetrat summo omnium dolore, immo interdum intra quadrantem horæ præ dolore occidit, quo et ipse Lundini 1728 laboravi. Animal nonnisi rude siccatum vidi. Animalibus chasticis videtur proprietatibus affine. Quomodo æra petat, unde decidit a solstitio æstivali in hyemale, nullus dixit.*"

STOBÆUS

Stobæus, by some means or other obtained intelligence of the vigils of his pupil, and did not know what to think of him. Linnæus was always a brisk student, fond of company, and of a merry convivial turn. The professor took it therefore into his head, that he set up so late to play at cards with his upper servants, or take some other diversion with them. His well-meaning mind resolved to disuade him from such an indecorous conduct for a young gentleman. In consequence of this resolution, he quite unexpectedly entered the apartment of Linnæus at a very late hour. But, what was his surprize, when, instead of finding him engaged in the company of the *quick*, he found him surrounded with the productions of departed great men; and intrenched, as it were, with the works of the greatest botanists, such as Cæsalpinus, Bauhnius, Tournefort, &c. By this unexpected scene he grew still fonder of the youth, and gave him full and entire permission to make use of his library.

Linnæus did not neglect profiting by these literary treasures, and by the instruction of his professor and benefactor. During the time he had spent at *Lund*, his mind had become more enlightened; but, at the same time his desire of seeing and learning was more increased. The first, and most ancient seat of the Swedish Muses, the University of *Upsal* (distant seventy-five *Swedish* miles from *Lund*) presented fresh opportunities to gratify his laudable wishes. He certainly could not expect there to be immediately so well circumstanced as he had been at *Lund*, which he had resolved to quit. Notwithstanding his passionate love of study conquered all other considerations. His resolution being sanctioned by paternal consent, Linnæus took his departure for *Upsal*, at Michaelmas, 1728, a place where he at first suffered many misfor-

misfortunes and adverse chances, but ultimately became the theatre of his greatness.

He arrived at *Upsal,* with a considerable store of knowledge; but his finances were slender, and such as they were, from the vivacity of his temper he could hardly manage them to advantage. Meanwhile he pursued his favourite study with all possible zeal, free from care and anxiety respecting his bodily support. His professors were OLOF or OLAUS RUDBECK, jun. and ROBERG. They were both old men; a circumstance, which, in several instances, proved fortunate to LINNÆUS. The greatest adept in natural history, and especially in botany, in *Sweden,* was OLAUS CELSIUS, a clergyman, first professor of divinity, and afterwards head of the chapter of *Upsal.* When LINNÆUS first began to reform natural history he described him in a letter to BARON HALLER, as the only botanist of his country *. At first the youth hoped, in vain, to profit by the learning of this great man, who was then at *Stockholm* on official business. He was, therefore, obliged to continue his career without any guidance except that of his own genius. The works of the immortal men of the two last centuries now served to enlighten his progress.

A twelvemonth had scarcely elapsed, when LINNÆUS saw himself reduced to the most calamitous and distressed circumstances. What little substance he had brought with him was expended, he could expect no supplies from home, his debts and the cares of providing for his livelihood increased, and no chearing prospect promised a mitigation of his.

---

* *In Suecia nullus est botanicus, præterquam* OL. CELSIUS, *primarius Theologiæ Professor, qui absque generibus plantas amat, muscos sedulo quærit. Rudbeckius enim decrepitus est.* This letter to Baron HALLER is dated from *Hartecamp,* near *Leyden,* May 1, 1737.

D   hapless

hapless fate. In the compassionate beneficence of his countrymen
and fellow-students, he found, however, some temporary relief in his indigent state. He picked up a meal here and there, and was glad to cover
himself with their left-off clothes. He had not even a sous to purchase a
pair of shoes. Imperious necessity compelled him to have recourse to
the trade which his father had once resolved to bind him to. He put
cards in the worn-out shoes which were given him by his comrades, and
stitched and mended them with the bark of trees, to enable him at least
to go out to collect plants. No great, or eminent man of our age, not
even BENJAMIN FRANKLIN, the *American* printer, ever struggled
with so many difficulties and adversities, while endeavouring to reach
the towering height at which his genius made him aspire. VOLTAIRE,
HALLER, NEWTON, and LEIBNITZ, had parents who were possessed
of property to smoothe their path. In the installation-speech made by
LINNÆUS in 1741, on entering on his office of professor, he offered
public thanks to Providence for having so wonderfully supported and
relieved him under the hardest pressure of poverty, and in other misfortunes*.

Difficulties and adverse circumstances have frequently been the
school in which great men have been formed, and they also helped
to build the greatness of LINNÆUS. - A less energetic character would
have been crushed by despair; but our hero found in them fresh in-
centives to perseverance and fame. The struggle against fate roused
his every endeavour. He continued his vigils and exertions in his
darling science. " Methinks," says the celebrated Dean BÆCK, " LIN-

---

* *Gratias tibi, Deus omnipotens ago, quod in vitæ meæ cursu, inter gravissima pauper-
tatis onera et alia quævis incommoda omnipotento auxilio tuo mihi semper adfuisti.*

" NÆUS

" NÆUS saw FLORA in all her beauties on a throne, he saw her holding
" forth a wreath to crown his head ; all Nature in her magnificence bade
" him draw nearer ; but he saw the whole, as it were, at a most remote
" distance. He was obliged to penetrate the labyrinth of DÆDALUS
" to seek the thread which could guide him to the right path through
" so many wanderings."

When the poverty of LINNÆUS had risen to its highest pitch, fortune
and his distinguished conduct offered him at once a charming prospect.
OLAUS CELSIUS had returned from *Stockholm*. He visited the botanical garden. LINNÆUS was present, spoke of the plants, described
them with an exactness surprising in a student, and upon nearer conversation displayed such extensive knowledge as struck CELSIUS with
astonishment. He made farther enquiries into the circumstances and
conduct of the young man, heard of his distress, and became his benefactor.

LINNÆUS was received into his house, where he obtained, gratis,
board and lodging. CELSIUS was likewise a great adept in the
Eastern languages, and then prepared his *Hierobotanicon*, a work in
which the plants and trees mentioned in Holy Scripture were to appear,
and which was published in the years 1745 and 1752, in two volumes,
did great honour to its author, and forms an appendix to the *Hierozoi-
con*, published by BOCHARD upon the animals whose names appear in
the Bible. LINNÆUS bore an active share in the collection of this
learned work, and gave such literary assistance as no other student
could have better afforded. This was one of the chief motives which.
made CELSIUS take him into his house. To complete this task, LIN-
NÆUS had the free use of the library of CELSIUS, which in botanical

works

works was one of the richest and most valuable in *Sweden*. He also had the advantage of receiving the immediate instructions of his protector, and of being able to take his advice in all difficult cases. Upon the whole, CELSIUS treated him with paternal care, and gave him various proofs of his benign favour on many subsequent occasions. In return for such kindness, LINNÆUS, among all his patrons cherished most the memory of this venerable man. He never spoke of him without expressing his reverence and gratitude. CELSIUS died, like LINNÆUS, in the full enjoyment of his celebrity, on the twenty-fourth of June, 1756, at the advanced age of seventy-six years, and found always among his academical colleagues in his former pupil the warmest and most grateful of friends.

TOURNEFORT was the only botanical author to whom LINNÆUS stood thus far indebted for the greater and more solid part of his knowledge. The sovereign empire which that great writer had acquired in botany, since the latter end of the last century, began now to totter. The young student at *Upsal* conceived the idea of creating a new system of doctrine. It was a Frenchman who inspired him with this new thought. It was VAILLANT, one of the most penetrating botanists, who died too soon for his scientific fame, and for the botanical discoveries and elucidations which he gave as demonstrator of the royal botanical garden at *Paris*, where he departed life in the year 1722. We shall have occasion, in the course of this work, to make more ample mention of him.

Thus far the division of the vegetable reign had been made from the various parts and properties of the plants, from their fruits, from the number of the petals of their flowers and blossoms, &c. Till then, TOURNEFORT,

TOURNEFORT, the professor of VAILLANT, had been the greatest systematical botanist. This man founded the system of division upon the form and quality of the flower or blossom, a side from which Frenchmen are apt to consider many things; and his method was predominant at that epoch.

By some lucky incident a small work of VAILLANT on the structure of flowers, fell into the hands of LINNÆUS *. Till now he had examined the plants by their bloom, according to TOURNEFORT's system; but without granting implicit faith to the received usage and authority, he directed his attention and enquiries on the remaining parts of the plants, especially on their generative parts, the *stamina* and *pistilla*, which had, to that very hour, been considered as insignificant. The flowers contain threads with a head at the top, commonly called the *stamina*, on which reposes a *dust bag*. The latter contains a floury dust, which, in point of its destination is very analogous to the male seed of animals. In the middle we generally find protuberances, which are frequently jagged and glutinous in the upper part. These are the *pistilla*, or *dust-ways*, which, with the *stamina*, or *dust-threads*, are the most essential when a plant is to bear fruit. If the fruit is to turn out well, the dust must fall out of the bag from the *stamina* or dust-threads on the cicatrice or jagg, by which the fructification is effected. The *stamina* or dust-threads are therefore the male, and the *pistilla* or dust-ways the female parts of plants.

* VAILLANT's *Sermo de Structurâ Florum*, Lugd. Batav. 1718.

The

The ingenious observations which VAILLANT made on the sexes of the plants attracted the notice of LINNÆUS, refined and confirmed his own remarks, kindled a fresh light, and soon, in a lucid interval, put into the young man's mind the thought of a NEW SYSTEM, by which a better order in the division of plants might be introduced, if this division were made from their sexes, from the number of stamina or dust-threads and pistilla or dust-ways, a system—(SYSTEMA SEXUALE)—of which he became afterwards the creator, which bears his name, and was acknowledged in course of time as the best and most exact method, universally adopted by botanists, and even preferred to the most modern ones.

The ideas of a better theory, which VAILLANT had hinted, guided now LINNÆUS in his botanical observations. He began to consider the plants, especially from their new and unimproved side, by their sexes, by the number of stamina, and compared them with the ancient system, and the divisions which had till then been used. The farther he brought his enquiries, the more deficient did he find the ancient system, and the more consistency did he discover in his own thoughts; in short, the greater, the more powerful were the attractions of his own plan. The sexes of plants now occupied his thoughts day and night; and the fresh knowledge which he obtained by this survey, soon paved him the way to a better fortune.

In the summer of 1730, a disputation was held before Bishop WALLIN, on the copulation of trees *(de nuptiis arborum)*. LINNÆUS was present. The subject of the controversy was quite familiar to him. None found it more pleasant, nor had any one at *Upsal* studied it better than himself. He composed, therefore, a small written treatise on the sexes of the plants, replete with new and curious observations. OLAUS RUDBECK, jun. then professor of botany, heard of this treatise. He was struck with the spirit of observation, and the solidity and novelty of the knowldege of our young author, which advanced him farther in his academical career.

The father of the new friend of LINNÆUS was OLAUS RUD-BECK, who died at *Upsal* on the 12th of December 1702, as professor of botany. *Sweden* had long been without a man of such great erudition, and such bold and heterodox a spirit of enquiry as his. He was the first celebrated naturalist of his country, and became the founder of the botanical garden at *Upsal*. He travelled at the expence of Queen CHRISTINA, and collected a vast quantity of herbs and plants. He intended to publish these in twelve volumes with wood cuts, under the title of *Campi Elysii*; and bestowed for a considerable time the utmost pains and diligence on their description and publication; but the great fire which broke out at *Upsal* in the year 1702, destroyed this literary treasure, of which nothing remained but two *folio* volumes, which afterwards became a great curiosity *. His grief at this loss accelerated his death in the same year. He was also author of the famous historical work, intituled *Atlantica, sive Manheim, vera Japheti posterorum sedes ac patria*, consisting of four volumes in folio; a work equally rich in learning and singular paradoxes, in which RUDBECK attempts to prove

* They were published at *London* in July 1789, by Dr. JAMES EDWARD SMITH, Proprietor of the LINNÆAN Museum and Herbals, under the title of—*Reliquiæ* RUDBECKIANÆ, *sive camporum Elysiorum libri primi, quæ supersunt, adjectis nominibus* LINNÆANIS—folio.

that

that *Sweden* is the Atlantis of PLATO, the Paradise of ADAM, and the native country of the ancient northern and southern nations, including the Greeks and Romans.

OLAUS RUDBECK, the son of the former, born on the 15th of March 1660, who had taken his degrees at *Utrecht*, succeeded his father in his academical functions. During the first years he made botany his chief pursuit. He afterwards applied to philology, in which he made great progress, and intended to publish a great philological work, intituled *Lexicon Harmonicum*, when death arrested his career on the 23d of March 1740. When he first took LINNÆUS under his protection, he had attained his seventieth year. Going out and giving lectures became equally difficult for him, and he wished for an assistant. In point of botany he could have found none more able than LINNÆUS. The perusal of his treatise, and a nearer trial of his abilities, determined OLAUS to fix his choice upon him.

He took LINNÆUS into his house, where he gave lectures for him in the botanical garden in the year 1730. It did great honour to a young student only twenty-three years of age, to become the representative of a venerable academical institutor. He supplied his place with every mark of approbation. The vivacity of his instructions, the novelty of matter, charmed his audience, and this charge, *ad interim*, became to the young lecturer a fresh incentive to improvement, and a school of his own cultivation. He stood indebted to the venerable old man under whose roof he was placed, for a more extensive knowledge of ornithology; he had a collection of all the Swedish birds, and gave lectures on them. LINNÆUS always continued to

make

make botany his principal study; but it was decreed that he should likewise establish a better order in the other reigns of Nature, especially
among the different classes of the animal reign. The new plan of a botanical reform, and the theory of the sexes of the plants, consequently
remained the object of the thoughts and enquiries of Linnæus. He
became acquainted with the difficulties and infinite trouble that would
attend the introduction of a new order ; but the charms of invention, the
prospects of honour and fame, doubled his zeal, and rendered pleasant
his labours. He began to build the foundation of his system, and
wrote several treatises on the classes and genera of the plants, which
afterwards were published in *Holland*, and served to disseminate his
system of reform.

Linnæus, during his abode at *Upsal*, had the good fortune to meet
with a young friend, to whose zeal and rivalship he owed a great deal.
This was Peter Artedi, equally conspicuous for his eminence in a
certain branch of natural history, and his unhappy fate. He was born in
the year 1705 in *Angermania*, likewise of poor parents, and behaved
at the college of *Hernasand* in the same manner as Linnæus did at
Wexicoe, preferring the study of nature, especially that of fishes, to all
other accomplishments. In 1724 he came to *Upsal*, to study divinity,
but he soon exchanged this science for natural history. Linnæus
himself describes the history of this friendship with those sentiments
of liveliness and cordiality which fully evince its value. " In the
" year 1728," says Linnæus, " I came to *Upsal*. I asked what student
" was most eminent for his knowledge in natural history. The name of
" Artedi was heard every where; he had studied there several years
" before me. I felt the most ardent desire to see him. On paying him

E   " a visit

" a visit I found him pale, downcast and weeping because his father had
" just died. Our conversation soon turned upon plants, stones and ani-
" mals. The new remarks he made, the knowledge he displayed, struck
" me with amazement. I solicited his friendship, he wished for mine.
" How valuable, how happy was our intercourse! With what pleasure
" did we see it cemented! If one of us made some new observation, he
" communicated it to the other; not a day elapsed without our re-
" ceiving reciprocal instruction. Rivalship increased our diligence and
" researches; though we lived at a great distance, yet it could not pre-
" vent us visiting each other every day. Even the dissimilitude of our
" character turned out to advantage. His temper was of a more
" serious cast. He excelled me in chymistry, and I outdid him in the
" knowlege of birds and insects, and in botany."

ARTEDI finally confined his botanical studies to that division of the
vegetable reign which treats of the *plantæ umbelliferæ, (umbelliferous*
plants), in which he pointed out a new method of classification, which
was afterwards published by LINNÆUS. But the chief object of his
pursuits, which transmitted his fame to posterity, was the empire
of NEPTUNE, or the knowledge of the natural history of fishes, called
Ichthyology. Even in this branch of science LINNÆUS first stood
up his rival, but found himself so far exceeded in point of abilities
by his friend, that he relinquished to him this province, on which the
latter afterwards bestowed all his juvenile labours. " Thus," says
BAECK, " these two young rival geniuses divided among themselves
" natural history, as the Romans once had done the domination of
" the world."

ARTEDI had projected the happy plan of introducing a new method and classification in Ichthyology, which cheered and strengthened LIN-NÆUS in his design to effect the same in botany. The zeal of reform animated both in their new hypotheses, and both were equally fortunate in their exertions and discoveries, but not in their fate. Fate, relentless Fate parted them—they once more had the joy to meet, but far from their country; the imperious mistress of men tore, by the . most melancholy accident, a friend from LINNÆUS, who was the companion and promoter of his studies, and the delight of his academical life.

Meanwhile a new prospect opened itself before LINNÆUS, to extend his learning. In 1710, when the plague raged at *Upsal*, and forced the students to fly from this university, a private literary society was instituted under the auspices of OLAUS CELSIUS, which was fully incorporated in 1719, and confirmed by royal sanction and privilege in the year 1728. This society was in its flourishing infant state, and for this reason the zeal for public researches and enterprizes was the greater at that period. Its chief tendency was to objects of domestic natural history. Among all the Swedish domains, none was more unknown in point of its productions and natural curiosities than the remote, vast, and wild region of *Lapland*. Already in the preceding century pains had been taken to remove this want of knowledge. OLAUS RUDBECK senior, undertook in the year 1695 to travel through this extensive northern province at the expence of CHARLES XI. king of *Sweden*. He collected many natural curiosities, which were, however, destroyed by the great fire at *Upsal* in 1702, with

the

the *Campi Elysii*. It was proposed to compensate for this loss. Under the immediate protection of the States, the Academy of Sciences came to a resolution in 1731, to send another traveller to make discoveries in *Lapland*. CELSIUS and RUDBECK had proposed a young gentleman for this purpose, and their choice fell on him, who united their good wishes and the greatest abilities—our LINNÆUS.

SECTION

SECTION III.

———

LINNÆUS RECEIVES A SUM OF MONEY TO DEFRAY HIS TRAVELLING EXPENCES.—
DIFFICULTIES ATTENDING THE SCIENCE OF BOTANY.—DESCRIPTION OF HIS
JOURNEY.—DANGERS AND OBSTACLES.—VISITS THAT PART OF LAPLAND
WHERE SOME FRENCH ASTRONOMERS ASCERTAINED SOME YEARS AFTER THE
FIGURE OF THE EARTH.—CONTINUES HIS PEREGRINATION THROUGH THE
NORTHERN ALPS.—ANECDOTE.—COMPARISON WITH BARON HALLER'S JOUR-
NEY IN THE ALPS.—LINNÆUS RETURNS TO UPSAL.—EXTENT OF HIS JOURNEY,
AND OF THE BENEFITS WHICH RESULTED FROM IT.—PUBLISHES HIS FIRST
WORK, THE FLORA OF LAPLAND.—JOURNAL OF HIS TRAVELS REMAINS UN-
PRINTED.—IS ELECTED A MEMBER OF THE ACADEMY OF SCIENCES OF UP-
SAL.—BEGINS TO DELIVER LECTURES.—GAINS APPLAUSE.—IS ENVIED.—NICHO-
LAS ROSEN BECOMES HIS ADVERSARY.—THEY FORBID HIM TO READ LEC-
TURES.—HE CONCEIVES THE DESIGN OF STABBING ROSEN.—DISTRESSED AND
UNFORTUNATE CONDITION OF LINNÆUS.—ANECDOTE.—FATAL SENSIBILITY
OF HIS MIND.—MAKES FRIENDSHIP WITH BARON REUTERHOLM AT FAHLUN.—
MAKES A JOURNEY THROUGH DALECARIA.—HISTORICAL ACCOUNT OF HIS
JOURNEY.—JOURNAL UNPRINTED.—LINNÆUS RETURNS TO FAHLUN.—GIVES
LECTURES ON MINERALOGY.—CONTRACTS FRIENDSHIP WITH DR. MORÆUS.—
FALLS IN LOVE WITH HIS DAUGHTER.—THE YOUNG LADY GIVES HIM MONEY
TO ENABLE HIM TO TAKE HIS DEGREE OF DOCTOR AT A DUTCH UNIVER-
SITY.—PREPARES FOR HIS DEPARTURE.

A Journey through *Lapland* is certainly one of the most difficult and
most disagreeable that can be made in Europe. A thousand might have
declined the offer of going such a journey. But LINNÆUS, from
his love of fame, and fired with an enthusiastic desire of making
some farther progress in his favourite science, deemed himself happy
in such an opportunity. No premium or reward having been offered for making this journey, and the travelling money being very
small, were additional motives to have rejected the offer. Indeed the whole sum devoted to this expedition did not amount

10

to more than one hundred *Swedish platens*, or to seven pounds ten shillings sterling at farthest.

If there be a science which to raise its votary to celebrity requires the courage of enthusiasm, and the patience of labour and difficulty, that science is botany. The divine, the lawyer, the philosopher, the *bel-esprit* can become great men in their own closets; the astronomer by observing the spheres of the worlds from the observatory can gain an immortal name; but it is not thus with the botanist and natural historian. Nature requires the personal contemplation and scrutiny of her secrets and curiosities. Hence the goddess of no science had ever so many zealous lovers, no science so many who fell victims to their devotion of study, as that of natural history.

LINNÆUS accepted the proposal of the journey in autumn of 1731, and visited in winter professor STORÆUS, his late benefactor at *Lund*, and his parents, who were now more reconciled to him, and smiled at his progress. Thence he returned to *Upsal* in April, to prepare every thing for his peregrination in the *Siberia* of his country.

Immediately on the return of spring, which seldom chears the year at *Stockholm* before May, he commenced his journey on horseback, on the second day of that month, that he might not be over-fatigued when he arrived at the place of his destination. He took his route to *Gevali*, through the North-eastern province of *Norland*, along the gulph of *Bothnia*. From thence he was to proceed North-west to the Southernmost province of *Lapland*, called *Umea Lapmark*; but spring had not visited this district at the latter end of May. The country was replete with the dreary scenes of winter, and threatened the traveller with disappointment and destruction. People persuaded LINNÆUS not

to

to expose himself, but wait the full return of summer. His courage was blind to difficulties, and so impatient his desire of making some new discovery, that he was irresistibly induced to visit those tracts which had seldom or never been visited before.

Having waited a few days at *Hernafand*, the chief town of *Angermania*, on the Bothnian gulph, in expectation of milder weather, he commenced his wanderings on foot, and travelled alone through the above-mentioned province of *Lapland*. Trees, herbs, animals, mountains; in short, every novelty and curiosity of Nature which offered itself, became the objects of his observation and attention. The prophecies made to him respecting this undertaking he now experienced to be but too well founded. Every difficulty which could be thought of occurred to cross his enterprize. The rivers which he was to pass over being still swelled, and as rapid as torrents, he frequently found his life in danger; the country which is every where intersected with bogs and forests could not stop him; all these obstacles were heightened by the inclemency of the climate, the want of provisions, and frequently by that of a sheltering place to rest his head upon in those desert tracts. LINNÆUS thought himself the happiest of men if when tired and exhausted with his daily peregrinations he could at night find the cot of some *Laplander*, to still his hunger and to repose his wearied limbs!

Undaunted by all these obstacles and dangers he continued his journey through the other provinces of *Lapland*, through *Pithea* and *Ulua Lapmark*. If we consider that this *Canada* of *Sweden* does not contain a single town, but thirty-two scattered dwellings or villages, we shall be able to form to ourselves some idea of the inhospitable and

desert

desert state of those regions. LINNÆUS did not travel through cultivated fields, but through a country whose surface is deeply covered with snow during the greatest part of the year, containing a few solitary huts, abodes of the greatest poverty, but contentment, whose tenants have no notion of superfluity, nor of many wants; in short, through a country where the human race is still in a rough, uncultivated state. The manners of the inhabitants with whose language he soon got acquainted, their hospitality and good-nature which he praised, the diseases which he found among them, and their modes of cure, œconomy, &c. became the object of our traveller's attention.

The same northern districts through which LINNÆUS was now travelling, were visited four years after by that celebrated society of Southern astronomers and philosophers who ascertained the figure of the earth, and glorified SIR ISAAC NEWTON in his grave. This great man had maintained in the last century by an ingenious theory, that the earth was flat and pressed inwards about the poles. The great Italian astronomer CASSINI, whom the liberality of LOUIS XIV. brought to Paris from Bologna, by several mensurations attempted to refute NEWTON's hypothesis. To decide this contest, this learned expedition was undertaken at Paris, through the endeavours of Count MAUREPAS, an expedition which will ever be memorable in the annals of literature.

CONDAMINE was dispatched from Paris to Peru with another society, to measure there the degrees beneath the equator, and MAUPERTIUS, OUTHIER, CLAIRAUT, CAMUS, and MOUNIER, repaired to Tornea in Lapland, whither they were accompanied from Upsal by ANDREW CELSIUS, the Swedish astronomer. The result of
                                                        both

both these voyages and observations, was a full confirmation of NEW-TON's opinion, that the earth is a spheroid, higher towards the equator and more depressed about the poles.

> " Newton in the starry sky,
> " Newton saw them, and from the heavens,
> " Bade them confirm his discovery
> " To the astonish'd world."

Let us return to our traveller. Having explored the interior parts of the provinces of *Lapland*, LINNÆUS directed his steps to the alpine mountains which part *Norway* from *Sweden* and extend from the Frozen Sea to the southern province of *Warmeland*, in a latitude of between ten and twenty, and a longitude of two hundred Swedish miles. The obstacles and dangers which he had overcome, could not at all be compared with those presented by this steep and rocky region, whose summits are the throne of winter, and whose remote and interior parts were seldom trod by the foot of man. But even this dreary district had the greatest allurements for LINNÆUS.

He continued courageously those arduous travels, bidding defiance to dangers and difficulties, disregarding the nipping frost of the mountains and the heat of the vallies. He turned his most serious attention to the third part of natural creation, the mineral reign, to the better order and division of which his reform was likewise to extend; and having reached the northern boundaries, he visited the mines and obtained fresh knowledge. The fruits which he reapt from his excursions, were so attractive to his mind, as to induce him to go as far as the shores of the North Sea, whither two good-natured *Laplanders* followed him as his guides and interpreters. He then set out on his re-

F

turn

turn by a different way, through the mountains, and exhausted with
hardships, fatigue and hunger, reached *Lulea* on the eleventh of August.

" All my food in those fatiguing excursions, which cannot be eased
" by voluntary repose or riding," says LINNÆUS in the account which he
gave of his travels in the year 1771, to his worthy friend and pupil,
Doctor and Professor GIESKE at *Hamburgh*, " consisted for the most part
" of fish and rein-deer's milk ; bread, salt, and what is to be found every
" where else, did but seldom recreate my palate.   One of the greatest
" nuisances which I met with in *Lapland*, was the immense number of
" flies. I used to keep them off by drawing a crape over my face.
" For want of this necessary article I must have been forced to
" swallow numbers of these insects with every breath. The *Laplanders*
" have a specific of their own against those unpleasant intruders;
" they besmear their hands and face with a kind of rosin.   This num-
" berless quantity of teazing insects is not without its utility; they
" serve as food to the birds of passage ; and the latter are a valuable
" branch of the *Laplander's* subsistence. I remained a whole fortnight
" on the banks of the river, which is about four times as broad as the
" ground on which *Upsal* is erected. I found it, as far as my sight could
" reach, entirely covered with wild geese, ducks, &c. The *Laplanders*
" have nothing to do but to catch and kill them, a resource which
" affords abundant supplies both in winter and summer."   .

He chose at *Upsal* the motto, *Tantus amor Florum*—THUS GREAT IS
THE LOVE OF FLOWERS; and if ever a motto was verified and confirmed, LINNÆUS has done it by the present. " Surely, he," says
                                            BAECK,

BAECK, " must be a faithful lover of FLORA who suffers so much in
" her service, and is contented with a favourable smile of his beloved
" one, as LINNÆUS was with a plant growing on the brink of some steep
" waterfall, to which he climbed up in danger of his life, or with some
" unknown moss concealed in profound caverns or clefts."

The journey through Lapland was the first and most difficult of the
six different travels of LINNÆUS. He spoke himself of it afterwards,
when he assumed the functions of his academical office in the year 1741,
in the following expressions : " There is no important nor considerable
" province of *Sweden* through which I have not roamed with great fa-
" tigue and bodily exertion. My journey through *Lapland* was particu-
" larly toilsome : and I own that I was obliged to sustain more hardships
" and dangers in this sole peregrination through the frontier of our
" northern world, than in all the travels which I undertook in other
" parts, though not without fatigue and weariness. But having once sus-
" tained the toils of travelling, I buried in the oblivion of *Lethe*, all the
" dangers and difficulties which I had suffered. The invaluable fruits
" which I reaped from these excursions, compensated for every toil *."

The best comparative image of the *Alps* of *Lapland*, is presented by
those of *Switzerland*. But how many excellencies and prerogatives

* *Nulla facile est nobilior Suecia Provincia, quam ego non perreptavi, perlustravi, etsi
non sine corporis viriumque defatigatione eximia. Iter quidem Lapponicum maximi mihi con-
stitit laboris ; et fateor, necessum mihi fuisse, plus devorare molestiæ ac periculi, vagando per
unam hanc mundi nostri arctoi oram, quam per reliquas omnes, quas unquam genitum contigit
mihi obire terras in extero orbe, nec tamen et ipsas absque delassatione viriumque jactura a me
calcatas. Sed—exatlantis itineribus, mox omnis defuncti discriminis ac molestiæ me quasi
Lethæâ cepit oblivio, compensante hæc omnia fructu inæstimabile, quem ex bis viarum erroribus reportavi.* LINN. AMOENITAT. ACAD. Vol. II.

have

have not the latter, in preference to the inhospitable and desert tracts
of *Lapland!* The description given by Baron HALLER of his *Alpine*
tour, and of the hardships which the botanist must encounter in
Switzerland, is the only apt comparison which can be drawn with
the *Lapponian* journey of LINNÆUS; a description, that in most instances can be applied to the latter, except in the narrative of hardships, which the reader must fancy to have been greater and more
complicated in *Lapland.*

    " Among all the botanists," says HALLER, " the botanist of
" *Switzerland* finds the greatest difficulties. That country exhibits an
" infinite variety ; and the excursions made there cannot be deemed
" pleasure-walks. M. VAILLANT, who composed the catalogue of
" plants in the environs of Paris, and a great many other botanists who
" have written similar works, only found pleasure. They visited fine dis-
" tricts, villas, parks, pleasant woods, and returned from their excur-
" sions in the full enjoyment of every domestic comfort; their labour
" was mere recreation. But it is quite another case in *Switzerland.*
" The traveller must climb up the *Alps* through dreadful cliffs, descend
" from these with still greater danger, suffer on the summit of the moun-
" tains the most piercing frost, which almost chills the blood, and re-
" turn afterwards to the vallies, where he is almost suffocated with heat.
" In all these excursions one is exposed to a constant intemperature of
" the climate. For the clouds, which generally rest on the *Alps,*
" emit almost every day, hail or thunder; or the brows of those huge
" mountains are covered with thick fogs, which prove still more
" dangerous, because they conceal the paths, or rather the slightest

        * Baron HALLER's Bibliotheque Raisonnée, tom. ix, p. 266.

                                                    " tracks.

" tracks. For regular highways and roads are not to be found in
" those wild regions. The least cloud or fog can mislead the travel-
" ler: and if he loses his only right track, for there is seldom
" more than one, he may surely give himself up as lost. In all this
" he is deprived of every commodity, and must go without bread
" or bed. The night is spent in huts. The inhabitants are, indeed, as
" hospitable as the Greeks of yore; they share with strangers their
" usual food—nay, even their dainties. But what dainties!—Milk, and
" sometimes curds. For those who drink water it is an excellent beve-
" rage, being the purest and finest in the world. But the nights are very
" unpleasant. The coldness and roughness of the boards, which supply
" the place of beds, render them almost insupportable. Notwithstanding
" such hardships, there have always been persons who wished to face
" them. Those mountains, covered with perpetual ice, those rocky py-
" ramids, covered with everlasting snow ; those awful, obscure valleys,
" from which pour down a great number of torrents among a thousand
" cascades ; those natural fountains and reservoirs, which surpass by far,
" every thing which the most powerful monarch could procure ; those
" deserts, whose calmness and solitude is not even interrupted by the song
" of birds, those numerous flocks, the image of innocence. In short,
" all this has a something moving, splendid and majestic. One remem-
" bers it with pleasure, and feels, by some secret magic, a desire of re-
" turning and renovating such lively and pleasant ideas by fresh contem-
" plation. Every other journey of a similar extent is but uniform, if
" compared with the present."

All the hardships enumerated in this description, cold and immoderate
heat, hunger, want of commodities, and numberless dangers attending

the

the trackless wilds, presented themselves in the journey of LINNÆUS, but none of the above mentioned charms and rural delights, of which *Lapland* is entirely destitute.

LINNÆUS arrived at *Lulea*, where he took rest for a few days, and then continued his travels. Coming thither he had visited the western provinces on the Gulph of *Bothnia*, and he now directed his way towards the eastern districts through *Tornea* into *Finland*.

Having passed through *Carleby, Vasa, Christianstadt* and *Bjoerneborg*, he reached *Abo*, the capital of the grand dutchy, where he crossed over the Gulph, and after six months travels, of more than eight hundred German leagues in extent, he returned to *Upsal*, towards the latter end of October 1732. He had so well managed his travelling money, as to have been able to defray out of it the expences of getting made a large fur dress, called by the Swedes *Lapmud*, and for which he brought rein-deer-skins with him.

The intention of his journey was most completely fulfilled. *Lapland* is a country as poor in plants as in other productions. LINNÆUS had, however, discovered upwards of one hundred of the former, which were either entirely unknown or undescribed before. But the objects of his attention were not only confined to plants; they included also the curiosities of the animal reign; the domestic arrangements and usages of the inhabitants, their mode of living, and many other civil and moral subjects. He set down all these remarks in the diary which he kept on his journey. This valuable production has likewise remained unprinted. It is written in the *Swedish* language; and after the author's death it became, with his natural collection and other manu-

scripts,

scripts, the property of Doctor J. E. SMITH, of *London*. Several auditors of LINNÆUS obtained this manuscript for their use in their medical and œconomical treatises and labours. Its contents, with regard to botany, have, however, been made public by LINNÆUS himself in two works.

One of these works became the first which appeared in print with the name of LINNÆUS, and is an official document, in which he presents an account of his journey. It is a catalogue and short description of the plants of *Lapland*, under the title of *Florula Lapponica*. Even in such a small work LINNÆUS had already relinquished the system of TOURNEFORT. He described the plants not by their flower or blossom, but according to his own favourite plan, by the sex, the number of stamina, or dust-threads, and the pistilla or dust-ways, which he was obliged first to examine himself. From this small work, the beginning of the epoch of botanical reform, and the introduction of the modern sexual system is to be dated. But this first stone towards the raising of the new Colossus, was too little and too unimportant to deserve particular notice; the more so, as it was concealed in a remote and distant country. Much more was required to be done in order to excite general attention, to make this new structure better known, and to render it the general pattern.

The Royal Academy of Sciences received very favourably this first specimen of the exertions of the juvenile tourist. The two different parts of the *Flora of Lapland*, were inserted in their transactions 1732 and 1734; and to give LINNÆUS a token of their gratitude and esteem they elected him one of their members. Some recent increase of knowledge derived from those travels, and the honour of being elected academician,

academician, were the only rewards which LINNÆUS obtained for his toils. Having surmounted so many dangers and difficulties, he hoped to find repose and better fortune at *Upsal*; but instead of these, fate overwhelmed him with fresh adversities.

Ambitious to shine in the science which he professed, and endeavouring to secure the means of decent support, he began in the year 1733 to give lectures on botany, chymistry and mineralogy. On the latter science he was the first at *Upsal* that ever gave regular lectures. Novelty of matter, the different view in which he represented botany, and the solidity and clearness of his doctrine, gained him uncommon approbation.

This very distinction, so justly acquired, turned out to his prejudice. Envy and rivalship, combined with self-interest, gave rise to all the violence of animosity. LINNÆUS had not taken his degrees, which excluded him from the right of delivering public lectures. Had he been a genius of the second order, he might have expected to meet with indulgence; but as matters stood, he became too obnoxious to his competitors, who were determined to check his rising fame. A young man became at once the rival and accuser of LINNÆUS. His name was Doctor NICHOLAS ROSEN. He had succeeded professor RUDBECK in his anatomical and physical office. The applause which LINNÆUS received militated against ROSEN's reputation. He informed against him before the senate of the university, and insisted that, in virtue of the academical statutes, LINNÆUS be no longer suffered to give public lectures. He was summoned to appear before the senate; several members were in his favour; but ROSEN pleaded the inviolability of the

2

statutes,

statutes, which the senate were bound to enforce, by forbidding Lin-næus to continue his lectures.

This was a blow which hurled down in a moment the brightest hopes of our hero. His glad prospects changed into dreary views. His ambition was hemmed in the sphere of its operations, and his active diligence at once bereft of the only means by which he could support himself. No wonder if the wrath of Linnæus burst forth in a most unbounded manner. In the access of his rage he forgot himself, his future happiness, and every moral consideration. When Rosen left the senate, Linnæus waited on him, with desperate fury drew his sword, and was ready to run it through the body of his enemy, had not the bye-standers fortunately wrested from him that instrument of his vengeance. This violent step excited universal notice. Rosen, who was a member of the academy, complained of this gross assault, and of this daring violation of the laws of public safety. The drawing of the sword was alone sufficient to annihilate the whole subsequent plan of botanical reform. The rigor of the law threatened Linnæus with proscription, and he could never afterwards have made his appearance at *Upsal.* The bad consequences of this decree were, however, warded off by the friends and protectors of Linnæus. Olaus Celsius interposed, allayed the resentment occasioned by this event, and brought matters so far that punishment was changed into a bare reprimand.

Linnæus was now spared, but he still cherished the idea of vengeance. His sanguine temper almost drove him to desperation. Still did he meditate the design of stabbing Rosen if he should meet with him in the streets. While this desperate resolution had insinuated

itself

itself into his mind, he awoke one night in agonizing consternation—his fancy replete with dreadful images—he once gave a serious thought to the horrid idea, and reason conquered the effervescence of passion. From this moment he became more fortunate—as he himself confessed afterwards—and this very occurrence induced him to write a particular diary, under the title of *Nemesis Divina**.

LINNÆUS and ROSEN became afterwards professors almost at the same time, and both were men of eminence. The recollection of this scene of animosity became as little extinct as the secret rivalship which attended the career of their studies, when they once became colleagues. ROSEN acquired a well merited reputation, both in the branches of physic, and as an author, he was appointed Dean of the College of Physicians like LINNÆUS, and created a nobleman by the name of *Rosen von Rosenstein.* He died the 16th of July 1773†.

                                                                        If

---

* I have collected this anecdote from a conversation which LINNÆUS once had with a celebrated pupil of his, and which he related in these words:—" Hoc interficiendi consilium " quum in animo volverem, noĉte quondam e somniis emergens, altius reputavi—et inter- " mittere statui. Ne faeias dixi ; *Deus vindex erit.* Et ex eo tempore omnia in melius ver- " gebant."

† ROSEN was born on the first of February, 1706, in a village near *Gottenburgh,* where he frequented the college in 1718. His father was a preacher ; ROSEN was destined for the church, but disliked the studies of divinity as much as LINNÆUS. Physic was his favourite science. His principal professor was KILIAN STOBÆUS at *Lund.* Having resided four years at the university, he went to *Stockholm,* and became tutor in a nobleman's family. In 1728, assessor MARTIN died at *Upsal,* when ROSEN became substitute professor of physic. Before he took upon himself this new office, he made a tour through *Germany, Switzerland, France* and *Holland,* where he was made doctor at *Harderwyk,* in 1730. In the spring of the follow-ing year he entered on his professorship at *Upsal,* became member of the Society of Sciences there, was received a member of the Royal Academy of *Stockholm,* in 1739 ; in 1740, he be-came ordinary professor for *Rudbeck*; in 1757, he was created a knight of the order of the Polar Star, and ennobled in 1762; when Queen LOUISA ULRICA gave him the name of
                                                                        ROSENSTEIN,

If LINNÆUS had chosen to continue his lectures, he must have taken his degree of doctor; but this was not in his power for want of money. He had more than enough to do to support himself. Amidst these adverse circumstances, there was still one hope left for him. The office of substitute professor of the university of *Lund* had become vacant. He took pains to obtain this charge, and STOBÆUS and other professors supported his claims; his efforts proved, however, fruitless, and another obtained that wished-for happiness.

His situation now became as wretched as before, but his courage and serenity continued the same. The consciousness of his eminence, the remembrance of the darker but still more pleasant prospects of futurity, 'the idea of his bold plan of reform which he still continued to work upon, and the hope of a future comfortable subsistence, animated his resolution and fortitude in combating adversity.

These virtues allayed likewise the rigor of his fate. The former pupils of LINNÆUS lamented his situation. Several of them resolved in the year 1733 to make excursions in the mountainous countries, and they put LINNÆUS at the head of the enterprize, which had for its tendency a farther knowledge of the mineral reign. This excursion extended to *Garpenberg, Averstal, Bitzberg,* and especially to *Fahlun,*

ROSENSTEIN, and chose his coat of arms. He gained great celebrity as a physician to the Royal Family of *Sweden,* and received in the year 1769, for his inoculation of the small pox at court, a reward of 100,000 rix dollars, from the states of the kingdom. His motto was, Without Thorns, " *Sine Spinis.*"—In his last illness he requested the medical assistance of LINNÆUS. His country lost in him one of the greatest physicians. The academy of *Stockholm* had a medal struck to his memory, with this inscription: *Sæculi decus indelibile nostri.* He published the *Method of Curing the Diseases of Children,* translated into German, English, Dutch, French, and Italian: also, *A Medical Repository of Domestic Medicine for Families and Travellers.*

the

the capital of *Dalecarlia*, famous for its rich copper-mines, the most celebrated in *Sweden*.

This was the place, where he laid the foundation of his temporary and subsequent prosperity. He was introduced to Baron REUTER-HOLM, Governor of the Province. This nobleman delighted in the studies of nature; and chiefly spent his leisure hours with the produ&ions of the mines. His charge as dire&or of the mines became more lucrative in proportion to his knowledge of their produce. He saw LINNÆUS, admired his uncommon talents, and grew very fond of him. He had two sons, whom he felt a strong desire of having instru&ed and improved in all the principal œconomical and mineral processes. He resolved, therefore, to, let them travel. LINNÆUS had already explored *Lapland*, acquired experience, and made observations and discoveries. The Baron's sons could not have found an abler guide, and his choice fortunately fell upon him.

Several other young men associated with those young nobles in the excursion. It took place in the spring of 1734, under the dire&ion of LINNÆUS. Each of the young travellers had assigned to him a particular and separate branch of observation. Their way was dire&ed to the Eastern part of *Dalecarlia*, thence to *Norway*, through the mountains, where the mines at *Roraas* occupied their attention for a long time. To view them was the chief obje& of their journey. From hence they returned, by another road, through the West of *Dalecarlia*, to *Fahlun*.

It was at first proje&ed to publish all the observations of the travellers in a colle&ion, but this plan was never executed. LINNÆUS kept a particular journal; but this, like that of his journey through

Lapland, was never printed; partly, because he was prevented from publishing it by other occupations; partly, because he did not choose to publish his juvenile observations after he had gained such universal celebrity. His Dalecarlian diary was consulted as a manuscript by his pupils, and the botanical remarks were inserted in his own works. A particular fruit of this journey was a list of the pasture herbs, which was afterwards prepared for the public eye under the title of *Pan Suecus*, and inserted in the second part of the *Amœnitates Academicæ*.

LINNÆUS, having no prospect of support at UPSAL, remained on his return from this journey, at *Fahlun*, where he established a little college under the auspices of Baron REUTERHOLM. He began to give lectures on the art of assaying metals, and upon other branches of mineralogy. In a town situated in the mountains, like *Fahlun*, the novelty of those instructions excited interest. Theory came to the assistance of the near occasion of practice and experiment. LINNÆUS, considering the smallness of the place, found a sufficient number of pupils, and earned applause, money, friends, and protectors.

The most interesting and most important connexion which he formed here was with a young lady. It was she who fixed his wavering career, and became afterwards his consort and companion through life. LINNÆUS wrote to Baron HALLER the history of this connexion and courtship;—and who would not wish to hear it in his own words.

" Returned from my journey*," says he in this letter, " I took up " my residence at *Fahlun*, the capital of *Dalecarlia*, began to give lec-

" tures

* *Fatto itinere redii in primariam urbem istius provinciæ Dalecarliæ, Fahlunam; docui mineralogiam, amatus ab omnibus permansi per mensem. Erat ibi medicus quem divitem dicere*

" tures on mineralogy, was universally beloved, and remained there a
" whole month. The physician of that district passed for a rich man.
" Considering the poverty of the province, he could justly be deemed
" opulent. His name was MORÆUS, eminent for his learning and skill
" among the Swedish physicians (LINNÆUS called him afterwards in
" one of his dissertations the *great physician of the Swedes, magnum*
" *gentis nostræ medicum).* Physic, especially practical medicine, was the
" science which he esteemed and preferred above all others. He grew
" fond of me. I visited him frequently, and always met with an amicable
" reception. He had two daughters. SARAH ELIZABETH, the eldest,
" was a beautiful girl. A certain Baron had paid his addresses to her,
" though without success. I saw her, was amazed, smitten, and fell
" in love. My caresses and representations won her heart. She promised
" her consent, and vowed to be mine. But as a poor young man I was
" much perplexed to ask her of the father. At last I ventured. Mo-
" RÆUS consented and refused. He loved me, but not my uncertain
" and adverse fate. He finally declared, that his daughter should re-
" main unmarried three years longer, and at the expiration of that time
" he would give his ultimate decision."

Thus LINNÆUS had a bride in the twenty-seventh year of his age.
Little did old MORÆUS think, how great a man his son-in-law would

dicere non erubescebat vulgus, immo erat inter omnes in ista pauperrimâ provinciâ ditissimus,
nomine MORÆUS, vir etiam inter Sueciæ medicos, doctrinam si spectes, facile primus. Vir iste
nullum vitæ genus medicinæ inferiorem (praxin hic spectans) esse, millies pronunciavit; me
interim amabat. Adii domum ejus, non semel gratus ipsi hospes. Filiam habuit (et aliam ætate
inferiorem) pulchram, quam ambiebat Liber Baro quidam frustra; vidi, obstupui, præcordia
intima sensi attonitus novis intumuisse curis. Amavi, illa tandem victa blanditiis votis, &c. &c. -
et me amabat, promisit, dixit fiat. Pat rem adloqui erubescem pauperrimus, dixi tamen;—
Voluit et noluit, me amabat pater, non mea fata, dixit: intacta permanebit per tres annos,
dicam tum demum. Letter to HALLER, *Stockholm,* September 12, 1739.

once

once be! Botany appeared to him too uncertain a branch of fame and support. He, therefore, advised LINNÆUS to apply himself more exclusively to the theoretical and practical study of physic. It then became necessary for the latter in order to see crowned the most ardent of his wishes, by the possession of his beloved, to take his degree of Doctor before the expiration of the limited period. Want of money had rendered this impossible, notwithstanding his multifarious learned exertions. Love helped him to conquer these difficulties. In the year 1733, he had the good fortune, through the friendship and influence of professor WALL-RAVE, to obtain a pension arising from a foundation made in the university of *Upsal*, by one WREDE. This pension amounted to sixty dollars per annum*. He strained every nerve to obtain a continuation of this benefaction, but his efforts proved unsuccessful. His ELIZABETH became however his support. She procured him about one hundred dollars out of her savings, arising from the liberality of her father. To this, LINNÆUS added what little money he had laid by from his pension and lectures†. With this stock he was to travel into a distant country, and to acquire the title of doctor. At that time it was customary in *Sweden* for students to take up their degrees in foreign universities, a fashion in some respects attended with expence, in others productive of utility. The Swedish physicians used then to become graduates in *Holland*, and generally at the University of *Harderwyk*, which was the least expensive. LINNÆUS was therefore, preparing for his departure to that

---

* The pensions granted by the crown to the students at *Upsal*, amount to forty-five. Private pensions, called *Stipendia Magnatum*, there are now thirty and some odd.

† In a letter to BARON HALLER already mentioned, LINNÆUS himself says: *Exivi patriam 36 nummis aureis dives.* By *Nummi aurei*, LINNÆUS always meant ducats, the usual gold currency of *Sweden*. According to FABRICIUS, it made a sum of one hundred ducats.

2   country.

country, which by the concurrence of auspicious circumstances became the abode of his fame, and the theatre of his primary greatness. ·

But before we can follow him on his journey, and in the career of his reform, it is necessary for the sake of a better view, to promise an historical episode, or a concise history of the fate and state of the science of botany at that time—a science which has since been entirely changed by his discoveries.

SECTION

SECTION IV.

A SHORT HISTORY OF BOTANY.

AMONG THE GREEKS.—THEOPHRASTUS, THE FATHER OF BOTANY.—HIPPO-
CRATES.—DIOSCORIDES.—AMONG THE ROMANS.—PLINY.—VIEW OF THE PRO-
GRESS OF BOTANY.—OBSTACLES.—WANT OF SYSTEMATICAL DIVISION.—FATE OF
THIS SCIENCE IN THE MIDDLE AGE.—ITS REGENERATION IN THE FIFTEENTH
CENTURY BY THE GERMANS.—BRUNFELS.—BOCK.—FUCHS.—THE SIXTEENTH
CENTURY.—CONRAD GESNER, THE FATHER OF MODERN BOTANICAL HISTORY.
—HIS SINGULAR DESTINY.—CULTIVATION OF BOTANICAL GARDENS.—BOTANI-
CAL EXCURSIONS.—THE GERMANS ARE THE FIRST WHO PUBLISHED THE FLORAS,
OR COLLECTIONS OF PLANTS OF CERTAIN COUNTRIES.—CLUSIUS THE GREAT-
EST BOTANICAL TRAVELLER IN THE SIXTEENTH CENTURY.—AFFLUENCE OF
BOTANICAL MATERIALS.—WANT OF A NEW SYSTEM.—CAESALPINUS, AN ITA-
LIAN, FORMS ONE.—CASPAR BAUHIN, A SWISS, THE FIRST UNIVERSAL WRITER
ON BOTANY.—THE SEVENTEENTH CENTURY.—JUNGIUS.—MANY JOURNIES TO
PROMOTE NATURAL HISTORY.—MORISON AND RAY, ENGLISHMEN, THE FIRST
AUTHORS OF MODERN SYSTEMS.—RIVINUS.—TOURNEFORT, THE MODERN LE-
GISLATOR IN BOTANY.—ACCOUNTS RESPECTING HIM AND HIS SYSTEM.—
VAILLANT HIS PUPIL.—HIS INGENIOUS OBSERVATIONS ON THE GENERA, OR
SEXES, OF PLANTS.

THAT same region of Eastern Europe, whence the Muses by ferocity
and warlike rage were driven, towards the middle of the fifteenth century, to seek an asylum in other distriéts of this part of the globe, and
which has been the seat of Ottoman ignorance and barbarism ever
since; that same region which, in the time of the Greeks, became the
genuine soil of all the sciences, was also the cradle of botany. It
owes its first cultivation to THEOPHRASTUS, that eminent philosopher

H   who

who acquired immortal fame by his moral chara&eristic sketches. He
was born at *Eresus*, in the island of *Lesbos*; lived in the third century
before the birth of CHRIST (between the 97th and 123d Olympiad);
and was a disciple of PLATO and ARISTOTLE. Through his distinguished talents he became dear to the latter, who constituted him heir
to his library, and successor in the Peripatetic school. He preferred the
love of Nature to the abstruse pursuits of philosophy. He undertook
several journies for the purpose of promoting natural knowledge; and
the fruits of his labours terminated in two valuable works on natural
history and the generation of plants *, which have been preserved to
this day. In these he gives a descriptive account of upwards of
500 plants. A century before him HIPPOCRATES had already been
the pride of his nation; but the studies and discoveries of this original genius were almost exclusively confined to the human frame, its
diseases and cures. As the oracle of the sick, whose advice and attendance was requested from all quarters, he chiefly bestowed his attention on those produ&ions of Nature, which, by their medical virtues,
were calculated to engross his principal concern.

Thus THEOPRASTUS was and remained the first learned botanist who
flourished in *Greece* during its independence and republican freedom.
The fall of the latter had for its mediate consequence the decline of
the sciences. Several centuries elapsed without THEOPHRASTUS having a successor or rival of his fame. At last an Asiatic arrogated to

* Περὶ φυτων ισοριας, seu Historiæ Plantarum, lib. ix. cum commentar. J. C. SCALIGERI et
J. BODÆI a Stapel, *Amsterdam* 1644. Of the xth book we have only fragments,
φωτιχῶν αιτιῶν βιβλια η, seu de Causis Plantarum, lib. vi. His complete Greek works first
appeared with those of ARISTOTLE at *Venice*, by A. MANUCE, from 1495 till 1498, six
volumes in folio. The best Latin translation is that of DAN. HEINSIUS, *Leyden*, 1613.

himself

himself the merit of pursuing farther the career of the celebrated LESBIAN. This was DIOSCORIDES, a native of *Anazarbe* in *Cilicia*. He lived in the first century after the birth of CHRIST. Medicine was his profession. He was the first who bestowed the utmost attention by enquiring into the medicinal properties of plants. He made them the object of several travels through various provinces in *Europe* and *Asia*. His work on the medical virtues of the plants *, which rendered him the literary father of the *Materia Medica*, remains as a valuable monument of his greatness. His travels into remote countries had enabled him to make more observations than THEOPHRASTUS. He described upwards of 600 plants.

The *Greeks* were in all sciences, especially in natural history, and in the scientifiic representation of botany, the original predecessors and teachers of the Romans, their conquerors. The latter, at the most flourishing epochs of their universal monarchy devoted themselves more than ever to the Muses. The less known and less cultivated goddess FLORA, found only among them one great votary, who, by his meritorious exertions, preserved his name even beyond the grave. This was PLINY the elder, of *Verona*, a man universally eminent in *Roman* literature, and especially in natural history. The large classical work which he wrote on this subject is principally appropriated to the vegetable reign, which it occupies from the 11th to the 19th book. In point of rich collections and keen observations he excelled all the Greeks. By his own avowal, his natural history is a compilation from

---

* Περὶ ὕλης ἰατρίχῆς, de Materia Medica, lib. vi. first published by A. MANUCE at *Venice*, 1499, in folio; afterwards by J. A. SARACENUS at *Frankfort*, 1598, folio. The most modern and best edition is by the late Baron VON KOLLAR, *Vienna*, 1770, with plates.

about

about 2500 different authors. This, in some measure, proves that the
Romans were not without naturalists, though their fame had perished
with their works. PLINY was too soon wrested from the lap of the
science which he cultivated with so much zeal and success, for he fell
a victim to his curiosity on Mount *Vesuvius*, in the 56th year of his
age, and the 79th after the birth of CHRIST.

These were the most eminent and most celebrated botanists of antiquity. The pains they took, the collections and discoveries by which 🐦
they first opened the career of this science, however meritorious, could
not but be considered as the efforts of beginners. No study was less
susceptible of being brought by them to a certain criterion of perfection than that of botany and natural history in general. *Rome* was not
built in a day; nor could the edifice of this science be raised in so
sudden a manner. It required materials from all countries on earth,
which demanded to be minutely viewed, examined, and arranged. The
Romans were the masters of the ancient world; but they had only a
slight and superficial knowledge of the smallest part of it; in proportion to the *Greeks* they had but few connexions with foreigners; every
body was uncultivated but themselves; the art of printing, and that of
engraving on copper and wood, had not yet been invented;—all these
were material obstacles to a successful and marked progress in natural
history.

The plants which were known and discovered by the ancients, though
they amounted to some thousands, were still but very few, and an
almost imperceptible part of an infinite whole. They solely consisted
of the plain collections of southern produce, mostly gathered on the
frontiers of two parts of the world, *Europe* and *Asia*. The number of
all

all the plants growing on our globe is certainly unlimited, and can only be alledged upon supposition and conjecture. LINNÆUS counted afterwards 10,000 species of them, and described upwards of 8,000. One of his subsequent adversaries, the French botanist, ADANSON, who made several discoveries in his *African* travels, estimated the number of those plants which were known, but not properly discriminated, at 18,000, and that of the unknown ones at 25,000. If we admit this calculation, which bears every plausibility of being too high in number according to ADANSON, and too low according to the LINNÆAN scale, only choose a medium between both extremes, the result arising from it will furnish a decisive proof of the scanty provision which the ancients have made for this division of the store-house of natural knowledge. They described the plants, but required longer and more various observations to represent their internal structure, properties, and distinctive marks. In other respects they formed their collections without order, without any particular classification; a circumstance which proved extremely painful and laborious to the subsequent lovers of botany. The small quantity of materials amassed by the ancients, remained a rough chaos, which waited to receive its more direct limitation and arrangement from some creative hand. There was no branch in which such a chaos could be more detrimental than in the history of Nature, the mother of so many numerous families, races and offsprings, among which a limited distinction and classification could alone elucidate the original descents, and their various branches and affinities.

In a state thus debile and infirm, botany was handed down to a barbarous and superstitious æra, in which the cultivation of the sciences

was

was the least of all concerns. The *Mahometans* and *Arabs* were the
only nations who would give them a partial reception. But they were
fonder of practical physic than botany, which was almost totally forlorn,
and abandoned of course.

After a lapse of near fifteen ages, botany was rescued with other
sciences in the middle of the fifteenth century from her widowed state.
The printing and engraving on wood, and the discovery of *America*, came
to her assistance. The *Germans* were the foremost to draw her from
oblivion. The first representation of plants in wood-cuts made its appearance at *Mentz* towards the latter end of the fifteenth century, and
an *Italian Flora* in 1485 was printed at *Padua* *.

In botany the ancients could less be the guides and patterns of the
moderns than in the other sciences. The latter were too little acquainted with the discoveries of the former; their descriptions were
unintelligible, and mostly related to unknown southern plants. They
had no classification, no system; it was not known where they classed
this or that plant, which of either they meant in their description, and
of course their discoveries remained unprofited by and lost. Hence it
became necessary to regenerate, as it were, the whole science of botany, and to collect and describe fresh materials for that purpose.

In this point the *Germans* likewise were the first in setting an example to other nations. A native of *Mentz*, of the name of OTHO
BRUNFELS, professor at *Strasbourg*, and afterwards first physician in
the city of *Bern*, who died in the year 1534, became the first modern

---

* Hortus Sanitatis seu de Herbis ac Plantis, in quarto, printed at *Mentz*, by P. SHOEFFER.
Herbarius Pataviæ impressus, anno Domini 1485, also with wood-cuts.

restorer

restorer of botany at the commencement of the sixteenth century.
He published a collection of plants faithfully drawn after nature *.
At the same time EURICIUS CORDUS, a *Hessian*, professor of the
university of *Marbourg*, who died at *Bremen* in 1535, signalized himself by his botanical merits. VALERIUS CORDUS, his son, who died on
his-travels through *Italy*, was a conspicuous naturalist, and torn too
early from the bosom of science in the 29th year of his age.

The footsteps of the latter were followed by two other *Germans*,
JEROME BOCK, physician in the small town of *Hornbach* in the Dutchy
of *Wurtemberg*; and LEONARD FUCHS, a *Swabian* professor at *Ingolt-
stadt*, and afterwards at *Tubingen*, whom CHARLES V. Emperor of *Germany*, created a nobleman on account of his rare talents. The former
departed life in 1554, the latter in 1566. Both of them had made collections of plants which they published †. Thus was botany restored by
the southern *Germans* in the first half of the sixteenth century. They
were, however, all excelled in point of copiousness of knowledge, ingenuity of observations, and richness of materials, by a *Swiss*, their co-
temporary. This was the *Polyhistor* of his age, and especially the prince
of modern natural history in general, CONRAD GESNER, a name, whose
splendid celebrity has been propagated by many learned and meritorious
rious descendants and successors down to this present day. Adversity

* This work was printed at *Strasbourg* in 1532, in two volumes, folio, in German; afterwards in Latin, under the title " Herbarum Hical Icones ad Naturæ Imitationem Imitatæ."
Strasbourg, 1532, three volumes, folio.

† Von FUCHS De Historia Stirpium Commentarii Insignes, *Bazil*, 1542, in folio.—JEROM
BOCK's New Herbal, in German, printed at *Strasbourg*, 1539; and a second edition printed
at the same place in 1546, folio. Baron HALLER gives the following character to BOCK:
" Nemo tot plantos ante vidit et descripsit, nemo vires veriores addidit illo."

also

also raised him to greatness. He was born at *Zurith* in 1516, and intended at *first* to study divinity. He came to *Strasbourg*, but so great
was then his poverty, that he thought himself very fortunate in being
received as servitor to a professor. Love became the umpire of his
destiny, and directed all his subsequent enterprizes. He entered the
state of matrimony in the 20th year of his age, though without having
wherewithal to support himself. His poverty rose to the highest pitch.
He resolved to quit the theological career which he had hitherto pur-
.sued. He went to study physic at *Montpellier*; was made doctor, and
afterwards professor of physic in his native place. No country but
Switzerland could have furnished him with better opportunities of
making botanical observations, nor did GESNER let them escape.

Among his botanical works there is a remarkable catalogue of plants*.
His great philological knowledge first enabled him to give them a nomenclature in several languages. He was also the first who introduced
the method of classifying plants by their flowers and fruit. No literatus
of his age was more diligent and more fertile than GESNER; and the numerous works which he published, were, as I may say, but a beginning
of his scientific harvest. He left behind a much superior number
of writings, part printed, part in manuscript. He was prevented
finishing them by the plague, which swept away his valuable existence
in 1565, in the forty-ninth year of his age.

After the Hessian literatus E. CORDUS, who was the first professor of
physic in the university of *Marburg*, GESNER was also the first who
cultivated a private botanical garden for his own use. But the first

---

* Catalogus plantarum, Latine, Græce, Germanice, et Gallice, Tigur. 1542, in quarto
His posthumous works were published by SCHMIDEL, under the title of " Gesneri Opera
" Botanica, Norimbergæ, 1754 and 1759," 2 vol. folio.

                                                          public

public establishment of this kind, was made at the university of *Padua*, in 1540. This public example set in *Italy*—an example so evidently useful to physicians and natural philosophers, was imitated before the close of the sixteenth century by medical gardens at *Zurich, Turin,* and *Montpellier.* In this manner the science of botany now became a regular academical study.

During the latter half of the sixteenth century, its novelty and pleasantness gained it several lovers in most of the Southern countries of *Europe.* Collections were made, plants described, voyages of natural discoveries in other parts of the world undertaken, and the charms of Flora created an enthusiasm, which bade defiance to all dangers and difficulties. Mr. WIELAND, born at *Koenigsberg,* in *Prussia,* who afterwards assumed the name of GUILANDINUS in *Italy,* made a voyage into *Asia* and *Africa,* under the protection of a rich patrician at *Venice;* but on his succeeding voyage to *America* he was captured by a Barbarian pirate, and carried a slave to *Algiers.* A lover and professor of a science to which he afterwards fell a martyr, FALLOPIO, professor of Botany at *Padua,* generously paid his ransom. GUILANDINUS became the successor of his deliverer in his professorship, and died at *Padua* in 1589.

PROSPER ALPINUS, a Venetian, who a few years after succeeded GUILANDINUS as professor, became equally eminent for his zeal in botany and natural history. He made a voyage to *Egypt,* as physician to the Consul of the Republic, and brought back with him several learned productions*; he died in the year 1617. One of the first and

* De Plantis Ægypti, Venet. 1592, quarto.—De plantis Exoticis, Libr. II. Venet 1627, quarto.—Historiæ Naturalis Ægyptiorum Lib. IV. *Leyden,* 1735, quarto.

most

most expensive public voyages to *America* was made by Don Francis Hernandez, a Spaniard, first physician to Philip II. King of *Spain*. The object of this voyage was a physico-natural exploration and description of *Mexico*, on which the Spanish government bestowed 60,000 ducats. The result of this voyage was not published till some time in the seventeenth century *.

Among the learned of the different nations, the Germans also distinguished themselves by travels undertaken for the improvement of natural knowledge. Among others, Leonard Rauwolf, a native of *Augsburg*, who died as physician to the army in the Austrian service, in 1596, became eminent as a diligent observer on his travels in *Asia*, and the Eastern countries of *Europe*, from 1573 † till 1588.

They were likewise Germans, who conceived the useful idea of rendering the curiosities of nature, and the indigenous plants of certain provinces, the exclusive object of their attention, and to describe them in separate collections. The first who set an example in this respect, was George Fabricius, the Saxon historian, who died in the year 1571. In his historical description of *Misnia* ‡, he gave a short catalogue of the indigenous plants and animals of that province. But this was only one single good idea of a secondary plan. The first regular

* Franz. Ximenes 4 libros della Naturaleza y Virtudes de las plantas y animales, que estam recevidos en el uso de Medecina en la Nueva Espanna, &c. &c. con lo que el Dr. Hernandez escrivio en lengua latina, *Mexico*, 1615, quarto.—The whole works of Hernandes were afterwards published under the title: Plantarum, animalium, mineralium Mexicaniorum historia, *Roma*, 1651, folio, with 800 cuts.

† Description of his travels through the East, especially *Syria*, &c. in German, 1583, four parts in quarto.—His dried collection of plants was afterwards published by the Dutch Botanist J. T. Gronov, under the title of " Rauwolfii Flora Orientalis, *Leyden*, 1755. octavo.

‡ Rerum Misnicarum, lib. vii. *Lipz.* 1569 and 1660, quarto.

I

and original pattern in this branch, was published by CASPAR SCHWENK-FELD, born at *Greifenberg* in *Silesia*, who died as physician at *Gorlitz*, in 1609. He gave a full description of the animals, plants, and minerals of *Silesia**.

Among the itinerant naturalists of the sixteenth and all preceding centuries, none distinguished himself more by an indefatigable zeal, and a variety of observations and discoveries, than a Belgian. His name was CHARLES ECLUSE, born at *Arras*, in 1526. He was to have studied law, but bestowed all his diligence and the resource of his fortune upon botany, travelled almost through the whole East and West of *Europe*, including *Portugal, Spain, France, England, Germany, Hungary*, &c. had several times his arms and feet fractured, owing to the zeal and curiosity which guided his peregrinations, and died finally at an advanced age in 1609, as professor of botany at *Leyden†*.

During a period of about one hundred and fifty years, a considerable provision of materials for natural history had been made. These materials were more considerable than any ever before collected, discovered, and published by the ancients. Notwithstanding all these advantages, botany remained an uncultivated republic. Threatened with troubles in proportion to the increase of its population, it wanted what the ancients had never introduced—a constitution, a collection of laws to preserve order, and the necessary divisions and distinctions between the numerous species, races, and families, in order to fix the preser-

* Historia Stirpium Silesiæ—et ejus Fossilium. *Lipz*, 1600.—Theriotropheum Silesiæ in quo animalium vis et usus perstringuntur, *Lignicii*, 1604, quarto.

† He wrote the following works: Historia rariorum plantarum per Hispanias observatarum, *Antw.* 1576, in octavo.—Per Pannoniam, Austriam, &c. *Antw.* 1583.—Historia plantarum Rariorum, 2 vol. folio, *Antw.* 1601, &c.

vation

vation and closer kaowledge of the whole. The plants were jumbled
together, those which were analogous were separated, and the heterogeneous ones united; no part of them had the special privilege of being
considered as the distinctive mark of its species; their internal structure had been but little examined, and the use of their names applied
without system, appeared so confused and corrupted, that this great
resource proved rather a burden than a help to memory.

The natural politics of an Italian, first felt after GESNER the inconvenience occasioned by this defect. This was ANDREW CÆSALPINUS,
born at *Arezzo*, in the district of *Florence*, in 1519, first professor of
physic and botany at the University of *Pisa*, and afterwards first
physician to POPE CLEMENT VIII. at *Rome*, where he died 1603.
The idea of such a want, being besides a lover of order, which he had
learned to value in the school of ARISTOTLE, made him conceive the
thought of rendering himself the legislator of the confused botanical
commonwealth. This task, however, baffled his strength. His genius
was inventive, but his knowledge of botany neither original nor universal. He missed both leisure and opportunity. CLUSIUS had discovered more fresh plants than he ever was acquainted with. His herbal did not contain nine hundred species, a fact fully proved by the
Florentine Botanist MICHELI, who had it in his possession. A provision of this kind was too small to give a comprehensive view of botany, and the knowledge which CÆSALPINUS acquired of the internal
structure of plants, was too secret and too defective to point out the
most perfect order. He was only directed by the fruit, and mostly by
that part on which the shoots or germins repose. This system had its
defects, but it brought CÆSALPINUS much nearer to the truth, and he
                                                    discovered

discovered more real similarities, more natural classes than all the botanists who preceded, and many who followed him. His work on
plants *(De Plantis, Lib. XVI. Florent.* 1583.*)* still remains a valuable
monument of ancient botany. " Cæsalpinus was a great man," says
Linnæus with enthusiastic affection, " What signal service did he
" not render by first opening the career!—His short descriptions,
" by which he distinguishes himself from all others, please me parti-
" cularly. He has always some oddity of his own*."

With the close of the sixteenth century a man appeared, who
had long ago been expected by botany in its confused state, who
did not shrink from the herculean labour of collecting into one regular
mass its numerous and scattered treasures, of exhibiting them at one
view, and giving a knowledge of the botanical world and all its discoveries. This was Caspar Bauhin, the second great botanist produced by *Switzerland.* He was born in the year 1560, at *Basil,* made
a tour through *Italy* and *Germany,* and was appointed professor of
botany and anatomy in his native place, where he died in 1624.

His elder brother, John Bauhin, first physician the Duke of *Wir-
temberg,* acquired also a great literary reputation in botany. The principal works, by which he gained a lasting name in the annals of that
science, were his representations of plants, and especially what he
called the exhibition of the botanical theatre †, a work which took up
almost all his life-time, and was the fruit of fourteen years collections
and labours. It served to facilitate the study of botany and to promote

* Cæsalpinus mihi magnus; quantum erat, primam condere gentem !---Ille mihi maxime
placet, ejusque breves description.s, quibus discedit ab omnibus aliis, tamen semper habet
aliquid singulare. Epistolæ ab eruditis viris ad Hallerum scriptæ, Vol. I. *Bernæ,* 1773.

† Phytopinax, *Bas.* 1596, quarto.---Pinax Theatri Botanici, *ibid.* 1623.

it's

its knowledge. BAUHIN was not the creator of a system, but he reformed many abuses and defects, especially the confusion of names.

He collected the synonymous terms of 6000 plants, which various
authors had assigned to them of their own accord. This prevented
the manifold mistakes which had till then been made by botanists, who
took several descript plants for non-descripts, and gave them new
names, only because they had been described too much and too va-
riously. BAUHIN himself made several mistakes in this new method,
which are however, considering the whole extent of his merits, worthy
of being overlooked.

LINNÆUS himself represents the fate of botany under an ingenious
simile : " Botany," says he*, " is a plant of the genus of the palms,
" which sometimes do not bloom for a whole century, and bear fruit
" at a late period. Botany first put forth some shoots in the reign of
" ALEXANDER, was afterwards transplanted to Rome, continued to
" prosper, but grew no farther, and began to fade, when they ceased
" to foster it. It was then transported into Arabia, and yielded, for
" the first time, in the sixteenth century, a slight frail blossom in
" Italy—(CAESALPINUS)—a blossom which could be blasted on its
" short and thin stalks by the least gust of wind, and bore no kind of
" fruit. In the seventeenth century it began to germinate, pro-
" duced only a few leaves and no mark of bloom; but in the
" spring of this golden age, when the snow had scarcely been melted
" the trunk put forth blossom, and the latter a fruit—(CASPAR BAU-
" HIN) which almost came to maturity."

* In the preface of his Bibliotheca Botanica, *Amsterd.* 1738.

This

This fruit procured contentment. A pause ensued in the farther cultivation of botany. The learned thought it was sufficient, if they knew and called the plants by the names which BAUHIN had given them. The ravages of the thirty years war, the theatre of which was chiefly in Germany, had no progressive influence on the arts and sciences of peace, especially on botany. Among those men who thought freely of botany, and consulted their own spirit of inquiry, there was one at this period in *Lower Saxony*, of the name of JOACHIN JUNGIUS. He was born at *Lubeck* in 1586, first professor of Mathematics at *Giesen* and *Rostock*, afterwards professor of Physic at *Helmstaedt*, and died as Rector at *Hamburgh*, in 1657. His spirit accustomed to mathematical accuracy, bestowed more attention on the internal structure of plants, he made more ingenious remarks in * his writings, and was the first who had some of the fundamental ideas of the system, which was finally introduced by LINNÆUS.

But during the latter half of the last century, a new epoch commenced in botany as well as in many other sciences. The former acquired more enthusiastic lovers, even among those nations who till then had hardly taken any notice of it. Thus far its empire had solely been extended to the productions of Europe; but now the first zealous beginning was made, to obtain knowledge from the other parts of the world. The English, Dutch, and French, being the first commercial nations, had the best opportunities, and took care to profit by them. RUMPHIUS, HERRMAN, RHEEDE, KAEMPFER, MARGRAF, SLOANE, PLUCKENET, BROWN, SHERARD, CATESBY, CLAYTON,

* Isagoge Phytoscopica, *Hamb* 1678, quarto.—Farther, Doxoscopiæ Physicæ Minores, seu Isagoge Physica Doxoscopica, *Hamb.* 1662.

TOURNEFORT,

Tournefort, Dodart, Plumier, Feuillee, Boccone, and many others travelled to remote countries and islands, and acquired merit in natural history. With the love of collecting natural curiosities, which spread more and more throughout *Europe*, the botanical gardens became also more numerous. In *England*, those of *Oxford*, *Chelsea*, and *Kew*; and in *Holland*, those of *Amsterdam*, *Leyden*, and the *Hague* were established.

The advantage accruing from these voyages and travels, augmented to an uncommon degree the botanical materials, and rendered them twice as copious as they had been before. Hence a proper systematical method became the more necessary to avoid a Babelonian confusion among the different writers in that science. It required a better compass to extricate oneself from such a labyrinth, and according to these wishes the epoch of systematical botany arrived.

The Britons were the first who opened this systematic tract in Robert Morison and John Ray, or, as he called himself in Latin, Rajus, both of them originally divines. Morison was a native of *Aberdeen* in *Scotland*, born there in 1620. He remained a staunch loyalist during the civil wars which distracted *England*, and served even as a soldier; a situation of life which he could never forget, owing to a dangerous wound he had received. He afterwards went to *France*, where he was made director of the royal garden at *Blois*, returned to *England* in 1660, and was appointed professor of botany at *Oxford*. His end was tragical. While riding in a curricle through the streets of *London*, it was overset, and himself thrown on the pavement, by which fall he fractured his skull in 1683. Linnæus drew his character and merits in a letter to Baron Haller, written in the year 1737, in the

following

following expressions: " MORISON was a vain, self-conceited, but
" nevertheless, a meritorious man, since he revived an antiquated
" method *. If you compare the genera of TOURNEFORT, you will
" easily see what the latter owed to MORISON; it was at least an obli-
" gation as great as that which MORISON owed to CÆSALPINUS, even
" allowing TOURNEFORT to have been a most scrupulous enquirer.
" With all the good things which MORISON borrowed of CÆSALPI-
" NUS, he seems to have differed from him in point of a systematical
" knowledge of Nature, whereas CÆSALPINUS paid greater atten-
" tion to the distinctive marks of plants †."

RAY, an Englishman, born in the county of *Essex* 1628, the rival of
MORISON, was a much superior genius. Divinity was his professional
study; but this sacred pursuit did not make his fortune, owing to the
spirit of opposition which he manifested in the contentions of the
church. He travelled through *Germany, France* and *Italy*, and afterwards directed his exclusive application to botany and natural history,
in which he wrote more than any other of his countrymen ‡. He died

in

---

* MORISONUS vanus fuit et inflatus, tamen nunquam non laudandus, qui viviviscere fecit
methodum demortuam. Confer *Genera* TOURNEFORTII, et quid MORISONIO debuit facile
agnoscas; tantum certe ac CÆSALPINO MORISONIUS, licet fidus fuit examinator TOUR-
NEFORTIUS. MORISONIUS omnia sua, quæ bona à CÆSALPINO habuit, videtur in eo dis-
cessisse, ut observaret concatenatam affinitatem, naturæ magis quam characteres.—Baron
HALLER gives the following opinion of his system: " *Methodus* MORISONII *penes*
" *nulla est.* Veras errores vix detexit, nisi quando ad genera veriora stirpes revocavit. Id
" vero habet commodi, quod plures stirpes habeat quam BAUHINUS."

† See MORISON'S *Plantarum Historia Universalis, Oxon.* 1678, two vols. folio; and *Hortus Regius Blesensis, London,* 1669, octavo.

‡ *Methodus Plantarum emendata, London,* 1703 and 1733, in octavo. *Synopsis Me-*
K   *thodica*

in 1705, in the 77th year of his age, after having acquired great celebrity.

LINNÆUS gave a still more unfavourable opinion of him. He draws his character in the above mentioned letter as follows: " RAY cer-" tainly was a most laborious man in collections and descriptions; but " in that branch of botanical knowledge which relates to the genera of " plants, he was less than nothing; and in the examination of flowers a " mere nonentity. Compare the first edition of his botanical system " with the second and third. Every thing it contains he borrowed from " TOURNEFORT. I am at a loss to divine why nobody takes notice of " the discoveries of CÆSALPINUS, and wishes to ascribe every thing " to RAY *. Both MORISON and RAY derived their botanical systems " from the fruit of plants."

To these authors of systems may be added AUGUSTUS RIVIN, a Saxon, professor of botany at *Leipzick*, where he died in 1723, in the seventy-first year of his age. He classified the plants by the number of their petals or the leaves of their flowers, and divided them into eighteen classes—a division subject to many material defects†.

thodica Stirpium Britonnicorum, London, 1690. Historia Plantarum Generalis, London, 1693.

* Certe vir laboriosissimus in colligendo, describendo, &c. at in *genericis* minus nihilo, in examinandis floribus plane nullus. Quæso, confer ejus primam editionem *Methodi* cum secunda et tertia, ubi a TOURNEFORTIO edoctus fuit omnia. Nescio cur nullus CÆSALPINI observare potuit inventa.—See a full opinion on the merits of RAY in Dr. RICH. PULTENEY's Historical and Biographical Sketches of the Progress of Botany in *England*, from its origin to the introduction of the LINNÆAN system. Vol. 1, *London*, 1790, octavo.

† His principal botanical writings are—*Introductio Generalis in rem Herbariam. Lips.* 1690. *Ordines Plantarum Irregularium Flore Monopetalo, Tetrapetalo et Pentapetalo. Lips.* 1690.

1

Thus

Thus different structures were raised to reduce into order the stores
of natural productions, and to facilitate a comprehensive view of them;
but, as in all former fabrics, there was no formal and regular perfection
in them. The chambers were not sufficiently commodious for common
use, and the division of the whole was destitute of solidity and precision.

A greater architect arose, who excelled all his predecessors. This
was JOSEPH PITTON DE TOURNEFORT, a Frenchman, born at *Aix*
in *Provence* in 1656, whose genius was wholly created for botany.
His parents had destined him for the church, but TOURNEFORT, like
our LINNÆUS, ranged through the fields and collected plants instead of
going to school. He was left fatherless at the age of 21. He now devoted himself entirely to his inclination, studied at *Montpellier*, where
the botanical garden was of great service to him; made a tour through
Languedoc, Dauphiny and the *Pyrenees*; was appointed professor of the
royal botanical garden at *Paris* in 1683; visited *Spain, Portugal, England* and *Holland;* undertook to travel from 1700 to 1702 at the expence of LOUIS XV. into *Greece* and *Asia*, whither he was accompanied by A. GUNDELSHEIMER, a native of *Anspach*, and physician to
the King of *Prussia*, and died at last in a state of celibacy in the year
1708. His death was occasioned by a catastrophe similar to that which
befel MORISON, his chest being crushed by a carriage which suddenly
passed by him.

Before he set out on his travels he published a new botanical system which soon attracted universal attention. He divided the plants
into twenty-two classes, which he determined by the different forma-

K 2   tion

tion of the flower, and their orders he ascertained by the fruit. His system of reform principally consisted of the following points and topics:

He divided all the plants, which were known to him, from the quality of the flower *(corollæ)* into classes, which his predecessors had limited by the fruit, and these classes he subdivided into orders. He arranged the genera by solid, distinctive marks, which he borrowed of the fruit; gave them fixed generical names, and placed the species, with their manifold variations, under the genera *. Thus, when the lovers and professors of botany met with a flower or plant unknown to them, the guidance of this system enabled them to get acquainted with the class by the structure of the flower, with the order by the quality of the fruit, and by the examination of both fruit and flower with the species. This classification was of infinite service, in affording uncommon aid to the memory and judgment †. His system also remained in general acceptance to the time of LINNÆUS; and many learned men took pains to mend its defects.

While TOURNEFORT was still dignified with the title of the oracle of botany, one of his pupils made himself conspicuous by his heterodox ingenuity. Too soon, however, was he torn from the lap of the sciences to have erected himself a throne upon the ruins of that of his master.

* See *Reformatio Botanices*, LINNÆO *proposita a* J. M. REFTELIO, 1762; *in Amoenital.* Acad. vol. vi. page 306.

† The work which contains this system, is the master-piece of TOURNEFORT, entituled *Elemens de Botanique, ou Methode pour connoitre les Plants. Paris*, 1694, three vols. octavo, and rendered afterwards more complete, under the title of *Institutiones rei Herbariæ. Paris*, 1700, three vols. quarto.

This

This was SEBASTIAN VAILLANT, a Frenchman, born at *Vigny* in *Isle de France*, in 1669. His poverty made him apply rather late to his favourite study. He first was an organist, then a surgeon, and afterwards secretary to FAGON, first physician to LOUIS XIV. He learned a great deal of this man, made his fortune through him, being appointed demonstrator of the plants in the royal botanical garden at *Paris*, under ANTHONY DE JUSSIEU, professor of botany, whom he soon after excelled by his superior talents and merits. VAILLANT died at *Paris* in 1722. He only published two small pamphlets in which he did not encompass with peculiar judgment the whole reign of botany, although he displayed many new and original observations in them. LINNÆUS stood much indebted to his ingenuity and observations upon the internal structure of plants and their sexes, and always remained his warmest defender. " I own," says LINNÆUS, in a letter to Baron HALLER, " that I never read an author more accurate than VAILLANT, nor one " who invented more novelty in botany, laboured more, and obtained " less reward than him *."

TOURNEFORT was and remained the prince of botany; but upon nearer investigation there were many imperfections and flaws found in his system. Soon after him many articles of his were changed, new names and new classes introduced, and fresh methods planned. But those who embarked in such enterprizes were men not half so ingenious nor half so penetrating as TOURNEFORT. The botanical commonwealth was threatened with fresh barbarism and ravages, had not a different legislation brought about a total reform.

* Ego fateor, me nullum adhuc legisse, qui VAILLANTIO accuratior fuit, qui plura nova invenit in botanicis, qui plus laboravit, qui parcius præmium reportavit.

Such

Such were the fates of botany—such its state—when Linnæus prepared to travel to *Holland*, where he undertook the reform, which pro-
gressively extended to the two other reigns of Nature, both animal
and mineral.

SECTION

SECTION V.

HAVING spent his winter months in visiting his friends and rela-
latives, in preparing his academical dissertations, and arranging the
collections of his materials of reform, which he considered as his most
valuable treasures, LINNÆUS began in April, 1735, his travels to

foreign

foreign countries, which the laws of love and ancient custom had rendered necessary, and which became pleasant by the happy prospects of his farther improvement and the enterprizes he had planned. But he could then as little foresee the advantageous circumstances thrown in his way by auspicious fate to favour his remarkable career, as he could measure the long space of time which he was to pass afar from his country.

He set out on his tour to *Holland* from *Fahlun,* through the Southern provinces of *Sweden, Copenhagen, Jutland, Schleswick,* and *Holstein* to *Hamburgh.* Here he rested himself for some time. His zeal of knowledge outweighed all other considerations. He saw the literary curiosities and natural collections at *Hamburgh,* and met with a most amicable reception on the part of the respective proprietors and other connoisseurs and lovers of natural history.

Among these was Dr. JOHN PETER KOHL of *Altona,* afterwards professor at *Petersburgh,* who when advanced in life returned to the former place, where he became the benefactor of the college, and enriched it with a large and fine library. At *Hamburgh,* he found the Burgomaster JOHN ANDERSON, Doctor GEOFFRY JÆNISCH, and JOHN VON SPRECKELSEN *, all eminent men, with whom LINNÆUS carried on a literary correspondence. The great library and collection of natural curiosities which belong to the latter, chiefly engrossed his attention—afforded him utility and entertainment—but at the same time involved him in a pleasant dilemma.

---

* Several foreign literary productions have very improperly represented SPRECKELSEN, by the title of Burgomaster; he was only Secretary of Council. Professor DILLENIUS of *Oxford* has also misstated his death in a letter to HALLER, written in 1746. SPRECKELSEN had a correspondence with the greatest Naturalists and Botanists of the age.

It

It had till then been universally believed, that SPRECKELSEN was possessed of a singular phenomenon; but the keen eye of the young traveller, replaced this pretended prodigy into the rank which it should never have relinquished, namely that of a curiosity and a fine production of art. It represented, and was deemed to be a serpent with seven heads. Upon close inspection, LINNÆUS discovered that those seven and extraordinary heads, far from being natural, were merely factitious. He found that they consisted of nothing but the jaw bones of weasels artfully covered with serpent's skin, regardless of the palpable difference which subsists between the structure of the jaw bones of weasels and of serpents.

Thus the phenomenon of *Hamburgh* all on a sudden ceased to be a wonder; a circumstance which proved somewhat fatal both to SPRECKELSEN and LINNÆUS. The seven heads had stamped a great value on this serpent. It had been the pledged security for a loan of ten thousand marks, and now it became scarcely worth one hundred. This event occasioned many schisms and embarrassments. It was finally insisted on, that LINNÆUS should prove before an academical *Forum*, that the serpent was not a phenomenon. In this crisis Dr. JAENISCH gave him the friendly advice to quit *Hamburgh* with all possible speed, in order to avoid all useless delays and litigations. LINNÆUS followed this advice, and was frequently after heard to say: " I only had one " friend at *Hamburgh*; this was Dr. JAENISCH; for he was a true " friend to me*." Thus commenced the travels of LINNÆUS with adventures and unexpected accidents, thus was he obliged, on account of his genius and better penetration to leave a city where he had so-

* " Doctor JÆNISCH unicus fuit amicus, quem Hamburgi habui; verus enim fuit amicus."

L   journed

journed with great pleasure for about a month, notwithstanding such a delay little corresponded with his pecuniary resources.

He now continued his journey to *Holland*, and at the end of May reached *Harderwyk* in *Guelderland*. Botany had always been his chief study, and physic that of his leisure-hours. Even in the latter he displayed his original spirit of investigation. He had chosen for his thesis of installation a new hypothesis of the causes of the cold intermitting fevers, especially in his own country. In this dissertation he assigns as one of the principal causes, the water impregnated with argillous substances;—an hypothesis, which he took pains to render valid by many arguments and ingenious asseverations. "These," BAECK says, "make "one willing to credit the author, though the principal point might "still be subject to doubt." The envy of the celebrated WALLER, his countryman, raised afterwards a thousand objections to this dissertation. After a triple examination and public defence of his treatise, LINNÆUS obtained on the 24th of June, in the 28th year of his age, that dignity which he had long ago deserved *. BARON HALLER, one of the greatest geniuses of our age, whom LINNÆUS respected as a friend and dreaded as a rival, had it conferred upon him nine years before at *Leyden*, in the 18th year of his age.

The chief end for which LINNÆUS had undertaken this journey with the assistance of his future bride, was now accomplished. His intended father-in-law had advised him to return to *Sweden* immediately after he had taken his degree of doctor, to settle there as a practical physician. LINNÆUS was willing to comply, but he would not quit

---

* HYPOTHESIS NOVA *de Febrium intermittentium causa, quam pro gradu doctoris obtinendo proposuit* CAR. LINNÆUS, *Suecus*; *Harderovici Die* 24. *Jun.* 1735.

Holland before he got acquainted with its principal literati and other remarkable objects.

He went from *Harderwyk* to *Leyden,* which is the first Dutch university. Having lived too high at *Hamburgh,* his poverty now constrained him to hire a garret and live extremely low. At the same time he looked out for friends and acquaintance, and soon found them. Among these were ADRIAN VAN ROYEN*, Professor of Botany; Doctor, and afterwards BARON VAN SWIETEN, one of the oldest and most favourite pupils of BOERHAAVE; young LIEBERKUHN from *Berlin,* then a student at *Leyden,* afterwards celebrated by his accurate microscopic observations and anatomical curiosities; farther ISAAC LAWSON, a Scotchman, whose loss like that of LIEBERKUHN, the sciences had too early to mourn, and Doctor JOHN FREDERICK GRONOV, afterwards senator and burgomaster of *Leyden.*

The latter, who was also a well versed lover of botany, encouraged and induced LINNÆUS to enter the lists as author, in which, having been supported by a concurrence of many favourable circumstances, he soon formed a great and splendid epoch. Among the various writings which he had long ago collected and projected in *Sweden,* he first published the plan or prospectus of the classical work which became afterwards the universal code of natural history. His SYSTEMA NATURÆ † appeared on fourteen folio pages. It was the foundation stone of the edifice, which was on subsequent occasions so symmetrically and so beautifully finished and aggrandized by its architect, and enlarged by foreign artists.

* He was made Professor after BOERHAAVE, who resigned his Professorship on account of his age, in 1732; he was born in 1705, and died in 1779.

† Systema Naturæ, sive regnia tria naturæ, systematicæ proposita, per classes, ordines, genera et species. *Lugd. Batav.* 1735. folio 14.

LINNÆUS

LINNÆUS had only given a view of the three reigns of nature,
with a better division and order, but this already manifested his
vast and inventive genius. The small work, which made the beginning of his reform, created universal attention, and was received with the greatest applause. The author, however, could
not conceive the least hope of making his fortune in *Holland*. His
pecuniary resources were almost exhausted. He was preparing to return to his native country, although no charming prospect invited him
thither. The most eminent man then at the University of *Leyden*, and
who made a great epoch in its annals, was HERMANN BOERHAAVE, the
general oracle of medicine. LINNÆUS had particularly wished to see
and converse with him, but it was in vain. Indeed there was no room for
surprise at his disappointment. No Minister could be more overwhelmed
with intreaties and invitations, nor more difficult in granting an audience
than BOERHAAVE. His menial servants reaped advantages from this
circumstance; for them an audience was always a profitable money-
job; by the weight of gold it could alone be accomplished. Without a
douceur it was hard for any stranger or foreigner to gain admittance.
LINNÆUS was quite unacquainted with this method, and had it not in
his power to make presents. Owing to BOERHAAVE's infinite occupations,
and the strict regularity which he observed, Ambassadors, Princes, and
PETER the GREAT himself, were obliged to wait several hours in his
anti-chamber, to obtain an interview*. How much more difficult must it

have

* The following historical and chaÆeristic anecdotes of this great man, will perhaps not
be unpleasant to the reader. BOERHAAVE was born in 1668, at *Voorhout*, near *Leyden*.
His father was a preacher, and had destined his son for the same sacred function. But the
inclinations of the latter to study divinity; however great his progress appeared in the beginning, was rather more compulsive than spontaneous. Like LUTHER, who, vowed to
study divinity, during a tempest in which a friend of his was struck dead by a flash from the
bursting element, so BOERHAAVE met with an accident which made him resolve to renounce

his

have been for the young Northern Doctor, allowing him his usual spirit of liberality, to aspire at the honour of admittance. Notwithstanding all these obstacles he obtained it last. He sent BOERHAAVE a copy of his new-published system. Eager to know the author of this work, who had likewise recommended himself by a letter, he appointed LINNÆUS to meet him, on the day before his intended departure, at his villa, at the distance of a quarter of a league from *Leyden*, and charged GRONOV to give him notice of his intention. This villa contained a botanical garden, and one of the finest collections of exotics. LINNÆUS punctually attended to the invitation.

his theological career. One day, in an excursion, some man wholly engrossed the conversation on divinity, especially on SPINOSA, whom he called the Heretic of *Amsterdam*. BOERHAAVE, who had long heard with silence the rantings of this stranger, asked at last, "whether "he had ever read SPINOSA?"—"the stranger answered in the negative;" every person present laughed at him. This man to avenge himself, called our ingenious enquirer a *Spinosist*, which involved him in disagreeable disputes. BOERHAAVE, immediately upon his father's death, which happened in 1683, began to apply himself exclusively to the study of physic, in which he afterwards became the most eminent man, not only of the age he lived in, but of many preceding centuries. He took his degree of doctor in the 25th year of his age, and was appointed professor of Physic, at *Leyden*, in 1701. Here he remained, declining the most advantageous offers made him from abroad. His celebrity extended from *Europe* to other parts of the globe. He even received a letter from *China*, directed *A L'illustre* BOERHAAVE, *Medecin en Europe*. His school became the seminary of the greatest physicians. Extremely active and plain, he was in other respects a downright Dutchman. His whole wardrobe consisted of a couple of suits, which he used to wear till they became three [?] His Dutch-built stature, his old shoes, his loose hair, and the large crab-stick, which [?] always with him, made him pass for some person of a low description, though he was one of the richest individuals at *Leyden*. He left his daughter, who was married to Count TOMS, upwards of a million of florins. His necessitous circumstances, during his youth, had rendered him very parsimonious. He was, however, extremely beneficent to the poor. After having accumulated the greatest merits in medicine, and benefited mankind in general, he died in the 70th year of his age, on the 30th of September, 1738. See the following works respecting BOERHAAVE:—Account of the life and writings of H. BOERHAAVE, by Dr. BURTON, *Lond.* 1746, octavo.—A. SHULDEN's Oratio Academica in memoriam H. BOERHAAVII, *Lugd. Bat.* 1738, octavo.----Essay sur le Caractère du Grand Medecin; ou eloge critique de M. H. BOERHAAVE, (par M. MATY) *a Cologne*, 1747, in octavo.

L   BOERHAAVE

BOERHAAVE, who was then sixty-seven years old, received him with gladness, and took him into his garden for the purpose of judging of his knowledge.

He showed him as a rarity the *Crategus Aria,* and asked if he had ever seen that tree before, as it had never been described by any botanist. LINNÆUS answered that he had frequently met with it in *Sweden,* and that it had also been already described by VAILLANT. Struck with the young man's reply, BOERHAAVE denied the latter part of his assertion, with so much more confidence as he had published himself that work of VAILLANT s *(Botanicon Parisiense, Lugd. Batav.* 1727, fol.) with notes of his own, and firmly believed that tree had not been described in it. To remove all doubts, and to give all possible sanction to what he advanced, BOERHAAVE immediately fetched the work itself from his library—and to his extreme surprise found the tree fully described in it, with all its distinctive marks. Admiring the exact and enlarged knowledge of LINNÆUS in botany, in which he seemed even to excel himself, the venerable old man advised him to remain in *Holland,* to make a fortune which could not escape his talents. LINNÆUS answered that he would fain follow this advice, but his indigence prevented him from staying any longer, and obliged him to set out the next day for *Amsterdam,* on his return to *Sweden.* He took his leave of BOERHAAVE, and this visit unexpectedly became the source of his fortune, of his eminence, and of that botanical reform which the frowns of fate, and the cares of providing for his daily subsistence, had not thus far permitted him to accomplish.

What the Italian poet METASTASIO says, respecting the happiness or misfortunes of man, and the vicissitudes of destiny by which the greatest

enterprises

enterprises are so frequently decided, may be with great propriety applied here to LINNÆUS.

> " Nel cammin di nostra vita,
> " Senza i rai del ciel cortese
> " Si smarrisce ogn'alma ardita,
> " Trema il cor, vacilla il piè.
>
> " A compir le belle imprese
> " L'arte giova, il senno ha parte ;
> " Mà vaneggia il senno e l'arte
> " Quando Amico il ciel non è.

LINNÆUS set off from *Leyden* to *Amsterdam*, there to embark for his country. BOERHAAVE had given him a letter of recommendation to his pupil JOHN BURMANN, then Professor of Botany in the capital of *Holland.* BURMANN was then occupied in completing a description of plants of the island of *Ceylon.* On account of BOERHAAVE's recommendation, LINNÆUS met with a friendly reception ; but he happened to surprise his new patron, just at a time when he was overwhelmed with occupation, and the latter begged, therefore, LINNÆUS to come to see him once more before his departure, and to excuse him then for not being at leisure. LINNÆUS complied. At this second visit the conversation turned upon botany. " Would you wish to see my " plants ?" asked BURMANN—so LINNÆUS relates this anecdote " With great pleasure," replied I. BURMANN showed me a shrub— adding: " This is a rarity." I took one flower, examined it, and observed that it was a species of bay. " No, no," replied BURMANN. " But indeed it is," observed I; these are the blossoms of the Cinnamon tree, *Laurus Cinnamonum.*—" To be sure they they are," said BURMANN, " but as to bay"—Here I interrupted, and convinced him that it

a   belonged

belonged to the species of bays. We examined other flowers; he objected, but I refuted his objections, and persuaded him. At last, he asked me; " Will you help me in my *Ceylon* collection ? Will and " can you stay at *Amsterdam* ?" Linnæus informed him that his poverty rendered it absolutely impossible. Burmann had already grown so fond of him and his acquirements, that he generously offered to board and lodge him in his own house, free from all expence.

Linnæus, enlivened with the hope of making perhaps his fortune in *Holland*, and delighted with a situation which could procure him so many opportunities of enlarging the knowledge which had been constantly the object of his exertions, accepted with gratitude the hospitable offer. Though fortune offered him no settled prospects, yet he could return to *Sweden* in spring with both more advantage and greater convenience. He entered the house of Burmann, where he found a considerable collection of natural curiosities, and what was more valuable still, a select library of books relative to botany and natural history in general. These became of service in the completion of several of his works, among which was comprised his Botanical Library *(Bibliotheca Botanica)*, published by him three years after, and dedicated to the friend who had shown him so much kindness. He found an opportunity partly to requite those favours to the son of Burmann, who studied under him at *Upsal*, in the year 1759, and inherited the dignity and fame of his father. Among the many distinguished members of Burmann's family, we deem it proper to mention the meritorious Philologist Peter Burmann, who was a son of the protector of Linnæus.

With

With labor and social recreation the winter-season glided very pleasantly away in *Holland*, and the ensuing year 1736 opened with a prospect which totally changed for some time the resolution of LINNÆUS to return to his country. BOERHAAVE, who had been informed that he was at *Amsterdam*, having already evinced towards him affection and esteem, now granted him his patronage. Doctor GEORGE CLIFFORT, Burgomaster of *Amsterdam*, and one of the Directors of the Dutch East India Company, the most zealous lover of natural science, expended vast sums of his princely fortune to procure plants and natural curiosities; and was, in this respect, like SHERARD in *England* as a private gentleman, the most distinguished and most extraordinary person in *Holland*, and perhaps even in all the world. These treasures, brought from all quarters of the globe, he he hoarded up in his Museum and botanical garden at *Hartecamp*, a villa belonging to him near *Harlem*. But these valuable articles were still left without order or scientific description. CLIFFORT wished for a man adequate to fulfil this task.

BOERHAAVE was his physician. CLIFFORT one day paid him a visit at *Leyden.* " Shall I give you some good advice," said the former. " You have plenty of every thing, yet there is one thing alone you ha"·· " not got to render your life completely happy. You are accustomed · " live high, hence you are so frequently troubled with hypochondriac " complaints. You must keep a physician of your own, to prescribe and " order your diet, and to take daily care of your health—in cases of a " more serious nature he may consult me."—" Well proposed!" replied CLIFFORT, " but where shall I find such a clever and skilful man ?"— " Never mind, this I shall make my own business. I know a young " Swede, who is now at *Amsterdam*, it is him I shall recommend as the

M   " best

" best to answer your purpose. Besides, he is also an excellent botanist,
" and will arrange your garden at *Hartecamp*."

CLIFFORT quite charmed with this proposal, lost no time in having
it executed. BURMANN and LINNÆUS were invited to come to *Harte-*
camp. They went into the garden, and saw the plants and hot-houses,
which contained many rare and curious productions from the *Cape of Good*
Hope. LINNÆUS examined and pointed out those which were known,
and those which were new. His display of knowledge struck and enraptured CLIFFORT. The conversation on botany was prolonged, and
the parties then went to the library. BURMANN found there the second part of an excellent work written by Sir HANS SLOANE, entitled
The Natural History of Jamaica, which he had not yet seen. " I have
" two copies of this work," said CLIFFORT, " and you may have this,
" if you will give me LINNÆUS by way of exchange."

CLIFFORT now offered terms to LINNÆUS, consisting in a proposal
of free board and lodging, and a pecuniary allowance of one ducat a
day, or 1000 florins per annum. An offer of this nature could not
leave room for hesitation. Who could have been more rejoiced than
LINNÆUS, at finding a sphere of operation so eligible for, and coinci-
dent with his wishes.

Before we accompany LINNÆUS to his new residence at *Hartecamp*,
which became the school of his greatness, we shall first mention a catastrophe which rendered the year 1735 for ever memorable to him.

When he still resided at *Leyden*, he had the unexpected pleasure of
meeting there ARTEDI, the friend of his youth, and the companion of
his studies. The latter had left *Sweden* before LINNÆUS in 1734, and
went over to *England* for the purpose of making greater improvement

in ichthyology, the science to which he had wholly devoted his labours.
From *England* he came to *Holland*, where he wished to take his degree
of Doctor, but want of money prevented him, and his family circumstances were still more unfavourable than those of LINNÆUS. The
latter became his patron. He recommended him to the celebrated
apothecary SEBA, at *Amsterdam* *, a peculiar lover of natural history, who
had collected a great quantity of natural curiosities, and began to describe
them, but needed some assistance owing to his advanced stage of life.
SEBA received ARTEDI as his assistant. " No sooner," says LINNÆUS,
" had I finished my *Fundamenta Botanica*, than I hastened to commu-
" nicate them to ARTEDI; he shewed me on his part the work which
" had been the result of several years study, his *Philosophia Ichthyologica*,
" and other manuscripts. I was delighted with his familiar converse;
" meanwhile overwhelmed with business, I grew impatient at his
" detaining me too long. Alas! had I known that this was the
" last visit, the last words of my friend, how fain would I have tarried
" to prolong his existence!"

In a short time after, on the 25th of September 1735, ARTEDI was
in company at SEBA's—he left his house to return home—the night
was dark, unknown the way—he comes to the brink of canal
not inclosed with rails, in which he falls—his shrieks and moans
not heard—the struggles of his agony are unwitnessed—he falls, far
from his native land, in the bloom of youth, a y̆ of w that element the inhabitants of which were so familiar to him, an to th better

---

* SEBA died on the 21st of May, 1736, in the 74th year of his age. The work which
chiefly distinguished his name in the scientific world, is entituled *Locupletissimi rerum Naturalium thesauri accurata descriptio, et iconibus artificiosissimus expressio*; Amstelod. tom.
iv. with 449 plates.

knowledge

knowledge of which he had devoted the whole diligence of his life, and
spurned all obstacles. Next day his body is found; LINNÆUS informed of his fate hastens to the spot, and with a torrent of tears
beholds the inanimate remains of the best of friends, and causes them
to be committed to the tomb.

When ARTEDI and LINNÆUS were at *Upsal*, they had already reci-
procally constituted themselves heirs to each others books and manuscripts. LINNÆUS was now ready to assert his right, that he might
rescue, at least, the fame of his deceased friend from oblivion. But the
landlord of ARTEDI, at whose house his situation had compelled him
to contract some small debts, would not deliver up his effects, which he
threatened to sell by public auction. Through the generous liberality
of CLIFFORT, the wish of LINNÆUS was accomplished. CLIFFORT
purchased the manuscripts, and made him a present of them. The
principal one was the general work on fishes *; which LINNÆUS published in 1738.

" Who could have been more adequate to this task," says LINNÆUS,
" in the preface, " than the man to whom the style, the ideas, and whole
" method of ARTEDI were so familiar ? How fortunate shall I deem
" myself, if I have perpetuated the memory of my deceased friend, and
" rescued from oblivion a work which is one of the best and most
" meritorious of its kind. ARTEDI has rendered his science the most
" easy, though it is one of the most difficult. May there be more
" ARTEDIS to describe the animal reign with similar exactness !"

* PETRI ARTEDI, Sueci Medici Ichthyologia, sive opera omnia de piscibus—Edid. CAROL.
LINNÆUS, Lugd. Batav. 1738, in small quarto.

In the beginning of the spring 1736, LINNÆUS went to the villa of *Hartecamp*, where he passed so many glorious and pleasant hours. There study was his greatest delight. Surrounded by treasures from all quarters of the globe, a great part of which he had never seen before, encircled with a most select and valuable library devoted to his use; uncontrouled in all his arrangements; seconded by a patron equally beneficent, and ready to procure every thing which could be either missing or wished for; plants, good living, *Leyden, Amsterdam,* and *Harlem* in proximity—how could LINNÆUS, thus situated, wish for a more charming and more advantageous situation any where else! In this Paradise, as he called it, the great projects he had conceived were brought to maturity. Hesitating, whether he should dedicate his services to ÆSCULAPIUS or to FLORA, he resolved to consecrate them wholly to the latter.

When he sojourned at *Amsterdam,* he finished a small work which he had begun while a student at *Upsal,* and which was considered as the harbinger of his reform. It consisted of his *Fundamenta Botanica,* which appeared in 1736, on 35 pages in twelves. The theory of the science of botany was reduced by it to 365 aphorisms, and he displayed in these the basis of his new system. Fifteen years after the same work appeared, augmented with elucidations, and a description of the parts of plants, and their technical terms, under the title of *Philosophia Botanica.*

Nearly at the same time, when this elementary book appeared, LINNÆUS published his *Bibliotheca Botanica* (in 153 pages in twelves), for the perfection of which he stood chiefly indebted to the libraries of SPRECKELSEN at *Hamburgh,* BURMANN at *Amsterdam,* GRONOV at

Leyden, and Clifford at *Hartecamp.* Though it contained some imperfections, yet there was not a completer nor better digested repertory extant to that period. Linnæus gave in it a system of botanical researches, divided into sixteen classes, extracted from upwards of 1000 books, all the materials being systematically arranged.

The publication of the third work of Linnæus was occasioned by a rare foreign plant in Clifford's garden. This was the banana-tree *(Musa Paradisica),* the blossoms of which had only once or twice appeared in *Europe.* He gave a better and more methodical description of it under the title of *Musa* Cliffortiana, *Florens Hartecampi, prope Harlemum, Lugd. Batav.* forty-six pages in quarto, with two plates, one of which exhibits the whole plant, the other its parts of fructification.

These were the learned productions of the diligence of Linnæus in 1736. With them was diffused his celebrity; while his innovations attracted universal notice. But nobody could then suspect that great revolution which was to subvert the domination of Tournefort, and to hurl down with it so many grandees and plebeians in the republic of botany. The Germans did justice to the egregiousness and merits of our Swede, and the Imperial academy of naturalists at *Vienna,* which is one of the most ancient learned bodies, was the first of the foreign societies which admitted him that same year as a fellow-member, under the honourable title of Dioscorides the Second, names which have at all times been customary in that academy, and were made to keep pace with the celebrity of each member.

The amenities of the summer of 1736 were considerably heightened for Linnæus, by a journey to *England,* which he undertook towards

the

the latter end of July, at CLIFFORT's expence. No country could offer greater aliments for his desire of knowledge, nor was there one he had more anxiously wished to visit than this happy island. CLIFFORT's intention of enriching his garden with foreign, and especially with North-American plants, which were cultivated in the nurseries of *Oxford* and *London*, and of establishing fresh connexions for the benefit of his museum and garden, coincided with the desires of LINNÆUS. CLIFFORT, who did not like to be long deprived of the latter, limited the time of his absence to the short period of eight or twelve days. But LINNÆUS was eight days on his passage from *Rotterdam* to *Harwich.* He arrived at *London* with a letter of recommendation from BOERHAAVE to Sir HANS SLOANE, Bart. then the greatest amateur and collector in natural history, and afterwards founder of the British Museum. This letter is still carefully preserved among the archives of that museum. The substance of this letter, to the honour of LINNÆUS, and as an exact opinion of that great man, respecting the genius of our young botanist, deserves particular mention : " *The bearer of* " *this letter,*" says BOERHAAVE, " *is alone worthy of seeing you—alone* " *worthy of being seen by you. He who shall see you both together, shall* " *see two men, whose like will scarcely ever be found in the world* *."

But notwithstanding a recommendation couched in such expression as BOERHAAVE, whose mind was unsullied by flattery, had never written before, and which Sir HANS SLOANE had never received of any foreigner, LINNÆUS did not meet with that warm and friendly reception which he had fancied. The old Baronet did not seem quite

---

* LINNÆUS qui has tibi dabit Litteras, est unice dignus, Te videre, unice dignus, a te videri. Qui vas videbit simul, videbit hominum par, cui simile vix dabit orbis.

pleased

pleased with Boerhaave's compliment and the presence of the young
man, who wished to raise his learning above all others, and to subvert
the orthodoxy of botanical science †.

He

† Sir HANS SLOANE was a native of *Killylengh* in *Ireland*. He early distinguished
himself by his peculiar talents in natural history. RAY and the celebrated SYDENHAM
were his professors and friends. In 1685 he was chosen member of the Royal Society and of
the Royal College of Physicians at *London*. Two years after he accompanied the Duke of
ALBEMARLE as governor to *Jamaica*, and was the first who distinguished himself by his
knowledge of the natural history of that island. He described its physical curiosities in two
valuable works, *Catalogi Plantarum, quæ in Insula Jamaica, sponte proveniunt, Lond.* 1696;
and The Natural History of *Jamaica*, two vols. *Lond.* 1707 and 1725, with 174 copper-plates.
On his return in 1689, he was elected physician of Christ Hospital, created a baronet, appointed
first physician of the army, first physician to GEORGE II. and in the year 1726 president of
the Royal Society, in the room of Sir ISAAC NEWTON. Thus the greatest man was replaced by the most remarkable. Sir HANS had been admitted a member of the Royal Academy of Sciences at *Paris* in 1708. He was the HIPPOCRATES of *London*; his activity was
indefatigable, and as a fortunate inventor of many medicaments, he extended his fame beyond
the grave. He terminated his celebrated career in the year 1753, in the 93d of his age.
Philanthropy and patriotism were the leading features of his character. The beautiful botanical garden at *Chelsea* was left by him to the Company of Apothecaries, on condition of
their introducing every year fifty new plants, till their number should amount to 2000.
Whenever he had two copies of the same work in his own library, he presented one of them
to the library of the College of Physicians of *London*, or to that of *Oxford*. His collection
of natural curiosities was the richest a private individual was ever possessed of. His library
consisted of 50,000 volumes. The catalogue of his natural collection formed eight volumes
in quarto, in which 69,352 curiosities were described. This treasure, which, according to his
own expression, was destined to magnify GOD and benefit mankind, he made over by his will
to the nation, on condition that his children should receive the sum of 20,000l. sterling. The
nation acceded to the terms proposed by the testator. Parliament granted the sum required,
and the whole of those precious collections were incorporated with the British Museum.
The sums which Sir HANS had expended upon them amounted to upwards of fifty thousand
pounds, and those articles which he received as presents to ten thousand pounds. If his
BRITANNIC MAJESTY would have hesitated to accept of his cabinet at the rate of twenty
thousand pounds, his will ordained that it should be offered at the same price, 1. To the
Royal Society of *London*. 2. To the University of *Oxford*. 3. To the College of *Edin-
burgh*. 4. To the Royal Academy of Sciences at *Paris*. 5. To the Imperial Academy of
Petersburgh. 6. To the Royal Academy at *Madrid*. 7. To the Royal Academy at *Berlin*. 8.
In case all these academies should have declined the offer, article by article was to have been
sold by auction. The British parliament passed an act on the 5th of April 1753, to pay

the

He had followed RAY's system ever since the last century, and observed the alphabetic order in his collections. He was too old, in fact, and too self-sufficient to feel any inclination to learn the innovations of our young man, and to do homage to the laws of his system. He very readily permitted LINNÆUS, as he did other foreigners, to see his cabinet; a treasure unequalled in its kind all over the world. He also showed him his herbal, which consisted of near 250 divisions.

One of the principal motives of the journey of LINNÆUS to England, was the botanical garden at *Chelsea*. CLIFFORT wished to procure some foreign plants from it. The great botanist PHILIP MILLER, who died on the 18th of *December*, 1771, in the 80th year of his age, was then keeper of that garden. LINNÆUS waited on him, MILLER conducted him into the garden, showed him the plants, and gave them their ancient and inaccurate names. LINNÆUS was silent, his silence was ascribed to ignorance, and MILLER jocosely said to one of his acquaintance: *Sure, the botanist of Burgomaster CLIFFORT is a great man,—he knows nothing at all of plants.*—LINNÆUS heard of this, and saw MILLER again, firmly resolved to teach him to know better. MILLER made use a second time of the ancient names. " Why do you apply these, pray?" asked LINNÆUS, " we have better " and conciser appellations."—MILLER still retained the ancient terms, was somewhat offended at the lesson he had received, but began however, to conceive more esteem for the knowledge of LINNÆUS.

the said sum to his two daughters, to purchase at the same time the manuscripts collected by HARLEY, to add to these collections COTTON's library; to erect a particular edifice to keep them in, by raising the expences by means of a lottery of seven hundred thousand pounds sterling—this is the origin of the British Museum.

The

The latter visited him a third time, and met with a more pleasant and polite reception, obtained the plants which he requested for CLIFFORT's garden, kept up ever after a friendly acquaintance and correspondence with MILLER, and the garden of *Chelsea* was finally arranged according to the LINNÆAN system.

From *London*, LINNÆUS went to *Oxford*. The greatest and most ingenius botanist in that University, was, at that time, JOHN JAMES DILLENIUS, by birth a Hessian, formerly professor of botany at the University of *Giessen*, who died in 1747. He met with the same patronage on the part of a rich Englishman, which LINNÆUS did on the part of CLIFFORT. This patron was WILLAM SHERARD, whose brother JAMES was also a great lover of natural history. SHERARD, as a private man, was the most zealous promoter of natural science England could then boast of. He had long resided at *Smyrna* as Consul, and he collected a great number of plants and natural curiosities. On his return to *England* he established the celebrated botanical garden at his seat at. *Eltham*, which was described by DILLENIUS. *(Hortus. Elthamensis, Oxon.* 1732.*)* He intended to continue the great work of BAUHIN *(πιναξ Theatri Botanici)*, but death arrested him in his enterprize in 1738. To render his collections useful to posterity, he deposited a sum of money to establish a professorship at *Oxford*, for the purpose of describing and arranging those collections. DILLENIUS obtained this office, he took upon him the prescribed literary labour, but could not accomplish it. His time was mostly taken up by his natural history of Mosses, *(Historia Muscorum, Oxon.* 1741). a classical work, in which more than 600 species of mosses are described, by which

which he made an epoch in natural history, and raised a lasting monument to his fame.

LINNÆUS waited on DILLENIUS, and found him in company with another gentleman; who, as he afterwards learned, was no other than WILLIAM SHERARD. He addressed DILLENIUS in Latin, and apologized for his ignorance of the English language. After some short conversation, DILLENIUS said to SHERARD in English:—*See, this is the young man who confounds all botany.*—LINNÆUS understood this, as the word *confound*, so analogous to the Latin of *confundere*, was made use of; he feigned, however, not to understand him. They then went to the garden. LINNÆUS took great notice of a plant which he had not yet seen *(Anthirrhinum Minus)*. He asked DILLENIUS what plant it was? " That is more than you can tell me?" answered the latter.— " Yes I can tell, if I may be permitted to take off a flower and ex- " amine it."—" Take one and welcome," said DILLENIUS. LINNÆUS took one and gave it the right name. DILLENIUS prepossessed by the pride of his own knowledge, continued to treat our luminary with great coolness and reserve.

The latter despaired of ever gaining his friendship, and obtaining presents of plants for CLIFFORT's garden. His travelling money was also very nearly expended. He went therefore on the third day to DILLENIUS, and intreated him to let his servant hire a coach for him to return to *London*, as he could not speak English. The servant was dispatched. " Before I go," said LINNÆUS, " I have one favor more " to request: pray tell me candidly, why did you tell the man who " was with you the day before yesterday, that I was *the person who* " *confounded all botany.*" Astonished and thunderstruck! DILLENIUS

N 2   :ndeavoured

endeavoured to deny what he had said, and to turn the conversation on some other subject, but LINNÆUS insisted on an explanation.

" Well," said DILLENIUS, " come along with me." He went to
his library and showed LINNÆUS his work : entituled *Genera Plantarum*, of which GRONOV, without his knowledge, had sent him one
half of the printed sheets. Every page was marked in different places
with the letters N. B.—" What do these marks signify ?" asked LIN-
NÆUS.—" They signify all *the false genera of plants in your book.*"—
" They are not false," replied LINNÆUS, " or if they are, I beg you
" would teach me better; I will thankfully receive your correction."—
" Very well, let us try."—They went in the garden. DILLENIUS took
up a plant called *blitum*, in his and others opinion it had three stamina.
LINNÆUS examined the flower, and found, according to his assertion, that it only had one.—" Psha! such a thing may happen in one
flower," exclaimed DILLENIUS,—but it was so with all.—Several
plants were now examined, and the genera given by LINNÆUS proved
to be accurate. This effected an entire change in the conduct of DIL-
LENIUS. " You must not be gone so soon," said he " I wish you
" would assist me in arranging and classing SHERARD's collections."
LINNÆUS saw those collections, remained some time longer at Oxford, and received of DILLENIUS all the plants he wished to have
for CLIFFORT's garden.

DILLENIUS would not however publicly accept the LINNÆAN
system. Old age added to the pride of experience, scouted the idea
of reform, and sought rather to follow error than truth. But this literary discordance did not diminish the esteem which DILLENIUS had

2

conceived

conceived for LINNÆUS, though it was not preserved quite uncontaminated by envy.*

To this interesting acquaintance may be added several other connections at *Oxford* and *London*, which were useful to CLIFFORT, and in process of time equally advantageous to LINNÆUS. A friendly intercourse was cultivated and improved between the latter and professors COLLINSON, MARTYN, RAND, EHRET, and other persons who make a conspicuous figure in the annals of literature. Enriched with knowledge and a collection of natural treasures, he returned to *Holland*, towards the end of September, and was most joyfully received by CLIFFORT.

Impelled by his celebrity, by the contradictions he had experienced, and animated with the flattering idea of becoming the creator of a new system, and the legislator of botany, LINNÆUS now began to pursue with all possible exertion the career which conducted him to greatness. NEWTON had conceived the original thought of splitting the rays of light. To prove its possibility, and to render valid a new truth, he spared no expence in having the finest instruments made, and bestowed days and nights on the object of his invention. Such is the

* The following passage of a letter, which DILLENIUS wrote to BARON HALLER, on the 13th of October, will sufficiently evince the acrimony of his temper. *Linnæi Floram Suecicam nondum vidi. Non est unius hominis conscribere Floram universi regni. Canis festinans, &c. Vidisti procul dubio Orchides in actis Suecicis, partum egregium, quem facile pessumdabis. Vereor tamen, ne nihil agas; est enim homo, - - - - - - ne quid gravius dicam. Scribit ad me quotannis fere semel, nil nisi semina efflagitans, licet ipse nulla mittit. Mihi plurima; sed an fecerim operæ pretium, bacreo. Inhiat tantum generibus novis et multa petit, quæ nunquam apud nos semina, immo nec flores ferunt; ignarus rei hortensis. Specierum ipsi parca cognitio; novi tamen bene merita et a morem in plantas ob quæ ipsi bene cupio.* Epistol. ad HALLER. Vol. II. p. 299. To understand this answer, we find it incumbent on us to say, that LINNÆUS had criticised HALLER in the *Flora Suecica* in a strong and pointed manner.

· ivity

activity and enthusiasm which characterize genius, and without which
no great enterprise can be encompassed. " A system which is to bear
" our name," says HALLER, " an opinion issued from our own head,
" effects with the learned what ambition has effected with ALEXANDER.
" Labor, time, skill, all the energy and force of mind are applied
" cheerfully and without contradiction as soon as our system becomes
" more certain, more pleasant, and more probable. Who would have
" counted and fixed the stamina.in flowers almost numberless, had they
" not been the essential part of the new sexual system of LINNÆUS,
" and the principal source of rendering it perfect and universally pre-
" dominant !"

It required a strong and forcible progress to bring about such revolution. And in fact, no time, during the whole life of LINNÆUS, was
more distinguished by an extraordinary activity, none more fertile for
the republic of science than the year 1737. It was in the course of
this same year, when LINNÆUS published about 200 printed sheets.
Such a deal of writing would have been no novelty, and the young
Swede had long before been excelled in it. But what constituted its
pre-eminence was, that the six works, which LINNÆUS published in the
course of this year, and which diffused the reform of botany from *Hartecamp* throughout *Europe*, were all originals, and by more than one
half large classical works; replete with the most difficult researches,
new representations, and accurate critical doctrines. It would have
done infinite honour to his diligence, had he only produced one of those
works in a whole twelvemonth. The plans and materials for some of
them had certainly been previously collected ; but the whole required
to be digested and arranged. All those labours could not prevent him
                                                    from

from giving proper attendance to CLIFFORT's garden, and receiving the frequent visits of strangers from *Leyden* and *Harlem*.

The *Genera Plantarum* was the first work of LINNÆUS, which made its appearance after his return from *England*, in the beginning of 1737, and in the completion of which he had spent the last months of the preceding year. It was published at *Leyden* on 384 pages in octavo. He limited in it the characters of the genera of plants, according to the number, form, situation and proportion of their generative parts, rectified the names of the genera by those distinctive marks which were always true to nature, and applicable to any system which might have been adopted for the limitation of the classes and orders. Had he not done this, such a change would only have created more confusion and disorder. Having thus applied proper names to the genera, he also began to alter the names of most of the species. LINNÆUS, according to his own assertion, had till then, examined the characters of near 8000 plants. The labour and extent of such circumstantial researches at such an age as his, deserve reflexion. Upon the whole, he had described in the above work, upwards of 935 genera of plants. This number was afterwards augmented by one half in the eleven different editions, with his own and foreign additions. In the same year he published a supplement to it, (*Corollarium Generum*) in which he described 60 new genera. To this he also added a concise view of the sexual system (*Methodus Sexualis*). LINNÆUS, as we had occasion to observe before, had already inserted after his return from *Lapland*, a concise list of the plants of this extensive Northern region in the transactions of the royal society of *Upsal*. In the month of April 1737, a precise description of them appeared at *Am-*

3

sterdam

sterdam on 372 octavo pages, which from motives of gratitude he dedicated to that learned body of his country.   The plants were described
in it agreeable to the new sexual system, with a special index of their
native soil, and their utility in medicine and husbandry, and embellished with a striking representation of fifty-eight of the most curious
plants, on twelve large copper-plates, engraved at the expence of that
academy.   In the introduction the author gave a brief physico-geo-
graphical description of *Lapland*, and in the work itself many interesting remarks on the manners, diseases, and mode of living of the inhabitants, interspersed with other miscellaneous strictures.   At the so-
licitation of GRONOV, he permitted one of the Lapponian plants,
called *campanula serpillifolia*, to be, after his own name, denominated
Linnæa, and represented on a plate of that work *.—An honour which
he so well deserved !

   LINNÆUS soon after conferred similar honours on other celebrated
men, in the valuable work by which the object of his residence at *Hartecamp* was completed, and a flattering monument raised to the name
of his patron.   This was the description of CLIFFORT's garden, *Hortus Cliffortianus*, printed at *Amsterdam*, on 501 pages in folio.   It was
first intended to be published in quarto, and some sheets still in the possession of Doctor J. E. SMITH at *London*, printed off in that form,
corroborate this assertion.   The size was, however, soon found im-
proper and inconvenient, and CLIFFORT spared no expence to bring
forth the repertory of his treasures in a most elegant shape.   The representations of the plants were engraved on thirty-two plates, by the

* This plant which is generally called *Linnæa Borealis*, has been engraved in the frontis-
piece, after nature, from a specimen which the Translator procured of Dr. J. E. SMITH,
the proprietor of the LINNÆAN collections.

                                                              celebrated

celebrated EHRET, which rendered the work dearer than any other ever published by LINNÆUS. CLIFFORT made presents of copies of this work to his friends and principal acquaintance. The few copies which were left to the booksellers, were sold by them at twenty-three crowns per copy.

LINNÆUS had arranged the plants in this work after his own system. A meritorious undertaking—as, by it, more light and greater order were diffused. The celebrated Swiss botanist GESNER*, one of the foreign friends of LINNÆUS, gave the following opinion of the *Hortus Cliffortianus*, in a letter to BARON HALLER. " An excellent production indeed, " full of ingenious opinions, and as replete with erudition as any bo- " tanist can possibly display. What pleases me most, is, that the author " —(a thing never done with regularity by any preceding botanist)— " gave besides the names of the species their principal characteristics†."

One of the greatest evils in botany, which had thus far rendered that science a maze of difficulties, and threatened it with Babylonian confusion, was the vague and barbarian technology which prevailed in it. " It resembles a chaos," said LINNÆUS, " the mother of which is ig- " norance, the father custom, and the fosterer prejudice."—Bold enough to hurl into ruins that gothic structure to which several living old artists had contributed, and to exhibit the grounds of his innovations and reforms, he published his *Critica Botanica* at *Leyden*, on 228 pages,

* JOHN GESNER was born at *Zurich*, on the 18th of March, 1719, and died on the 6th of May, 1790.

† Opus sane egregium et acerrimi judicii, nec minoris eruditionis, quo difficulter Botanicus carebit; mihi perplacet, ab eo (Linnæo) in nominibus specierum notas earum essentiales exhiberi, quod ante quisquam botanicus recte præstiterit. See Epist. ad Alb. HALLERUM, vol. ii. *Bernæ*, 1773, p. 6.

of

oɛtavo.—This was a full and classical commentary on the fourth part
of his *Fundamenta Botanica* already published. He examined in it the
names of the genera, species, and bastard species of plants, pointed out
inaccuracies, confirmed the good ones, rejeɛted the bad, and established
certain rules, and a new method for the denomination of plants.

" Botanists," says LINNÆUS, in the third letter which he wrote to
Baron HALLER, on the 8th of June, 1737, " have hitherto wholly ne-
" gleɛted the language of their science. Since TOURNEFORT, more
" than a thousand generical names have been changed and introduced.
" What cause have I to change them? None, but because they are
" not founded on proper grounds and definite laws. The greatest part
" of the names of the species of plants are, doubtless, wrong, and if
" these are to be changed, why should not the same be done with the
" false names of the genera! Our successors in the republic of botany
" will ultimately cease to give implicit credit to the authority of the
" ancients. Why should we retain the ell-long names of *Monolasiocal-*
" *lenomenophyllorum, Hypophylocarpodendorum,* &c. and other barba-
" rian jargon?"

This reform, however rational and meritorious, met with many con-
tradiɛtions at first on the part of those whose pride and self-love were
aggrieved by it, and who thought it beneath their dignity to receive in-
struɛtion from a youth. We shall hereafter speak more amply on this
subjeɛt. The celebrated professor LUDWIG, at *Leipzig,* wrote soon
after the following letter to Baron HALLER : " What is your opinion
" of the *Critica Botanica* of LINNÆUS? He certainly is a severe, but
" sometimes a fortunate censor of botanists. I like his representations,
" yet

" yet I cannot in all points agree with him*." The energy of truth and and the goodness of his cause soon got the upper hand. Opposition could not triumph over the majority of the impartial, and the reform of LINNÆUS was introduced with his ameliorated botanical technology.

One of the greatest philosophers of this century, who found the utmost delight in nature, expresses himself in the following manner respecting this new technical language : " It has been objected," says J. J. ROUSSEAU, " that this nomenclature was not *Ciceronian*. But this ob-" jection would only then find any reasonable grounds, if CICERO had " written a complete treatise on botany. All those terms are, whether, " Greek or Latin, expressive, concise, sonorous, and by their great pre-" cision, form even elegant constructions. In the daily practice of the " art we find all the utility of its new language, which is as much conve-" nient and necessary to botanists as algebra to the geometricians." LINNÆUS published another little work, which was a description of CLIFFORT's orchard *(Viridarium Cliffortianum)* ; and he then resolved with impatience to return to his future bride, by quitting *Hartecamp,* which had till now been his elysium, at the expiration of the year 1737. He had rendered this villa the most curious in *Holland,* but the period of its fame was but of a short duration. CLIFFORT, by his liberal sacrifices to nature and art, found himself at last in unpleasant circumstances, and the glory of *Hartecamp* vanished with him. The villa itself remained in possession of his family. His son, who was chosen afterwards Burgomaster of *Amsterdam,* did not follow with equal en-

---

* Professor LUDWIG, who by his medical talents acquired such high distinction, says in his letter to HALLER, " *Quid de Critica Botancia Linnæi sentis ? Rigorosus quidem, sed sae-* " *pissime felix botanicorum censor est*; *non displicent quæ protulit, licet non in omnibus cum* " *ipso sentire queam.*"

† See ROUSSEAU's preface to his botanical dictionary.

thusiasm

thusiasm his father's inclination. In remembrance of LINNÆUS, his portrait, after life, and in a Laplander's dress, is still preserved there. From the original, drawn at CLIFFORT'S, several copies were executed. In these portraits LINNÆUS had the most grotesque appearance. It represented him with boots of rein-deer-skin, about his body a girdle, from which was suspended a Laplander's drum, a needle to make nets, a straw snuff-box, a cartridge-box, and a knife; his neck was bare; his head was covered with a grey round hat; his hair was of a stiff brown colour; over his hands he wore Laplander's gloves; and in his right he held a plant, red from within and white from without*.— This portrait did not bear the least resemblance to LINNÆUS in his age and maturity of manhood, except the piercing hazel eyes, and the wart on his right cheek.

BOERHAAVE had thus far been the author of his good fortune in *Holland,* and resolved farther to become his promoter and benefactor. The charge of a physician in ordinary in the Dutch colony of *Surinam,* in *South America,* had become vacant. It was only in BOERHAAVE's power to recommend a successor. He offered this place to LINNÆUS, who, owing to a desire of propagating and enjoying his celebrity in *Europe,* and deterred by the unpropitious climate of that colony, thought proper to wave it. He proposed a friend of his, a German, of the name of BARTSCH. This was a youth of great parts, and a most amiable character. LINNÆUS had got acquainted with him at *Leyden;* grew as fond of him as of ARTEDI, and instructed him farther in botany, of which he became a rare and most enthusiastic professor. BARTSCH gladly accepted the charge, and sailed in the summer of 1737

* *This was the plant called after his own name, Linnæa Borealis.*

I

for

for *Surinam*, where he fell six months after a victim to the climate, and a worthless and bad treatment. Greatly moved at the loss of a friend, with whom he had spent many an agreeable hour, of whose happiness, diligence and friendship he had such high expectations, and from whom he hoped to receive so many curiosities and discoveries from that part of the world, LINNÆUS resolved to render his memory immortal, by giving to a plant the appellation of *Bartsia*, after the deceased's own name.

LINNÆUS left *Hartecamp* to go with CLIFFORT to *Amsterdam* on private business, and thence, at the end of October, to *Leyden*. Here, he visited among others, his friend professor VAN ROYEN. BOER-HAAVE had also been VAN ROYEN's patron, and resigned many years before, the professorship of botany in his favour. VAN ROYEN had for many years been welcome in BOERHAAVE's family; but love at last broke and destroyed all those friendly connexions. He made proposals of matrimony to Miss BOERHAAVE the sole heiress of the great man of that name, and beyond doubt, the greatest fortune then at *Leyden*; but his offer was rejected. He now became quite embittered against BOER-HAAVE and his family. The botanical garden at *Leyden* had long before been arranged and described agreeable to BOERHAAVE's own method *. VAN ROYEN did afterwards every thing he could do against him and his memory, and resolved to regulate the academical garden by the LIN-NÆAN system.

While he was occupied with this project, LINNÆUS waited on him. VAN ROYEN offered him board and lodging free, and an annual salary of 800 florins, if he would stay and assist him in the performance of his plan. " Fain would I stay with you," replied LINNÆUS, " but I do

* Indices Stirpium Horti Academici Lugduno—Batavi, *Lugd. Bat.* 1710 and 1720, quarto.

" not

" not choose to arrange the botanical garden after my own method.
" My obligations to BOERHAAVE are too great, and I have too
" much respect for his memory." VAN ROYEN insisted on having
the garden altered. " Well," said LINNÆUS " let us project some new
" system, which shall be neither BOERHAAVE's nor mine, but which
" may be considered as your own." This proposal pleased, and thus
originated, after the publication of CLIFFORT's garden, the new description of the botanical garden at *Leyden*, and ROYEN's new system
of botany, of which, strictly speaking, LINNÆUS himself was the author *.

LINNÆUS profited by his stay at ROYEN's to publish two other
works. The one friendship imposed on him as a duty, and the
other had for its tendency to put in a clear light the prerogatives of his
system, and to establish its predominance.

The first was the production of the diligence of his ill-fated friend,
the ichthyology of ARTEDI, which appeared in the beginning of 1789
at *Leyden*; a work, which in LINNÆUS's own opinion, is unequalled in
the natural history of fishes. The second was the *Classes Plantarum*,
which LINNÆUS published in the same year on 656 pages, octavo.
In this work he presented a general and circumstatial view of the sixteen universal and thirteen partial systems till then introduced in botany, from GESNER and CÆSALPINUS, the first systematical botanists
down to his own time. He criticised the classifications of MORISON,
RAY, DILLENIUS, KNAUT, RIVINUS, RUPP, LUDWIG, HERMANN,
BOERHAAVE, TOURNEFORT, VAILLANT, SHEUCHZER, MAGNOL and

---

* Floræ Leydensis Prodromus, exhibens Plantas quæ in Horto Academico Lugduno—Batavo
aluntur. *Ludgd. Bat.* 1740.

PONTEDERA,

PONTEDERA, shewed the errors and excellencies of each, and added the genera of plants according to the different authors in the margin of his own system.

He soon had the pleasure to see his aspiring ambition gratified, and the sway of his method acknowledged. His friends, VAN ROYEN and GRONOV were the first who followed his dictates. The former published in 1739 a description of the plants of *Virginia (Flora Vir-giniæ)*, in the completion of which he had been assisted by LINNÆUS, and his technical nomenclature and descriptions. Thus with *Sweden* *, the Dutch were the first who did homage to this new botanical constitution, though it was rejected by some proud aristocratic malecontents.

The great number of friends and connexions whom LINNÆUS had found in *Holland*, afforded him fine prospects and secured his subsequent welfare. The Dutch wished to prevail on so valuable a man not to leave their country. It was proposed to him to make a botanical voyage at the expence of the republic to the *Cape of Good Hope*, with the promise of giving him on his return, a professorship of botany in a Dutch university. But LINNÆUS also slighted this offer, because he violently longed after his country, and after those bright hopes which he flattered himself to realize there.

The beginning of the year 1738 was the dullest time LINNÆUS passed in *Holland*. Formerly he always was of a serene, unruffled and cheerful temper; but now disquietude and melancholy preyed upon him. The celebrity which he had gained, the remonstrances of his friends, in short, nothing could raise his depressed spirits. The hercu-

* At *Stockholm* was published J. EBERH. FERBER, Medici, Hortus Agerumensis, Secundum Methodum Sexualem Linnæi. 1739, octavo.

lean labours to which he had dedvoted the elapsed year, could not but act with malign influence upon his health. Towards the close of January he was seized with a violent fever, which lasted upwards of six weeks. In March he visited *Hartecamp* for the last time, to enjoy the sweets of the vernal year, and to effect a complete restoration of his declining health.

CLIFFORT had visited him during his illness at *Leyden*, and seemed displeased with his residing in that city. " If it was your wish to stay " longer in *Holland*," said he, " I had the first right to your company, " and could have paid you your annual stipend as formerly."—During the latter part of the time LINNÆUS resided at *Hartecamp* he received a ducat per day.

His extreme application to study, was considered by his friends as the source of his discontented and sickly condition. But the sole and real cause of his disquietude and illness was SARAH ELISABETH, his intended bride. He had corresponded with her during the whole time of his stay in *Holland*. Her letters to him were constantly forwarded by one of his friends. As we have already observed, his future father-in-law had fixed the marriage at the expiration of three years, which were already elapsed, and LINNÆUS still remained abroad in the fourth year. His friend, to whom the letters of his ELISABETH were entrusted, and for whom he had obtained a professorship, endeavoured to take advantage of this long absence, and to obtain the hand of Miss MORÆUS for himself, by representing that her lover would never return to *Sweden*, and by so doing he almost had his wishes sanctioned by her father's consent. Fortunately another friend of LINNÆUS interposed for him, confirmed the reliance upon his constancy and fidelity, and thus dislodged this trea-

cherous

cherous rival. LINNÆUS himself related this threatening incident, which was like to have proved sinistrous to his passion, in a letter which he wrote a twelvemonth after to Baron HALLER *.

He intended to pay a visit to HALLER at *Goettingen*, and to professor LUDWIG at *Leipzic*, on his way back to *Sweden*, and had proposed to himself to pass through *Upper* and *Lower Saxony*, and the Danish dominions. Both, according to his promise, expected him with impatience. But he altered his resolution. Being so near the confines of *France*, he would not miss this opportunity of seeing *Paris*, where he had previously made several acquaintances by his correspondence.

He reached that capital in the beginning of May, where ANTHONY and BERNARD DE JUSSIEU, two brothers, were the principal botanists. The former was the successor of TOURNEFORT, and died in 1758, and his brother in 1777. They gave LINNÆUS a most kind and flattering reception, though ANTHONY was a bigotted adherent to TOURNEFORT's system, and too old to begin to learn a new one. Through them he became acquainted with the most eminent French literati, and saw all the botanical and other natural curiosities at *Paris*. He also saw the herbals of TOURNEFORT, VAILLANT, the two JUSSIEUS, and of SURIAN, a French physician, who had made two voyages to *America* with PLUMIER the jesuit. He visited the public libraries, and the private ones of ISARD and others; was introduced to the great entomologist REAUMUR,

* Permansi in Belgio, ut novisti; interim amicus meus summus, Cl. B... Litteras amicæ meæ ad me per tabellarios continuo transmittebat; sanéte præstitit. Ultimo anno 1738, quo apud VAN ROYEN vixi, (quod erat quarto anno; non enim sucer plures quam tres concessit annos) et hoc quidem nutu sponsæ, sibi proximum judicavit B ... esse, mea enim recommendatione factus fuit professor; mox me non reversurum in patriam demonstrabat; Sponsam meam ambiebat, fere obtinuit ni intervenisset alius, fallaciam qui prodidit; punitus et ipse fuit mille satis adversis. Epistol. ad Hallerum, vol. i. p. 415.

who

who invented the new thermometer; examined with BERNARD DE JUSSIEU all the curious plants in the botanical garden; and in a word, every thing which his curiosity could wish to have seen in so short a time. He wrote to HALLER " I have seen here so many public and " private libraries in natural history, that I am already enabled to pub- " lish a second edition of my *Bibliotheca Botanica*, since my fresh know- " ledge of books is much greater than it was before."

Paris, from its predilection for TOURNEFORT and VAILLANT, gave but little credit to the botanical reform of LINNÆUS: " He is a young " enthusiast," they would say, " who confounds all, and whose sole " merit consits in having plunged botany into a state of anarchy *." " Don't laugh, good people," said the French naturalist GUETTARD, who penetrated deeper than the rest into the spirit of the LINNÆAN me- thod, " don't laugh at LINNÆUS, the time will come when he will laugh at you all." A truly pathetic anticipation—for the same young Swede who now afforded them merriment, became afterwards, in de- spite of their sarcastic jokes, the master of his science in *France*,—and the late royal garden at *Trianon* was arranged according to his own sys- tem, in preference to that of the French botanists.

LINNÆUS was treated in the most friendly, cordial and affectionate manner by BERNARD DE JUSSIEU, whom he never ceased to corres- pond with. " I heard with pleasure," says Dean BAECK, who was at *Paris* in 1743, " in what high terms BERNARD DE JUSSIEU spoke of " LINNÆUS, whom he always used to greet by the title of our good " friend."

---

* C'est un jeune enthousiaste, qui brouille tout, n'a d'autre merite et de gloire, que d'avoir mis l'anarchie dans la botanique.

It

It was to his friendship Linnæus stood also indebted for an honour which was so rare and distinguishing for a young foreigner. He was admitted a correspondent member of the French academy of sciences. He left with some reluctance a city where he had enjoyed so much pleasure and entertainment. He had promised Baron Haller to visit him on his return from thence; but the impatience and constancy of his amorous flame recalled him to his country. After one month's residence in the French metropolis he went on board a ship at *Rouen*, in which, after a passage of five days, he reached *Helsingburg* in *Scania*, whence he set out to *Stockholm*.

Never was there a genius of the North who returned from foreign countries to his home, loaded with so many encomiums and laurels.

SECTION

SECTION VI.

———

OPPONENTS, AND LITERARY CONTESTS OF LINNÆUS.

BARON HALLER.—FIRST LETTER OF LINNÆUS TO THE BARON.—CONNEXION
BETWEEN THESE TWO GREAT MEN.—FRIENDSHIP, RIVALSHIP, AND OPINIONS
OF HALLER.—G. E. HALLER, HIS SON, WRITES AGAINST LINNÆUS.—L. HEISTER
AT HELMSTADT.—HIS RESENTMENT AGAINST LINNÆUS.—EXCITES HIS PUPIL,
PROFESSOR SIEGESBECK, AT PETERSBURG, AGAINST HIM.—AN ACCOUNT OF
THIS MAN.—HIS LITIGIOUS WRITINGS.—THEIR RIDICULOUS CONTENTS.—IS RE-
FUTED BY GLEDITSCH AND PROFESSOR BROWALLIUS.—HEISTER ENTERS THE
LISTS AGAINST LINNÆUS.—SEEKS TO DISPLAY HIS CELEBRITY BY A WORK OF
BURKHARD.—SEXUAL SYSTEM OF LINNÆUS.—IDEAS OF THE ANCIENTS RESPECT-
ING THE SEXES OF PLANTS.—JUNG.—MILLINGTON.—CAMERARIUS AND BURK-
HARD.—THE LATTER STARTS IDEAS ON THIS HEAD, WITHOUT SUCCESS.—LIN-
NÆUS UNACQUAINTED WITH JUNG'S WORKS. — ANECDOTE. — LIST OF THE
OTHER PRINCIPAL OPPONENTS OF LINNÆUS—KLEIN—CRANZ—ALSTON—PON-
TEDERA—SPALLANZANI.—ADANSON—COUNT DE BUFFON.—EXQUISITE POLITE-
NESS OF COUNT DE BUFFON TO LINNÆUS, JUN.—WALLER, A PUBLIC ANTA-
GONIST OF LINNÆUS IN SWEDEN. — PUBLISHES AN ACADEMICAL TREATISE
AGAINST HIM.—CONTENTS OF THAT WORK.—TURNS OUT TO THE AUTHOR'S
PREJUDICE.—ANECDOTE.—ANYMOUS DEFENCE OF LINNÆUS.—ITS CONTENTS.—
HIS METHOD OF REVENGING HIMSELF ON HIS ADVERSARY.—HIS PRUDENT
CONDUCT IN EVERY ATTACK.

REVOLUTIONS are never effected in the bosom of peace and
perfect concordance. They occasion convulsions, and these more or
less violent storms. Thus it happens in the political world, and still
more so in he republican domains of literature, where every one is at
liberty to give his vote. In the political world, the triumph of revolutions depends on the resolution and superiority of power. In the republic

republic of literature, it depends on the energy of truth, which is of
course the most arduous and the more honourable of the two. Where
such victories are obtained, opponents and rivals are seldom wanting.
As Homer had his Zoilus, Luther his Ecks, and Sylvester
Prierias, Bayle his Jurien, Voltaire his Frerons, and Wolf
a Lang, and his partner, as antagonists;—how very consistent was it
with the order of things, that the young Swede, who rose to the glorious
dignity of a reformer, should have had his adversaries too. Without
proclaiming him the infallible oracle of the wide range of his science—
for he had and must have had his defects—we discovered but too often
in the literary feuds directed against him that spirit which generally
animates and characterizes them. The love of truth was used as a
cloak, and envy, party-spirit, self-interest, and passion, as chief motives of the controversial disputes of his adversaries. But his conduct, amidst those attacks, was more prudent than that of many a great
man who either preceded or came after him. Agressions he could
not prevent, but he impeded the breaking out of a war, whose burthen
must have proved disagreeable, and whose issue could have added
no fresh laurels either to his honor or to his merits.

We shall now take a general view of his opponents, and the attacks
which took place at the first period of his reform in *Holland;* we will,
at the same time, communicate all the subsequent contests and feuds
which his passive conduct prevented from becoming rancorous struggles.
This we will do, that we may hereafter follow him with uninterrupted
quietude in the course of his meritorious life.

The first whom he dreaded as an enemy, and had afterwards great
reason to revere as the sincerest well-wisher and lover of his prosperity,

was

was Baron ALBRECHT HALLER. LINNÆUS had first got acquainted with him by a botanical treatise which HALLER published in the year 1734, in a periodical work, at *Nuremberg*, entituled : *Commercia Litteraria**. Fear and anxiety, more than esteem, made him, in 1737, correspond with this young man, who in the preceding year had been appointed professor of the new-founded university of *Goettingen*, which was the first step to his greatness.

LINNÆUS had heard of his friend GRONOV, at *Leyden*, a report that HALLER intended to write against his new system. He therefore wrote a letter to him from *Hartecamp*, dated on the 5th of April. The contents of this letter characterize too much his cast of mind for us to omit it here :

———" I have just received intelligence of your intending to declare " hostilities against me. Permit me, therefore, to come to a more cir- " cumstantial explanation with you on this subject. I could' wish to " avoid, as much as possible, your displeasure and your attacks. Much " rather would I choose to side with you. Nothing would be more " unpleasant to me than to be your adversary. PEACE BE WITH US! " Ever since your name has been known to me, I always felt the highest " esteem for you. To my knowledge, I never have done aught that " might have given you offence. Why will you then challenge me to " fight? say, what could make me incur your displeasure? I will give " you satisfaction.—PEACE BE WITH US !

" Should my innocent SEXSUAL SYSTEM be the cause of this war, " it would be a very unjust one: I have never pretended that the

---

* Ad rei Medicæ et Scientiæ Naturalis incrementa. This work appeared in 15 volumes quarto, from 1731 till 1745.

2   " method

.\

" method was natural. Become yourself a creator of a similar system,
" and I will immediately acknowledge you. If you have remarked
" greater faults in me, I forgive you your superior wisdom. Who
" could perambulate, without erring, the wide spread domains of nature?
" Who could observe every thing with sufficient accuracy? Correct me
" in a friendly manner, and you shall have my best thanks. I have
" done all I could do. A great tree cannot bear a lofty top when
" only it first begins to shoot forth. I have already made myself
" known to all the principal botanists. They have all encouraged me,
" and none would oppress my insatiable desire of getting acquainted
" with nature. Should you be more obstinate than all those? In your
" treatise in the Journal of *Nuremberg,* your disposition appears to me
" too elevated, too sublime, ever to permit you to avail yourself of
" the ignorance of others to promote your own greatness*."

    " Forbearing to contend with me, you will do much better to com-
" municate your profound learning and knowledge of nature to the
" world. This will surely be more honourable to you. Look back
" on the history of botanists. Proud of their skill and inventions,
" they would not remain quiet and peaceable when they first appeared
" on the stage. Long have I been of that opinion, but now I know
" better. After the lapse of a few years, the former became so com-

---

* Si quos alios in me vidisti errores, Tu sapientior, hæc ignoscas. Quis caruit erroribus,
in diffusissimo Naturæ constitutus campo? Quis sufficientes habuit observationes? Moneas
hæc amice, et tibi gratias agam. Feci, quæ potui, nec fastigium summum acquirit vasta
arbor, prima qua erumpit tempestate. Innotui Botanicis certe primariis omnibus dudum;
me erexerunt omnes, nec meum insatiable discendi naturalia, desiderium fregit ullus. An
tu hisce omnibus durior? Videris mihi ex tua dissertatione magis nobilis, quam ut te jactares
super ignorantiam aliorum. Epistol. ad Hallerum, Vol. I. p. 234, et seq.

" plaisant

" plaisant and so polite, that they would not offend any person with a
" single word.

" I have perhaps been the only one, who after your own method,
" acquired his learning without a master.   I am still a learner, and
" you will indulge me for not having yet become learned.   If science
" can be acquired by your method, I am also in hopes of it by my own*,
" Finally I much doubt whether you or any other accademical pro
" fessor can derive any benefit from quarrels.   The first endeavour of
" a teacher should be to procure the confidence and respect of his
" audience.   But if his pupils see him in error, how dangerous will
" it prove to his authority!   What man, however learned or accom-
" plished, has not been justly censured for having censured others.
" It always leaves some stigma behind.

" Consult the history of all literary champions, and show me but one
" who ingratiated himself with the world by his feuds.   MATTHIOLUS
" might in his time have been a great man, had he not given himself
" to litigiousness.   What could RAY and RIVINUS do with their quar-
" rels?   DILLENIUS still laments that the latter compelled him to enter
" the lists; and did his victory add any thing to his celebrity?   Another
" sent him a challenge some time after, but he wisely declined accept-
" ing it.   The ingenious VAILLANT endeavoured to pave himself the
" way to glory by the downfall of TOURNEFORT.   How much greater
" would he have been, had he not acted thus!

" I shudder at the idea of entering a combat.   Because, whether you
" vanquish or are vanquished—prejudice and blame will always attend

* Ego demum fui et forte solus, qui secundum istam a te datam methodum absque præ-
ceptore ullo, quæ novi, addidici. Disco adhuc; ignoscas quod doctus, etiamnum non
evaserim. Si doctrina, tua methodo, comparari queat, spes doctrinæ etiam apud me elucet.

" your

" your lot. Who triumphs without scars? To me, and perhaps to you
" the time is too valuable to be spent in disputes. I am also too young
" for them. If you once take up arms, you must not lay them down
" till the conclusion of the war, and this once began might last till
" death. And all this *weighty* and *serious* struggle—how would it appear
" in the eyes of posterity at the expiration of half a century?—As a
" tale, as a mere joke! I am not ashamed of being taught better by
" you—Behold him, whom you wish to make your enemy, and who
" once more solicits most earnestly peace and your friendship.

  " But should the rumour circulating be without foundation, I most
" earnestly beg your pardon, for having troubled you with these ample
" representations."

  The fear of LINNÆUS was panic, and the report turned out to be
an idle story. HALLER wrote immediately to inform him of his
friendly disposition in the warmest expressions, and to assure him,
that it never entered into his head to molest him in his laudable career.
LINNÆUS in return, sent him a letter of thanks on the first of May,
in which he paid the following compliment. " I feel an uncommon
" pleasure in the falsehood of the report. You only and DILLENIUS
" I could wish never to be mine enemies. For you both have read
" the same book which I read—you have read Nature.—As to other
" botanists who can only boast of book-learning, I do not value them,
" however great their erudition might be."

  In the same year this scientific zeal brought on a short interruption
of their friendship. HALLER had sent LINNÆUS a copy of his dissertation of inauguration on the method of studying botany *(de Methodo
studii Botanici; Goett.* 1736.) LINNÆUS, in an unguarded moment, too

                                                              proud

proud of his confidence, and still more animated with a desire of sport-
ing his own knowledge, returned an answer, with a criticism, in which
he hinted at several erroneous assertions, and manifested his predilection for his own system. · " Rest assured," said LINNÆUS, " that
" as a stranger, I love and esteem you with all my heart, you will not
" therefore, take it amiss, if, in a friendly and confidential manner, I
" say a few words, respecting your excellent treatise*." But HALLER
was displeased, and manifested his displeasure to him at his amicable
severity.

LINNÆUS hastened to appease his resentment. He did not expect
that his critique would be so ill received†. In a letter to HALLER,
written on the 8th of October, he says : " Do not believe that I write
" against you from enmity. I take Almighty God to witness, that
" there is no botanist whom I esteem, revere, and love more than you.
" So think not ill of me. If I have selected the names of all the
" genera of which you have a different opinion, it was not to censure
" you, but to know the truth, and to confirm myself to it on future
" occasions. I only beg here that you may no farther think of all
" which gave you offence in my last letter. You shall never have

---

* Si persuasus sis, me, quem vidisti nunquam, te ex animo amare magnifice facere, nec
ægre feres, si pauca tecum loquar de tua dissertatione, certe magni laboris pere.¯

† Ne putes me ex studio inimica mente contra te scribere. Testor omnipotentem Deum,
me nullum Botanicum majori in pretio, honore et amore habere quam te! Sentias itaque
non de me male! Excerpsi ex tuis generibus nomina circa quæ dissentisti a me, non ut te
reprehenderem, sed ut certior fierem et in tempore me corrigerem—Unice oro, rejicias a
tua mente omnia, quæ ultima epistolate offenderunt. Nunquam habebis apud me causam
iræ; me amabis dum -me presentem videas, meumque animum. Quanti ego te fecerim, vel
me absente coram te declarabunt, vel quidem mihi inimici. Doleo maxime quod in me læsus fuerit
tuus in me generosus animus; culpam deploro, veniam precor! Spero te hisce satisfactum,
quod si sis, et amicus ret antea. Epistol. ad HALLER. Vol. I. p. 337.

" occasion

" occasion to be angry with me, you will like me if you see me in person,
" and come to get acquainted with my way of thinking. My very ene-
" mies must own in my absence how much I esteem you. I lament ex-
" tremely my having offended your noble disposition towards me, I
" regret my fault, and crave your pardon. I hope this explanation will
" afford you satisfaction, and you will, as formerly, remain my friend."

And so did HALLER remain the friend of LINNÆUS. He gave him
the noblest and most egregious proofs of his friendship. Their mutual
correspondence continued till 1750. Three years after, HALLER left
Goettingen, and returned to *Bern,* his native city. A collection of
critical disquisitions, which HALLER's son published against LINNÆUS,
during four years, reckoning from 1750, seems however to have been
the cause which broke off that correspondence.

The personal and reciprocal esteem and attachment between these
two great men, was not unfrequently disturbed by jealousy and literary
discordance. Considering the difference of their genius and way of
thinking, it could not happen otherwise. That poet who sung with
such beautiful philosophy the vanity of HONOUR, would not have been
the *polyhistor* of the age, had not a sense of that same honour guided
him on the path of fame. With all the discretion and sedate grandeur
of his temper, he was not insensible of its sweets and its value.

As to LINNÆUS, glory was the soul of all his endeavours, and the
idol of his affections. He rose to be the monarch of botany, and
claimed universal homage. HALLER followed his own method in that
science. How could it therefore have been possible that public disputes, reproaches, and petty attacks should not sometimes have broken
out between them.

" LINNÆUS"—

" LINNÆUS"—says the Chevalier ZIMMERMANN, " a pupil and
" friend of HALLER, with whom he was well acquainted by several.
" years domestic connexion,—had in the course of a few years pulled
" down the whole structure of botany, that he might erect on the ruins
" of his predecessors his own system; he rejected every thing foreign
" to his own precepts, and sent the greatest botanists into a school,
" where they were first to learn the signification of the names he had
" created, and the laws of his system. HALLER, with placid eye, saw
" this mighty dictator step forth; he was not insensible of the necessity
" of a reform, but saw at the same time, that he went too far. He fol-
" lowed LINNÆUS where ever he thought the truth was his guide,
" but where the latter only dealt in hypotheses, he there quitted him.
" The plurality of methods," said he, " is not hurtful, unless they grow
" too imperious, like the LINNÆAN system."

This pride of LINNÆUS in his science, this exclusive authority which
he maintained, and the unfriendly and rigorous animadversions which
sometimes attended his sway, excited the displeasure of HALLER, and
gave him frequent opportunities to indulge himself in strong censure. We
shall quote here some of those criticisms, as we should otherwise offend
against candor and truth, and expose in a diminitive light the great
merits of LINNÆUS, were we to pass over in silence the reproaches
and objections raised against him.

BARON HALLER having been somewhat severely treated in the
critique given by LINNÆUS, in the year 1745, of the *Flora Suecica*, expressed himself as follows in the review of the *Fauna Suecica*: " The
" unbounded dominion which LINNÆUS has assumed in the animal
" reign, must upon the whole appear disgusting to many persons. He

1   " considered

" considered himself as a second ADAM, and gave names to all the
" animals after their distinctive marks, without ever caring for his pre-
" decessors. He can hardly forbear to make *man a monkey*, or *the*
" *monkey a man*."

At a later period he gave the following critical opinion and review.
" LINNÆUS always accuses those who find fault with him. But has
" he not caused his merits to be depreciated, by suppressing all bo-
" tanical names given by foreign authors except a few, nay, even
" those denominations which are palpably better than his own? Has
" he not trampled upon the inventions of those, who would not be
" guided by his rules, omitted mentioning their new invented plants,
" and not pointed out their improvements? Has he not judged very
" severely of many learned men, even in sciences which have never
" been his province? Has he not refused to adopt, as long as possible,
" several species of plants which he reckoned among the bastard-
" species, and at last adopted several of them? We wish that LINNÆUS,
" with his great industry and vivifying genius, may so far conquer his
" temper, as to place some confidence in men endowed with eyes and
" genius like himself, though they live in more southern countries, and
" remember in general, that all sciences like botany, are a republic."

These two censures are fully characterised by a spirit of asperity and
resentment. Wounded self-love did not a little contribute to their
publicity. HALLER was the panegyrist, but more frequently the censor
of LINNÆUS in those works, which furnished him with an opportunity
of venting his spleen. He, however, vindicated himself from the reproach of jealousy against LINNÆUS a few years previous to his death.
" It appears from the letters of LINNÆUS," says he, " in the preface
" prefixed

" prefixed to the publication of his latin correspendence, how little
" jealous I have been of that man, even when he provoked me with
" his contradictions. I feel, therefore, some pleasure at having it in
" my power to refute those unjust charges by LINNÆUS's own testi-
" mony*." This resentment, manifested by epistolar correspondence,
did not extend to the professorial chair, nor to representations and
opinions in written works.

Whatever was neglected by the father to show himself the public opponent of his northern friend, was accomplished by his son GOTTLIEB
EMANUEL HALLER. He first dedicated his time to the study of
physic, but afterwards distinguished himself as an able civilian. He
did not long survive his father, and died as High Bailiff of *Noyon* in
the canton of *Bern*, April 9, 1786. He commenced his career as an
author, in the 15th year of. his age, by several tracts directed against
LINNÆUS. They formed no epocha nor reform, and contained only
several observations stamped with the genius of the father.

A more violent and more implacable adversary, whose unruly spirit
frequently interrupted the peace of the literary world, was professor
LAWRENCE HEISTER, at *Helmstadt*, who died in that city in 1758, in the
76th year of his age.—A man distinguished by his merit in anatomy
and surgery; but as unskilful in the science of botany, as he was
conspicuous in the former. He always considered himself as a great
botanist. His self-love was of course easily offended. He followed
RAY's system, and had introduced many new changes and fresh appellations in the vegetable reign; but the reform of LINNÆUS levelled

---

* Ex LINNÆANIS Epistolis apparet quam non invidus in virum fuerim, etiam cum suis
objectionibus me lacessivisset; neque displicuit mihi injustam accusationem proprio LINNÆI
testimonio refutare.

2.   them.

them with the dust. When the latter published his *Genera Plantarum*
in 1737, HEISTER, fired with indignation, wrote thus to HALLER:
" LINNÆUS rejects all the characters defined by his predecessors, and
" introduces new names to those plants on which the best ones have
" already been bestowed; will there be many to follow such inno-
" vations?"—and LINNÆUS mentioned in his system: " that all the
" botanists considered the fructification in plants as the basis of good
" order, HEISTER alone accepted, who fixed the genera by the petals."—
All this could not be granted; war was therefore declared.

HEISTER thought it unworthy of his fame to commence hostilities
himself. He left it to a champion, one of his pupils, Doctor JOHN
GEORGE SIEGESBECK, who at his recommendation was appointed Professor of Botany at St. *Petersburgh.*—This man's celebrity turned to
his shame, and his insignificant name was only kept in remembrance,
owing to the greatness of the genius whom he so much strove to lessen.
His conduct, as an opponent, was the more impudent, as he was himself destitute of that knowledge which might have made him a competent judge of learning. The celebrated GMELIN, who lived at the
same time at *Petersburgh,* delineates his character in these words:
" SIEGESBECK has scarcely a superficial knowledge of botany, he un-
" derstands the writings of others as little as he knows himself. He is
" contented with the bare names of plants suggested to him by his sterile
" brain, destitute of all penetration.*"

LINNÆUS had for some time carried on a friendly correspondence
with SIEGESBECK; but the allurements and examples of HEISTER,

---

* SIEGESBECKIUS nec primis labris Botanicen degustavit, nec quid scribant alii, nec se
ipsum i: teligit, contentus solis plantarum denominationibus, quas sterile et doctrinæ orbum
ingenium ipsi suggerit. Epistol. ad HALLER. vol. ii. p. 110.

soon

soon made every sentiment of amity vanish. Even in the year 1737,
his critical zeal brought forth a very violent pamphlet against LIN-
NÆUS, which contained few arguments, but a most copious deal of
nonsense and ribaldry*. He combated in this work the New Sexual
System of LINNÆUS in a manner peculiar to himself. LINNÆUS had
maintained in this system—that in the animal as well as in the vegetable reign, there were frequently several males to one female :—
plures mariti; una fœmina in eodem thalamo.—" What man in the
" world," declaims SIEGESBECK against this well-expressed proposition,—" will ever believe that God Almighty should have introduced
" such confusion, or rather such shameful whoredom for the propagation
" of the reign of plants. Who would instruct young students in such a
" voluptuous system without scandal †?"

LINNÆUS having obtained a copy of this invidious production, complained of it in a letter to HALLER, in the following satyrical expressions : " I wish to God, SIEGESBECK had written those things be-
" fore I published my first treatise! I would then have learned in my
" youth, what I must now learn in my manhood, namely, not to write,
" to hear others and be silent myself. What could induce me to be
" so foolish as to bestow so much time, so many days and nights upon
" a science, to reap such fruits—to become after all the derision of the
" world! SIEGESBECK affords no arguments; his whole book is one un-
" interrpted strain of declamation. Whether I answer or am silent,

* Botanosophiæ Verioris Sciographia ; cui accedit ob argumenti analogiam Epicrisis in
Linnæi Systema Plantarum, &c. *Petrop.* 4to.

† Ecquis vero unquam credet, tales confusiones, vel si mavis *scortationes* quasi detestabiles
in Regno Vegetabili ad propagationem a D. O. M. esse subordinatas? Ecquis Methodum
talem lascivam studiosæ juventuti sine offensa poterit aperire?

R   " both

" both points would throw a stigma upon my honour. He knows
" nothing of argument, rejects my sexes of plants, laughs at my cha-
" racters, and challenges all the botanists, to declare if they compre-
" hend them *."

All real botanists understood the LINNÆAN characters, save SIEGES-
BECK. LINNÆUS acted the wisest part—he made no reply to his in-
vectives. The intrinsic value of his works and his reform contained
the best defence. What SIEGESBECK had done by challenging LIN-
NÆUS, was in process of time taken up voluntarily by other men.
Doctor JOHN BROWALLIUS, Professor of the University of *Abo* in
Finland, and afterwards bishop in that city, and Professor GLEDITSCH at
Berlin, vindicated his cause against the litigious quibbler at *Petersburght*.
He had also provoked and charged GLEDITSCH, who very prudently
treated him with the same contempt. And what were the consequences
of this Russian quarrel?—The domination of LINNÆUS spread farther
with his fame—and SIEGESBECK became every where unpopular and

---

* Utinam SIEGESBECKIUS hæc scripsisset, dum primum edideram tractatulum; addi-
dicissem juvenis, quod senex addiscere cogor,—abstinere a scribendo, audire alios, tacere
ipse. Quæ me dementia cepit, qui tantum consumsi temporis, tot horas, noctesque in artem,
tales quæ proferat fructus,—ludibrium ut evaderem orbi!—Argumenta ejus nulla sunt, sed
exclamationes totum per librum. Si respondeo aut taceo, commaculor utrinque; rationes
non intelligit; negat sexum; ridet meos characteres, et provocat omnes, an ullus eos intel-
ligat?—Epist. LINN. ad HALLER. vol. i. p. 361.

† This was done in the following works:—J. BROWALLII examen epicriseos in systema
plantarum sexuale Linnæi, auctore SIEGESBECKIO, *Aboæ* 1739.
J. G. GLEDITSCH Consideratio Epicriseos Siegesbeckianæ, *Berol.* 1740, in 8vo.
BARON HALLER wrote the following words at the bottom of the title page of SIEGES-
BECK's Epicrisis:—" In parte prima opusculi RIVINI Methodum contra RAIUM et DIL-
" LENIUM defendit; in altera in methodum LINNÆI invehitur, *quam vereor ut ubique in-*
" *tollexerit.*"

ridiculous, was dimissed in 1747 from the Russian academy of sciences, and died a private man.

Meanwhile HEISTER felt an inward satisfaction at the quarrel of which he had himself been the author. Though no victory ensued, yet he rejoiced in the teazing violence of the aggressions. In other respects, he was prudent enough not to show himself directly in the field of litigation. He screened himself behind his pupils, whom he had influenced with his spirit of resentment. With these he held disputations at *Helmstadt* replete with acrimony, and pointedly levelled against the northern reformer*.

Doctor MOEHRING at *Ievern*, an able botanist, gave his opinion of those hostile dissertations, in a letter to HALLER, in the following words : " They are a mass of turbulent verbosity ; the smallest minutiæ
" are attacked in them, and matters censured which LINNÆUS himself
" only pointed out as plausibilities, and which none of his opponents
" have thus far been able to expose in a clear light. If those literary
" brawlers had but so deservedly exerted themselves in botany as
" LINNÆUS, they would see, that it is easier to criticise, than by
" dint of the most arduous observations to discover truths and give
" new elucidations. How much better would it be, to remain an entire
" stranger to honours than thus impudently to attempt to lessen the
" reputation of another. Thus far can envy and party-spirit mislead
" us mortals !"

---

* These were L. HEISTERI Dissert. sistens meditationes et animadversiones in novum systema botanicum Sexuale LINNÆI; Respond. P. C. GOECKEL, *Helmst.* 1741.—Dissertatio de nominum plantarum mutatione utili ac noxia, Resp. J. E, SANDHAGEN, *Helmst.* 1741, and several others.

HEISTER had at last, the satisfaction of making a discovery from which he promised himself the greatest triumph and hoped to dwindle into nothing, both the fame of LINNÆUS and his system of reform. A letter had fallen into his hands, which JOHN HENRY BURKHARD, first physician to the Duke of BRUNSWICK WOLFENBUTTEL, had written to LEIBNITZ, and caused to be printed in 1702. In this letter, BURKHARD, with great ingenuity, had already given some ideas of the sexes of plants and of the system the formation of which was afterwards fully accomplished by LINNÆUS. But at the same time BURKHARD was never of opinion, that a new system of botany, might be introduced from the parts of fructification of plants *. He set forth the proposition of deriving the division of their classes from the flower, and their orders from the fruit. HEISTER was not remiss in divulging his discovery. He caused a new edition of BURKHARD's letter to be printed in 1750, with a circumstantial introduction, in which he directed all the shafts of his resentment against LINNÆUS, and represented the novelty of his modern sexual system, with the most sarcastic irony†. Thus all notable inventions and reforms have

---

* The following are BURKHARD's own words on this subject:—Quoniam autem partes genitales minus sunt conspectæ, nec spectantium occulos facile alliciunt ; consultius esse duco, si earum conformatio in comparatione stirpium prætermittatur et vesicularum tantum seminalium situs et numerus attendatur, et quidem non ubivis, sed in plantis tantummodo, quæ flores imperfectos ferunt, nbi constituendis classibus æque inservire poteruut, ac in floribus perfectis petalorum situs ac numerus.

† The following is the title of BURKHARD's letter, which is become a literary scarcity : J. HENRICI BURKHARD Epistola ad LEIBNITZIUM, qua characterem plantarum naturalem nec a radicibus nec ab aliis plantarum partibus minus essentialibus, peti posse ostendit, simulque in comparationem plantarum, quam partes earum genitales suppeditant, inquirit. Guelpherb, 1701. 32 pages in quarto.

mct

met with envious persons, who took a delight in rendering the fame of originality an object of dispute.

HEISTER's malign reproaches against LINNÆUS, on this occasion, were really unmerited. The little production of BURKHARD, quite a literary phenomenon, had never been mentioned in any botanical work, had never acquired much publicity, and how could it therefore be considered as the source of the modern system of LINNÆUS. The writings of JUNG, or JUNGIUS, whom we already mentioned above in the history of botany, and who published them in the last century, were in a similar manner alledged against the prince of botanists. But this charge was of as little validity as that of BURKHARD's letter. When LINNÆUS, then a young student at *Upsal*, projected his new botanical plan, he had never once seen those works, and we can adduce convincing proofs of this assertion. Doctor GIESEKE at *Hamburgh*, who heard the lectures of LINNÆUS in 1771, mentioned once, in familiar conversation, the writings of JUNG; and, especially, his principal botanical work— *Doxoscopiæ Physicæ minores*. LINNÆUS replied that he was utterly unacquainted with it. GIESEKE, after his return sent him this work, upon which LINNÆUS thanked him in a letter of the 24th of December 1774, in the following words : " Three days ago I received your rare present " of JUNG's *Doxoscopiæ* which I never saw before. I thank you for " this work in the most obliging manner. I see the author has been a " very laborious and ingenious man for his age." In honour to his name, LINNÆUS junior, called afterwards a new North-American plant, *Jungia*.

That some ideas of the sexes of plants had already been hinted before, is an incontrovertible fact, and LINNÆUS did not him-

self

self deny it*. The ancients, as PLINY records†, had some notions of such a system. Besides JUNG, another German of the name of CAMERARIUS, Professor at *Tubingen*‡, and Sir THOMAS MILLING-TON, Professor at *Oxford*, had already given some ideas of the sexes of plants, during the last century, nay there is even a remoter instance §. Sir THOMAS MILLINGTON's observations had been communicated to Dr. GREW, but they were never printed.

VAILLANT displayed these ideas with more ingenuity than all his predecessors. But what difference is there between publishing a mere thought—and forming, completing, and rendering it the leading star of an universal reformation. Had this been accomplished by JUNG, CAMERARIUS, or Sir THOMAS MILLINGTON, their names would have shone in perpetual lustre, and no LINNÆUS would then have been wanted. But it was he that really entered that immortal career, which was only pointed at in distant obsurity; it was he that took upon himself with infinite pains, the numberless observations which became necessary to attain the proposed end ‖.

He

---

* Exacte dicere, quis primus sexum plantarum invenerit, res esset maximæ difficultatis. Veteres cognoscebant sexus; sed parum solida erat cognitio. THOM. MILLINGTON, circa annum 1676, primum verum inventorem hujus doctrinæ fuisse dicunt ; at nihil de ea tradidit. Nemo autem melius VAILLANTIO, magno illo botanico, accurate rem ostendit, quamvis argumentis non demonstraverit.—LINNÆUS in the solution of the prize question *De Sexu plantarum.*

† Arboribus, immo potius omnibus quæ terra gignat herbisque etiam utrumque sexum esse, naturæ diligentissimi tradunt. Plin. Hist. Natur. Lib. xiii. Cap. 4.

‡ Epistola de Sexu plantarum. *Tubingæ*, 1694, twelves.

§ Already in the year 1592, a Polish literatus of the name of ADAM ZALZIAWISKY, maintained the difference of the sexes of plants.

‖ ADANSON, one of the most distinguished French opponents of LINNÆUS, did him complete justice with regard to his sexual system, by saying : " Though the idea of a system " founded

He had already completed in *Holland* the best part of his design. The sway of his new system became wide-spread and predominant in a few years. There were, however, men among most nations of Europe, who did not agree, or were at least discontented with the laws of the new constitution of natural history, and who loaded LINNÆUS with censure and blame. Nothing, however, could have been more natural in a science which had never been thoroughly learnt, never reduced to mathematical uniformity and perfection; in a science where opinions were frequently as different as the heads whence they sprung—finally, in a science for which ADANSON alone proposed sixty-five systems, though none of them has been received. Among the German Anti-Linnæans, we ought especially to reckon Dr. KLEIN at *Dantick*, who in 1742 published a treatise against the new classification of the animal reign: H. CRANZ, professor of botany at *Vienna*, a violent *antipode* in most of his numerous botanical works; and among those who conducted themselves with more moderation and dignity, M. de NECKER and Dr. HACQUET, without mentioning here the criticisms of many other Germans.—Among the English we remark Professor CHARLES ALSTON of *Edinburgh*;—among the Dutch CAMPER;—among the Italians, Professor JULIUS PONTEDERA at *Padua*; SPALLANZANI and Dr. CYRILLI at *Naples*;—among the French, especially ADANSON*, and the celebrated Count de BUFFON, who died on the 16th of April 1788†.

" founded on the sex of plants be due to BURKHARD—yet the execution of this system is new
" and belongs to LINNÆUS." See ANDANSON's *Familles des plantes.* Par.1763, 8vo. v. i. p. xii.
* LINNÆUS wrote thus of ADANSON to GESNER at *Zurich*: " He is either mad or intoxi-
" cated:"—*insanit aut non sobrius est.* HALLER on the contrary called him *a fine head and a
worthy rival of* LINNÆUS.—*Lepidum caput, et æmulum Linnæo dignum.*
† See BUFFON's *Discours sur la maniere de traiter l'histoire naturelle.*

1   This

This great man in the violence of his attacks and criticisms, was chiefly hurried away by jealousy. His ambition also induced him to behold, even the fame of HALLER, with an envious eye. Notwithstanding this, he revered the greatness of LINNÆUS, and honoured his memory. He gave a convincing proof of his respect to LINNÆUS the younger. In 1782 the latter came to *Paris*, where the Count gave him a most cordial reception. The royal cabinet of natural history was shut almost to every body; but BUFFON shewed him all that was remarkable; and on his expressing a wish to see the royal botanical garden, he wrote to LINNÆUS, jun.—*that on that day he would be spoke to by none but him.*

Even *Sweden* did not want for persons who envied the good fortune and greatness of LINNÆUS. His only open and avowed enemy in that country was JOHN WALLERIUS, the great mineralogist, who died in 1785. In the year 1741 he published an academical treatise at *Upsal*, which was entirely levelled at LINNÆUS*. He laid down twenty propositions, in which several assertions and representations of LINNÆUS, in his System of Nature, in the Flora of *Lapland*, in his Dissertation on Cold Fevers, and in a treatise inserted in the transactions of the academy of *Stockholm*, were treated with ridicule. He began with the thesis, that man cannot be classed among the quadrupeds. Then follows a critique on the LINNÆAN division of the

---

* This treatise, which is extremely rare, and almost entirely unknown in every part of *Europe* except *Sweden*, has been communicated to the author by Mr. EHRHARDT, botanist to his BRITANIC MAJESTY in *Hanover*. The author has since inserted it in the following work, which he published at *Hamburgh* in 1792, in 8vo.—" Collectio Epistolarum CAROL. " A LINNE ad Viros Cl. scriptarum; accedunt opuscula pro et contra LINNÆUM scripta, " extra Sueciam rarissima."

mineral

mineral reign into three classes, which WALLERIUS had divided into six. " LINNÆUS," says he, " has planned his classification more from " a spirit of innovation than from well-founded truth. His hypothesis " that stones were never created is also false. LINNÆUS has asserted, " that the intermitting fevers, especially in the province of *Upland*, " are endemical." WALLERIUS endeavours to turn this proposition into ridicule as an hyperbolic representation, and alledges a chronological list of the distempers at *Upsal*, which had been communicated to him by professor ROSEN, in behalf of his dissertation.

WALLERIUS hoped to gain celebrity by the different contents of this treatise, and to make his fortune, but it only served to undermine both. LINNÆUS enjoyed too much popularity and protection at *Stockholm*, for this worthless injury of his reputation to please or to remain without consequential resentment Had WALLERIUS had ten times more merit it would not have been valued, owing to this literary feud. He felt its sinister effects for upwards of ten years, and it was not till after the demise of FREDERICK I. that he obtained the ordinary professorship at *Upsal*, which had so long and so vainly been the object of his ambition. The real cause of this aggression was occasioned by his rival's concurrence to obtain the professorship of physic, to which LINNÆUS was appointed.

These circumstances evince sufficiently the profound indignation which WALLERIUS's attacks had excited in LINNÆUS. He felt them the more poignant as they proceeded from a countryman and an academical colleague. In order to avert the unpleasant sensations which WALLERIUS might have created in the mind of persons who were strangers to the merits, distinction, and celebrity of LINNÆUS abroad,

s   and

and to triumph over his rival in the vacancy at *Upsal*, he published a small work, under the title of *The Opinion of the Learned World on the Writings of* CHARLES LINNÆUS, M. D." *(Orbis Eruditi Judicium de Car. Linnæi M. D. Scriptis).*

This is the only peculiar apology which LINNÆUS ever wrote in his own behalf, and also the only production which he published in an anonymous manner. However numerous and common the greatest part of his other works are, yet as extremely scarce is this performance even in *Sweden* *. It seems neither to have been known to HALLER nor to other naturalists, at least they never mentioned it, and there are scarce two copies to be met with in all *Germany*. The contents of this pamphlet being equally remarkable and unknown, they deserve a more particular account.

The title contains the symbol or motto of LINNÆUS, taken from VIRGIL: " To raise fame by deeds, is the task of the noble-minded:" —*Famam extollere factis—hoc virtutis opus*; and on the back GRONOV's inscription on the image of LINNÆUS :

   " *Ne succumbe malis; te noverit ultimus Ister,*

   " *Te Boreas gelidus.*"

—" In spite of fate—from the Danube's mouth to the frigid North, shall thy name be known."

Then follows a short view of the principal incidents of our hero's life, and a list of the different works which he till then published, with their divers editions, making altogether twenty-one, besides the names of those who have publicly accepted and vindicated the LINNÆAN

* I am indebted for the communication of this pamphlet to the friendly kindness of Dr. KNOES at *Upsal*. It is printed in one sheet, small octavo, without numerical figures or the year.

system—

system—Van Royen, Gronov, Ferber, Browallius, Gleditsch, afterwards communicates all the printed or written epistolary opinions and attestations given respecting him by twenty learned men.

Among these are the most eminent botanists, and some men of the most distinguished celebrity in their respective science, namely, five Dutchmen, professor John Van Gorter at *Harderwyk*, Herman Boerhaave, Van Royen, Gronov and Burmann at *Amsterdam*;— four British literati, Sir Hans Sloane, Bart. president of the royal society of sciences at *London*, professor Dillenius at *Oxford*, and the two physicians Lawson and Donnel Jacob;—four Frenchmen, the celebrated pathalogist and botanist De Sauvages at *Montpellier*, A. Jussieu of *Paris*, professor Barrere at *Perpignan*, and professor Gravel at *Strasbourg*;—two Swiss, Baron Albrecht Haller and John Gesner;—and five Germans, J. Gleditsch of *Berlin*, Dr. Breyne of *Dantzick*, professor Lange of *Halle*, counsellor Otto Menken at *Leipsic*, and professor Kohl of *Hamburgh*. We deem it important to insert here the substance of the most remarkable of these testimonials.

VAN GORTER *

Was the promoter of Linnæus. When he took up his degree of doctor of physic, Van Gorter expressed himself thus in the diploma:

" The undersigned does certify, that he has remarked in the learned " Swede, now doctor of physic, Charles Linnæus, uncommon know-

---

* He was also some time first physician to the court of *Russia*, and died in 1762. His son David held the same office, and died in 1783.

" ledge

" ledge and erudition, not only in all the different branches of physic,
" but also in botany.

" Witness my name, &c. &c.

HERMANN BOERHAAVE,
In a Letter to Linnæus, *dated January* 13, 1737.

" The sight of your work (the *Genera Plantarum*) excites admira-
" tion, and exhibits a performance of infinite diligence, extraordinary
" industry, and incomparable knowledge. I cannot sufficiently praise
" its utility. *Whole ages will extol its worth, the good will imitate it,* and
" all men will use it with advantage.—Your botanical works bid de-
" fiance to mortality and to all Aristarchuses."

VAN ROYEN,
In his Preface to the Flora Leydensis, page 16:

" The fifth system in botany has been produced according to the
" sexes of the plants, from the stamina and pistilla, by Charles Lin-
" næus, the prince of all the botanists of his age. Superior to all, he
" reformed the whole of botany, diffused fresh light over all its parts,
" and purged it of its impurities. Never has that science appeared
" in such a beautiful and transcendent lustre as at present."

Letter of recommendation written by Van Royen *to* M. de Jussieu,
7th May, 1738, *when* Linnæus *set out for* Paris.

" Behold Charles Linnæus, the prince of botany, if ever one
" existed. Who does not know him yet, may know him by experience.
" This excellent man, so distinguished, so well versed in all parts of

1   " natural

" natural history, is the bearer of this letter.   I recommend him in the
" strongest manner to you and to your kindness."

SIR HANS SLOANE, BART. P. R. S.

In a Letter to LINNÆUS, *December* 20*th,* 1737.

" I am so uncommonly pleased with your *Flora Lapponica,* that I
" very much wish to see the other parts of the natural history of that
" country completed, and publicly described by you *."

DILLENIUS,

In a Letter to LINNÆUS, *dated August* 18, 1737:

" Your *Flora Lapponica* I have received, seen, and read with great
" pleasure.   I wish to GOD we had more such Floras brought forth
" with similar diligence and care.   In this you have shewn that you
" are the man †."

DE SAUVAGES,

In a Letter to LINNÆUS, *the celebrated Restorer of Natural History,*
dated September 10, 1737:

" I congratulate you myself, and the learned world, and heartily re-
" joice at your having undertaken labours so extensive and momen-
" tous.   But I am astonished, and can hardly see how so young a man
" as you could publish so many and such various works, a single one

---

* Flora Lapponica speciatim mihi tantopere arridit, ut maxime cupiam, cæteras illius re-
gionis partes Historia Naturalis intueri tua exaratus manu, publiceque luci datas.

† Vidi accepi et legi *Floram* tuam *(Lapponicam)* multa cum voluptate ; utinam plures
istius modi nobis prostarent, tali studio et cura elaboratæ ; in hac te virum præstitisti.

" of

" of which, to conclude from your letters and your celebrity, ought to
" gain you an immortal name."

In a second Letter, March 15th 1740.

" I have frequently been speaking of you to my colleague, professor
" MAGNOL. He holds you in reverence. Doctor LE MONIER, of
" *Paris*, who, by the KING's commands is collecting plants here, calls
" you a *divine, an adorable man—virum adorandum.* I congratulate
" you, that JUSSIEU, that zealous adherent of TOURNEFORT, has
" arranged the royal botanical garden at *Paris*, according to your sys-
" tem. I now esteem him the more, since he is obsequious to the
" truth. An uncommon and extraordinary thing indeed! He so old
" —and you so young—and both botanists! Ah! how much do the
" noble botanists excel the splenetic and envious physicians!"

In a Third Letter, dated August 12, 1740.

" Your name is now most copiously quoted by the literati of our
" nation, and your writings are eagerly sought after. He that is in
" possession of them, conceals and preserves them in the most careful
" manner, and does not communicate such treasures.

" Were I to express the pleasure which I felt in the perusal of
" your works, it would take up several letters to describe it. Your
" merits are far above my encomiums. I want eloquence to represent
" them. I dwell, therefore, in mute admiration. All my colleagues
" are astonished when they hear what you have done at your time of
" of life. There never was a man who could write in so short a time,

" so

" so many valuable works. I hear that the *Herrmanian* garden at
" *Leyden* is also arranged according to your system. To speak candidly,
" you are a real CHARLES XII. in natural history ; yet with this diffe-
" rence, that you have subjugated the botanical world for ever."

BARON ALBRECHT HALLER *

In six letters to LINNÆUS, from April 14, 1737, to the 9th of
January, 1738, calls him an excellent and true—nay, the first, greatest,
most eminent, and most accurate, botanist.

In a Letter to LINNÆUS, April 7, 1738 :

" What do you care for SIEGESBECK! Was there ever a man, who
" embarked in a new and grand enterprize unenvied? Is there not
" plenty of great characters who do justice to your merits? Did you
" ever hope to please every one, even the SIEGESBECKS? Cheer
" up and presevere, continue to embellish the sciences in which you
" have acquired so much real celebrity."

HALLER *in his Act. Germ. Erudit. Page* 288.

" We feel pleasure to premise, that there has never a been book
" written in this science, which can be compared with the *Genera*
" *Plantarum* of LINNÆUS. Its whole plan is unborrowed, unattempted,
" and original. It is built on the strictest examination of 8000 plants.
" But what LINNÆUS has done none has ever attempted or thought
" of."

GLEDITSCH,

GLEDITSCH,
In a Letter to LINNÆUS—THE GREATEST OF BOTANISTS—*April* 20, 1740.

" I do not disallow that the examples of LINNÆUS are a Gordian
" knot for all those who hate to take pains, and do not choose to burden
" their weak minds with plain ideas and representations."

FREDERICK OTTO MENKEN,
In a Letter to LINNÆUS, *May* 5, 1736:

" I participate with pleasure in the approbation granted to you with
" emulation for your various excellent works in botany and natural
" history, not only by your own countrymen, who so well know how to
" value men of genius, but also by my fellow-citizens of *Leipsic.*
" Success to the noble science whose boast you are, whose lustre you
" make shine, and which flourishes through you, and expects so many
" new honours in your name !"

REVIEW OF THE CLIFFORTIAN GARDEN,
In the Acta Eruditorum of 1739, *Page* 256.

" A valuable work, which, from its display of science and erudition
" cannot be sufficiently praised. We are at a loss which we are to
" extol most, either the distinguished zeal of the collector in promoting
" the progress of science, and the immense sums which he has be-
" stowed on this public monument of his garden, or the admirable and
" happy genius of the celebrated author, the DIOSCORIDES of our
" times.

times. The moderation of CLIFFORT which restrained LINNÆUS in the preface, restrains us also from conferring our encomiums on him, because none but another LINNÆUS could praise a LINNÆUS*. His fame is so wide-spread that it needs no comment. His writings and his ingenious system, by which the minutest and formerly unknown parts of flowers and fruits are brought to light, sufficiently speak for him. France venerates him, elected him a correspondent member of the Royal academy of sciences, *Holland* parted with him with reluctance, and *Sweden* receives him again gladly in her bosom. The work before us contains a collection, an epitome of all the works hitherto published by LINNÆUS, and affords uncommon elucidations in the history of the vegetable reign.

The public quotation of such opinions and testimonials, was the properest expedient which LINNÆUS could choose, to render his countrymen attentive to his merit and distinction, and at the same time the most eloquent defence which he could make against the aspersions of WALLERIUS.

The attacks of the whole phalanx of his foreign opponents could not induce him to accept a challenge. The method of his vengeance was equally original and piquant. He sat enthroned above the whole reign of vegetation. With the plants he transmitted honour and disgrace to posterity. To beautiful plants he assigned the names of his friends, and to the pernicious and inferior ones he gave the names of his enemies. As an instance of this particular, we only need quote here the *Siegesbeckia, Heisteria, Bufonia, Adansonia,* and *Pontederia.*

* *Nec LINNÆUM alius, quam LINNÆUS collaudet.*

T   The

The attacks of his opponents were by no means indifferent to his ambition; yet he thought it more prudent to commit them to oblivion, than to acquire notoriety in defence of his name. His whole way of thinking in this respect, he expresses in the best manner in a letter to BARON HALLER, written in the year 1748*, when the latter had a dispute with the Aulic Counsellor HAMBERGER of *Jena*, about respiration.

" If you will listen to the counsel of a sincere friend, I advise you
" to give up the dispute with HAMBERGER and his whole set. Nay,
" that man is not your equal. The more he is beneath you, the more it
" aggrandizes his reputation and his notability, which is otherwise com-
" pressed in a very small sphere. BOERHAAVE, our great pattern never
" replied. I still remember what he told me."—" Never," said he,
" answer attacks. I promised to take his counsel, and found it
" answered well. Your time, my dear HALLER, is too precious to the
" public. You can do more for science than hundreds of others.
" The plurality of men judge of matters which they do not understand.
" How do kings wage war ? Their very conquests are attended with the
" loss of many thousands of subjects. Thus it is with the learned. If
" even they triumph, it happens by lessening their influence and merit. Be
" our assertions true or false, they will so remain, whether we defend them
" or not. Children, now occupied with infant sports, will judge us when
" once we are gone. The hypotheses of HAMBERGER will never be
" permanent if they are erroneous, however much they may enjoy the
" transitory triumph of deluded fashion. Remember the disputes of our
" ancestors in botany. Does not the very perusal of them inspire with

* Epist. ad HALLER, vol. ii. p. 409.

2.   " disgust.

" disgust. People are in some measure fond of reading attacks, but they
" generally dislike the aggressor, they despise and laugh at him.   You
" may do as you please; I only advise you, for my part, as a friend.
" A general must not protract a war to too great lengths. He frequently
" brings the enemy to do that which he did not expect.   Thus HAM-
" BERGER might gain friends, who would attack all you do, and furnish
" him with stratagems, which, till now, he never could think of."

The tolerant conduct of LINNÆUS towards the introducers and partisans of other botanical systems, became publicly manifest during his
reform in *Holland.*   " There are," writes he, " several systems in bo-
" tany, some easier, safer and more commodious in certain points, others
" more general.   I do not know what blindness has brought men to see
" every other system with an indignant eye.   It is much to be wished
" that every beginner would habituate himself to all systems.   If the
" plants have been examined according to them all, the beginner can ripen
" his opinions, which so seldom happens, owing to the predilection gene-
" rally bestowed upon one single system, in preference to all the rest*."

When LINNÆUS, at an advanced period of life, published for the
last time, in the year 1766, his SYSTEM OF NATURE, that monument of
his immortality, he concluded it with the following declaration of his
past conduct.   " I have ranged through the thick and shady forests of
" nature, I have to and fro found sharp and perplexing thorns, I have
" as much as possible avoided them ; but learned at the same time, that

---

* Hinc omnes methodi addiscendæ sunt,—Nescio, quid fascinat homines ut non possint al-
teram methodum videre absque perturbatione.—Optandum foret, ut tyrones omnibus as-
suescerent methodis.—Postquam examinaverint juniores Botanici plantas secundum omnes
methodos, apti sunt ad ferendum matura de singulis judicia, quæ tam raro alias occurrunt,
cum communiter apud omnes unica in pretio sit methodus, reliquæ autem minus. See Præfat.
ad Classes plantarum. *Lugd.Bat.* 1738.

" foresight

" foresight and attention do not always conciliate perfect and entire safety.
" I have therefore quietly borne the derision of grinning satyrs, and the
" jumps of monkies upon my shoulders. I have entered the career and
" completed the course assigned by fate*."

* Intravi densas umbrosasque Naturæ sylvas, hinc inde horrentes accutissimis et hamatis
spinis; evitavi, quotquot licuit, plurimas; at neminem tam esse circumspectum didici, cujus
non diligentia sibi ipsi aliquando excidat; ideoque ringentium Satyrorum cachinnos, meisque
humeris insilentium cercopithecorum exultationes sustinui. *Incessi Viam et quem dederat
cursum fortuna peregi.*

SECTION

SECTION VII.

RESIDENCE OF LINNÆUS AT STOCKHOLM.—BEGINNING OF HIS ACADEMICAL LIFE AT UPSAL, &c.

LINNÆUS RETURNS TO SWEDEN.—SETTLES AT STOCKHOLM.—IS RIDICULED AND CALUMNIATED.—BEGINS TO PRACTICE PHYSIC.—UNPLEASANTNESS OF HIS SI-TUATION.—HALLER OBTAINS FOR HIM THE PROFESSORSHIP OF BOTANY AT THE UNIVERSITY OF GOETTINGEN.—THE BARON'S LETTER TO LINNÆUS.—ANSWER MADE BY LINNÆUS.—HAPPY TURN OF HIS FATE.—COUNT TESSIN BE-COMES HIS PROTECTOR.—THE CURE OF THE COUGH MAKES HIS FORTUNE.—ANECDOTE.—IS APPOINTED PHYSICIAN TO THE ADMIRALTY AND BOTANIST TO THE KING.—JOINS IN WEDLOCK WITH MISS MORÆUS.—FOUNDATION OF THE ROYAL ACADEMY OF STOCKHOLM.—HIS CONCERN IN THIS INSTITU-TION.—IS ELECTED FIRST PRESIDENT.—HIS SPEECH ON HIS RESIGNATION OF THE PRESIDENCY.—OTHER LEARNED LABOURS.—DEATH OF OLAUS RUDBECK AT UPSAL.—LINNÆUS ENDEAVOURS TO SUCCEED HIM, BUT TO NO PURPOSE.—HIS JOURNEY TO THE ISLANDS OF OELAND AND GOTHLAND.—PROFESSOR ROBERG AT UPSAL RESIGNS.—LINNÆUS SUCCEEDS HIM.—HIS SPEECH OF IN-AUGURATION.—EXCHANGES HIS FUNCTIONS AS PROFESSOR OF ANATOMY FOR THE PROFESSORSHIP OF BOTANY.—BIRTH OF HIS SON CHARLES.—GOES TO UPSAL.—BOTANICAL GARDEN, ITS BAD STATE, ITS TOTAL AMELIORATION AND DESCRIPTION.—THE GARDEN IS BEAUTIFIED AND ENLARGED IN OUR TIME.—LETTER OF DONATION SENT BY GUSTAVUS III. LATE KING OF SWE-DEN.—HONOURABLE MENTION OF LINNÆUS IN THAT LETTER.—FRESH AC-COUNT OF THE BOTANICAL GARDEN AT UPSAL.—COLLECTION OF FOREIGN TREASURES.—FLOURISHING STATE OF THAT GARDEN UNDER DERRICK NIET-ZEL OF HAMBURGH, GARDNER UNDER LINNÆUS.—CELEBRITY OF THE UNI-VERSITY OF UPSAL.—FOREIGN PUPILS OF LINNÆUS.—ESTABLISHMENT OF A CABINET OF NATURAL HISTORY.—PRESENTS.—LECTURES OF LINNÆUS.—MORE LEARNED LABOURS.—HE PUBLISHES HERMANN'S HERBAL.—TRAVELS THROUGH WEST-GOTHLAND AND SCHOENEN, OR SCANIA.—FLORA AND FAUNA SUECI-CA.—LINNÆUS IS ELECTED MEMBER OF THE ACADEMIES OF MONTPELLIER, TOULOUSE AND BERLIN.—SEVERAL MEDALS STRUCK BY THE SWEDISH GRAN-DEES IN HONOUR OF LINNÆUS.—MEDAL OF COUNT TESSIN—IS APPOINTED DEAN OR PRESIDENT OF THE COLLEGE OF PHYSICIANS.—MOTIVES OF HIS PREFERMENT.—DEATH OF THE FATHER OF LINNÆUS.

AFTER an absence of three years and an half, LINNÆUS returned to his country, and reached *Stockholm*, in September 1738. The thought of his arrival made his heart vibrate with the utmost joy. He

now

now expected to reap honours and respect, as the reward of his long
noble exertions. But how soon did he experience the truth of the
adage, which tells us, that a prophet is no where less valued than in
his own country. The treatment which HALLER met with on his first
return to *Bern*, and that which fell to the share of many other great
men, was also reserved for LINNÆUS. Celebrated and respected
abroad, he now was a stranger in his native land, and the sport of obloquy and derision. The winter of 1738 nipt the laurels he had
gathered in *Holland*. The rude climate of *Sweden* did not seem propitious to their growth. For the sake of his daily support he now began to follow the advice of his intended father-in-law, by applying himself to the practice of medicine. But ÆSCULAPIUS, at his first setting
out, proved as unkind as Flora. Nobody would entrust a botanist
with the curing of patients.

This perplexed situation still continued in the beginning of
1739. HALLER resolved to become the benefactor of LINNÆUS. He
reserved for him his own professorship of botany at *Goettingen*.

The following are the contents of the letter, which HALLER had
already written to him, on the 24th of November 1738.

" Be happy in your destinies! You, of whom Flora conceives greater
" hopes than of all other botanists. Return once more to gentler
" climes! If ever my country recalls me to its bosom,—and this I hope
" will be the case—I have pitched upon you, if you like the offer, to be
" the heir of the garden of this city, and of all my dignities. I have
" already mentioned it to those at whose disposal all is left *."

And

---

* Tu a quo Flora sperat plura quam ab omni alio botanico, utere quæso felicibus fatis, et
aliquando ad mitiora climata redi. Si unquam me patria repetit, et spero repetituram, te
quidem,

And in another letter, dated January 19, 1739, he mentioned again what follows.

" My determination of giving up the garden still remains the same. " I shall only stay here a few years longer, and can leave it to none that " is worthier than yourself *."

Had this letter come to hand a few days sooner (it had been sent with the preacher of the German congregation at *Stockholm*), *Sweden* would, perhaps, have lost the man, who afterwards became its boast, and the Hanoverian university would have enjoyed the distinguished honour of possessing the two greatest academical professors of our age. LINNÆUS did not, however, receive the letter till the 12th of August 1739, when his circumstances had changed much for the better, which induced him to decline the offer.

The kindness of his friend, and the unforeseen chance of so fine a prospect abroad, could not but make a deep impression upon him. Animated with the most lively sense of heartfelt gratitude, he returned the following answer to HALLER:—" A thousand times have I praised " HERMANN † in his grave. While TOURNEFORT was yet unprovided " for, he was so uncommonly generous as to offer him his own place, " and to seek another. HERMANN came afterwards to *Paris*, and " TOURNEFORT in honour of him ordered the fountains to play in " the royal garden. But how moderate was this gratitude towards the

*

quidem, si tunc placuerit conditio, destinavi horti hæredem et quælitcunque honoris, et eam sententiam coram eis locutus sum, in quorum manu sunt omnia.

* De horto eadem mihi sententia est, ego quidem paucis annis his versabor, neque unquam tradere potero digniori. See *Orb's Eruditi Judicium de* C. LINNÆI, àl. D. *Scriptis*, page 9.

† HERMANN was a German, and professor of botany at *Leyden*, where he died in 1615.

" magnanimous

" magnanimous friendship of HERMANN! And what shall I now say
" of you? You take a liking to a foreigner, invite him to come to
" you, and offer him an academical dignity and a professorship, and even
" the botanical garden. A brother cannot be kinder to a brother, a
" father cannot treat better his only son. I have had intercourse with
" many men; many have shewn me affection, but none so much
" kindness as you. I would express my gratitude in words, but I am at
" a loss where to find them. For ever shall the memory of your name
" be sacred to me, and to others after me*.

To this letter of thanks LINNÆUS also added a short narrative of his
adventures, with the following account of his residence at *Stockholm*,
and the happy alteration in his circumstances, which we shall communicate here as the best historical account to continue our biography.

" I took up my residence at *Stockholm* *. Every body laughed at my
" botany. Not one could tell how many restless nights and toilsome

---

† Quid de te dicam ipse? Peregrinum amas, vocas, professoriam dignitatem et munus
et hortum sere offers. Vix frater fratri, vix pater hoc filio unico. Uno verbo, plures mor-
tales vidi, multi me amarunt, nullus mihi obtulit tanta, quanta tu. Verbis grates redderem,
si possem. At sancta mente servabo, dum vixero, et alii post me, tuum nomen.

† Sedem fixi *Holmiæ*, irrisus ab omnibus ob meam botanicen. Quot insomnes noctes et
laboriosas horas transegerim, nullus dixit; quam vero a *Siegesbeckio* eram annihilatus, omnes
uno ore acclamabant. Incepi praxin exercere valde lente; non erat, qui vel servum mihi
curandum obtulit. Sed brevi fata cessabant adversa, et post diuturnas nebulas Phœbus.
Emersi, ad primates acceritus, cessere omnia secunde; nullus æger sanabatur, me non præ-
sente; pecunias accepi; ab hora quarta matutina in seram vesperam ægros adii, noctes apud
ægrotos consumsi. Heu! dixi, *dat Æsculapius bona omnia, Flora vero solos Siegesbeckios*;
interdixi Floram; quæ collegi adversaria æterno pulvere sepelienda millies decrevi. Mox
primarius medicus classis navalis constitutus fui; conventus civium mox me botanicum re-
regium, publice quo ducerent botanicen in regia sede *Stockbolmiæ* dixere, stipendio annuo
auxerunt. Incepi iterum amare plantas. Sponsam adii tum meam quinquennem, tam dignus
thalamum intravi sponsæ et uxoris. Socer tamen sat pecuniis ipse delectatur, nec genero
facile concedit; sed nec opus habeo; et quis a me generatur, habebit. Epist. ad HALLE-
RUM, vol. i. page 415.

2

" hours

" hours I had bestowed on it; but every corner resounded with the
" humiliating lesson I had received from this SIEGESBECK. I began
" to set up for a practitioner, but my success was very slow. They
" would not even employ me in a servant's cure. But in a short time,
" adversity ceased to persecute, and after many clouded days, the lucid
" sun broke through my obscurity. I rose,—was called to the great,—
" every thing turned out prosperous; no patient could be cured with-
" out me; from four o'clock in the morning till late at night, I visited
" the sick, spent nights with them, and earned money. Alas! said I
" Æsculapius *affords all that is good, but* Flora *yields but* Sieges-
" becks. I renounced botany, and resolved a thousand times to de-
" stroy all my collections for ever. Soon after I was appointed first
" physician to the fleet, and after a short lapse of time the States chose
" me botanist to the King, and assigned me an annual salary to teach
" that science at *Stockholm* *. I now grew fond again of plants, and
" married my bride, who, after five long years, still thought me worthy
" of her love. My father-in-law, however, is dearly fond of money,
" be does not like to part with it. For my own part I can do with-
" out, and thus leave it to my offspring."

The cure of a long, and now, alas! a fashionable distemper of a friend,
which was effected in a fortnight, paved LINNÆUS the way to fortune in
his practice. This recovered patient recommended LINNÆUS as an able
physician to his numerous acquaintance. Among these were several of the
same description who complained of weakness in the breast, and abstained
on this account from drinking wine. They applied to LINNÆUS, he re-

* This salary amounted to one hundred ducats per annum, and was chiefly granted him as
a reward for his learned exertions abroad.

stored

stored them, and they could afterwards enjoy their glass with the best. This circumstance made a great impression on the jovial circles. His reputation increased, and no physician was thought more able than LINNÆUS in curing all *pectoral* complaints.   He was called to the lady of an aulic counsellor, troubled with a cough.   LINNÆUS prescribed a remedy which she could carry by her, for constant use.   This lady was one day at court on a card party with queen ULRICA-ELEONORA.   While playing " she put something into her mouth.   " What is this ?" asked the Queen.—" A remedy against the cough, may it please your Majesty; " I always find myself much relieved after using it."—The Queen had a cough at that very time.   LINNÆUS was called, he prescribed the same remedy, and the Queen's ailment disappeared.—Thus did the cough first introduce him to court, and there advance his prosperity.

The patron to whom LINNÆUS stood indebted for his recent good fortune, was that celebrated statesman Count CHARLES GUSTAVUS TESSIN, who educated the late King of *Sweden*, and terminated his meritorious career on the seventh of January 1770.   He was well versed in the sciences and a great lover of natural history.   To his attention and favour *Sweden* owes the display of the greatest genius which it ever produced.   LINNÆUS always found in him the kindest and most zealous protector, through whose interest he obtained all further dignities and honours.   To transmit the remembrance of those benefits to posterity, he enumerated them in a public manner in the last edition of his System of Nature, which he dedicated to this noble friend.   " He received me," says LINNÆUS, " on my return, when I " was a stranger in my own country, he obtained for me a salary from " the States, the appointment of physician to the admiralty, the profes-

2

" sor

" sor of botany at *Upsal*, the title of dean or president of the college of
" physicians, the favour of two Kings, and recommended me by a medal
" to posterity *.

The manner in which Count TESSIN first avowed himself the protector of LINNÆUS deserves particular mention. Having made himself known at Court by the cure of the cough, the Count, who was
already acquainted with his distinguished rank in science, sent for him,
and after a long conversation asked him, if he did not wish for some
office, or if he would like to petition for any place, as the diet was then
assembled. " The charge of physician to the admiralty is now vacant,"
replied LINNÆUS, " but it is destined, as I hear, for another." " But
" that other shall not have it," replied the Count; and a few weeks
after, on the the 14th or 15th of May, LINNÆUS received the diploma
of physician to the Navy and botanist to the King.

Having thus acquired a settled income, which was farther increased
by his medical practice, he hastened to obtain his bride. Old Mo-
RÆUS was now very glad to give his consent without much intreaty,
and the hymeneal bond was sealed on the 26th of June.

The same year which favoured him with the smiles of fortune,

* Ille me, peregrinum in patria, reducem excepit ;
  Ille mihi stipendium ab ordinibus regni expetiit;
  Ille mihi spartam medici classis procuravit;
  Ille mihi munus quo fungor conciliavit;
  Ille mihi titulum quo distinguor paravit ;
  Ille me ad serenissimos Reges introduxit;
  Ille me cusso numismate posteritati commendavit.
      " Ille meas errare boves, ut cernis et ipsum
      " Ludere quæ vellem calamo permisit agresti.

See *Systema Naturæ*. edit. xii. *Holm.* 1766.

proved

proved equally propitious to his name and to the state of the sciences
in *Sweden*. The corporate scientific bodies under royal authority and
protection had only been instituted the preceding year at *London* and
Paris. The most modern of the capitals in the north of *Europe, St.
Petersburgh*, was the first, which, under the auspices of PETER THE
GREAT, obtained in the year 1724 the distinguished and earliest honour of such a corporate literary body. LINNÆUS, by soliciting a
similar establishment at *Stockholm*, now strove to attain the same merit
and honour which LEIBNITZ and HALLER had acquired by the institution of the academies at *Berlin* and *Goettingen*. He was well acquainted with the learned at *Stockholm*, and with those grandees
who loved the sciences. A general scientific zeal gave birth to the
idea of raising a learned corporation. The most active promoter of
this plan was a young man of noble birth and great parts, Count A. G.
HOEPKEN, who held afterwards the dignity of counsellor of state and
chancellor of the university of *Upsal*, with distinguished merit, and
died on the 9th of May 1789, in the fiftieth year of the existence of
the academy of *Stockholm*, and in its first jubilee *. The society which
in the beginning only consisted of six members, held their first meeting
on the second of June 1739—and LINNÆUS had the honour of being
elected president. None could have been worthier of that distinction
than himself; none of the members had so well deserved of any one
science, and gained such early celebrity as he. The fixed period for the
duration of the presidency was limited by the statutes to three months
only. LINNÆUS resigned his charge on the third of October, and
made on that occasion a speech in his mother tongue, on the remarka-

* Count GYLDENSTOLPE is now his successor.

bles

bles in insects*. This speech contained excellent observations and the most beautiful sketch of the œconomy and wisdom of nature. " The author of this speech," says the Chevalier Bæck, " was an ani-" mated and sprightly painter, who captivated his readers, and excited " in them a kind of ecstatic rapture."

This society, however small in the beginning, soon rose to the most honourable public greatness. The number of its members kept pace with its fame; and through the patriotic exertions of Count Tessin, it was raised to the honourable title of Royal Academy of Sciences at *Stockholm* on the 31st of March 1741. This example set by *Sweden* soon excited the emulation of *Denmark*. The royal Danish academy was consequently instituted in 1742 at *Copenhagen*, under the direction of the beneficent Count of Holstein, then minister of state. The learned society of *Stockholm* was not gifted with any particular funds on the part of the crown, nor did its members receive annual salaries. The only stipends allowed were those assigned to the professor of natural philosophy, and to the two secretaries. These, besides the prizes and prize-medals, were drawn from the fund arising from presents or legacies. The members had already published their transactions, which at the expiration 1779 amounted to forty volumes, and have been translated into German, French, and other languages, and are continued down to the present time. These transactions contain the richest store of useful knowledge and discoveries. This advancement of the sciences in that country is originally due to Linnæus.

Having enjoyed the utmost popularity in the capital of *Sweden*, and being blest with the resources of a plentiful income, Linnæus was not

* Oratio de Memorabilibus in Insectis. Vide Amœnitates Academicæ, vol. ii.

quite

quite so well pleased with his situation as might have been expected. He was, upon the whole, fonder of meddling with plants than with patients. His love of Flora was still prevalent, notwithstanding the bad return which that goddess made him when he first became her votary in *Sweden.* The garlands of fame which she had made for him, leaving him to expect others more beautiful, still possessed too many attractions. In 1740, he published a new edition of his *Fundamenta Botanica,* and dedicated that work to DILLENIUS, HALLER, VAN ROYEN, GRONOV, JUSSIEU, BURMANN, and AMMANN professor of botany at *St. Petersburgh.* We mention this trifling circumstance, because it shows the scale of gradation of the merits of the most eminent botanists of that time, and their rank in the esteem of LINNÆUS.

His wishes had long been directed towards that university of his country where he had laid the foundation of his greatness, and suffered so many vicissitudes in the smiles and frowns of fortune. On the 3d of June 1740, his former protector, OLAUS RUDBECK junior, departed life in that city, by which demise the professorship of botany became vacant. It was this office which LINNÆUS desired in preference to all others. He offered himself a candidate, made interest, but was disappointed. The laws of equity, and the university statutes opposed his success. NICHOLAS ROSEN, his former antagonist attained this academical charge, as he had taken his degrees before LINNÆUS, and rendered himself more meritorious at *Upsal,* by a longer residence and active service.

Meanwhile LINNÆUS did not want for protection. The diet which assembled in the beginning of the year 1741, extended also their deliberations, to a mode of lessening the foreign productions

duꞓions of art, and of promoting the progress of the domestic manu-
faꞓures of *Sweden*. They resolved, that travels be undertaken through
those Swedish provinces which were the least explored. The question,
who was the most capable person to be charged with the execution of
the enterprize, was soon decided. The choice fell on LINNÆUS, who
accepted the offer. His first tour was to the islands of *Oeland* and
Gothland. He set out on this exploit, in the spring of 1741, accompanied by six naturalists. He had particular instruꞓions to examine
all the plants and produꞓions, which might be useful in dying, œconomy, and medicine, and to see if there was not a kind of earth in those
islands fit for the fabrication of porcelain-ware. The zeal of LIN-
NÆUS even exceeded the bounds of his charge, he discovered many
new plants, colleꞓed a great variety of observations on the antiquities
of those islands, their mechanical arts, the manners of the natives,
their fisheries, and many other objeꞓs; but he was not able to accomplish the chief end of his voyage. He could find no porcelain earth,
as the soil of both islands consists of a calcareous earth and chrystal
rocks. His tour was however of great utility; the states gave him a
public testimony of their satisfaꞓion, and four years after, he published
the narrative of this tour*.

The infirmities and advanced age of a man finally realised those
hopes of LINNÆUS, which had been frustrated in the preceding
year. Soon after RUDBECK's death, M. ROBERG, senior of the University of *Upsal*, and professor of physic and anatomy, requested his
dismission. His request was granted with the appendage of his whole

* There is a German translation of SCHREDER, published at HALLE in 1763 in 8vo from
" the Swedish original, entituled " *Car. Linnæi Oeländska och Gothlandska Resa*," *Stockholm*, 1745, large oꞓavo.

salary,

salary, as he had exercised his academical functions longer than the
fixed term of thirty years*. LINNÆUS put up for this vacancy,—and
through the interest of Count TESSIN, obtained the professorship of
physic and anatomy in 1741, being then in the 34th year of his age.
Though this office was not what he absolutely wished for, yet it put him
in a better situation of exerting himself to obtain what he really wanted.
Owing to his multifarious professional avocations, his young spouse
went to live with her parents at *Fahlun.* It was thence he received the
welcome tidings which rewarded his conjugal happiness. His lady presented him with a young heir, on the 20th of January 1741, who was
baptized after his own name, and remained the only male offspring that
survived him. Having become a father, he now set off in September
with his family to *Upsal,* the theatre of his fame and his constant residence.

On the 17th of October, he assumed his professorial functions with a
discourse, occasioned by his late peregrination. He expatiated on the
use and necessity of domestic tours†. He displayed the wide range
of objects, which *Sweden* contained for the study of Physic, Natural
History, Mineralogy, Zoology, Botany, and Œconomy; and depicted,
in living colours, the bounteous gifts of nature, with which, he said, we
had nothing else to do, but to observe and convert them to our own use.

ROSEN had not been remiss in his endeavours to obtain an ordinary
professorship, and to prefer the present certainty, to the incertainty of
the future. He was to teach botany, and LINNÆUS anatomy. Such

---

* There is a fund for two professors at *Upsal,* who have done the duty of their office for
thirty years. The widows of professors receive a kind of pension paid them in corn.

* Oratio de peregrinationum intra prtriam necessitate. See Amœnitat. Academic. Edit.
Schreber. Erlang.

an

an appointment militated against the call and will of the muses. To make each of them great and useful in his own branch, a change of offices was requisite. Both were sensible of the impropriety of their respective stations, and by a friendly agreement, with the consent of the Chancellor of the University, the two professorships, whose emoluments were equal, were mutually exchanged in the beginning of 1742. Thus LINNÆUS was raised to that sphere of operation which he considered as the happiness of his life, and which was so adequate to his zeal and endowments. He directed his first efforts towards the improvement of the botanical garden at *Upsal*, which had been established after the middle of the last century by the celebrated Swedish naturalist OLAUS RUDBECK senior. The novelty of the enterprise afforded to the latter great applause and support. Through the liberality of King CHARLES GUSTAVUS, and the zeal of the Chancellor of the University, the garden was soon put in a good state. It still remained in an improved condition in the reign of CHARLES XI. The two RUDBECKS, both father and son, enriched it with the plants they had collected in their travels. But at the beginning of the present century it ceased to be one of the most flourishing botanical gardens of *Europe*. The dreadful conflagration which converted the best part of *Upsal* into a heap of ruins in 1702, destroyed it entirely. During the unfortunate reign of CHARLES XII. there were no hopes of its establishment. There was, indeed, no money to purchase plants. RUDBECK grew old, and none remained after him to take care of it. In short, the garden had decayed into a tract of pasture ground to graze the sheep and cows. It did not even contain fifty foreign plants.

Linnæus now became its second creator. In a few years he raised such a temple to Flora as had never before graced that northern tract. With the gardens at *Paris*, *Oxford*, *Kew*, *Leyden* and *Hartecamp*, it became at last, one of the most beautiful and most valuable in *Europe*. All that had been formerly refused to advance the progress of botany, was now granted out of respect to the great man who was the boast and soul of that science. His zeal kindled fresh fervor in others. Count Charles Gyllenborg was then Chancellor of the University, a nobleman of great scientific acquirements and a special lover of botany. He began to conceive and cherish a particular fondness of that science on a journey which he made during the last century to *Lapland*, with Rudbeck junior He considered the celebrity of the University of *Upsal* as inseparable from his own fame. He saw in Linnæus a man who could increase this celebrity, got acquainted with him at *Stockholm*, helped him to his professorship, and always remained his sincerest and most zealous protector. On his account the Swedish government resolved to spare no expences for the total improvement of the botanical garden. Baron Charles Harlemann, the king's architect furnished the plan. The latter was also a professed friend of Linnæus, and by the intercession of several great men, it was further resolved to build a dwelling-house for the professor of botany adjoining to the garden. Thus Linnæus, having the family of nature so near him, he could give them much better attendance, and study their peculiarities, and communicate their knowledge to his pupils. The execution of the proposed plan was begun in 1742, and completed in the course of the following year. On the 18th of July, 1743, Linnæus took possession of his new and beautiful premises.

In

In the year 1745 he gave a description of the new garden, with all its dispostions and establishments, mentioning in the most grateful terms all those who had contributed to its restoration and embellishment*. The garden was not laid out on a very extensive scale, but arranged in a tasty manner. We shall here communicate a concise description of it, given by a learned traveller, who visited *Upsal* in the year 1771.

The academical garden of *Upsal* has been arranged by LINNÆUS. An iron gate of excellent workmanship leads to it from the high road. At the top of the gate the Swedish arms, and those of Count GYLLENBORG, who has so zealously promoted its restoration, are displayed. From within a spacious yard presents itself to view; on the right stands the dwelling of LINNÆUS, who is the director of the garden, on the left appear some other buildings. A straight avenue leads by another gate to the garden, which is parted from the yard by an elegant wooden inclosure. The garden itself is laid out in a superb style. Its most considerable part consists of two large tracts of ground. One of them contains the perennial plants; the other those from which the seeds are annually gathered. Each of these tracts is divided into forty-four beds, surrounded with a low hedge and little doors. The plant-house is situate eastward. It is divided into the plant-hall *(frigidarium)*, which lies in the centre; into the thriving-house *(caldarium)*, and the hot-house *(tepidarium)*, which form the northern wing, and the gardner's cot, which forms the southern wing. To the west lies the thriving-bank *(vaporarium)*, and to the south the glass-bank; the sun-

* Descriptio Horti Upsaliensis, *Upsal*, 1745 Vide Amœnitates Academicæ, vol. i. In this work the garden is represented on a plate.

house

house *(solarium)*, lies facing the ponds, into which fresh water is conveyed by pipes. The southern apartments of this edifice contain the
large cabinet of natural curiosities belonging to the royal academy
of sciences, which are very considerable *.

The

* The botanical garden of *Upsal* underwent many material alterations after the death of
LINNÆUS, during the latter part of the reign of the late King of *Sweden*. The conspicuous
zeal and munificence of the latter, in ameliorating the state of the sciences in his kingdoms,
went so far, that works were carried on upwards of four years to beautify the botanical garden at *Upsal*, to add fresh edifices for keeping the plants, and splendid structures for preserving the natural curiosities. He also ordered that the house occupied by the professor of botany be enlarged and rendered more commodious. GUSTAVUS III. came himself to *Upsal*
to inspect all the buildings of the academy. He frequently repeated his visits, and found
that the botanical garden, as it then stood, was but ill adapted to its utility, both in point of
situation and extent. The Chevalier THUNBERG, professor of botany at *Upsal*, confirmed
his Majesty's opinion by his own remarks. It was finally resolved to adopt an entire plan of
alteration in the summer of 1787, at which time the King was at *Upsal*. His Majesty gave
orders that this plan be immediately put into execution, and the ditch for the foundation wall
was begun in June, and advanced so far under the immediate inspection of Professor PROS-
PERIN that the foundation stone could be laid as early as the 6th of August, 1787.

GUSTAVUS III. himself performed the ceremony with suitable splendor and solemnity.
His Majesty was attended by most of the courtiers and grandees. He repaired to the botanic
garden, received the homage of the professors, and delivered to the Archbishop of *Upsal*,
UNO VON TROIL, as commander of the order of the Polar Star and pro-chancellor of the
university, the grant of the ground. The pro-chancellor made a short address of thanks.
The King then laid himself the foundation stone; after a certain number of medals had
been put in its inside, he threw three trowels of mortar upon it, then handed the trowel to
Count CRAHN and to the rest of the grandees in his suite.

The letter of donation which GUSTAVUS III. presented to the university is verbatim as
follows:

" WE GUSTAVUS III. by the Grace of God, KING of the *Swedes*, *Goths* and *Vandals*,
" Lord in *Norway*, Duke of *Schelswick* and *Holstein*, &c. &c. &c. do certify by these pre-
" sents, that, even during our minority we looked with pleasure and attention upon the most
" ancient seat of learning in the North, our University of *Upsal*, and that during the course
" of our reign we took care to promote its splendor and increase. Besides our own satis-
" faction, and besides the honour of accomplishing that, which the two greatest Kings whose
" names we bear endeavoured so carefully to effect, we not only found an opportunity to
" teach our beloved son, by our own example, to value the happiness of governing an en-
" lightened nation; but also to enjoy the daily satisfaction of seeing the Swedish geniuses

" rise

The greatness and celebrity of the director of this garden required a gardner of competent skill and abilities. It was not beneath the dignity of LINNÆUS

" rise to the most perfect knowledge of the sciences. To attain this end we have examined
" and viewed the constitutions of the University, to see which of them might require a change
" or an alteration. We found that it was necessary that the botanical garden, with its col-
" lections, should be removed to some more convenient spot, on account of its situation and
" extent. AS LONG AS THE LEARNED WORLD ACKNOWLEDGED IN THIS SCIENCE THE
" SOLE LAWS OF A LINNÆUS, HIS GREAT NAME AND HIS KNOWLEDGE SUFFICED FOR
" ALL. But, whereas, the discoveries are now augmented, and FOREIGNERS ILLUMINED
" BY HIS SCIENCE HAVE BEGUN TO RIVAL HIS COUNTRYMEN, HIS MEMORY, AND THE
" HONOUR OF THE UNIVERSITY REQUIRE SUCH PREPARATIONS WHICH MAY ENABLE
" HIS SUCCESSORS TO PROPAGATE HIS FAME. We have for this reason resolved, not only
" to defray the expence attending the establisment of a new botanical garden out of our own
" private resources; but also to add a grant of the ground of the pleasure-garden near the
" castle; besides 31,360 square yards of ground to the westward. We are, therefore, willing
" to alienate the said pleasure-garden and ground from us and the crown, and we do by these
" presents renounce every future claim and title thereto, presenting the same to our Academy
" of *Upsal* as an everlasting property and possession, on condition of its being used for the
" rearing and fostering of botanical objects. . This shall serve as a due notice to every one.
" In corroboration whereof we have signed this present grant with our own hand, and sealed
" it with our royal seal.

　　" Done in the Castle of *Upsal,*　　　　　　　　　" Signed GUSTAVUS,
　　　　" August 16, 1787.　　　　　　　　　　　　" E. SCHROEDERBEIM."

　　Respecting the amelioration of the botanical garden at *Upsal,* the CHEVALIER DE THUN-
BERG has favoured the author with the following account in a letter, dated *Upsal,* November
12, 1791.
　　" The ancient academical garden was situate in a very low ground, and the dwelling of
" the professor and the other buildings stood on a marshy soil. For this reason I intreated
" the KING, to grant the garden of the palace to the Academy of *Upsal,* and to have it
" converted into a botanical garden, which was done accordingly. The buildings for the pre-
" servation of the plants, the *Orangerie,* the hot-house, and the lecture room in which the
" bust of LINNÆUS will be put, the museum, the professor's house, &c. &c. are mostly
" finished, and will be quite complete in a few years hence. The old botanical garden is still
" in being; but the buildings, especially the *Orangerie,* are almost a heap of ruins. In the
" new garden I have ordered the perennial plants to be arranged and planted in three beds,
" and the annual ones in a field, according to the LINNÆAN system. The Swedish, the medi-
" cinal and other plants for the use of the medical and œconomical students, are contained in
" separate beds. Besides the natural curiosities preserved in spirits of wine, the academy
　　　　　　　　　　　　　　　　　　　　　　　　　　　　　　　　　　" was

Linnæus to have a man, who, in his art, was one of the first in *Europe*, and to whom he stood indebted for many useful instructions respecting the cultivation and nursing of plants. His name was Derrick Neitzel, a German, born at *Hamburgh* in 1703. He had arranged the principal gardens in *Lower Saxony*, and was afterwards employed by Cliffort at *Hartecamp*.

Linnæus had thus obtained the finest repository that could be wished for, but he only wanted the plants. His zeal, and the connexions which he had with the greatest botanists in *Europe*, soon remedied this defect, and rendered the garden one of the richest in *Europe*. In 1742 he introduced more than two hundred indigenous plants in it, and sent a student to *Norway* to collect there the most valuable botanical treasures. " Formerly," says Linnæus in a letter to Haller, " I had " plants but no money—and now, of what use is my money without " plants *?" This proves with what enthusiastic fondness Linnæus loved plants.

Soon, however, did his foreign friends gratify his wishes in a most eager and satisfactory manner. He received plants and seeds from

" hardly possessed any thing else, till I presented it with my collection of dried plants, " insects, birds, &c. &c." *

* Prior hortus situs erat loco maxime depresso et ædes demissæ loco paludoso. Ego igitur a Rege Clementissimo petii, ut hortus arcis regiæ academiæ donaretur proque hortu botanico instrueretur, quod et dudum factum est. Ardes pro plantis servandis (*Orangerie, the hot-house, &c*). Auditorium, in quo erigetur *effigies Linnæi*, museum naturalium, ædes professionis, &c. jam magnâ ex parte exstructa sunt, et post paucos annos omnino erunt paratæ. Prior hortus adhuc quidem existit, ædibus *(orangerie)* fere collapsis ; et novus hortus ita a me instructus est, ut plantatæ fuerint plantæ perennes in arcis tribus, et annuæ in unica, secundum systema Linnæanum ; præterea plantæ Suecicæ, officinales pharmaceuticæ, &c. in distinctis arcis plantatæ sunt, in usum medicorum et œconomorum. Præter naturalia, spiritu vini servata, museum academicum quidquam vix habuit, ante quam ego collectionem meam herbarum siccarum, insectorum, avium, &c. &c. Academiæ Upsaliensi donaveram.

* Ante habui plantas, non pecunias ; nunc quid juvant pecuniæ, ubi non plantæ ! *Epist. ad* Haller, vol. ii. page 147.

Haller

HALLER and GLEDITSCH at *Berlin*, LUDWIG at *Leipzic*, Dr. MOEHREN at *Yevern*, GESNER at *Stutgarth*, JUSSIEU at *Paris*, Professor DE SAUVAGES at *Montpellier*, DILLENIUS at *Oxford*, COLLINSON, MILLER and CATESBY at *London*, VAN ROYEN and GRONOV at *Leyden*, BURMANN at *Amsterdam*, GMELIN and AMMANN at *Petersburgh*, and afterwards from many others. The embellishing and enriching of the botanical garden at *Upsal*, was the favourite study of his life. His anxious and tender care triumphed over the rigour and inclemency of the frigid climate of *Sweden*. The plants which grow even in the most southern country were now cultivated in the garden at *Upsal*, which presented treasures from every quarter of the globe *.

Six years after the re-establishment of this garden, LINNÆUS in 1748 published its description. The number of the foreign species of plants amounted to one thousand one hundred. His genius diffused itself like the beams of the sun over the botanical world, and its beneficent influence gave warmth and animation, especially in *Sweden*. Besides him there was not a single eminent botanist in the whole kingdom. The lectures had hitherto been rather a matter of form than of instruction, and were not frequented. LINNÆUS came, and entirely changed the face of affairs. His genius charmed and formed others. FLORA was now more courted in *Sweden* than at any former period. Not only the votaries of ÆSCULAPIUS, but the students of other sciences bestowed now the utmost diligence and attention upon botany. The hall in which LINNÆUS delivered his lectures overflowed with a crouded audience. Through him the university of *Upsal* formed a new epoch,

* Hortus Upsaliensis, exhibens plantas exoticas, Horto Upsaliensi academica, a CAROL. LINNÆO illatas ab anno 1742, in annum 1748, &c. *Holm*. 1748, octavo, 3 6, &c.

3   The

The usual number of students was 500, which proportion continued also after his death. But during the septennial war in 1759, while LIN-NÆUS was rector for six months *, the number of students amounted to *one thousand five hundred*. To profit by his knowlege pupils came from *Russia, Norway, Denmark, Great Britain, Holland, Germany, Switzerland*, nay, even from *America* †. Thus he deserved well of foreigners, and became the benefactor of the muses at *Upsal*. He made summer excursions at the head of his pupils, who frequently attended him to the number of upwards of two hundred. They then went in small parties to explore different districts of the country. Whenever some rare or remarkable plant, or some other natural curiosity was discovered, a signal was given with a horn or trumpet, upon which the whole corps joined their chief, to hear his demonstrations and remarks ‡. What swelled his audience was a fine regulation made in his time at *Upsal*, in consequence of which all the young students of divinity and country rectors were obliged to learn the elements of botany and domestic medicine, that they might be able to act as physicians in remote districts where regular medical assistance could not speedily enough be procured.

It was through LINNÆUS that *Upsal* obtained its celebrated botanical garden and a public cabinet of natural curiosities. The patriotism of

* Rector and pro-rector are two different offices at *Upsal*. The rector is personally at the head of the academical government, and the pro-rector is his immediate predecessor in office, who, in case of necessity, administers his functions *ad interim*.

† Nec majori unquam morum sanctitate conspicuus fuit coetus mille et quingentorum studiosorum hoc frequentantium Athenæum. See *Amoenitat. Acad.* vol. x. *Erlang.* 1790.

‡ Herbat'ones Upsalienses, in *Amoenitat. Acad.* vol. iii. Also Travels into *Poland, Russia, Sweden* and *Denmark*, by W. Cox, A. M.

2   the

the great and learned could not intrust their treasures to better care than that which LINNÆUS took. Count CHARLES GYLLENBORG was the first who set an example of liberality, by contributing towards that museum.

Count CHARLES GYLLENBORG was descended of an ancient and respectable family, one of whose members was created a count in the reign of CHARLES XII. The name of the former is in various respects celebrated in the history of *Sweden*. The display of his political fame was made at *London*, where he resided for several years in quality of ambassador from the court of *Stockholm*. Here his conduct brought upon him a singular misfortune. By command of GEORGE I. he was taken into custody on the 9th of February 1717. It was reported that from some letters which had been intercepted, it appeared that the Count carried on a conspiracy with the enemies of his Britannic Majesty and the partisans of the late Pretender. The British court in the letter which it delivered to the foreign ambassadors, in justification of its conduct, expressly stated, that the Count had endeavoured to spirit up his Majesty's subjects into a rebellion against their sovereign. A commission was appointed to enquire into this charge, but upon examination no solid proofs appeared against him. Meanwhile his epistolary correspondence with Baron GOERTZ, who fell a victim to his machinations in the year 1719, and with Baron SPARRE, and other Swedish ministers, was published. In the first letter GOERTZ confessed he was the author of " *The Remarks of an English Merchant*," a work which had excited great sensation at that epoch. Owing to the interference of the French cabinet, and the representations of other courts, Count GYLLENBORG was released in July 1717, and sent back to *Sweden* in an English ship.

Y	.	As

As soon as he arrived at *Stockholm*, the British ambassador was likewise liberated from confinement, as the Swedish court had thought proper to use reprisals.

GYLLENBORG afterwards waited on King CHARLES XII. whose favour he had long ago gained by his zeal and abilities. He was appointed with Baron GOERTZ, minister plenipotentiary at the conferences of pacification which were opened with the court of *Russia* in the isle of *Aland,* but which terminated without success. In the year 1719 he was raised to the dignity of high chancellor of *Sweden.* In the beginning of the following year he also acted an important part in the negotiations respecting the acession of FREDERICK I. to the throne, and gained constantly greater influence during the reign of this monarch, who appointed him counsellor of the Swedish empire and chancellor of the university of *Lund*, and in the year 1739, when a great change took place in the senate and ministry, in which he took an active part, he was made president of chancery, minister for the foreign and home departments, and soon after chancellor of the university of *Upsal.* Count TESSIN, who was then ambassador at the court of *Versailles,* received, in a short time after, the appointment of vice-president of chancery. Count GYLLEMBORG died between sixty and seventy years of age. He was an able minister, an erudite author, and a fellow of the royal society of *London.* Death snatched him away on the 14th of December 1746, too soon for the university of *Upsal,* to which he left his cabinet of natural history, remarkable for a great number of amphibies and corals. During the latter part of his life he had the honourable satisfaction of seeing his example of munificence imitated by FREDERICK ADOLPHUS, then Prince Royal of *Sweden,* who presented the

university

university of *Upsal*, with a considerable collection of curious animals, fishes and insects; farther by NICHOLAS GRILL, a merchant at *Stockholm*, who bequeathed to the same university a valuable collection of natural treasures, the produce of *North America*; especially some rare serpents which had been collected at *Surinam*. These presents were in course of time considerably increased by the Chinese curiosities of LAGERSTROEM at *Gottenburgh*, and by several other gifts. To do honour to the donors, and to enlarge the knowledge of natural history, LINNÆUS described these sundry collections *. In a short space of time the number of presents became so very great, as to induce the Swedish government, upon some representations made by LINNÆUS, to order a separate building to be raised in the year 1748, for the purpose of preserving them.

LINNÆUS now divided his diligence into the occupations for his pupils, for his country, and for the learned world at large. We will compress the sphere of his exploits to the year 1750, to see what he did to advance the above mentioned purposes.

He was not, nor did he wish to be such an universalist as HALLER; and nature remained his sole study. His application was entirely bestowed upon her productions. He gave lectures on botany, natural history, the medicinal virtues of plants, the *Materia Medica*, and on the diætetic and knowledge of diseases. His delivery was a pattern for a professor in point of energy, instruction and entertainment. " Science," said BÆCK, " streamed with peculiar pleasantness from his lips. He

---

* Amphibia GYLLENBORGIANA, Jul. 18, 1745. Museum ADOLPHO-FREDERICANUM, May 31, 1746. Surinamensia, GRILLIANA, Jul. 18, 1748. Chinensia, LAGERSTROEMIANA, 1754.—See *Amœnitates Academicæ.* Vol. i. ii. iv.

                                                    " spoke

" spoke with a conviction and perspicuity which his deep penetration,
" his clear notions and ardent zeal inspired him with. It was impossi-
" ble to be near him without attention, without participating in his
" enthusiasm. He communicated to his pupils the greatest part of the
" ideas and materials of the thirty disputations which were held under
" him till the year 1750. They contained real treasures and elucida-
" tions of science."

The new established academy of *Stockholm* owed partly its existence
to the zeal of LINNÆUS, and found in him the most active promoter
of its flourishing and respectable state. From the year 1739 to 1750
he caused twenty-five treatises to be inserted in its annals, relative
to several remarkable animals, plants, and other Swedish natural
curiosities. He was also a most active co-operator in the royal society
of *Upsal*, among all the learned corporate bodies, which first admitted
him a member, and made him its secretary for several years. During
the same period he enriched its transactions with twelve theses or treatises (*Acta Erudita Upsaliensia*).

His reputation as the most eminent botanist was now decided. Of
the truth of this assertion he obtained a very flattering proof, which at
the same time furnished him with an opportunity of renovating the fame
of a German then in his grave. Mr. AUGUSTUS GUNTHER at *Copenhagen*, had in his possession a most capital herbarium from the *East Indies*, consisting of five volumes. He had enquired of several botanists
after the collector, but none could tell him who he was. He sent,
therefore, the whole to LINNÆUS, to make use of it in the composition
of his System of Nature. The latter found upon strict examination,
that it was the herbal of PAUL HERRMANN, professor of botany at
                                                          Leyden,

Leyden, who, during the last century had been sent to the *East Indies* in the year 1670, and collected those plants during his seven years residence in the island of *Ceylon.* The numbers in this herbal related to the *Museum Zeylanicum,* which appeared after HERMANN's death in the year 1717. LINNÆUS published the description of the whole collection in 1747, after it had lain in concealment for upwards seventy years *. It contained six hundred and sixty plants, which were arranged according to his new system. Including the work of his friend BURMANN, *(Thesaurus Zeylanicus Amstelod,* 1738), and that of HARTOG the Dutchman, who made a voyage to *Ceylon,* at the expence of Doctor SHERARD, there is no country nor island in *Asia* whose natural history is better described than this.

In all *Europe,* and the world in general, no country was better described than *Sweden*—and all this had been done by LINNÆUS. The Swedish government derived the most essential benefits from his talents. In the spring of 1746 he made a tour to *West Gothland.* He travelled more than 300 German leagues, and in the following year published the result of his observations †. In the summer of 1749, he visited *Scania* or *Schonen,* the most southern of the Swedish provinces ‡. This was the sixth and last tour which he made in his own country. Thus LINNÆUS became the father of a beautiful and most accurate natural statistic of his own country. Before he set out on his two last tours, he published a description of the Swedish plants §, with an index

* Flora Zeylanica, sistens plantas Indicas Zeylonæ Insulæ, quæ olim lectæ fuere a PAULO HERMANNO Professore Botanico Leydensi. *Holm.* 1747, n. 2½.

† C. LINNÆI *Wästgöta Resa*; as Riksens Ständers befalning förrättad. *Stockholm,* 1747, in *Swedish.*

‡ LINNÆI *Skånska Resa,* förrattad 1749. *Stockholm* 175 , also in *Swedish.*

§ *Flora Suecica, exhibens plantas per regnum Sueciæ crescentes, &c. Holm.* 8ve. p. 392.

1

Illustrating

illustrating their medical and œconomical properties, the place of their growth, and their Swedish and provincial denominations. GMELIN, in a letter to HALLER said, he was very much pleased with that work, which was a fresh proof of the astonishing diligence of LINNÆUS*. This first edition contained a description of 1140 plants, and in the second, their number was augmented to 1296.

A twelvemonth after the publication of this Flora, followed a description of the Swedish animals, birds, amphibies, fishes, insects and worms†; a work which he had already began to collect, while a student at *Upsal* in the year 1730. There had never appeared so general and complete a zoology of any country. The first edition contained 1350 articles. By his own discoveries and the observations of his pupils, this number was increased, in a second edition, fifteen years after, to 2266. This last edition presented the following state and proportion of the animal reign in *Sweden :* 1691 species of insects, 198 of worms, 195 of birds, 77 of fishes, 53 of sucking animals, and 25 of amphibies. Entire and absolute perfection cannot possibly be expected in a work of this description. BÆCK justly observed, that something is still left to be added to it by the diligence of posterity; but that at any rate the honour belongs in preference to him who first paved the way to such perfection.

The beginning of the academical career of LINNÆUS, so celebrated for writings, travels and reforms, so replete with patriotic and scientific activity, did not remain unrewarded. His merits were now honoured

* *Flora* LINNÆI *placet. Est enim stupendæ ejus diligentiæ novum argumentum. Epist. ad* HALLER. Vol. ii. p. 250. HALLER however did not like the work.

† *Fauna Suecica,* sistens animalia Suecicæ regni, &c. *Holm.* 1746.

and

and acknowledged, not only abroad but also at home. In 1743 he was chosen member of the Academy of Sciences of *Montpellier*, where he kept up his friendly correspondence with Professor DE SAUVAGES; seven years after he was elected member of the society of *Thoulouse*, and in 1747 member of the Royal Academy of *Berlin*. In the same year he caused similar honours to be bestowed on several of his learned friends in *Sweden*: HALLER, JUSSIEU, SAUVAGES, GESNER, GMELIN, CLAYTON, COLLINSON, and VAN SWIETEN were received members of the Royal Academy at *Stockholm*, an honour which had, for the first time been conferred upon foreigners. LINNÆUS received a testimony of respect in his own country, which had never yet been bestowed on any of his academical predecessors,—a distinction, which on account of its unprecedented singularity, became the more flattering and encouraging to him. Four patriotic grandees, Counts EKEBLAD, HOEPKEN, PALMSTIERNA and Baron HARLEMAN, caused a gold medal to be struck in his remembrance. One side represented the bust of LINNÆUS with this inscription:

CAROL. LINNÆUS. M. D. BOT. PROF. UPS. ÆTAT. XXXIX; on the other side these words: " CAROLO GUSTAVO TESSIN ET IMMORTALITATI EFFIGIEM CAROLI LINNÆI CL. EKEBLAD, ANDR. HOEPKEN, N. PALMSTIERNA, ET CAR. HARLEMAN. DIC. MDCCXLVI.

LINNÆUS was highly fond of the portraits of great and celebrated men. He had collected many of them in his travels abroad. In the apartments of his house those of the most remarkable botanists were exhibited to view. In 1746 a print of HALLER was published in

copper-plate.

copper-plate. LINNÆUS requested a copy of this portrait of HALLER himself, and sent him one of his gold medals in return.

The dedication of this medal to Count TESSIN, was both an honour well deserved, and a happy idea, much to the advantage of LINNÆUS. His exalted patron was encouraged in a most flattering manner in the continuance of his patronage. Charmed with the noble example of his patriotic fellow-citizens, he also gave LINNÆUS, in the following year, a token of veneration, which was equally honourable to himself and to the object for whom it was destined. He ordered a medal to be struck, representing on one side, the bust of LINNÆUS, and on the other three crowns, on which the sun casts his beams, with this simple but eloquent motto: *Illustrat—He illumines**.

Before LINNÆUS received those marks of private respect of Count TESSIN, the latter had already rewarded him with royal favour. Professor ROSEN, the colleague of LINNÆUS, furnished the Count with an opportunity. ROSEN, assisted by the advice of HALLER, had saved the life of the late King. That Prince was born on the 26th of January 1746; in the second month he became so ill that all hopes of his recovery were given up. ROSEN was called from *Upsal,* and insisted that the prince's nurse be immediately discharged. The College of Physicians was against his determination, but found itself compelled to give its assent;—in a short time after the prince recovered— and ROSEN was rewarded with presents, an annual pension of 500 dollars, and the title of Dean of the College of Physicians. ROSEN

---

* This medal is of silver, and about the size of a Dutch gilder. In the three crowns, which are a fine allusion to the domination of LINNÆUS in the three reigns of nature, are several of her attributes. In the first, the heads of an eagle, a lion and a whale are very conspicuous, and the two others bear plants and fragments of minerals.

was

was then the only man who bore this title in *Sweden.* He having saved the life of so great a prince deserved great favours. In this case the court could not overlook his colleague LINNÆUS, who among all the learned men of *Sweden* had rendered himself most deserving in the learned world. At the instance of Count TESSIN, LINNÆUS likewise obtained the title or *Archiater,* or Dean of the College of Physicians, on the 19th of January 1747.

His father,—who in his youth, had designed LINNÆUS for an apprentice to a shoemaker!—now saw his son thus honoured by the great men of the kingdom, raised to dignities, his fame spread all over *Europe,* and his name rendered immortal. The father of LINNÆUS died at *Stenbrohult,* May 12, 1748, aged 74. Long ago would his memory have perished but for his great son, who was at first the torment, but afterwards the delight and boast of his life.

z   SECTION

SECTION VIII.

EXCURSIONS OF THE NORTHERN LITERATI.—HISTORY OF THE TRAVELLING PUPILS OF LINNÆUS.

LINNÆUS was of the number of those great men who exhibited the most eloquent picture of the strength of the human powers and endowments, and who proved by their own example, what the genius and activity of a single individual is capable to accomplish. Let us

remember

remember a LUTHER, a VOLTAIRE!—and who is not astonished at the influence which they had over their age and over so many nations! LINNÆUS kept pace with them in proportion to his science. He was the reformer of botany, and became the greatest and most universal promoter of natural history that ever existed. Never has so much been done for that science in so short a space of time as at the period in which he flourished, and immediately after him. What he did directly, for his own part, had never yet been done by any naturalist before him. His lecture-room became the nursery of eminent and celebrated men. The eloquence of the master enraptured and won his pupils. His enthusiasm, his thirst for science, became their own, and he gave them opportunities to exert those qualities. *Sweden* obtained and acquired by him a new celebrity,—it became famous by the transmigration of the learned, unexampled in any other country. From *Upsal* the disciples of LINNÆUS travelled to all quarters of the globe to study nature, and to disseminate the knowledge of her treasures. We shall here give a brief sketch of those itinerant Swedes, and of the other celebrated disciples of LINNÆUS, since they form one of the principal and most glorious periods of his life.

" If I look back upon the fate of naturalists," says LINNÆUS*, " must I call madness or reason that desire which allures us to seek " and examine plants? The irresistible attractions of nature can alone " induce us to face so many dangers and troubles. No science ever " had so many martyrs as natural history. PLINY, the prince of " nature among the Romans, plunged into the fiery abyss of Mount " Ætna†, SIMON PAULI from his love of plants broke his leg;

* See C. LINNÆI, *Critica Botanica*, p. 81.

† PLINY died, by all accounts, on the sea shore near *Stabiæ*.—*Translator.*

2   " CLUSIUS,

" CLUSIUS, an enthusiast equally unfortunate, was thrown into irons,
" and robbed of all his treasures in *Barbary*; GUILLANDINI was
" taken by pirates; the Dutch Consul RUMF died blind in the island
" of *Amboyna*, where he preferred his toils to all the wealth of the uni-
" verse; LIPPI was murdered in the wilds of *Æthiopia*; STELLER
" fell a victim to his exertions in *Siberia*; GMELIN was thrown into
" a dungeon by the Tartars; LOWITZ impaled; SCHEUCHZER left all
" the conveniences of life to gather grasses, exposed a thousand
" dangers, on the *Alps*; TOURNEFORT exchanged the luxuries of *Paris*
" to range through the wilds of *Turkey*; a BANKS, a FORSTER, and
" other cotemporaries are equal to, nay they excel TOURNEFORT in
" point of enthusiasm; because they exchanged smiling fortune at home
" with the threatenining dangers of foreign climes, in barbarous and
" unknown regions; RUDBECK lost his collections in the fire of
" *Upsal*, and died of a broken heart; PLUMIER suffered shipwreck;
" BANNISTER was hurled headlong down a rock in *Virginia*; BARELLI,
" MICHELI, DONATI, VAILLANT and others, without number, fell a
" sacrifice to their scientific exertions in natural history."

The pupils of LINNÆUS augmented the number of victims of science.
We shall begin with those whose ill-fated career deserves most to be
lamented.

Sweden stands indebted to Count TESSIN for the preservation of the
great professor at *Upsal*; likewise for the numerous peregrinations of
his pupils. The patriotic disposition of many of his fellow-citizens,
imitated afterwards his example. He requested of the Swedish East-
India Company at *Gothenburgh*, to let every year a young naturalist
make a voyage to *India* in their ships, free from expence; a request

made

made by so great a man, was instantly complied with, MAGNUS LA-
GERSTROEM, a great lover of natural history, was then director of that
company, and the academy of *Stockholm* afterwards received him as
one of its members. He gratified every wish of LINNÆUS; took
the young travellers under his special protection, and charged the cap-
tains of the ships to serve them whenever they found an opportunity.
LAGERSTROEM even brought it so far, that they could purchase natural
curiosities in *China* at the company's own expence*.

The first of the pupils of LINNÆUS, who profited by this opportunity to visit a remote part of the world, was C. TERNSTOEM,
a young man who seemed to be born to collect natural curiosities. In 1745 he embarked at *Gothenburgh* for *China;* but fell
a victim to the climate, even before he could reach the place of his
destination. He died at *Poulicandor,* towards the close of 1745.

Soon after LINNÆUS became the instrument of a second voyage.
He represented in his lectures, in the most eloquent and persuasive manner, the extraordinary merits and great celebrity which a young student might obtain by travelling through *Palestine,* and by enquiring
into and describing the natural history of that country, which was till
then unknown, and had become of the greatest importance to interpret
the bible, and to understand eastern philology. This certainly was an

* Regiæ Cancellariæ, simul regiæ tunc temporis Scientiarum Academiæ Præses, Comes
TESSIN, cum Societate Indica convenit, ut quotannis cum navibus liceret mittere juvenem,
naturæ sacris initiatum, in Indias, Societatis hujus impensis ; quod, quamvis ab initio insuetum
facile tamen evenit, opere et favore nostri M. LAGERSTROEM, qui non modo summo favore amplexus est ejusmodi naturæ curiosos, sed in mandatis dedit navium gubernatoribus,
ut his inservirent, quacunque liceret regione, ut finem obtinerent propositum ; immo quod
magis est, jussit Societati subjectos socios, suis propriis impensis emere, quæcunque in China
occurrerent singularia ad locupletandam Scientiam præstantissimam. *Amœnitates Academicæ,*
vol. vi. Edit. Schreber, p. 232.

Herculean

Herculean and dangerous enterprize.   Nevertheless there was a young man whose courageous zeal was bent upon this expedition.

His name was FREDERICK HASSELQUIST, then a student, and afterwards doctor of physic.   The lively representations of LINNÆUS, and the obvious importance of the voyage itself, soon rendered it an object of patriotic concern.   There being no fund arising from the liberality of the crown, private collections were made, which poured in very copiously, especially from the province of *East Gothland*, the native country of the young traveller.   All the faculties of the university of *Upsal* also granted him a stipend.

Thus protected, he commenced his journey in the summer of 1749. By the interference of LAGERSTROEM, he had a free passage to *Smyrna* in one of the Swedish East Indiamen.   He arrived there at the conclusion of the year, and was received in the most friendly manner by Mr. A. RYDEL, the Swedish Consul.   In the beginning of 1750 he set out for *Egypt*, and remained nine months at *Cairo* the capital. Hence he sent to LINNÆUS and to the learned societies of his country, some specimens of his researches.   They were published in the public papers, and met with the greatest approbation, and upon the proposition of Dean BAECK and Dr. WARGENTIN, Secretary of the Royal Academy of Sciences, a collection of upwards of 10,000 dollars in copper-money was made for the continuance of the travels of young HASSELQUIST.   Counsellors LAGERSTROEM and NORDENCRANTZ, were the most active in raising subscriptions at *Stockholm* and *Gothenburgh*.   In the spring of 1751, he repaired to his destination, and passed through *Jaffa* to *Jerusalem*, *Jericho*, &c. He returned afterwards through *Rhodus* and *Scio* to *Smyrna*.   Thus he fulfilled all the ex-

3   pectations

peƈtations of his country, but he was not to reap the reward of his toils. The burning heat of the sandy deserts of *Arabia* had affeƈted his lungs; he reached *Smyrna* in a state of illness, in which he languished for some time, and died February 9, 1752, in the 30th year of his age.

The fruits of his travels were, however, preserved through the liberality of a great princess. He had been obliged to contraƈt debts. The Turks, therefore, seized upon all his colleƈtions and threatened to expose them to public sale. The Swedish Consul prevented it. He sent with the intelligence of the unhappy exit of his countryman, an account of the distresses under which he died;—and at the representation of Dean BÆCK, Queen LOUISA ULRICA granted the sum of 14,000 dollars in copper-specie, to redeem all his colleƈtions *. They arrived afterwards in good preservation at *Stockholm*, consisting of a great quantity of antiques, Arabian manuscripts, shells, birds, serpents, inseƈts, &c. and were kept in the cabinets at *Ulrichsdale* and *Drottningholm*. The specimens of the natural curiosities of these museums being double or treble in number, LINNÆUS obtained some of them, and published the voyage of his ill-fated friend†, and honoured his memory with a plant which he called from his name *Hasselquistia*.

The plan which LINNÆUS had first projeƈted, and which HASSELQUIST on account of his illness was not able to execute alone, was soon after revived by a German. Professor MICHÆLIS of *Goettingen*, one of the greatest adepts in the Eastern languages, who from the great

* See the introduƈtion to the Flora Palæstina, in the Amœnitat. Acad. vol. iv.

† Fred. Hasselquist Iter Palestinum, *Stockholm*, 1757, 8vo.

respeƈt

respect which Count Hoepken entertained for him, was created a knight of the polar star in the year 1775, demonstrated the necessity of obtaining a more extensive knowledge of that country, which had been the theatre of most of the events related in Holy Scripture; and he brought it so far, through the interference of the Danish Ministers Counts Bernstorf and Moltke at *Copenhagen*, that an expedition was made into *Arabia*, which will always be recorded in the history of Frederick V. King of *Denmark*, as a striking and honourable testimony of his liberality and zeal in the promotion of the sciences. Five persons were chosen for this purpose, viz. Counsellor Niebuhr, professor Forskal, professor Von Haven, professor Cramer, M. D. and Baurnfeind, the painter. The former had been proposed by Counsellor Kæstner, and the two latter by Michælis. Forskal was a native of *Sweden*, a pupil of Linnæus, and well versed in the Eastern languages, which he had studied under Michælis at *Goettingen*. He was soon after appointed professor at *Copenhagen*, and heard the lectures of Linnæus upon natural history at *Upsal*. The voyage was commenced in 1761; *Arabia Felix* proved as unfortunate to these naturalists as it had once proved to Hasselquist. Forskal sent a letter, with some dispatches to Count Bernstorf, on the 9th of June, 1763, in which he gave him a precise account of the Arabian balsam of *Mecca*. These were the last dispatches which he ever sent to *Denmark*. One month after, on the 11th of July 1763, he departed this life, in the 31st year of his hopeful age. The fate of his companions was equally fatal. Death snatched them all away in *Arabia*, except M. Niebuhr, who afterwards published an account of this memorable voyage. The observations of Forskal were not lost. His surviving

A a   friend

friend published them * at *Copenhagen*, and the interesting contents of his last letter were communicated to LINNÆUS †, who called a plant after his name—*Forskahlea Tenacissima* ‡.

Thus three of his young pupils found an early grave in. *Asia*. The ashes of a fourth were destined for another part of the world. However flattering the choice of FORSKAL to act as a naturalist in the Danish voyage to *Arabia* must have been, yet the selection of another pupil of LINNÆUS proved equally honourable to our luminary. Application was made to him from the west of *Europe*, from *Madrid*, for an able botanist. He chose for this purpose a young Swede of the name of PETER LOEFLING, who went to *Spain* in 1751, where he

* Flora Ægyptiaco-Arabica, *Havn.* 1775, 4to.—PETRI FORSKAL Descriptiones Animalium, Avium, Amphibiorum, Piscium, Insectorum, Vermium, quæ in Itinere Orientali observavit; *Havn.* 1776.—All published by Counsellor J. A NIEBUHR.—Symbolæ Botanicæ, seu Plantarum, tam earum quas itinere, imprimis Orientali collegit PET. FORSKAL, quam aliarum recentius detectarum exactiores descriptiones, auctore M. WAHL, profess. &c. *Havn.* 1790, fol. cum 25 tab. æn. pars. I.

† See *Opobalsamum Declaratum. Upsal,* 1764. In the *Amœnitat. Academ.* vol. vii.

‡ Counsellor NIEBUHR sent LINNÆUS a copy of FORSKAL's work as soon as it was printed. Apprehensions had been entertained in *Sweden* lest his observations should be lost in *Denmark*. The royal academy of sciences of *Stockholm* received M. NIEBUHR as one of its members, out of gratitude for the pains he had taken to preserve the name and celebrity of the unfortunate FORSKAL. LINNÆUS himself, who was quite overjoyed at the publication of the observations of his late pupil, sent him a letter of thanks for the copy he had presented him with. M. NIEBUHR, in a letter to the author of the present work, expresses himself thus : " That FORSKAL was a worthy and excellent pupil of LINNÆUS, whose name he " never mentioned without reverence, is a fact which needs no repetition. It is sufficiently· " proved by his labours and observations. I doubt not but it will entitle him yet to the praise " of posterity. And this was my wish when I endeavoured to preserve his memory in the " literary world."—LINNÆUS might certainly have chosen a better plant than the *Forskalhea tenacissima* to perpetuate the memory of his pupil. That it contains an allusion to the character of the deceased, the Swedes themselves do not deny. Great men have great whims, and LINNÆUS had his, especially in the denomination of plants.

1

acquired

acquired great merit in his profession of botanist to the King, and in advancing natural knowledge. The Spanish government wished to profit still farther by his talents. In 1755 he was sent to *South America*, to travel through the different Spanish settlements and possessions, and to explore their natural produce; but scarce had he been a twelvemonth in that southern region ere he fell a victim to its climate. He died February 11th, 1756, in the flower of youth, aged twenty-seven years, and crowned with merit. LINNÆUS was singularly affected at the loss of him. Among all his travelling disciples he was one of the most zealous and most learned botanists, and none had a finer opportunity to enrich his science *. He left to his great teacher at *Upsal* the the melancholy pleasure of publishing his voyage, and dedicating to his memory a plant which he denominated *Loeflingia* †.

LINNÆUS did not live to hear of the tragical exit of another of his pupils, who, like LOEFLING, revered him as his promoter. This was J. P. FALK. He was born in *West Gothland* in 1730, and came to *Upsal* in 1751, to study natural history. His diligence and poverty were equally great. He was as much distressed as LINNÆUS once had been. The latter did for FALK what CELSIUS and RUDBECK had formerly done for himself. He took him into his house and made him tutor to his son, afterwards professor LINNÆUS. In the year 1759 he made a tour to *Gothland*. The good fortune of FORSKAL induced him two years after to go to *Copenhagen*, in hopes of being chosen a member of the society of the Arabian travellers. His hopes were, however, frus-

* Nullus erat facile huic anteferendus, vel amore plantarum vel sola eruditione botanica, nullique similis occasio concessa fuit. *Amœnitat. Acad.* vol. vi.

† PETRI LOEFLINGII *Iter Hispanicum. Stock.* 1748, octavo.

trated,

trated, and he returned to *Upsal*, where he published in the year 1762 his *Planta Alstroemeria*. In the following year the horizon of his fate became somewhat more serene. Through the recommendation of LIN-NÆUS he was called to *Petersburgh*, to be inspector of the cabinet of natural curiosities belonging to M. KRUSE, first physician to the Empress of *Russia*, and counsellor of state. He suffered shipwreck at *Narva*, and lost the best part of his effects. In 1765 he was made professor of the medical college and inspector of the botanical garden. His unbounded passion for study had a very sinister influence upon his health. He became subject to obstructions in the abdomen, and consequently to extreme fits of melancholy. He shot himself on his last travels through the Russian empire, at *Casan* in *Tartary*, in the night of the 20th of March 1774. Thus despair terminated the life of a man who had been too great a slave to science ever to enjoy happiness and social hilarity *.

To the above ill-fated persons may be added the celebrated J. J. BJOERNSTAHL. He certainly made the *Belles Lettres* his chief study, yet at the same time he had frequented the LINNÆAN lectures upon natural history. After twelve years peregrination he ended his career on the 12th of July 1779, in the forty-ninth year of his age, at *Solonichi* in *Macedonia*. The patriotism of his countrymen honoured his memory by medals, and his tomb with a marble monument.

These were the six pupils of LINNÆUS, the six ambassadors of FLORA, who were stopped in their mission by premature death. We shall now speak of those whose destinies proved more auspicious.

* See J. P. FALK's Supplements to the Topographical Knowledge of the Russian Empire. Narrative of his Travels from 1768 to 1773. *St. Petersburgh*, 1786, octavo, in German.

Besides

Besides LOEFLING, two other pupilsof LINNÆUS made a voyage to *America.* The principal among these was PETER KALM. A patriotic thought of LINNÆUS occasioned his voyage *. He well knew that a species of mulberry tree *(morus rubra)* grew wild in *North America,* and rose to a fine height in the open districts of *Canada.* The situation and climate of that country are much analagous to that of *Sweden.* The importation of raw silk in this latter kingdom was reckoned at twenty thousand Swedish pounds, which consequently drew out of the national coffer the sum 250,000 dollars per annum†. LIN-NÆUS proposed to the royal academy of *Stockholm* a voyage to *Canada,* to learn, among other things, whether or not the American mulberry trees and the silk-worms which feed on them could be transplanted in *Sweden* with advantage. Patriotism soon executed this proposal. The royal academy of sciences, the universities of *Upsal* and *Abo,* the magistrates of *Stockholm,* and the commercial college of the states contributed liberally to defray the expences. LINNÆUS chose KALM, who was then a student, and had already made himself known by his observations on domestic natural history, to undertake this voyage. He set out in October 1747, and passed from *England* to *North America,* where he remained three years. In 1751 he returned in good health to his country, where he published an account of his voyage ‡, and took upon him the functions of professor of natural

* See the Introduction to the Treatise upon the *Phalæna Bombyx,* in the *Amœnitat. Acad.*

† From an account of the Economical Journal published at *Stockholm* in the year 1790, it appears that the importation of foreign silk amounts at present to thirty-two thousand pounds per annum, of course to the annual sum of 350,000 dollars, Swedish currency. However in consequence of the late severe edict issued by the Regent this trade is now quite at a stand.

‡ KALM's voyage to *North America,* vol. iii. translated into English by FORSTER. *Lond.* 1771.

history

history at the university of *Abo*, in *Finland*, which charge LINNÆUS had previously obtained for him, and where he terminated his literary career in the year 1790. The mulberry-tree of *Canada* was by him introduced into *Sweden*, and cultivated in several gardens ; the Swedish government set a prize upon its cultivation in 1757, but the silk manufactures of that country never rose to a flourishing state.

Some time after KALM's return, Dr. ROLANDER, one of his colleagues, who had also been tutor to LINNÆUS, junior, made a voyage to *Surinam* and to the island of *St. Eustatius* in 1755; but his voyage was of no great utility, and he was one of those pupils with whose conduct LINNÆUS was most dissatisfied.

The melancholy fate of TERNSTROEM, HASSELQUIST and FORSKAL, who were cut off in the flower of youth in *Asia*, could by no means deter their countrymen. In 1750 OLOF TOREN made a voyage to the coast of *Malabar* and *Surat*, and some time after, PETER OSBECK, as chaplain of a Swedish East-Indiaman, sailed to *China*. Both returned safely with their treasures to *Sweden*, and published their observations*. The captain of the ship himself became conspicuous for his love of natural history and the zeal with which he served LINNÆUS. His name was ECKEBERG†. In 1765 A. SPARRMANN made likewise a voyage with him to *China*; he returned three years after, and from the year 1772 till 1776 made a voyage round the world with Capt. COOK and FORSTER—also to the coast of *Good Hope*, and into the interior parts of the South of *Africa*, by which his name became so celebrated‡. Much

* P. OSBECK's Journal of a voyage to the *East-Indies*, translated by. FORSTER.

† ECKEBERG's voyage to the *East-Indies*, and TOREN's tour to *Surate, Stockholm*, 1760.

‡ SPARRMANN's voyage to the *Cape* of *Good Hope, Stockholm* 1783, 8vo. *Swedish.*

about

about the same time a voyage was made to this latter country and the South-Eastern part of *Asia*, by one of the most distinguished pupils of the LINNÆAN school, then a physician in the service of the Dutch East-India Company. This was Doctor CHARLES PETER THUNBERG, that celebrated naturalist and worthy successor of his great teacher at *Upsal*, and of his friend LINNÆUS junior. He has been created a knight of the order of *Vasa*, since the year 1785 *.

Thus the spirit of LINNÆUS diffused itself from the North through all the zones of the earth, thus his name was spread by his disciples over most parts of the world, even in the Southern Indies. Some of his pupils were among the first who entered and explored the new discovered countries. One of them was SPARRMANN—and before him Dr. SOLANDER, who, after LINNÆUS, travelled through the *Alps* of *Lapland*, and accompanied, with Sir JOSEPH BANKS, the great and immortal Captain COOK in his voyage of discovery. He remained at *London*, where he held an office in the British Museum till his death, which happened in the year 1782 †.

† C. P. THUNBERG, M. D. F. R. S.—Travels in *Europe*, *Africa*, and *Asia*, especially in *Japan* during the years 1770 to 1779, are translated into English, in 3 vols. octavo. The Chevalier CHARLES THUNBERG commenced his travels, which lasted nine years, in August 1770, through *Norway* and *Denmark*, reached *France* in November, remained almost a twelvemonth at *Paris*, went from thence to *Holland*, embarked there for the *Cape of Good Hope*, and travelled three years through the interior parts of *Africa*; in 1775 he went to *Batavia* and *Japan*, and after a residence of sixteen months returned to the Island of *Java*, explored its interior parts during six months, went to (*Jon, · · · ·* also remained six months, and returned afterwards to his country by the *ape of Good Hope*, through *England*, *Holland* and *Germany*. His travels are the most interesting ever made by a native of *Sweden*. See the letter which LINNÆUS wrote to him in the *Collectio Epistolarum* C. A. LINNE, *Hamb*. 1792.

† See an account of the life and writings of Dr. SOLANDER, by Sir JOSEPH BANKS— also his Biography in the German literary journals of *Halle*, by Prof. G. FORSTER.—A medal was struck at *Gothenburg* in *Sweden*, by Baron ALSTROEMER representing the flower *Solandra*, with this inscription: JOSEPHO BANKS Effigiem Merito D. D. D. Cl. et Jo. ALSTROEMER.

In

In all those parts of the world, whence the Muses are not entirely banished, LINNÆUS became the modern teacher of natural history. His system was equally as well received at *Batavia* * and *Calcutta*, as at *New York* and *Philadelphia*. The friends of nature of all nations and all religions did homage to his system. His name and his doctrine became even known among the *Mahometans*. BJOERNSTAHL unexpectedly experienced the truth of this assertion. While he was at *Tharapia* in *Turkey*† he saw a Greek in a field, who was walking about with a book in his hands. He accosted him, and found with astonishment that the book which he held, was no other than the LINNÆAN *System* of *Nature*, the edition printed at *Halle* in 1761. The Greek whose name was DEMETRIOS, informed him, that he had formerly been first physician to the Pacha of *Egypt*; that five *European* learned men had been presented to him, among whom there was a botanist, with whom he had made several botanical excursions in the environs of *Cairo*, where they remained six months; that this same botanist had inspired him with the love of plants, made known to him the great man in *Europe*, (meaning LINNÆUS) and had shown him the way to collect and preserve plants.—The botanist whom DEMETRIOS alluded to was the ill-fated FORSKAL.

Not only the remotest quarters of the globe, but also many of the *European* states became the objects of the travels of the disciples of LINNÆUS. In 1752 MARTIN KOEHLER made a tour through into *Italy*; in 1760 ALSTROEMER visited the same country, *France* and

* At *Batavia* an extract of his system was printed with its technology in the Malay language.

† See J. J. BJOERNSTAHL's Letters, vol. iv. *Rostock* 1781.

Spain;

Spain; in 1758, ANTHONY ROLANDSON MARTIN * explored SPITZ-
BERGEN; UNÓ VON TROIL, now Archbishop of *Upsal,* made a tour
to *Ireland* in 1772; ROTHMANN to *France, Africa,* &c. FABRICIUS
to *Norway, England* and *France;* GIESEKE to *Great Britain* and
France; EHRHART through the territories of *Brunswick, Hanover,* &c.
FERBER through *Italy* and *Hungary;* besides many whose names would
form too long a list to admit of being inserted here.

The natural history of *Sweden,* however much LINNÆUS himself
had already done for its progress, was remarkably more advanced and
enriched by the travels and observations of his pupils.   Dr. SOLANDER
travelled through *Pithea Lapland;* MONTIN in 1759 to *Lulea Lapland;*
FALK and Dr. BERGIUS in 1752 to *Gothland;* KALM to *West Gothland,*
&c. &c.

Among his foreign pupils there were several Germans whose merits he
had most reason to boast.   Among them we reckon the following,
according to the chronological order in which they studied at *Upsal:*

1. Counsellor SCHREBER at *Erlangen,* frequented the lectures of
LINNÆUS about the years 1759 and 1760 ; and besides NICHOLAS
LAWRENCE BURMANN, the present professor of botany and physic at
Amsterdam, was the only foreigner who ever lived in the house of LIN-
NÆUS.   The latter gave him this character: *He was as penetrating as
any of the pupils I ever had under me.*

2. Professor FABRICIUS at *Kiel,* studied a. *Upsal* 1762 till 1764,
with the late Danish counsellor of state ZOEGA, who died in the year
1788.   LINNÆUS said of them: *If FABRICIUS comes to me with an*

* He died at *Upsal* as professor of anatomy, Sept 10, 1785.

insect,

insect, or Zoega *with a moss, I pull off my hat, and say—Be you my teachers* *!

3. Professor P. D. Gieseke at *Hamburgh*, frequented the Linnæan lectures in 1771, having taken his degree of Doctor at *Goettingen* in 1768. " *How much I loved and esteemed* Gieseke," said Linnæus afterwards to another of his German pupils, " *he himself cannot but* " *have known. I made him acquainted with the higher curiosities of nature,* " *and took no small pains in giving him lectures on the natural orders of* " *plants†.*"

4. F. Ehrhart, botanist at *Herrenhausen*, near *Hanover*, was one of the most confidential and most persevering pupils of Linnæus, at whose lectures he assisted between three and four years, viz. from the 20th of April 1773, to the 28th of April 1776, and the only native of *Switzerland* who perhaps ever studied at *Upsal*. For several years back that republic has been famous for being the native country of botanists and naturalists. Linnæus had acquired some of his knowledge from their productions. How great therefore must have been his joy to see the penetration of his genius and the fame of his science transmitted to posterity by a native of that country.

Among the Swedish pupils of Linnæus who settled in *Germany*, was the celebrated mineralogist, J. J. Ferber, professor at *Mitau*, and afterwards counsellor of the mines of the King of *Prussia*. He was

---

* Si Dominus Fabricius venit cum aliquo insecto, et Dominus Zoega cum aliquo musco, tunc ego pileum detraho et dico : estote doctores mei !—These are Linnæus's own words, copied verbatim.

† Quantopere Dom. Gieseke amaverim—et æstimaverim, ipsum fugere non potuit. Altiora ei tradidi, nec parum laboravi, quam prælegerem ipse ordines naturales plantarum.

born at *Carlscrona,* August 29th, 1743, and died at *Bern,* in 1791 *.—
Farther, the aulic counsellor and Chevalier Murray at *Goettingen,* who
was born at *Stockholm* June 27, 1740, and died May 22, 1791 †.

To the eminent German disciples of LINNÆUS may be added M.
MEYER at *Stettin,* and Doctors LEPPENTIN and J. GRUNOV of *Hamburgh.* The latter died in 1783.

These pupils esteemed and revered their master, who, in return, testified gratitude to their love and friendship to their merits. He conferred
upon them the greatest honour he could confer, by perpetuating their
names in the vegetable reign.   He thus glorified, for instance, his German pupils and friends, by the *Schrebera, Giesekia, Ehrharta, Murraya,
Jacquinia, Scopolia, Ludwigia, Gleditschia, Munchausia, Moehringia,
Trewia,* &c. &c.—His Swedish disciples and friends by the *Torenia,
Osbeckia, Solandra. Kalmia, Alstroemeria, Lagerstroemia, Browallia,
Celsia, Rudbeckia, Moraea, Bæckia,* &c.—His friends and the meritorious
botanists of *Switzerland,* by the *Halleria, Gesneria, Scheuchzeria:*—His
friends in *Great Britain,* by the *Sloanea, Sherardia, Dillenia, Collinsonia,
Milleria, Lawsonia, Ehretia, Ellisia, Hopea, Hillia, Sibthorpia,* &c.—
His Spanish pupils and friends, by the *Queria, Minuartia, Valetia, Orte-
gia, Salvadora, Ovieda, Monarda, Barnadesia, Mutisia, Hernandia, Xi-
mena,* &c.—His friends in *France,* by the *Sauvagesia, Jussiæa, Reau-
muria, Valantia, Dodartia Barreria, Isnardia, Guettarda, Gouania, Mag-*

---

* See FORMEY's panegyric on FERBER, read in the Royal Academy of Sciences at *Berlin,*
Feb. 3, 1791. German.

† Eulogium Jo. ANDR. MURRAY, in consessu, reg. scient. societ. recitatum die iv. Jan.
1791. A C. G. HEYNE, *Goettingae,* 1791. Twelve pages in quarto.

nolia,

nolia, &c.—His Dutch friends by the *Gronovia, Royena, Cliffortia, Boerhaavia, Swietenia, Burmannia, Gorteria,* &c.*.

Thus the majestic prerogative which LINNÆUS was possessed of, to confer titles in the vegetable reign, became an excellent means for him to honour merit and to demonstrate his friendship. But the use he made of this prerogative did not escape the eye of critical censure; and HALLER morosely complains of it in the following expressions:

" We find it very natural to assign to the genera of plants the names
" of celebrated men, and so far they ought not to be altered. But, as
" these names are the reward of labours generally unrewarded by the
" world, and an encouragement to devote oneself to such labours; and
" as no prince or minister is particularly honoured by having his name
" assigned to some herb or plant, we would reserve all those garlands for
" those alone who are real and experienced botanists. Nor would we
" ever assign such a denomination to the mere hopes conceived of men
" who have not passed the ordeal of merit; nay, we would by no
" means advance with a title, those whom experience may afterwards
" prove to be unworthy of such distinction. Above all, personal ser-
" vices, receptions into learned societies, presents, and casualties of
" this kind, ought by no means to be acknowledged with an honour
" which confers immortality, and is congenial alone to merit!"

* A list of plants thus denominated is to be found in G. R. BOEHMERI *Dissertatio de Plantis, in Cultorum Memoriam nominatis. Witembergæ,* 1770, quarto.

SECTION

SECTION IX.

REMARKABLE EVENTS OF THE LIFE OF LINNÆUS.

LINNÆUS DESCRIBES THE NATURAL CABINET OF COUNT TESSIN. — ULRICA
LOUISA, QUEEN OF SWEDEN.—HER EXTRAORDINARY LOVE OF NATURE.—
ESTABLISHMENT OF THE ROYAL CABINETS OF NATURAL HISTORY AT UL-
RICHDALE AND DROTTNINGHOLM.—LINNÆUS ARRANGES AND DESCRIBES
THEM.—IS ATTACKED WITH THE GOUT.—CURES THIS DISORDER WITH STRAW-
. BERRIES.—HIS OBSERVATIONS ON THE TÆNIA.—LINNÆUS DISCOVERS THE
ART OF MAKING PEARLS.—BOTANICO-PHYSIOLOGICAL ELUCIDATIONS AND
OBSERVATIONS RESPECTING THE SLEEP OF PLANTS.—ANECDOTE.—OTHER OB-
SERVATIONS AND HYPOTHESES.—COLLECTION OF HIS ACCADEMICAL DISSER-
TATIONS (AMŒNITATES ACADEMICÆ).—SOME ACCOUNT RESPECTING THEM.—
THE NUMBER OF DISSERTATIONS OVER WHICH LINNÆUS PRESIDED.—HE PUB-
LISHES HIS PHILOSOPHIA BOTANICA AND HIS SPECIES PLANTARUM.—ACCOUNT
OF THESE WORKS.—INTRODUCTION OF TRIVIAL NAMES.—BOTANY IS FACI-
LITATED.—THE MARGRAVINE CAROLINA LOUISA OF BADEN, A PECULIAR
LOVER OF NATURE AND A PROTECTRIX OF LINNÆUS.—OTHER FRIENDS OF
LINNÆUS AMONG THE FAIR SEX IN ENGLAND, FRANCE AND AMERICA.—
NATURAL CURIOSITIES SENT TO HIM FROM ALL PARTS OF THE WORLD.—
FARTHER IMPROVEMENTS IN THE ROYAL BOTANICAL GARDEN AT UPSAL.—
DONATI.—ANECDOTES.—LINNÆUS RECEIVES THE FIRST GREEN TEA-SHRUB
FROM CHINA.—SLIGHTS THE OFFERS MADE TO HIM FROM MADRID AND
PETERSBURGH.—IS THE FIRST OF THE SWEDISH LITERATI WHO IS CREATED
KNIGHT OF THE POLAR STAR.—COUNT HOEPKEN'S PANEGYRIC ON LINNÆUS.—
HE RECEIVES A PRIZE OF THE ACADEMY OF SCIENCES AT STOCKHOLM, AND
ANOTHER OF THAT AT PETERSBURGH.

WE now return to those remarkable occurrences peculiarly incident to the academical life of LINNÆUS, which, for the sake of a
more comprehensive view, we shall present in a period of ten years,
namely, from 1750 to 1760. His disciples became the priests and
teachers

teachers of nature in all parts of the world, through him the love of her productions animated the great, and penetrated even to the throne of his country.   Count TESSIN, his elevated patron, loved him and his science, especially the knowledge of the mineral reign.   He had collected a considerable cabinet of minerals the description and arrangement of which he left to the care of LINNÆUS.   This description appeared in 1753 in Latin and Swedish*, and to the honour of the author, Count TESSIN prefixed himself a preface to the work, dedicated it to LINNÆUS, and caused a copper-plate to be put in front of it, representing the medal which he ordered to be struck in honour of our luminary.

Under LINNÆUS the first royal museums were established in *Sweden*. We have already mentioned the present which King FREDERICK ADOLPHUS made to the academy of *Upsal,* while he was prince royal.   The love of nature was one of the favourite passions of that prince.   In a short time a great number of curiosities of the animal reign, especially foreign birds, amphibies, fishes, and insects were collected, and a cabinet built in the castle at *Ulrichsdale,* at the distance of half a league from *Stockholm.*   LINNÆUS had the honour to arrange it, and to publish a description of its contents in the year 1754 †.

The laudable example of this prince was followed by his excellent and accomplished Queen LOUISA ULRICA, sister to FREDERICK the GREAT.   She was, in general, the enthroned MINERVA of the Swedish Sciences. ‡ She also inspired the late king with the love of nature.

* Museum Tessinianum, *Holm.* 1753, folio.
† Museum Regis Adolphi Frederici, *Holm.* 1754, fol. 135, tab. 33.
‡ Doctor ROSEN in a letter to HALLER, written in 1753, thus expresses himself: " Regina " nostra clementissima, mirabili flagrat amore Historiæ Naturalis, et ex Hollandiâ imprimis " multum in eo studio apparatum sibi coemit."

She

She had a cabinet of shells, insects and coral collected at her own expence in her palace at *Drottningholm,* the slow increase of which rendered its treasures the more valuable. The oriental collections of the unfortunate HASSELQUIST were preserved in the same place. LIN-NÆUS also described this museum*, but not without taking the greatest pains. There was no curiosity in the kingdom which was not shown him, and he resembled ARISTOTLE before whom ALEXANDER the GREAT ordered a great number of curious animals to be brought, that he might describe them; but still greater than ARISTOTLE in this science, LINNÆUS profited better by the opportunity afforded him.

The two royal palaces of *Ulrichsdale* and *Drottningholm* still contain to this day the monuments of his labours and arrangements. The late King GUSTAVUS III. left those treasures of nature, which will ever shine as an ornament in those edifices, in the same order as LINNÆUS had described them according to his own system.

LINNÆUS chose the academical recess as the time for arranging the royal cabinets. There are two vacations every year at the University of *Upsal,* the summer vacation lasts three months, and the winter vacation six weeks. On those days of leisure, he used to go to *Ulrichdale* and *Drottningholm,* situate at the distance of about eight Swedish miles from *Upsal.* But some fell disorder threatened to prevent LIN-NÆUS from repairing thither, had not he fortunately discovered an efficacious remedy against it. In the summer of 1750, he was attacked with the gout. His fits were so violent as to deprive him of sleep for seven days and seven nights, nor could he ever keep his feet quiet for an hour together. The gouty matter circulated from one foot into the

* Museum Ludovicæ Ulricæ Reginæ, *Holm.* 1764.

other,

2

other, and thus gradually spread its poison in his hands and other limbs. Those who attended him began to despair of his recovery. All his appetite being gone, he one day took it into his head to refresh himself with strawberries ; he ate them, fell asleep, desired more of that fruit to be given him, and two days after rose from his bed entirely restored to health and vigor. In the course of the following summer he was again troubled with a relapse. He came to the palace, with a pale and distorted countenance. The Queen Dowager asked him if he wanted any thing.—" A pottle of strawberries"—answered he. The strawberries were brought him;—and the next day her Majesty saw him full of spirits and perfectly recovered in her museum of natural curiosities. Three years afterwards LINNÆUS had again several fits of the gout, but they were much weaker than formerly, and he always conquered their virulence with strawberries. He ate them every summer; they purified his blood, rendered his complexion more florid, and banished the gout for ever from his frame.

Exclusive of this new cure of the gout which casual experience had taught him, his penetrating genius found the way to many other discoveries. He first observed in the year 1748, that the worm *Tænia* belonged to the compound creatures, or to the animal plants ; that each of its limbs had a mouth and an anus. " I have examined the " *Tænia*," writes he in a letter to HALLER, dated September 13, 1748*, " and found fourteen of them alive and completely joined to each

---

* *Tæniam* examinavi et reperi quatuordecim vivas integras; quæsivi caput, quod omnes medici in lumbrico lato quæsiverunt, sed frustra; falsissimum est caput, quod Tulpius habet in observationibus. Et frustra quæritur caput, nam caput est in singulo articulo, et os in singulo articulo; in una specie subtus, in altera ad latus. Nullus mortalium potuerit intelligere hunc vermem, qui non intellexerit polyporum naturam, de quibus recentiores tam multa. Habet *Tænia* naturam polyporum et propagatur secedentibus articulis, dum quilibet articulus vivit et accrecit in perfectum corpus. Epist. ad HALLER. vol. ii. p. 411.

1   " other.

" other. In vain did I, like other physicians, look for its head; for
" the head and mouth are in each limb or division, in some down-
" wards, and in others side-ways. No mortal will be able to know this
" worm, unless he is acquainted with the nature of the *Polypi*, upon
" which so much has hitherto been written. The *Tænia* resembles
" them. It is propagated by the dying limbs; and every limb is ani-
" mated, and grows again to be a complete body."

As important as this discovery became to the medical world, as advantageous proved to LINNÆUS a second one, which he made in the
same year. He found out the art of making pearls. " I am at last
" acquainted," says he in the same letter to HALLER *, " with the man-
" ner in which pearls are generated in their shells. I can now bring
" it about, that each pearl-shell, (the *Mya Margaritifera* so abun-
" dantly found in the North Sea), which can be encompassed in one's
" hand, will, after a lapse of between five and six years, produce a
" pearl of the size of a pea."—He kept this secret to himself for a long
time. In the diet of 1762, it became a subject of public discussion,
and the states of *Sweden*, induced him, by the offer of a considerable
reward to communicate it to one of their representatives, a merchant
and director of the Swedish East India Company at *Gothenburgh*. It
does not however appear, that any considerable benefit was ever derived from this discovery. Doctor J. E. SMITH of *London*, the present proprietor of the LINNÆAN collections, is also in possession of the
manuscript which LINNÆUS wrote upon the generation of pearls. This

---

* Tandem intellexi, qua ratione Margaritæ nascantur et generentur in Conchis; et potero
jam efficere, ut quælibet concha margaritifera, quam licet in manu tenere, post quinque vel
six annos ferat margaritam magnitudine seminis e vicia vulgari. *ibid.*

curious

curious work is written in the Swedish language; and from its high
value, it may probably never appear in public.

The vegetable reign remained the favourite branch of the studies of
LINNÆUS. Propitious nature unravelled to his penetrating eye many
secrets and latent operations of the empire of Flora. His progress in
the knowledge of the physiology and the properties of the plants extended farther than that of any of his predecessors.

The similitude which the plants bore to animals, was partly the basis
of his system, the truth of which it confirmed in many respects. In
1754 he discovered that the plants are subject to a regular sleep, and
repose by night like the animals. A plant, (*Lotus Ornithopodioides*), the
seed of which had been sent him by professor DE SAUVAGES of *Montpellier*, occasioned this new observation. It bore two flowers. He
recommended the gardener to take the utmost care of them. Two days
after LINNÆUS returned late in the evening to see how they were
thriving. He looked, searched and could discover no flowers. The
next night he found them as invisible as before. The following morning he came and the flowers appeared as usual, but the gardener thought
they were fresh ones, as he had not been able to find any before, after
so many unsuccessful searches. This circumstance engrossed the attention of LINNÆUS. He visited again the fugitive flowers on the
third evening; they had again vanished, but he found them at last,
deeply wrapt up in and quite covered by some leaves. This only served
to excite his curiosity more and more. In order to surprise nature in
her wonders he perambulated the garden and the hot-house, in the
dead of some night, with a lanthorn in his hand—and there saw that
the

the greatest part of the flowers were contracted and concealed, and found that the vegetable reign was almost entirely in a dormant state[*].

The flower, as the most admirable and most curious part of the plants, had occupied him chiefly, and furnished him with the model of that new system, by which the vegetable reign obtained its male and female sexes, in the same manner as the animal reign. The truth of this system he corroborated successively by several irrefragable proofs and observations. He demonstrated, how the flower and fruit develope themselves as embryos, how there are even bastards among the plants, and how the mixture and bastard-species might be produced by putting the blossom-dust of one plant, upon the notch of fructification of another, in the same manner as we see the production of a mule by an ass and a mare in the animal reign. This is a palpable proof of the double sexes in the vegetable reign, which the French botanist *Adanson* would not in the least admit[†]. The objections and repre- sentations of M. NECKER at *Manheim,* against this discovery, are be- sides many others but too well known. According to the LINNÆAN method all the vegetable productions are propagated by seeds. He extended the same mode of propagation to the mosses, but could not accomplish those enquiries which were to make him triumph over his opponents. At last Dr. HEDWIG of *Leipsic,* the DILLENIUS of *Germany,* decided the contest in favour of LINNÆUS[‡].

---

[*] Somnus Plantarum, 1755; Amœnitat. Academ. vol. iv. of which an English extract by Dr. R. POLTENEY may be seen in the Gentleman's Magazine for 1757, p. 315.

[†] M. LINNE ignore-til, qu'il y a dans certaines plantes, comme dans les animaux, des familles entieres, où il n'y a point de sexe distinct, ni sensible, où tous les individus se mul- tiplient sans aucune fecondation.

[‡] See HEDWIG's Fundamentum Historiæ Naturalis Muscorum frondosorum, concernens eorum flores, seminalem propagationem, &c. Lips. 1782. 4to. also LUDWIGII Epistola de Sexu Muscorum detecto Lips. 1778. 4to.

One

One of the most ingenious observations of LINNÆUS in physical botany was his new theory of the origin of the blossoms. He considered them as a sudden display, happening all at once, of the leaves and the gems of plants, *(Prolepsis Plantarum)*, as the anticipation of a growth of five years. The lateral or side-leaves, spring, according to this theory, from those parts which would have produced the ordinary leaves in the following year, the calyx from the leaves of the third, the petals from the leaves of the fourth, the stamina from the leaves of the fifth, and the pistilla from the leaves of the sixth year. Thus this developement, according to the fabric of nature, would only be effected after a lapse of six years, were it not accelerated by the covers of the marrow of the plants, which contain too little of the alimentary juice to be able to follow its extension, and to prevent the thriving of the flower or blossom.

To these may we add many other observations upon the distinct parts and properties of plants. Thus LINNÆUS, for instance, demonstrated, how accurately flowers perform the service of a time-piece, in which the hour of the day can be precisely ascertained; he composed a calendar for the period when the plants thrive their blossom, *(Calendarium Floræ)* and pointed out from this calendar in what manner the time best calculated for certain labours of rural œconomy may be chosen, he presented the different sorts of the natural emigrations of plants, *(Coloniæ Plantarum)*, &c.

All these, and many other remarks and subjects which he left to the discussion of his pupils in the academical disputations, were collected and published by him under the title of *Amoenitates Academicæ*. The first part of this collection made its appearance in the year 1749, and the

the seventh and last in 1769. Disputations were held under him till
the year 1776.

The Aulic Counsellor SCHREBER of *Erlangen*, one of the greatest of
his pupils, who blended the fame of his master with his own, arrogated to himself the merit of collecting the scattered and unknown dissertations, treatises and speeches of LINNÆUS, with the writings of his
son. He published those valuable archives of natural history, and
augmented the *Amœnitates Academicæ* from seven to ten volumes. It
may justly be maintained, that there never was a professor of the age
under whom a series of disputations was held, more distinguished than
the above for originality, genuine discoveries, and rich scientific con-
tributions*. In the seven parts of the LINNÆAN collections, there
are altogether 150 treatises, the number of which, with more modern
additions, has been augmented to *two hundred*. Fourteen of them contain descriptions and lists of the flowers and plants of various countries and districts†. Thirty extend to certain genera and species of
plants, and the remainder treat of the natural philosophy and history of
botany, and a great number of them boast of medical, zoological, and
lithological contents.

During his residence in *Holland*, LINNÆUS had already given a concise theory of systematic botany in the work entitled *Fundamenta Botanica*, and completed afterwards several additional chapters in his aca-

* LINNÆUS presided during the whole of his academical career at 186 disputations,
WALLERIUS at 194, the Chevalier IHRE at 453, and professor AKERMANN at 516.—See
J. H. LIDEN's Catologus disputationum, in Academiis et Gymnasiis Sueciæ habitarum,
quotquot huc usque reperiri potuerunt, *Upsal*, 1778.

† Flora Anglica, Alpina, Palæstina, Monspeliensis, Danica, Capensis, Jamaicensis, Belgica,
Ackervensis, (Count TESSINS VILLA), Rybucensis, (a village in *Sudermania*), Plantæ
Surinamenses, Camtchatcenses, Africanæ, Herbarium Amboinense.

3 demical

demical dissertations. In 1751 he published commentaries upon them, which were at the same time a comprehensive view and justification of his whole system. This work is intituled *Philosophia Botanica*. After a short review of the principal botanists and their systems, he explains in twelve sections the different parts of the plants, furnishes examples to fix the characters of classes and orders, to discern the bastard species from the common species, to describe them accurately, and to arrange precisely their synonymy, &c. &c. All this displays the production of the hand of an experienced master, whose genius appears to be equally inventive, well regulated, and methodical. At the end of this valuable work LINNÆUS gives advice to young botanists, and adds instructions how to prepare herbals, to establish botanical gardens, and the best dispositions to be adopted in excursions and philosophical tours. This work remains a book of precepts for the botanical world, which becomes indispensably necessary to all those who wish for a fundamental knowledge of that science. ROUSSEAU, mentioning this production, says " It is the most philosophical book I ever saw in my life*.—*C'est le livre le plus philosophique, que j'ai vu de ma vie.*

Two years after appeared a work, which together with his *System of Nature*, became the immortal monument of his diligence and ingenuity both for his own age and for posterity, and which had occupied him for a long series of years. This was his *Species Plantarum*, published at *Stockholm* in 1753, with his portrait, in octavo, containing 1,200 pages.

* JOHN GESNER wrote on the 19th of June 1751, what follows to HALLER from *Zurich:* " LINNÆI philosophiam botanicam legi, plenam doctrinæ et experientiæ botanicæ, cum mul-" tis et novis et mutatis vocum determinationibus. Erant, quibus sibi multa vel nimia, aliis " nimis pauca tribuere videbitur."

It is an universal botanical repertory, a catalogue of all the plants till then known to LINNÆUS in different parts of the world, containing 7,300 species, without reckoning their variations. He dedicated this work to the King and Queen of *Sweden*, and was not himself insensible of its value and merit. " Never," said he in the preface, have I " retorted upon mine enemies the arrows which they let fly against me. " I have quietly borne offences of the satyrs, and the ironics and attacks " of malice. They have at all times been the reward of the labours of " great men; but they cannot hurt a single hair of my head. Why should " I not put up with these unworthies, when the greatest and most cele- " brated botanists, before whom they must bow down to the dust, have " loaded me with praises. My age, my profession, my character, do not " permit me to combat my opponents. I will bestow the few years I have " to live, upon making useful observations. Errors in natural history " will admit of no defence, nor can the truth be concealed. I appeal, " therefore, to the judgment of posterity."

What CASPAR BAUHIN had attempted at *Basil* in the beginning of the last century by his picture of the vegetable reign *(Pinax)*; what SHE-RARD had so much and so vainly wished to be executed with his great botanical collections by Professor DILLENIUS, was now accomplished by one man in the best manner possible. This work of LINNÆUS contains an universal representation of the most modern state of the vegetable rein; and of the discoveries which had till then been made in it, and reached the knowledge of our great luminary. " Posterity it- " self," says Dean BÆCK, " will once give its judgment, if it be neces- " sary to determine, if every thing published as new after the death of

2   " LINNÆUS,

" LINNÆUS, shall be really new." To be the more accurate, he mentioned only those plants which he had seen in herbals or gardens on his different tours in *Sweden, Holland, England,* and *France,* or which had been sent to him by his pupils. The rest he examined particularly, and as his work was wholly botanical, he forbore to add their sanative virtues, confining himself to mention their native countries, their synonims, their purity, &c. He also gave their most faithful representation, their time of duration, and the epoch of their discovery. It has been urged as a reproach against LINNÆUS, his not having sufficiently profited by the more recent observations of foreign authors; but it was easier to make this reproach than to prevent it. The work received many supplements in a second edition, and it can only be gradually enriched by the botanical discoveries of posterity.

One of the chief excellencies of this work was also the reformation of the botanical technology, which LINNÆUS effected by the energy of genius and expression. It consisted in the introduction of the *trivial names,* by which one or two adjectives at farthest, distinguish a plant from all its other relative species. Where these adjectives could not be applied, he gave the plants epithets borrowed from their inventors, or the place of their growth. In the margin of the long definitions of the distinctive marks of each species (*characteres specifici),* he added the modern trivial names. Professor RIVIN at *Leipzic,* once conceived an idea of such a reform [*]. But all the honour and merit resulting from it belongs to LINNÆUS, and it was the more favourably received, in pro-

[*] See RIVINI's Introductio Generalis in Rem Herbariam. *Leips.* 1690 and 1710.

portion

portion as men feel themselves inclined to prefer ease to difficulty and freedom to constraint *.

We will here exhibit an instance of the utility of those trivial names in a species of grass, which used to be called *Gramen Xerampelinum, Miliacèa, prætenuis ramosaque sparsa panicula, sive Xerampelino congener, arvense, æstivum ; gramen minutissimo semine.* LINNÆUS expressed clearly and distinctly the name of this grass by the two words—*Poa bulbosa,* and rendered its description more intelligible than could be done by the whole foregoing string of descriptive names.

"Nothing could be more disgusting and more ridiculous," says the philosopher of *Geneva,* "if a woman, or any of those men who are so "much like them, asked the name of some herb or garden flower, than "to throw up, by way of answer, a long train of latin words, which "sounded like a conjuration of hobgoblins †."

By this amelioration of language, by the easy and pleasant method introduced by LINNÆUS, the study of botany was uncommonly promoted and facilitated‡. It got rid of the deterring appearances of an

---

* See J. A. MURRAY Progr. duo : Vindiciæ Nominum Trivialium, Stirpibus a LINNÆO impertitorum. *Goetting.* 1782, octavo.

† Rien n'etoit plus maussade et plus ridicule, lorsqu' une femme, ou quelqu' un de ces hommes, qui leur ressemblent, demandoient le nom d'une herbe, ou d'une fleur de jardin, que ' la necessité de cracher en réponse, une longe tirade de mots Latins, qui ressembloient a des evocations magiques.—J. J. ROUSSEAU's *Preface de l' Edition de Botanique.*

‡ CONDORCET, in his Panegyric on LINNÆUS, expresses himself thus : "LINNÆUS has "been reproached with having rendered too easy the nomenclature of botany, and occasioned "thereby the appearance of a vast number of small works. This objection seems only to prove "what progress botany has made under him. Nothing, perhaps, evinces better how far a "science is advanced, than the facility of writing books of mediocrity on such a science, and the "difficulty of composing works which contain novelty of matter." See *Eloge de* M. DE "LINNE, in the l' *Histoire de l'Academie Royale des Sciences.* Paris 1 81, 74 pages in quarto.

arduous

arduous science.   Its vestment became more appropriated to its beauty.
Nature now gained friends among the ladies, and even on the throne.
Besides the Queen of *Sweden*, there was afterwards at the head of these
a young German Princess, who was the greatest female botanist ever
known.   This was CAROLINA LOUISA of *Baden*, Princess of *Hesse
Darmstadt*, whose early loss the sciences had to bewail in 1783, in
the thirty-second year of her age.   Her extraordinary love of the study
of natural history, and her respect for LINNÆUS are most authentically
attested in the following letter, which the late BJOERNSTAHL, his countryman, wrote during his residence at *Carlsruhe* in 1774:

   " I hear that you are spoken of every day at court.   You are the
" object of the conversation of the reigning Prince and Princess.
" They are not only lovers of natural history, but so versed in
" that science as to excite astonishment.   They can enumerate your
" whole system according to all its genera and species.   They know
" every tree, every plant in the hot-houses of this city, which are
" full of foreign and domestic plants, collected in all parts of the
" world, and completely classed and arranged according to your me-
" thod.

   " The Princess has an excellent cabinet of natural history, but she
" has nothing from *Sweden*, except the polar star, which illumines her
" path through the whole range of nature, I mean the works and writings
" of a celebrated Knight of that order.   I wish to GOD you or your son
" would come hither! .Her Highness has charged me to invite you
" both in her name.   She promises you a fine and commodious resi-
" dence, and hangings as beautiful as those at *Hammarby* (the villa of
" LINNÆUS).   For I mentioned to her Highness what fine flowers
                                                    " had

" had been sent to you from *England*, and that you had decorated your
" walls with them at *Hammarby*."

" Now to the most important point ! The Princess has lately began a
" work, and I am at a loss to guess whether it does greater honour to
" her scientific zeal, or to your System of Nature. She causes all
" your *Species Plantarum*, together with the parts of fructification of the
" plants, to be engraved in a most capital and most sumptuous style.
" Each plate costs four *Louis d'ors*, and represents one plant only, with
" its *pistilla* and seminal vessels represented separately, and the number
" of the plates will amount to 10,000. M. GAUTHER DAGOTI, an ex-
" cellent engraver, is very recently arrived here from *Paris*. The
" species of the *Veronica* are already finished, and executed beautifully;
" for the whole is done under the immediate inspection of the Princess.
" She is not only a great botanist, but there are also but few who equal her
" in the art of drawing. She examines every plate with the most scrupu-
" lous attention, and corrects the slightest blemish or fault. She after-
" wards paints the plants in the most lively colours. This work must, of
" course, become the most correct and splendid which ever graced the
" annals of botany, and will fully answer its title of *Icones Omnium*
" *Specierum Plantarum* C. LINNÆI.

" The Princess intends likewise to beautify with similar engravings
" your system of the animal reign. A present has been made to her of
" the description of the two Royal Swedish Museums, given by you,
" bound in a sumptuous manner, bearing on the outside the King's and
" the Queen's name, and the arms of *Sweden*. Her Highness sends you
" one of the plates representing a *Veronica* by way of specimen. She
" will be glad if it meets your approbation."

Besides those two Princesses, who did honour to their rare talents and accomplishments, LINNÆUS had also friends and correspondents among the fair sex in several countries. Among those at *Paris* we reckon Madame DU GAGE DE POMMERUIL and Mademoiselle BASSPORT; at *London* Lady ANN MONSON; at *Oxford* Mrs. BLACKBURNE; and at *New York, in America,* he had a most enthusiastic admirer in Miss COLDEN. As flattering as the approbation of the fair must have been to him, as gallantly did he acknowledge it. He preserved their names in the vegetable reign, and denominated amongst others, two beautiful plants *Monsonia* and *Coldenia.*

The celebrity of his name and his connexions in all parts of the world, were as much calculated for the advancement of science in general, as they proved pleasant to him, and above all, advantageous to the royal botanical garden. The latter became a northern paradise, which displayed the treasures and curiosities of nature from all quarters of the globe. No where could the student of botany find a more beautiful living repertory of science. To send to LINNÆUS the seeds of rare or new plants, was both esteemed an honour and a pleasure. Thus were plants transmitted to him, exclusive of those which he received of the above-mentioned persons, from *Astrachm* and *Kamtschatka* by M. DEMIDOFF, one of his Russian pupils, who obtained them from the collections of the two famous travellers, STELLER and LERCHE; from *Siberia* by GMELIN; from *Egypt* and *Palestine* by the ill-fated HASSELQUIST; from *China* by LAGERSTROEM, OSBECK and TOREN; from the island of *Java* by BASTOR and KLEINHOFF; from *Tranquebar* by KOENIG, one of his pupils; from the *Cape of Good Hope,* by his friend BURRMANN at *Amsterdam,* and by the Dutch governor TULLBAGH, and his pupils

THUNBERG

THUNBERG and SPARRMANN; from *Virginia* by GRONOV; from
Pensylvania and *Canada* by KALM; from *Jamaica* by Doctor BROWNE,
in whose honour he called a plant *Brownæa* and purchased his whole
collection; from *Mexico* by MUTIS; from the other parts of *South-
America* by MILLER; from *St. Eustatius* by DE GEER, for whom
they had been collected by ROLANDER; and even from the fifth part
of the world, or the new discovered countries in the South Sea, by
the celebrated FORSTERS, who with the immortal COOKE first landed
in those regions.

The celebrity of his name was in this respect of the utmost efficacy
to LINNÆUS, and frequently caused him the most rapturous joy. Among
others he received a great quantity of beautiful African seeds, through
one of the most singular adventures. DONATI, a young Italian naturalist, travelled through *Egypt* and the *Levant*, at the expence of
the King of *Sardinia*, at *Alexandria* he got acquainted with a handsome young lady, the daughter of a Frenchman, and fell in love with
her. The lady's brother begged to be permitted to travel with him.
DONATI granted his request, that he might obtain the hand of his
sister. But his intended brother-in-law made him his dupe, robbed
him of all his money and natural curiosities, and fled to *France*. But
not finding himself safe enough in that kingdom, on account of the
vicinity of the Sardinian dominions, he embarked again for *Constanti-
nople*. Often had he heard DONATI mention the name of the great
Swedish naturalist,—he therefore sent LINNÆUS from *Marseilles* all
the collections he had stolen; DONATI suffered shipwreck, and died
July 11, 1763, in the thirty-first year of his age.

There

There was no country in *Europe* of which he he did not possess the most remarkable vegetable productions. His Swedish herbal was completer than that of any of his predecessors. His pupils Bergius and Montin, and others already mentioned, augmented these treasures. The northern plants were seen flourishing by the side of those which grow in the hottest climates of the South. From *Italy* he received plants of Dr. Kaehler of *Alstroemer*, and Dr. Turra at *Vicenza*; from *Venice* of the Imperial Minister Rathger and others; from *Switzerland* of Gesner; from *France* of Seguier at *Peronne*, and of De Sauvages at *Montpellier*, who procured him likewise the herbal of the celebrated botanist Magnol; from *Spain* and *Portugal* of Loeffler and several Spanish botanists; from *Iceland* of Koenig, his pupil; from *Great Britain*, *Denmark*, *Holland* and *Germany*, of the numerous friends and acquaintances he had in those respective countries.

Among the foreign rarities which he transplanted and cultivated in the North, a Chinese plant was the most remarkable, as it had never yet been seen in *Europe*. This was the tea-shrub*. Linnæus had endeavoured many years to get possession of it; and took pains to raise it from seeds : he also hoped to obtain it by professor Gmelin with the *Russian* caravans from *China*, but in vain; Osbeck, some time after brought the tea-shrub with him as far as the *Cape* of *Good Hope*, where it was lost. The wish of Linnæus was however finally accomplished by his friend Capt. Eckeberg. This Swedish navigator, at his departure from *China*, had put tea-seeds in a flower-pot, which throve so well during the voyage, that Linnæus had the pleasure to receive a green tea-shrub at *Upsal* on the third of October, 1763.

---

* Amœnitat. Academic. Dissertat. Potus Theæ, A. P. C. Tillæus, 1765, vol. viii.

Besides

Besides the beauties of the vegetable reign, there was also at this university a collection of curiosities of the animal reign, which were increased in process of time by a civet cat, a casuar from *Ceylon*, and many others.

In the possession of these treasures and other conveniences of life, LINNÆUS was now as happy as his wishes could make him. He acknowledged his fortunate situation in a public manner.—" I thank " Providence," said he in a *programma*, in which he celebrated the anniversary of the king's birth-day in 1752, " which has guided my destinies, " that I now live, may that I live happier than a king of *Persia*. I tell " the truth, when I deem myself fortunate. You know fathers and fel- " low-citizens of this academy, that I am wholly occupied with this aca- " demical garden, that it is my *Rhodus* or rather my *Elysium*. There I " possess all the spoils of the East and the West which I wished for, " and which, in my belief, are far more precious than the silken gar- " ments of the Babylonians and the porcelain vases of the Chinese. " There I receive and convey instruction. There I admire the wisdom " of the creator, which manifests itself in so many various modes, and " demonstrate it to others*."

The royal family of *Sweden*, whose favour he had particularly gained by personal acquaintance, and by arranging the royal cabinets of natural history, increased his happiness, and rewarded his merits in the

---

* Deo optimo gratiam habeo, qui sic fata mea dispersavit, ut hoc tempore vivam, idque ita, ut Rege Persarum beatior vivam. Verum narro, dum me beatum censeo. Nostis, patres cive-que, quod in Horto Academico totus sim, quod hic mea Rhodus sit, aut potius hic meum Elysium. Teneo hic, quæ volo spolia Orientis Occidentisque, et nisi me fallo, id quod Babyloniorum vestibus, Sinensiumque vasis, longe est speciosius. Hic disco et doceo. Hinc summi opificis sapentiam ipse, aliis aliisque documentis se prodentem, admiror aliisque mon-stro. *Amænit. Academic. vol.* X. *Edit. Schreber. p.* 30.

3　　　　　　　　　　　　　　　　　　　　　　worthiest

worthiest manner. He was called to the remote kingdom of *Spain*, an honour never before conferred upon any Protestant *literatus*, there to be botanist to his Catholic Majesty at *Madrid*, and the terms proposed to him were of the most advantageous kind. His Spanish Majesty would allow him an annual pension of 2000 piasters, the free exercise of his religion, and create him a nobleman. This offer was made to him by the Duke de GRIMALDI, Prime Minister of *Spain* from the year 1773 till 1776.

The Duke's letter with the answer of LINNÆUS,—are both among the epistolar correspondence now in the possession of Dr. JAMES ED- WARD SMITH, of *London*. LINNÆUS considering what had been done for him at *Upsal*, considering the respect and favour which were shown him by the Swedish court, and on the part of his fellow-citizens, gene- rously declined accepting this flattering and honourable offer. He procured it to Doctor LOEFLING, one of his pupils, whom fate would not suffer to enjoy it long. Like the South-West of *Europe*, so did the residence of the vast empire of *Russia* wish to possess our lumi- nary. Proposals were made to him from *St. Petersburgh*, in conse- quence of which he was to have been professor of botany, and elected an ordinary member of the imperial academy of sciences, &c. But LINNÆUS had his reasons for slighting all these invitations, because his country truly valued and rewarded his merits.

He was raised to a distinction, which had never before fallen to the share of any Swedish man of letters. King FREDERICK I. founded in 1748 the order of the POLAR STAR for men of merit in the civil line, and FREDERICK ADOLPHUS his successor, granted it on the 27th of April 1753, first to LINNÆUS, in [preference to all other learned men. The

offer

offer made to him from *Madrid*, was soon after realized at *Stockholm*. On the 4th of April, 1757, he received a diploma, which raised him to the rank of the hereditary nobility of the kingdom, and he forthwith called himself DE LINNÆUS. Thus, from the humble condition of the son of a village preacher, he rose as high in rank and dignity, as the empire of the muses could possibly exalt him *.

When the new observatory was consecrated at *Stockholm*, the Aulic Counccllor Baron *Hoepken*, expressed himself in a speech, which he made before the King on the 20th of September 1753, in the Academy of Sciences, in the following words:—" Botany, during the longest period of its existence has been a fanciful and voluntary structure of memory, till it received certain foundations and distinctive characters of a man in *Sweden*, whose NAME I WOULD MENTION, WERE IT NOT KNOWN TO THE LEARNED WORLD, AND AS IMMORTAL AS THE SCIENCE ITSELF.

LINNÆUS reaped many other honours and rewards of his knowledge and merit, exclusive of those which have already been enumerated. In 1754 he wrote a treatise on the cultivation of the *Alps* of *Lapland*†. He demonstrated, how that ridge of mountains, which laid in a waste and wild state, and contained hardly an hundred species of plants, could be turned to great advantage, by the introduction of foreign trees and alpine plants, suitable to their climate and soil. He communicated this treatise to the academy of sciences of *Stockholm*. Count SPARRE had

* In the letters patent of knighthood LINNÆUS makes the 2044 families of inferior nobility then in *Sweden*.

† De plantis, quæ Alpium Suecicarum indigenæ, magno rei occonomicæ et medicæ emolumento fieri possint;—See transactions of the Royal Swedish Academy of Sciences of 1755, vol. v.

left prizes by his will, to be distributed for the best treatises on the promotion of agriculture and of the different branches of rural œconomy. No work could, in this respect, be more patriotic or more important than that of LINNÆUS. The first prize given since the making of this will was therefore adjudged to him, by the unanimous assent of the academy. It consisted of two gold medals, value twenty ducats, bearing the arms of Count SPARRE, with this inscription:

SUPERSTES IN SCIENTIIS AMOR FREDERICI HENRICI SPARRE.——THE SURVIVING LOVE OF THE SCIENCES OF FREDERICK HENRY SPARRE.

A still more distinguished honour, which was also a public triumph of his system, was afterwards conferred on LINNÆUS in *Russia*. The Imperial Academy of Sciences at *Petersburgh* set a prize of one hundred ducats, in the year 1759, upon the best treatise, in which the truth of the sex of the plants should either be confirmed or refuted; by new arguments and experiments, exclusive of those already known, and by which a preliminary historico-physical description of all those parts of the plants which contribute any ways towards the fructification and perfection of the the seeds should be communicated.—This problem interested too much the empire of the LINNÆAN system for its author to remain a quiet spectator. Versed in the subject which was to be decided, he wrote a treatise*, in which he proved the sex

---

* Sexum Plantarum (these were the expressions of the problem) argumentis et experimentis, præter adhuc jam cognita, vel corroborare vel impugnare, præmissa expositione historica & physica omnium plantæ partium, quæ aliquid ad fecundationem et perfectionem seminis conferre tradantur.

Printed afterwards at *Petersburgh* in 1760, in one volume quarto, 42 pages. See *Amœnitat. Acad.* edit. Schreve.. vol. x.

of plants with new and most irrefragable arguments.   The motto which
he affixed to this treatise, conveyed all the energy of his mind ; it was
Famam Extendere Factis—" To spread fame by deeds." The good
cause was triumphant.   The Imperial Academy, at their meeting on
the 6th of September, adjudged the prize to LINNÆUS, and thus did
homage to the truth of a system, which SIEGESBECK, one of its members, had with equal acrimony and ignorance formerly endeavoured to
destroy.

SECTION. X.

REMARKABLE OCCURRENCES ATTENDING THE LIFE OF
LINNÆUS, FROM THE YEAR 1760 TO HIS DEATH,
JANUARY THE TENTH, 1778.

MERITS OF LINNÆUS IN THE MEDICAL SCIENCE.—HIS VARIOUS MEDICAL WRIT-
INGS.—ANECDOTES.—UNFAIR CRITICISM OF M. VICQ D'AZYR.—REFUTATION
OF THAT CRITICISM.—APOLOGY OF ASSESSOR HEDIN.—MERITORIOUS EFFORTS
OF LINNÆUS IN THE NATURAL HISTORY OF THE ANIMAL REIGN.—HIS CLAS-
SIFICATION OF THE MINERAL REIGN.—HIS LAST LEARNED LABOURS.—LIN-
NÆUS WAS A MEMBER OF TWENTY ACADEMIES OF SCIENCES.—HIS WORKS
SERVE AS THE ELEMENTARY BASIS OF NATURAL HISTORY, ESPECIALLY IN
SPAIN AND PORTUGAL.—EXTRAORDINARY PRESENT MADE HIM BY LORD
BALTIMORE.—OTHER PRESENTS.—HIS GOOD CIRCUMSTANCES.—HIS PENSION.—
HONORARY BESTOWED ON HIM FOR HIS WORKS.—HIS RURAL ESTATES.—
RESPECTFUL HOMAGE RENDERED TO HIM BY SEVERAL SOVEREIGNS AND
MONARCHS.—VENERATION MANIFESTED BY THE FRENCH PHILOSOPHER, J. J.
ROUSSEAU FOR LINNÆUS.—LINNÆUS IS ELECTED A MEMBER OF THE SWEDISH
BIBLE.—COMMISSION.—HIS EXTENSIVE CORRESPONDENCE,—PARTICULARS OF
THE LATTER END OF THE LIFE OF LINNÆUS.—HIS LAST PUBLIC ORATION.
HIS ENTHUSIASTIC STUDY OF NATURE EVEN IN HIS OLD AGE.—BENEFICIAL
AND DETRIMENTAL INFLUENCE OF THAT STUDY UPON HIS HEALTH.—HIS.
LETTER TO MR. PENNANT.—HE SUFFERS AN APOPLECTIC STROKE.—ANECDOTE.
DECAY OF HIS MENTAL FACULTIES—HIS MISERABLE CONDITION,—OTHER
ANECDOTES.—DEATH OF LINNÆUS—HONOURABLE TRIBUTE PAID TO HIS ME-
MORY.—GUSTAVUS III. LATE KING OF SWEDEN, PUBLICLY LAMENTS HIS LOSS,
AND ORDERS A MEDAL TO BE STRUCK IN REMEMBRANCE OF HIM.—GUSTAVUS
III. IMMORTALIZES THE HONOUR OF LINNÆUS'S NAME IN THE HISTORY OF
THE UNIVERSITY AT UPSAL.—MONUMENT ERECTED TO LINNÆUS.—PRIZES
OFFERED FOR A PANEGYRIC UPON LINNÆUS.—QUEEN ULRICA LOUISA OF
SWEDEN. — ANECDOTES. — HONOURS PAID TO THE MEMORY OF LINNÆUS
IN FOREIGN COUNTRIES.—LINNÆAN SOCIETIES OF LONDON AND LEIPSIC.—
PORTRAITS OF LINNÆUS.—LEARNED INHERITANCE LEFT BEHIND HIM—COMES.
IN THE POSSESSION OF JAMES EDWARD SMITH, M. D, OF LONDON.—CIRCUM-
STANCES ATTENDING THE SALE OF THOSE TREASURES OF SCIENCE.—ANEC-
DOTES.—

WE have thus far considered LINNÆUS mostly in the light of a botanist. But this was not the only title which distinguished his fame.
He had renounced medicine as a practitioner, but as a theorist this
science derived the most essential benefits from his exertions. The
knowledge of diseases, *(pathology)*—their remedies or cures *(Materia
Medica)*—and the instructions how to preserve health by means of a
regular choice and judicious use of meat and drink, *(Diætetic)*—consti-
tute the three principal branches of physic; they are steps of knowledge which must be ascended by physicians if they wish to acquire
fame and eminence in their profession; and LINNÆUS acquired celebrity and extensive merit in those three different branches of medical
science.

We shall first take a view of his merits in the *Materia Medica.* The
best and most numerous remedies are drawn from the vegetable reign.
It is the chief arsenal in which Nature preserves her store of arms
against maladies. The animal and mineral reigns are but sparingly
provided with them. The accuracy or inaccuracy of the knowledge
of herbs and plants determine, therefore, the application of the medicines which are prepared from them; they determine also, in a great
measure, the restoration or sacrifice of afflicted humanity. As long as

botany

botany remained an irregular and tottering edifice, the *Materia Medica* mostly languished in the same condition. Thus a weak mother gave birth to a frail and puny daughter.

Linnæus became the modern creator of botany and natural history, and at the same time of the *Meteria Medica*. When he examined plants or other natural productions, their intrinsic properties and œconomical or medical virtues were generally the objects of his attention. And the fruit of his observations (the finest which his knowledge of nature could produce) became a general description of the great apparatus of remedies which are embosomed for the benefit of man's health in the three reigns of nature.

As the richest of those reigns, he first described the vegetable productions, especially those which grow in his own country; and in a like manner, sometime after, those sanative substances which exist in the animal and mineral reigns *. That spirit of precision and order which characterises all his works, is also highly conspicuous in those descriptions. The confused appellations which had till then prevailed with regard to many plants were now destroyed ; he assigned to every plant its real rank, its pharmatical and botanical names, the synonomy or bye-names given by the ancients, its native soil and properties, and an exact description of its sanative virtues. Many medicaments which have since been cried up as new discoveries, had long ago been known to Linnæus; for instance, a certain remedy against the *Tænia* was puffed and spoken of in

* *Materia Medica e Regno Vegetabili. Holm.* 1749.—*E Regno Animali. Upsal,* 1752. —*E Regno Lapideo. Upsal,* 1752. Respecting the first part of this work, John Gesner wrote to Haller in the year 1749, " Linnæi *Materiam Medicam* accepi, magno judicio, " non sine eximio usu digestum opusculum."

France as a great secret *, and purchased afterwards by the late King for a very considerable sum; yet LINNÆUS had long before discovered this remedy, and recommended it for use.

The compendium of the *Materia Medica,* especially that part of it which concerns the vegetable reign, has been enriched by him with observations and additions which he collected during a series of upwards of twenty years. Old age prevented him, however, from superintending the publication of a new edition. " I have nobody to " assist me," wrote he in the year 1771 to his friend Dr. GIESEKE. " If you will only stay with me this winter, I will then publish it. I " will read it to you, and you will write after me and arrange it in " proper order †." But this request could not be granted.

The two last treatises on the *Materia Medica* he caused to be inserted in the collection of his academical writings. They were afterwards printed as a separate work at *Venice;* and since that in *Germany,* by an eminent pupil of LINNÆUS, whose merits in natural history are universally allowed. This was the aulic counsellor SCHREDER at *Erlangen,* who calls it the Golden Book *(Liber Aureus).* HALLER, who, after BOERHAAVE, was the oracle of medicine, and a rigorous scrutinizer of the works of LINNÆUS, publicly enumerated the intrinsic excellencies of that work, which he praised as one of the best of the LINNÆAN productions. In process of time more voluminous and extensive works were written upon the *Materia Medica,* but LINNÆUS first lighted the torch which spread a new and beneficial light over the study of that

* Radix *Filicis Maris.*

† Neminem habeo qui me adjuvat in eo edendo. Sivis per hyemem mecum hic commorari, edam et tunc tibi prælegam, ut possis transcribere et in ordinem redigere.

science.

science. Notwithstanding this meritorious effort, which was duly acknowledged by the greatest masters, M. Vicq d'Azyr, secretary of the medical society of *Paris*, the panegyrist of Linnæus on the banks of *Seine*, gave the following dictatorial and abstruse opinion upon the abovementioned compendium of the *Materia Medica*: " Although he " (Linnæus) has made laudable efforts to introduce indigenous offici- " nal plants instead of exotics, yet we cannot help owning that this work " is little worthy of its author*."

The genius which seemed so entirely created for systematic order and description, farther displayed its eminence in pathology, which is another branch of physic. The necessity of a system, of a general rule by which diseases might be known and discerned according to their difference and manifold variations, had frequently occurred to his penetrating mind. An habitual practice of near three years at *Stockholm*, gave him a favourable opportunity of collecting observations. Dr. Thomas Sydenham, the British Hippocrates, had already pointed out in the last century, the essential advantages of a systematical nosology. " It would be a very good thing," says he, " if all " the diseases were reduced to definite and certain species, with as " much accuracy as the botanists have done with regard to the descrip- " tion of plants. †" Many were the opinions which had been given respecting the best plan of nosology. Some classed the diseases (the first

* Quoique il a fait de louables efforts, pour substituer des plantes indigenes aux étrangères, nous ne pouvons dissimuler, que cette production est peu digne de son auteur. See *Eloge de* M. de Linne, *par* M. Vicq d'Azyr, in the *Histoire de la Societé de Medicine*, vol. ii. *A Paris*, 1780, in quarto.

† Expedit, ut morbi omnes ad definitas et certas species revocentur, eadem prorsus diligentia ac ἀκριβεία, qua id factum videmus a botanicis in suis phytologiis.

and

and most imperfect idea) in their alphabetical order, others from the time of their duration, others from those parts in which they affected the human body, or agreeable to the causes of their existence and symptoms.

According to this latter method the late professor DE SAUVAGES, one of the best friends of LINNÆUS in *France*, published in 1739 a valuable work, which was highly embellished on subsequent occasions *. But before ever LINNÆUS obtained any knowledge of this work, he himself planned a systematic abridgment of nosology to serve him in his lectures, published it 1759 as an academical dissertation, by the title of *Genera Morborum*, and in 1763 as a separate work.

The whole class of envious persons at *Upsal* and in other parts of *Sweden*, found it strange and heterogeneous at first, to see the botanist LINNÆUS appear on the scene as a pathologist. They made very merry at his expence. But the goodness of his cause soon became triumphant. Dr. ROSEN, his colleague, had long studied the LINNÆAN *Genera Morborum*, and a few years after, used them as the standing rule of his lectures †.

" Of all men," says M. VICQ D'AZYR, " LINNÆUS should have " been the last to write on subjects which were foreign to him; be- " cause he had recourse to that spirit of detail, and to that aphoristic " and figurative style, which were considered as defects even in those " works which established his reputation ‡.

---

* Nosologia Methodica, Mo...pel. 1739. *Amst.* 1763, 5 vol. 8vo.—Farther augmented *Amst.* 1768, 2 vol. 4to.—Castigavit et auxit C. F. Daniel, tom. iii. *Lips.* 1791.

† See LINNÆUS's own words in the Supplements.

‡ Il etoit moins permis a M. LINNE, qu'à tout autre d'écrire sur les objets, qui lui étoient étrangers; parce qu'il portoit cet esprit de détail et de stile aphoristique et figuré, que l'on a regardé come des defauts même dans les ouvrages quiont établi sa reputation,

This

This opinion is too much stamped with gallic levity to require any kind of apology here. Patriotism, and the penetrating knowledge of two meritorious Swedish literati * have already satisfactorily vindicated the honour of their immortal fellow-countryman from the obloquy of the French panegyrist. They wanted neither the inventive powers of logic, nor the strength of syllogisms, in accomplishing this laudable end. A plain statement of facts constituted the best defence. Upon the whole, M. Vicq d'Azyr had not read the writings of Linnæus with that competent accuracy which must otherwise have enabled him to see in a proper light his merits as a theoretical physician.

" The *Genera Morborum*," adds Vicq d'Azyr, " are a nosological " picture in which Linnæus lavishes such a jumble of unusual and bar- " barous terms to class the diseases and even the slightest indispo- " sitions, that, upon a thorough perusal, the number of ills which " afflict the human race seem at least augmented by one half†."

With regard to the barbarous terms, it is a chimerical wish, to re-quire every expression to be Ciceronian in a medical nomenclature, or in a nosological manual. Linnæus was more studious of the precision than of the beauty of words. In his general division of diseases he re-duced them to eleven classes, thirty-seven orders, and three hundred and twenty-five species. Professor De Sauvages had upon the whole eleven classes, forty-four orders, and three hundred and fourteen

* Dr. Blom, in a Swedish work entituled *Samling of R? · och Upsatter uti Physique, &c.* *Gottenburgh,* 1781.—and S. A. Hedin, first physician to the king, in his work of Quid Lin-næo Patri debeat.

† Qu'ils sont un Tableau Nosologique, dans lequel l'auteur a employé avec une sorte de profusion une foule de noms inusités et barbares, pour classer les maladies et même les incom-modités les plus legères, de sorte, qu'en le lisant, il semble, que le nombre des maux, dont l'espèce humaine est affligée, est au moins augmenté de moitié.

species. It is strange that the French critic, perhaps from motives of patriotic predilection, seems to forget here, that one of his own country-men had, like LINNÆUS, magnified the number of diseases which de-solate mankind.

In the opinion of Dr. WILLIAM CULLEN, that great professor of pathology and the *Materia Medica*, who died at *Edinburgh* February 5, 1790, the *Genera Morborum* of LINNÆUS was the second systematic nosology after that of DE SAUVAGES. And the latter in a subsequent edition of his work, adopted himself all the descriptions and the new species of LINNÆUS. All his celebrated successors in pathology, a VOGEL, a SELLE, a HAARTMAN, a DANIEL, acknowledged with gratitude and impartiality the merits which LINNÆUS had acquired by his first efforts and knowledge in that science.

LINNÆUS fraught afterwards his system of nosology upon a more detailed plan. He also gave lectures upon the various species of diseases *(Species Morborum*)*. This plan however remained a manuscript, from which he dictated to his students. The chief result of his medical observations and lectures he published in 1766, under the title of *Clavis Medicinæ Duplex, Exterior et Interior, Holm.* twenty-nine pages in octavo. This work, small as it was, became a compendium of the whole science, and an epitomical sketch of the virtues and effects of medicines. " It was like an *Ilias* in *Nuce*," says Dean BÆCK, " but a nut somewhat hard to be cracked to get at the kernel." LINNÆUS himself confessed that he bestowed much labour upon this little production, and that medicine would still require a man's whole life, before its

---

* The following was the principle of LINNÆUS : *Genera ex Signis, Species ex causis.*—Jam si genera morborum probe nosti, speciem e causa determines, & nunquam falleris, ubi hoc potes. Sed hoc opus, hic labor !—

secrets could be brought to light. Of all the lectures Linnæus, those which he delivered upon this compendium required the most unremitting attention. Diætetic—as another most interesting and most useful branch of medicine, also occupied Linnæus. His travels had enabled him to make many experiments and observations upon that branch of medical study. " This science," wrote he to Baron Haller in 1744, " makes my delight, I have " collected more in it than I know any other to have done *". The whole course of his † diætetic lectures lasted three years each time.

He did not publish any general works upon this branch of physic It was however enriched with a considerable number of fine treatises upon single subjects, for instance, such as on the utility of motion, on the diversity of aliments, on bread, on the eatable plants of *Sweden*, on tea, coffee, chocolate, &c. &c. These tracts were defended by his pupils whom he furnished with the materials. He also made himself equally conspicuous in what is properly called medicine.

* In his meæ deliciæ ; in his plura collegi quam, quod novi ullus alius.—Already in the year 1740, Linnæus wrote thus to Haller : " Quid in diæteticis colligo tandem videbis, " in his per decem annos laboravi."

† Dr. Hedin, first physician to the Court of *Sweden* expresses himself in his Treatise : Quid Linnæo patri debeat *Medicina*, Ups. 1784, in the following manner :—" Illa hæc " acies ingenii elucet, ut fidem omnino superet, Medicinam, quam artem semper conjectura- " lem statuunt ignorantes osores, sub—Linnæi—manibus speciem physicæ experimentalis " induisse et assertis æque exploratis superstructum. Diffidendum tamen non est, opus hocce, " licet omni et admiratione et attentione nostra dignissimum, summis quibusdam medicis ali- " quo jure videri et difficile omnino comprehensu et praxi forsitan m mi adaptatum. Verum in " rebus tantæ indaginis raro sibi sufficit ingenium mediocre, nisi filum hoc Ariadneum per ob- " scuros scientiæ mæandros ab ipso auctore illustrissimo sequi di ceret. Hinc e t, quod, " qui censores agere voluerunt, notam ignorantiæ suæ prodiderint, quum, quæ proposita " fuerint, se v x intellexisse coacti sint ; quod ipsi cont git *Domino* Vic d'Azyr, *Corticale* " *Vitale* (*Clavis Medie* p. 5.) per cutem reddenti. Cui quam absona sit idea *vitalis cor-* " *ticalis*, nullum vel leviter in re medica versatum, fugere potest ; unde nec mirum, si de " utilitate hujus operis æque absona sit conclusio."

This

This is a summary view of the labours by which LINNÆUS acquired his medical celebrity in *Sweden*, and by which he formed the
greatest part of the young Swedish practitioners*. We now return to
his chief study, to natural history. FLORA was the fair deity to
whom he did homage in his youth, and to whose service he most
zealously continued to devote himself even in his old age. " But one
" single reign of nature," continues DEAN BÆCK, the celebrated
Swedish panegyrist of LINNÆUS, " was too confined a sphere for him
" to move in. With the same spirit and success he made conquests
" equally great in the animal reign. This reign was covered with still
" greater darkness, and remained a chaos of intricacy and confusion.
" GESNER, ALDROVANDI, and RAY, had spread over it some small
" streaks of a dawning light, but through LINNÆUS alone it first ap-
" peared as a serene and resplendent day. His animal system con-

* Dr. HEDIN comprises the merits of LINNÆUS in the *Materia Medica*, and in medicine
at large, in the following nine points :

I. *Simplicium* exactissimum dedit cognitionem, et quoad principia Botanica et vires, quæ
hactenus omnino inter desiderata Materiæ Medicæ erant.

II. Dudum nota et usitata propius determinare et ad species referre docuit.

III. *Nova indigena* introduxit, vel *frequentius* usurpare docuit, quo simul medicinam
domesticam per Sueciæ regiones usitatam breviter exposuit, et loca natalia plantarum apud
nos indicavit.

IV. *Exotica*, quæ usus medici sunt vel detexit, vel determinavit, ut nobis jam constet,
vel quibus in casibus, omnem impleant indicationem, vel quibus etiam excipiantur apris suc-
cedaneis, in quorum investigationem quam maxime erat intentus.

V. *Simplicium*, quoad multitudinem nimiam et usum rariorem, rigidissimam instituit
censuram.

VI. In venenatorum inquisivit usum, et dosin sensim determinare docuit.

VII. *Culturam* plantarum medicinalium ad unguem perduxit.

VIII. Modum colligendi et methodum exhibendi Medicamenta proposuit.

IX. Medicamentorum compositorum usum restrinxit.

See HEDIN's Collectio Epistolarum LINNÆI; accedunt opuscula pro et contra LINNÆUM
scripta extra Sueciam rarissima, *Hamb.* 1792, 8vo.

3   " sisted

" sisted only of a few pages i   beginni   the twelfth and last
" edition which appeared at *Stockholm* in 1767, at the expiration of
" thirty years after its first appearance, formed two large volumes,
" All the creatures of the animal reign then known, were arranged in
" it with as much accuracy and precision as the plants had been
" described in his botanical works.   Every animal with its cha-
" racteristics, its synonymous and trivial names, its country and prin-
" cipal qualities, could easily be found in it.   He taught us to distin-
" guish the species of the serpents by the number of their shields or
" scales, the fishes by the position of their fins, and was the first who
" ranged in due order the insects, those dumb and deaf instruments of
" nature, which collect in much larger numbers than any other living
" animals, and are in general only known by the mischief which we
" accuse them of committing upon us."

L INNÆUS also introduced a more convenient method of ordering the
testaceous animals *.   The stone-plants or corals were even before his
time mixed with the zoophites, worms, and insects.   LINNÆUS pointed
out their distinctive marks, and all were thus put in their proper place.   All
the animated beings were described on that muster-roll in such a manner
that the lover of nature on the frigid coast of *Greenland* might learn to
know by it even the smallest butterfly in the regions of *India*.

The merits of L INNÆUS in Mineralogy were, doubtless, very shin-
ing and eminent.   He was the first who established the genera in that
science, and precisely indicated their characteristic signs.   His mi-

* " LINNÆUS," says CONDORCET in his panegyric, " might doubtless have employed
" with regard to the animals the system which he used for the plants, but he was appre-
" hensive, lest, in spite of all the modesty and gravity which appeared in his lessons and his
" works, that method should too frequently offer to his pupils, images which naturalists
" themselves cannot always have the privilege to contemplate with total indifference."

neral

neral system, which was the latest received in his code of nature, consisted at the last edition in 1768, of two hundred and thirty-six oĉtavo pages. The treasures of this reign of nature are divided by LINNÆUS into three different classes; namely, in stones *(Petræ)*, minerals *(Mineræ)*, and fossils *(Fossilia)*, the latter into various orders, and the whole into fifty-four genera. LINNÆUS gave a singular hypothesis respeĉting the origin of stones, which was peculiar to himself. In his opinion, the water is the *prima materia* of the earth, and its sediment is clay. If sea-water be mixed with rain-water, the salty particles of the brine settle at the bottom like sand. Rotten plants are changed into a black dustlike earth; but all that belongs to the animal reign turns into chalk. LINNÆUS assigns these as the four principal matters from which all the rest spring by crystallization, solution, &c. &c.

This hypothesis, like his classification of the mineral system, met with many contradiĉtions. It cannot be denied, that LINNÆUS displayed in this part of natural history of which the classification is most difficult, less greatness than he did in all his other works, and for that reason did not become its legislator. During the latter part of his life, and since his death, many discoveries have been made in mineralogy, deeper knowledge has been acquired, and new means devised*. His countrymen WALLERIUS CRONGSTAEDT, BERGMANN and his own pupil,

---

* "LINNÆUS," says CONDORCET in his Eulogium, " classed the minerals almost entirely
" by their external forms: the chymists have made objeĉtions to this method, which it is
" very difficult to answer; but the naturalists, or at least the pupils of LINNÆUS, might
" have made objeĉtions equally powerful against a system of which the chymical analysis
" formed the first charaĉters; in other respeĉts when LINNÆUS published his method, the
" analysis of mineral substances had not yet been brought to that degree of perfeĉtion to
" which one of his countrymen, the celebrated BERGMANN, has since brought it.

the

the late celebrated FERBER, had acquired great names and high distinction
in the various branches of mineralogy, which had been the principal object of their study. In the same manner has he been far excelled by one
of his former pupils professor FABRICUS, who became the most eminent
entomologist. How many discoveries have there not been made within
these twenty years in the vegetable and animal reigns! but how little
can those gradations of progress, for which thanks are chiefly due to
him, diminish his greatness! To presume to censure a first-rate genius,
because somebody existed after him, who in certain separate branches
signalized himself to a superior degree, would be like venting the invidious spleen of ARISTARCHUS, it would be signifying that merit
ought never to be acknowledged*. What LINNÆUS said respecting
CÆSALPINUS, may be applied with more extensive propriety to him-
himself:

Quantæ molis erat, Romanam condere gentem!

LINNÆUS had laid the foundation to the modern and beautiful structure of natural history. To finish that edifice could not be the work of
one man alone. It is a task never yet performed, and left for improvement to all future generations. In this point LINNÆUS did as much
as his situation would permit. In the years 1767 and 1771, he published supplements to his botanical descriptions, and after the year 1774
gave accounts of single plants which had been sent him by his pupils. .

* "The system of LINNÆUS," says M. CONDORCET, " has no doubt some weak sides ;
" but till now, no other method has combined so many advantages; perhaps even the defects
" for which that system is censured, are inevitable in all artificial methods. Ought we
" for this reason to proscribe them and condemn ourselves to err grappling in the dark, be-
" cause the light presented to us, may sometimes be extinguished."
See *Eloge* de M. LINNE, in the histoire de l'Acad. Roy. des Sciences *a Paris* 1781, 4to.
p. 74.

These were the last fruits of the activity of a man whose whole life had been uninterrupted enthusiasm and merit. Meanwhile his fame spread all over the world, nay farther, perhaps, than that of any learned man of our age ever reached. He was every where freely acknowledged and revered as the first man in the science which he cultivated. The different academies of *Europe* vied with each other, which of them should first have the honour of electing LINNÆUS one of their members. He experienced also the flattering distinction which had never before been the lot of any Northern genius, to be received in 1762, as an ordinary member of the Royal Academy of Sciences of *Paris*, after he had been its corresponding member ever since the year 1738. This, for a foreigner, was deemed a very particular mark of respect by Barons LEIBNITZ, HALLER, VAN SWIETEN, and the great anatomist MORGAGNI at *Padua**. The Royal Society of *London* followed this example in the year 1763. In 1762 LINNÆUS also became a member of the British Œconomical Society, and in 1772 Honorary Member of the Physical College at *Edinburgh*. The Academy of *Florence* chose him in 1759, that of *Drontheim* in 1766, that of *Cell* in 1767, that of *Rotterdam* in 1771, that of *Sienna* in the same year, and that of *Bern* in 1772. He was elected Fellow of the Royal Patriotic Society in *Sweden* in 1775, and shortly before his death also became a member of the Medical Society of *Paris (Societe de Medecine)* which was first first instituted in the year 1776. The greatest academy in a distant part of the world, that of *Philadelphia*, also brightened her records by

* The person who replaced LINNÆUS in the Royal Academy of Sciences of *Paris*, was Sir JOHN PRINGLE, Bart. The only eminent men in *Sweden*, who could boast of such an honour after the death of LINNÆUS, were professor BERGMANN and the Chevalier WARGENTIN.

the

the honour of his name, in 1770. Thus was he (comprising the other scientific bodies mentioned before) member of twenty academies, namely, of three in *Sweden*, three in *Germany*, one in *Switzerland*, two in *Holland*, three in *France*, three in *England*, three in *Italy*, one in *Denmark*, and one in *America*.

From the river *Neva* to the *Tagus* in *Europe*, and in every other part of the world where Nature had friends, the works of LINNÆUS became the compass of the study of natural history. When a great number of reforms were introduced in the year 1771 at the university of *Coimbra* in *Portugal*, under the direction of the Marquis DE POMBAL, the royal ordinance issued for that purpose expressly stated, " That the works of LINNÆUS should be the pattern and basis " of all botanical lectures, because he was the best and greatest author " in that science." A similar change took place in the Spanish universities *. If we quoted these two countries as examples, instead of any other, we did it because the scientific achievements of the rest of *Europe*, penetrate so seldom, or at least so late and with so much difficulty beyond the *Pyrenees*.

Thus LINNÆUS reaped most plentifully those laurels which were the end and just due of his long and studious perseverance. The termination of his career now formed the finest contrast with its beginning. After having crossed so many thorny paths, he obtained the seat of honour and enjoyed peaceful fortune. His was the joy, to see in the year

---

* The Spanish professor of botany, A. CAPDEVILA, writes on this head to Baron HALLER in 1772 as follows : " In physiologicis per illustrem HALLERUM ; in botanicis CAROLUM LINNÆUM sequimur. TOURNEFORTII rei Herbariæ Institutiones, et CAROLI LINNÆI Philosophiam Botanicam legimus et relegimus ; hanc præferimus illis ob summam doctrinam et eruditionem eximiam.—*Epistolæ ad* HALLERUM, vol. vi. p. 100.

1763, his son CHARLES LINNÆUS, then in the twenty-second year of his age, appointed assistant professor of botany, with the promise that he should once be his successor.

Among the learned of his own country, he was a phenomenon of the first magnitude. What FERNEY and BERN were on account of VOL-TAIRE and HALLER, the remote city of *Upsal* became in a similar pro-portion with regard to LINNÆUS. No foreigner of quality or of any literary eminence passed though *Upsal,* without wishing to see him. Strangers of all denominations gave him the most flattering proofs of respect. Lord BALTIMORE, whose great fortune corresponded with his love of natural history, went from *Stockholm* to *Upsal* merely for the purpose of seeing LINNÆUS. He viewed the LINNÆAN collec-tions and after a few hours conversation with our luminary, conceived so high an esteem for him as to present him with a valuable gold snuff box set in diamonds. His Lordship's liberality and munificence did not stop here. On his travels through *Germany* he sent LINNÆUS a service of silver plate, or what the French call a *necessaire,* worth 2000 rix dollars, or upwards of three hundred pounds sterling. Such an act of munificence can only be the result of the generous sublimity of mind which so peculiarly characterises the inhabitants of the British isles.

LINNÆUS also received many proofs of the liberality and attach-ment of the richer class of his foreign pupils. Among the latter Messrs. DEMEDOROS and DEMIDOFFS, the sons of two most respectable and wealthy Russian families, signalized themselves in a peculiar manner. Owing to the universal love which LINNÆUS had gained, he even be-came the benefactor of his countrymen in our time. When the Swe-dish officers and soldiers, taken prisoners and dispersed over the Russian empire, in the late war, were exchanged in 1790, and at liberty to return to their country through *St. Petersburgh*, they met with the greatest support and encouragement, especially on the part of DE-MIDOFF, who resided in that metropolis, and exerted himself by rendering every service to those unfortunate Swedish warriors, whose gallantry he esteemed, and of whose country he still retained the most grateful remembrance.

The salary which LINNÆUS enjoyed, the property which he had acquired by his marriage, and the presents which were sent him by his pupils and admirers, made him one of the richest and most monied among the professors and inhabitants of *Upsal*. His annual stipend amounted to seven hundred *platens* or florins. To these may be added one hundred tons of corn and about twenty tons more, which were the produce of a prebendary estate; making altogether an annual income of about five hundred Swedish rix dollars, sometimes more and sometimes less, according to the price of the corn. During the latter part of his life the late King allowed him a double salary *. To these resources ought also to be joined the produce of his numerous writings, of which LAURENCE SALVIUS, a man of merit at *Stockholm*, was generally the editor, and by the care of the same person the first literary journal was introduced in *Sweden* in 1745, under the title of *Larda Tidningar.*

* The Chevalier THUNBERG thus expresses himself in a letter to the author from *Upsal*: " Professio Botanices quotannis LINNÆO hosce suppeditavit reditus: Frumenti 100, ut vocant " *tonnas*, et argenti 700 *(platar)* florenos, reditus villæ dictæ *Prabendebemman*, circiter " 20 tonnas frumenti, quod quidem censeri potest circiter 500 *Rdal* Succ. plus aut minus, " prout frumentum quotannis majori vel minori pretio vendebatur: ultimis tamen annis, ex " augustissimi regis gratia, in duplo LINNÆUS fruitus est hocce salario."

" REDITUS," says Professor THUNBERG, in another letter to the author, " Professionis " Botanices præter ædes publicas censentur circa 500 Imperiales Succ."

SALVIUS paid LINNÆUS for each printed sheet of his original works only the small sum of one ducat. But if it be considered, that on account of the small population in that vast kingdom, no great number of individuals are scientific readers, our surprise at so scanty a sum paid for such original works as those of LINNÆUS, will certainly abate. The foreign booksellers chiefly found his works the most profitable and most advantageous; and some of them still reap benefits from him, even after his death. Had LINNÆUS, as an author, received those sums which the publication of his works and their manifold editions yielded to the booksellers of every country, those alone must have made him worth a capital sum.

That rural amenity which always possessed the greatest charms in the eyes of the eminent men of all nations, and which may be looked upon as the just reward of merit in the decline of life—the possession of a villa—was also one of the first wishes of him who occupied himself solely with nature. Soon did his prosperous and flourishing circumstances gratify him with the accomplishment of this wish; he purchased the villa of *Hammarby*, at the distance of one league from *Upsal*. During the fifteen last years of his life he mostly chose it for his summer residence. There he kept, comparatively speaking, a little university. His pupils followed him thither, and those who were foreigners used to rent lodgings in the villages of *Honby* and *Edeby*, which were both contiguous to his villa. In 1769 he had a little edifice erected at the distance of a quarter of a league from his rural abode, upon an eminence, which commanded the prospect of that whole district. In this place he kept his collection of natural history, upon the contents of

x   which

which he delivered his lectures*.   He afterwards destined this country
seat as a dowry for his consort, who came to inhabit it after his decease.
He purchased at a subsequent period another villa of less extent called
Soefja.

The university of *Upsal* had the honour of having the late King of
Sweden, then Prince Royal, for its Chancellor, from 1764 to 1771.
This distinction it also enjoys at present in the heir of his throne.   When
GUSTAVUS went to *Upsal* he never left that place without favouring its
first genius with a long conversation or with a visit, which his Majesty
even frequently paid him at *Hammarby*.

During the late King's residence at *Paris*, LOUIS XV. congratulated
him upon the celebrated man whom his country possessed, and gave
orders to collect the seeds of the rarest plants in his celebrated gardens
at *Trianon*, as a present for LINNÆUS.   When GUSTAVUS returned
he took upon him the reins of government, which had devolved to his
care by the demise of his parent.   The present of seeds made by
LOUIS were punctually forwarded to LINNÆUS.

His Majesty, some time after his accession to the throne, came again
to *Upsal*.   After a period of upwards of thirty years academical services, LINNÆUS then intreated him, graciously to be pleased to accept
of his resignation.

But it was in vain for our luminary to represent, that the infirmities
incident to old age incapacitated him from being farther useful to the
university; his plea was rejected by the flattering objection, that *Upsal*

---

* He delivered those lectures to his foreign pupils who came in the summer from the villages to his museum, not in the grave and solemn habit of a professor, but as a friendly companion, frequently wearing his *robe de chambre*, slippers, a red fur cap, &c. &c.

ought

ought not to lose its chief splendor by his retreat. The King, at the same time made great amends to LINNÆUS, by rewarding him, as we have observed, with a double salary, and making him a present of two farms, with liberty to bequeath them to his heirs.

Two other great rulers of the North emulated the King of *Sweden*, by giving proofs of their respect to the celebrated professor at *Upsal*. The Empress of *Russia*, who, as judge of superior merit, became its remuneratrix, almost among every nation in *Europe*, sent presents to LINNÆUS. The King of *Denmark* zealously followed her example. MARIA THERESA, Empress of *Germany* and Queen of *Hungary*, and the King of *Sardinia*, complimented the Swedish ambassadors and other grandees who visited their courts, upon possessing a LINNÆUS, who was the pride of their country. FREDERICK THE GREAT, King of *Prussia*, also spoke in the highest terms of encomium of the prince of botany. Thus the son of a village preacher, whom persons jealous of his fame at *Stockholm*,—whom a SIEGESBECK and others wanted to turn into ridicule on account of his reforms,—thus was LINNÆUS honoured and revered by the greatest sovereigns of the age.

A philosopher, though not the most eminent, yet one of the most extraordinary of this century, J. J. ROUSSEAU, of *Geneva*, worshipped LINNÆUS as his idol. Having already adduced an instance of his enthusiasm for our luminary, we will communicate here by way of farther characteristic, the conversation which BJOERNSAHL had with him at *Paris* in the year 1770 *. " When I was with ROUSSEAU for the first " time," writes BJOERNSTAHL, " he asked me, if I studied botany?

* See BJOERNSTAHL's Letters, vol. i.

" Having

" Having told him that LINNÆUS had given me lessons at different
" times, he rose and exclaimed, " You know then my master and pro-
" fessor, the great LINNÆUS? If you write to him, assure him of my
veneration, and throw me prostrate before him—*(Et mettez moi a genoux*
" *devant lui).*—Tell him, that I know no greater man on earth; that I
owe him my health, nay, even my life." ROUSSEAU afterward shewed
" me LINNÆUS's *Philosophia Botanica,* saying, " This book contains
" more knowledge than the largest folio volumes. The books which
" come from the north generally abound with too much learning; but
" this one does not contain a single word which might be considered as
" unnecessary."—Such a panegyric from the mouth of the philosopher
" of *Geneva,* whose taciturnity seldom indulged itself in such flattering
" praise, struck me with unexpected surprise. At the name of LIN-
NÆUS he appeared to be quite enraptured; " I am (said he) a pupil of
" LINNÆUS, and deem it an honour." I asked him, what he thought
" of ADANSON? He answered, that the latter and CRANZ at *Vienna,*
" had both borrowed all their knowledge of LINNÆUS, and had
" attempted afterwards to lessen and calumniate his name, and been
" guilty of ingratitude to their master."

So lively a genius as that of LINNÆUS could never remain inactive.
His zeal continued as long as nature left any vitals in his frame. Even
in the year 1773 he took a share in an enterprise by which the late
King of *Sweden* distinguished the beginning of his reign as a lover of
science. A committee was appointed, consisting of six bishops, six
doctors in divinity, and eight other literati, charged with a better translation of the Bible into the Swedish language, and LINNÆUS was
chosen a member of this committee, for the purpose of ascertaining and

describing

describing the plants and other vegetable productions mentioned in the holy scriptures *. The late Chevalier MICHAELIS at *Goettingen*, whose dogmatic had been formerly confiscated in *Sweden*, and publicly burnt at *Upsal*, was also consulted in this enterprise.

Among all the learned of the north, LINNÆUS had the most extensive correspondence throughout *Europe*, and even in the other parts of the world. None but the greatest men whom this century produced with regard to the sciences, such as HALLER, BOERHAAVE and VOLTAIRE could come in competition with him in this particular. Some time before his death he made out a list of those men with whom he used to keep a regular correspondence. Agreeable to this list he corresponded with the following persons in *Germany*: The Margravine CAROLINA LOUISA of *Baden*, BASTER, VON BERGEN, BREYN and BRUCKMANN, at *Brunswick*; Count BRUMMER, BURKHARD, BUCHNER, and Professor J. A. GESNER at *Tubingen*; Professor GLEDITSCH at *Berlin*; Baron HALLER at *Goettingen*; Professor HEBENSTREIT at *Leipsic*; Professors HERRMANN and JACQUIN at *Vienna*; Professor GIESEKE and Doctors JÆNISCH, KAST, KOELPIN and KOHL at *Hamburgh*; Professor JOHN LANGE at *Halle*; Professor LESKE at *Leipsic*; LESSER, LEHMANN, LUDOLFF and Professor LUDWIG of the same place; J. E. MEYER and Dr. MOEHRING at *Yevern*; Counsellor VON MURR at *Nurenberg*; Professor MURRAY at *Goettingen*; Baron OTTO VON MUNCHAUSEN, MYLIUS, SCOPOLI, and Counsellor SCHREBER at *Erlangen*; SPENGLER and SPRECKELSEN at *Hamburgh*; WAGNER, WEIGEL, WEISSMANN and X. WULFEN. His correspondents in *Denmark* were, Messrs. ASCANIUS, Professor BRUNNICH, BUCH-

* See S. LONBOM's Utkast om Svenska Bibel Oefversatingar. *Stockb.* 1774, octavo.

WALD, and Professor FABRICIUS at *Kiel*; Professor FRUS ROTTBOEL, GUNNERUS, GUNTHER, Professor HORREBOW, C. F. HOLM, Professor KRATZENSTEIN, Professor O. F. MULLER, Mr. NEIBUHR, Professor OEDER, VON SUHM, Professor WAHL. and Counsellor ZOEGA at *Copenhagen*. In *Russia*, Professor AMMAN DEMIDOFF, DOMACHNEFF, GMELIN, KRASCHENNINNIKOW, LAXMAN, MOUNSEY, G. MULLER; and in the beginning SIEGESBECK. In *Great Britain*, Mr. ANDREW, Sir JOSEPH BANKS, Lord BALTIMORE, Dr. BROWNE, CHANNING, COLLINSON, Professor DILLENIUS, DONELL, EHRET, J. ELLIS, sen. Mr. FORSTER, as long as he resided in *England*, Dr. FOTHERGILL, Mr. GORDON, Dr. HILL, Professor HOPE of *Edinburgh*, HUDSON, LAWSON, LEE, Dr. LETTSOM, LIND, J. and PH. MILLER, MITCHEL, Mr. PENNANT, Dr. RUSSEL, Professor SIBTHORP of *Oxford*, SKENE, WALKER, WARNER, Rev. JOHN WHITE, of *Blackburne*, and Mr. WRIGHT *. In *Holland*, Professor ALLEMAND of *Leyden*; Professor BODDAERT at *Utrecht*; BOERHAAVE, BURMANN, at *Amsterdam*; CLIFFORT, J. VAN GORTER, Professor at *Harderwyck*; GRONOV at *Leyden*; VAN ROYEN, ROELL, VAN SWIETEN, VOESMAER and Professor WACHENDORFF. In *France*, Messrs. ANGERVILLE, BARRERE, DE BOMARE, DUCHESNE, CARRERE, CHARDON, CUSSON, GUAN, of *Montpellier*; GUETTARD, A. and B. DE JUSSIEU, LE MONNIER, MAYNARD, F. DE SAUVAGES, and the Abbé DE SAUVAGES. In *Spain*, Messrs. BARNHARDES, HORTEGA, QUER and MINNART. In *Switzerland*, Professors JOHN GESNER and SCHEUCHZER. In *Italy*, Messrs. BRUNELLI, DONATI, RATHGEB, the Austrian minister at

---

* Many of the above names are totally unknown to the Translator, who trusts his readers will excuse him if he does not prefix to the name of each person the respective title.

Venice,

Venice, Count SAGRAMOSO, SEGUIER, VANDELLI and Dr. TURRA. In *Turkey,* MORDAC. M'KENZIE. In *America,* BARTHRAM, CLAYTON, Miss COLDEN, Doctor GARDEN, of *South Carolina*; LOGAN BARTCH at *Surinam*; and MUTIS in *New Grenada.* In *Asia,* J. G. KOENIG at *Tranquebar*; and Messrs. RADEMACHER and NORDGREEN.

How much more would this list of one hundred fifty names be increased, would and could we add to it those persons to whom LINNÆUS sent single letters from *Sweden* and other countries, for the sake of making enquiries, or for similar purposes. It is to be regretted, that the correspondence of LINNÆUS, which was solely carried on to promote natural history, has not yet been published, at least in a select collection. That those letters would prove particularly interesting to botanists is a fact which precludes every doubt. LINNÆUS carefully preserved his letters, and they are actually in possession of Dr. J. E. SMITH*.

A Livonian, who travelled in *Sweden* in 1771, and visited *Upsal* on purpose that he might see LINNÆUS, gives the following account of our luminary's situation at that time, and likewise of his collections :

" Sir CHARLES LINNÆUS received me with great complaisance.
" He led a very bustling and active life; and I never saw him at lei-
" sure ; even his walks had for their object discoveries in natural his-
" tory. His collection of shells was very numerous, and consisted of the

___

* " I have long ago intimated this wish to Dr. SMITH, and he flatters me with its gratifi-
" cation some day by the following answer which he kindly returned to my letter : " The
" letters of LINNÆUS," says Dr. SMITH, " are about 3000. I project a publication of
" some of the correspondence some day; but it will require a careful revision before I give
" them to the public. I would not imitate the — — publication of HALLER's letters."
From a Letter of Dr. SMITH's to the Author.

" rarest

" rarest articles. His *herbarium* contained even then 7000 specimens,
" some of which were extremely scarce and curious. The plants are ar-
" ranged according to his own excellent system, and preserved in two
" presses divided into shelves, as he describes them in his *Philosophia*
" *Botanica.* His collection of fishes which he kept pasted on paper, was
" also considerable. He had, moreover, a numerous and choice col-
" lection of stones and fossils. But nothing could be compared with
" his collection of insects, in which not a single insect till then disco-
" vered in *Sweden* was wanting; and which contained likewise a great
" number of rare specimens from *China*, *Palestine*, *Surinam*, and almost
" from every quarter of the globe. He had also a good number of skele-
" tons and stuffed animals of the most curious kinds. His library is very
" numerous. In the hall of his dwelling house there are painted por-
" traits of several celebrated naturalists and botanists, and the plans of
" the most celebrated botanical gardens."

In the spring of 1772, the Chevalier MURRAY paid a visit to LIN-
NÆUS.—" Even then," says the Chevalier, when speaking of this visit,
" I found in that great man the same alacrity and vivacity of mind, and
" the same zeal to promote his favourite science, which I had formerly
" admired in him as a youth, and as his disciple. With regard to
" his opponents, who wished to diminish his celebrity, I found in him
" those sentiments of placability, and in general, that equity of opinion
" respecting the merits of other men, which, had they been heard, even
" by the most unjust and most rigorous critics, must necessarily have
" conciliated to him their love and affection *.

LINNÆUS

* *Eam tum in summo viro animi viriumque integritatem floremque, et illum in scientia sua*
locupletanda ardorem cognovi, quem juvenis olim et auditor miratus fueram ; et illum simul
in.

LINNÆUS gave even so late as 1772, a fine proof of the lasting vigour of his genius, which encompassed all nature; and at the same time of that liveliness of fancy which heightened the charms of his ideas. When he resigned on the 14th of December his functions of Rector of the University, which he had thrice exercised, he made an oration on the delights of nature, *(Deliciæ Naturæ).* He had composed this oration in a short time, though overwhelmed with a variety of other important business. The whole academical forum found it so beautiful, that the students of all the Swedish provinces sent deputies to him on the next day to intreat him to translate it into the Swedish tongue from the Latin. This was the fifth public oration of LINNÆUS, the first he made when he resigned his office as president of the Royal Academy at *Stockholm;* the second he delivered in 1741, the third in 1743, and the fourth in presence of the Royal Family of *Sweden* in 1759. He was no professed orator; but his language was that of nature and truth. Without displaying the embellishments and the art of a CICERO or a DEMOSTHENES this oration also captivated by its simplicity and energy, and occasioned rapturous admiration. As in his writings and in the professorial chair, so was he in his speeches, that systematic man, who concatenated phrase with phrase, and showed plainly the progressive course of his ideas. Nothing but death could dissolve his love and fondness of science, and his desire of obtaining the most minute knowledge of nature. In 1773 he wrote the following letter to Mr. PENNANT, the celebrated British Zoologist at *Lon-*

in adversarios, famæ ejus insidiantes, expertus sum in eo animum placabilem, et æquum in universum de aliorum meritis judicium, ut vel iniquissimus vel morosissimus censor hæc audiens, in amorem ejus raperetur necesse esset.—MURRAY in his Preface to the *Systema Vege-tabilium.*

don,

don, which will serve to illustrate and to characterize his liberality of mind.

Upsal, May 2, 1773 *.

" Long ago have I been informed, that my countryman Dr. TROIL
" has brought with him your presents, which I so eagerly expected.
" He lastly arrived here the day before yesterday, and delivered me
" your *Synopsis Quadrupedum* and your *Indian Zoology*. I return you
" my warmest thanks for each. I will peruse and re-peruse your *Sy-*
" *nopsis* a thousand times. I find much beauty and utility in it, and
" will study it thoroughly. After having read the work, I will ask
" you many questions, and never prove ungrateful to you. I will
" enter into no dispute about methods. Whether nature is Lutheran
" Calvinistic, Jewish, or Mahometan is all one to me, and the know-
" ledge of the species is the only thing I shall look to. I wish to God
" I could see your other works, especially that on birds, how much
" knowledge, which I am still deprived of, might I collect from them!
" Your INDIAN ZOOLOGY is a very beautiful work, with excellent
" figures of the rarest birds, and with the most accurate descriptions.
" Farewell—you'll hear more from me next time, &c. &c."

---

* Diu audivi, D. TROIL secum adduxisse dona tua, quæ avidissime expectavi. Redux tandem pridie ad nos accessit et mihi obtulit Synopsin tuam *of Qudruapeds*. (Chester 1771, in 8vo. with plates) et Zoologiam Indicam (*Lond.* 1769, in fol. with coloured plates). Pro singulis grates reddo, quas unquam possini calidissimas. Synopsin tuam legam et relegam millies. Multa in ea occurrent lectu mihi jucundissima et maxime utilia, quæ in succum et sanguinem vertam. Perfecto hoc opere, multa a te quæram; nec unquam nie ingratum senties. Non de methodo disputabo; mihi perinde erit, utrum naturæ color sit Lutheranus, Calvinianus, Judaicus aut Mahometanus: unice notitiam specierum quæram. O, utinam viderem reliqua opera tua, imprimis de avibus; quam multa inde addiscerem, quæ etiamnum me fugiunt! tua *Indian Zoology* perpulchra erat, pulcherrimæ figuræ rarissimarum certe avium, descriptiones etiam exactissimæ. Vale! &c.

Though

Though the enthusiastic violence with which L i n n æ u s exerted himself, and the excessive study of nature, which made him forget all other concerns, would often times prove detrimental to his health,— yet the charms of nature as frequently helped to restore it to its pristine vigor.   When he completed his *Philosophia Botanica*, in the summer of 1751, and in the following year, he had a most violent fit of the gout, and was obliged to keep to his bed almost totally deprived of the use of his limbs.   It was at this period, that his pupil K a l m returned from *North-America* with a great number of new plants and other natural curiosities.   The desire of seeing these treasures, and the delight which he felt when he actually saw them, was so great, as to make the gout fortunately disappear*.   The composition of the *Species Plantarum*, the most excellent and most laborious of his works, occasioned also an illness, which served to accelerate his death.   The constant silence which attended his studies, brought on the stone and the most excruciating pains in his right side.   When his pupil Ro- l a n d e r, returned from *Surinam*, he felt the liveliest sensations of joy.   R o l a n d e r had brought with him the Cochineal-tree *(Coffus Cochenillifer)*, on which were to be seen alive the insects from which the red colour used in dying scarlet is extracted.   This joy was however soon changed into the deepest sadness, owing to a mistaken care-

---

* The celebrated P e t e r W a r g e n t i n, Secretary of the Royal Academy at *Stockholm*, who died in 1783, wrote on this subject to B a r o n H a l l e r, August 12, 1751.—
   " Sane L i n n æ u m, jam hypochondrico malo et doloribus podagricis agonizantem re-
" suscitavit K a l m i u s, ostendendo solummodo insignem numerum plantarum rarissimarum,
" et quæ nondum ab alio Botanico fuerunt descriptæ.   Tantus amor florum !"
   L i n n æ u s himself related afterwards this occurrence to a friend in the following words:—
" K a l m i u s hic appulerat, altercque die monstrabat thesauros collectos.   Ego *parum* ad-
" *spexi*, quum in lecto me vertere non possem, sed tamen mirum in modum iis, quæ vidi,
" delectabar, idque ad reparandam sanitatem multum contulit."

fulness.

fulness. The tree had been removed to the botanical garden. Before
the gardener had received any instructions respecting its management,
he observed the insects, which were creeping upon its leaves, and
deeming them to be the destruction of the leaves, he gathered them
with great trouble and care, killed them, and thus annihilated the great
and bright hope which L I N N Æ U S had conceived of introducing cochi·
neal as a natural production into *Sweden*. This accident caused so
much derangement in his frame, as to be followed by a most violent
nervous head·ach.

Nature again operated by her magic power upon his health, even
when it was quite impaired and reduced in the year 1774*. Lieut. Col.
D A H L B E R G, who was afterwards knighted, returned from *Surinam*,
where he had remained for a considerable time on his estates, and brought
with him one hundred and eighty-six species of curious plants, the production of that country, as a present for the King of *Sweden*. They
had been preserved in a quite new and excellent way, in spirits of
wine, and still bore the fresh appearance of nature to such a degree,
that the most minute part of their flowers could be accurately examined. The King resolved to make a present of this valuable collection to the great naturalist of his empire, persuaded that there was

* L I N N Æ U S was in this instance exactly in the same situation as J. J. R O U S S E A U, who
wrote in 1767, in his moments of melancholy, the following letter :—" *Je dois ma vie aux*
" *plantes*; ce n'est pas ce que je leur dois du bon ; mais je leur dois, de conler encore avec
" agrément quelques intervalles, au milieu des amertumes, dont elle est inondée. Tant
" *que j'herborise, je ne suis pas malheureux* ; *et je vous réponds, si l'on me laissoit faire, je*
" *ne cesserai tout le reste de ma vie d'herboriser du matin au soir.*—J'herboriserai, mon cher
" hôte, jusqu' à la mort et au délà : *car s'il y a des fleurs aux champs Elysées,* j'en formerai
" des couronnes pour les hommes vrais, francs et tels, qu' assurément j'avois merité d'en
" trouver sur la terre."—See second Supplement à la collection des Oeuvres de J. J. R O U S·
S E A U, tom. iii. *Genève* 1789, p. 305 and 409.

none to whom it would prove more interesting. LINNÆUS penetrated with sensations of gratitude, composed a catalogue of those plants, which contained thirteen new genera, and upwards of forty new species. At the same time, he assigned the name of his royal benefactor to an American tree, whose beauty and loftiness corresponded with the greatness of he person whose name it bore*. He called this tree *Gustavia Augusta.*—This new appellation was the more expressive of his respect for his sovereign, as he had never before introduced the name of any monarch in the vegetable reign.

LINNÆUS, the darling of nature, was not so fortunate as FONTENELLE, HALLER, and VOLTAIRE, in finding her propitious to him till his last moment. His great mind, the energy and powers of his faculties, sunk into such a deep decline, that towards the last stage of his life, he was reduced to the helpless and feeble state of an infant. His fate was similar to, nay worse still than that of FRANKLIN. The two last years of his existence were, it might be said, but a slow and lingering obstinate struggle with death. While he gave lectures in the month of May 1774, in the botanical graden, he had an apopleĉic stroke, and fell into a swoon from which he did not recover for a long time†.

This

---

* Plantæ Surinamenses, *Upsal* 1775; resp. J. ALM; in the Amœnitat. Acad. Edit. Schrebers, vol. viii.

† A letter which LINNÆUS had written thirty-four years before this castastrophe, is said to have either occasioned or accelerated this fatal disease. In 1773 appeared the first volume of the letters, written in Latin, by men of literary eminence to BARON HALLER. LINNÆUS received this volume, and found that his letters and those particulars of his youth which he had formerly entrusted to sacred friendship and confidence were all inserted. Amongst others, he read with indignant surprise, a letter in which he had formerly described the history of his love, and added many other private transactions. (See *Epist. ad* HALLER. tom. i. p. 413, *Seq.*)—He had no sooner read this letter than he felt an extreme agitation, the apoplexy succeeded

This was the period at which his health declined entirely. In his younger days, he used to be afflicted with catarrhs and the tooth-ach, and in his maturity with the most violent meagrim ; but he now began to complain of a pain in the lower part of his back in his loins. In the year 1774 Mr. PENNANT, the celebrated Zoologist wrote to him, to intreat him not to forget his promise of writing the natural history of Lapland, which he had first made in the preface of his Flora Lapponica. The answer which LINNÆUS returned to Mr. PENNANT's request purported : " that it " would now be too late for him to begin.—Nunc nimis sero inciperem."

> " Me quoque debilitat series immensa laborum ;
> " Ante meum tempus cogor et esse senex."

His public activity continued however to last till 1776, when he had attained the 68th year of his age. Then the feeble and infirm state of his health suffered a fresh shock; his senses then seemed to be worn out, and his tongue, palsied as it were, almost denied its office. With that natural flow of chearfulness which was so peculiar to him, he thus describes his situation in his own diary:—" LINNÆUS " limps, can hardly walk, speaks unintelligibly, and is scarce able to " write."—Even in this melancholy and painful state, nature still remained his only comfort and relief. He used to be carried to his museum, where he viewed the treasures which he had collected with

ceeded soon after.—Such was the general assertion and inference of a great number of persons, when this melancholy accident happened at Upsal.—A celebrated foreigner, who was there at that time, seems to question that the publication of the letters written to HALLER should have had so fatal an influence upon the life of LINNÆUS;—" I do neither believe, nor have " I observed," says he, " that LINNÆUS felt any particular vexation at the printing of his " letters to HALLER."—It would be much more pleasant to us to refute than confirm such a disagreeable incident.

so

so much labour, and manifested a particular delight in examining the rarities and new productions, which during the latter part of his life had been brought him by M. MUTIS from *Carthagena* and *New Grenada*, and by his other pupils from the *Cape* of *Good Hope* and *Asia*.

In the winter of 1776, his deplorable condition rose to the highest degree of wretchedness. He had another apopleftic stroke, which almost deadened his right side, in which he had most frequently felt the pains. His situation exhibited the most melancholy picture of the decay of the human powers and greatness. His intellectual faculties wasted away like his body. The words which he uttered, HE, who in the prime of life had been the most systematic genius of this age, were for the most part a chaos of confused and unconnected ideas*. It now became necessary to lead, support, carry, dress and feed him by putting the viands into his mouth. His life began to prove an intolerable burthen. Having been a prey to such agonizing sufferings for upwards of a twelvemonth, and his illness having reached the climax of the most excruciating torture, occasioned by a fever and the stone, the GREAT LINNÆUS expired in a gentle slumber, in the afternoon, on the 10th of January 1778, after having led a life equally active and meritorious, of seventy years, seven months, and seven

---

* The following occurrence will farther serve to explain the miserable situation of LINNÆUS at the above mentioned epoch.—Those who are acquainted with the general customs of *Germany* and the rest of the Northern continent, well know, that every person of the better class keeps a memorial-book, in which it is usual for every stranger or friend of respectability to write down something to preserve his remembrance in the mind of the person who presents the book. On the 26th of September 1776, a foreign literatus laid before LINNÆUS his memorial-book. The latter having set down his name in it, scribbled underneath the word *Professor*, in the following mixed Greek and Latin letters:

Ρ ϙ ο φ ε ʃ ʃ o r.

The Author copied this from an authentic document.

days. With him died the most immortal man, whom his country ever yielded to the sciences. The year of his death was remarkable for the exit of several other great men. Voltaire and J. J. Rousseau died in that same year, and Haller terminated his bright career one month sooner than Linnæus, on the 12th of December 1777.

The death of Linnæus was an universal loss to the science of natural history—a loss to the University of Upsal, of which he had been the most celebrated professor for whole centuries, nay, since its very existence;—and, finally, a loss to the Swedish nation at large, which claimed him as her fellow-citizen. The mourning of the University was due to the great splendor which had fled with his spirit. His corpse was most solemnly removed to the cathedral of Upsal, and there committed to the tomb. All the professors, officers and students of the University followed his funeral;—and eighteen doctors, formerly pupils of Linnæus supported the pall. The Academy of Belles Lettres, History and Antiquities at Stockholm, which was instituted in 1753 and renewed in 1786, offered a golden prize medal worth sixteen ducats, for the best panegyric on Linnæus, either in verse or in prose, written in Latin, French or Italian. Already in 1786, a French specimen was sent in; but it afforded as little satisfaction as those which were delivered some time after. The Academy by command of the late King, offered a second golden prize-medal for the best Latin or Swedish inscription, to be engraved upon the monument which has since been erected to Linnæus, at the entrance of the new botanical garden* In the year 1781 a specimen appeared, but its composition

did

* The Author received the following letter on this subject, dated Upsal 1790:—" Rex noster " Augustissimus, proposito in Academia Regia Litterarum Humaniorum, Historiarum et Anti-
2   " quitatum

did not obtain the approbation of that learned body. Many other essays were afterwards delivered, but would not answer. At last, the academy received an elegant inscription, which was sent with the motto : " *At Pia Thura feram.*"—It was the production of Mr. GUNNAR BACK-MANN, a Swedish literatus, to whom the prize medal was adjudged according, by the academy at their meeting, held March 20th, 1792; and this inscription has been engraved upon the monument †.

The late KING, whose merits were so great, and who had esteemed LINNÆUS while he still was PRINCE ROYAL, and rewarded him as King, conferred farther honours upon his memory. When the Swedish diet was convened for the second time during his reign in the year 1778, he ordered his chancellor, at the opening of the *Pleni Plenorum,* or the four states of the kingdom, to read a sketch of his government and enterprises, during the six preceding years. In this sketch his Majesty mentioned the death of LINNÆUS in the following honourable and flattering manner :

" The University of *Upsal* has also attracted my attention. Always " will I remember with pleasure, that the chancellorship of that Univer-" sity was entrusted to me, before I ascended the throne ; I have also

" quitatum Stockholmiensi, duplici præmio et exteros et Indigenas ad certamen vocavit, tam " ad consignandum EULOGIUM LINNÆI, quam adi nscriptionem monumenti, in ejus honorem " erigendi, quorum tamen neutrum hoc usque tale Academiæ exhibitum est, ut præmio ornari " potuerit, Erigetur vero monumentum lapideum vel bustum LINNÆI in frontispicio novarum " ædium Horti et professionis Botanicæ nostræ Academiæ, quæ regiis impensis magnifice nunc " exstruuntur."

† Since the death of the late KING, the admirers of LINNÆUS in *Sweden* have raised a public subscription throughout the kingdom, to erect him a monument of Swedish norphyzy to LINNÆUS in the cathedral at *Upsal.* The CHEVALIER SERGELL has been charged with its execution, and considerable sums had already been subscribed in the beginning of 1794.

" in-

" instituted there a new professorship.—BUT. I HAVE LOST, ALAS !
" A MAN, WHOSE CELEBRITY WAS AS GREAT ALL OVER THE WORLD
" AS THE HONOUR WAS BRIGHT WHICH HIS COUNTRY DERIVED
" FROM HIM AS A CITIZEN. LONG WILL UPSAL REMEMBER THE
" CELEBRITY WHICH IT ACQUIRED BY THE NAME OF A LINNÆUS !"

On the 5th of December in the same year, the KING W. himself
present at the meeting of the Royal Academy of Sciences, when DEAN
BÆCK, one of the oldest friends of LINNÆUS, delivered the commemoration speech, which we had already occasion thus frequently to
mention in this work. The KING also rendered farther homage to the
merits of LINNÆUS by a gold medal which he ordered to be struck.
It was executed by the masterly hand of LYNNGBERGER, one of the
first artists Sweden ever produced. On one side the medal represented
the portrait of LINNÆUS, with the *Linnæa Borealis*, encompassed with
this inscription :

" CAROLUS LINNÆUS, ARCH. REG. EQUES AURATUS." On the
other side appears the figure of CYBELE, or nature in a sad and mourn-
ful posture, holding a key in her left hand, and surrounded with animals, plants, and other emblems of natural history. Among the animals a bear is to be distinguished, on whose back jumps an ape ;—
this is probably an allusion to the following latin words, already mentioned at the conclusion of Sect. VI. of this biography :—" *ringentium*
" *Satyrorum cachinnos, meisque humeris insilientium Cercophithecorum*
" *exultationes sustinui*."—It was in these words, our readers will remember, LINNÆUS had described his conduct towards his opponents
in the last edition of his SYSTEM OF NATURE. The forbear-
ance and greatness which characterized his conduct is extremely

a   well

well expressed on this medal. The bear, a noble Northern animal,
the fittest to represent him,—lies quite in a tranquil position, casting
a steady look upon the LINNÆA, and without seeming to take the
least notice of the jumps and teazing of the monkey. Around this em-
blem we see these words inscribed:

—" *Deam luftus angit amissi.*"

—" The goddess vents her grief at his loss."

The following words succeed immediately below the former:

POST OBITUM,

UPSALIÆ DIE X, JANUAR. M.D.CC.LXXVIII.

REGE JUBENTE.

After his death at *Upsal,* January 10, 1778, by the King's command.—
This medal is of the 17th size.

About seven years after, the great GUSTAVUS conferred a fresh
honour upon the manes of LINNÆUS. His name was then perpetuated
in the most distinguished manner, in the annals of the University of
Upsal, of which he had been the boast and glory for thirty-seven
years. When the late King came in 1787 to lay the foundation-stone
to the edifice of the new botanical garden in that city, the above
medal struck in honour of LINNÆUS was deposited within the stone,
along with some Swedish coins and medals relative to the King's coro-
nation, and to his administration as Chancellor of the University. This
dignity devolved on his accession to the throne to the present King,
then Prince Royal. His Majesty ordered the following inscription to
be engraved upon the copper sheet—which contained the coins :

GUSTAVUS

GUSTAVUS III.

UT BONIS ARTIBUS ET PRÆSERTIM SCIENTIÆ IN GENTIS LAUDEM, A CAROLO
LINNÆO AD FASTIGIUM EVECTÆ SIMULQUE MEMORIÆ CONSECRARET AU-
SPICIA, QUIBUS FILIUS

GUSTAVUS ADOLPHUS

ACADEMIAM UPSALIENSEM TUETUR, HAS ÆDES EXSTRUERE VOLUIT, PRIMIS
SUA MANU LOCATIS FUNDAMENTIS DIE XVII. AUG. M.D.CC.LXXXVII.

—" To promote the studies, and especially the science which Lin-
" næus, to the honour of his nation, has brought to the highest pitch
" of perfection, and to preserve the remembrance of the Chancellor-
" ship of the University of *Upsal,* the functions of which were exer-
" cised by the Prince Royal Gustavus Adolphus, these buildings
" have been raised, and the foundation-stone thereto laid, August 17th,
" 1787, with his own hands, by Gustavus III."

The honourable manner, in which the name of Linnæus was
mentioned in the letter of donation of the new botanical garden, has
been already stated in the seventh section.

The great and elevated Queen Ulrica Louisa, mother to the late
King of *Sweden,* who died in 1782, venerated Linnæus as devoutly
as her son. When Linnæus was alive, she had his portrait cast in the
form of a medallion by the celebrated Archeveque, exhibited in the
apartments of the palace at *Drottningholm,* in front of the portraits of
Klingenstierna, de Geer, and other illustrious Swedes *.

The

* " After the death of Linnæus," say Condorcet, " the King of *Sweden* caused a
" monument to be erected to him, by the side of that which the same prince had consecrated to

The memory of LINNÆUS was equally reverenced at home and abroad. JOHN HOPE, professor of Botany at *Edinburgh*, who died in 1786, opened his autumnal lectures in 1778, with a panegyric on LINNÆUS, and had a monument erected to him with this inscription:

"*LINNÆO POSUIT J. HOPE.*"

Professor ALSTON, his predecessor, had been one of the most rigorous anti-sexualists and opponents of LINNÆUS. A fine contrast appeared, however, under HOPE, and the same thing happened at *Helmstadt*, where BEIRIS, the successor of the implacable HEISTER, preached to his pupils the greatness of LINNÆUS, and instilled into their minds love and veneration towards him.

At the meeting of the royal academy of sciences at *Paris*, CONDORCET read a panegyric upon LINNÆUS; and M. VICQ D'AZYR made also his eulogium at the meeting of the Parisian medical society (*Societé de Médécine*), which was founded in 1776. The Chevalier THUNBERG had already, in 1779, sent to the royal academy of sciences at *Paris* some of the most interesting particulars of the life of LINNÆUS taken from his own diary. The purport of the contents of the panegyric delivered by M. VIQ D'AZYR, has already been circumstantially stated in the beginning of this section. The Duke DE NOAILLES

" DESCARTES (QUEEN CHRISTINA of *Sweden*, called the latter to *Stockholm*, where he
" died in 1650; but his remains were afterwards removed to *Paris*), who as neglected in
" his country after his death, as he had been disregarded there during his life, still expects
" of his fellow citizens those honours which foreign nations were eager to lavish upon him.
" See *Eloge de M. de* LINNÉ, *da   l'Histoire de l'Acad. Roy. des Sciences, Paris* 1781."—
The author of this biography knows nothing of this monument, and the plan of raising one
in the cathedral of *Upsal* is of a quite recent date.

caused

caused a monument to be erected in his garden in honour of LINNÆUS. It consists of a cenotaphium, or an empty tomb, on which stands the bust of LINNÆUS, and the plants *Linnæa* and *Ayenia* spring up by the side of it.

In the year 1787, a society of lovers of natural history assembled at *Paris*, under the name of *Societé Linnéenne*. Their intention was to cultivate and improve natural history, according to the LINNÆAN system, and to communicate to each other their observations and discoveries once a week. In this manner they endeavoured to render more general the system of LINNÆUS; the different branches of which, excepting botany, were but little known then in *France*. But this laudable institution could not expect to make any great progress as long as Count de BUFFON lived. It is well known, that BUFFON, who did not understand the LINNÆAN system, nor chose to give himself any trouble to understand it, had frequently censured LINNÆUS, and his influence over the royal academy of sciences being great and even general, no member of that learned body durst venture to say any thing in praise of the LINNÆAN system. The society, however, had long ago wished to erect a monument to LINNÆUS, their patron, in the royal botanical garden, where BUFFON resided; but these wishes availed nought as long the Count was in being. His death on the 16th of April 1788, and the French revolution which followed soon after, gave the society that liberty to follow their inclination, of which they had hitherto been deprived. Several members of the royal academy, who had till then assisted at the meetings of the society in a clandestine manner, now avowed themselves openly as members, and though, amidst the tumult and shocks of the revolution, it could but seldom assemble, though

many

many of the members were absent, yet the institution continued to sub-
sist, and the number of its members increased every day.

In the beginning of August 1790, the motion of erecting a monument
to LINNÆUS was again renewed; and as it was not convenient to bestow any considerable expences upon it at first, a resolution was entered
into of erecting a plain stone-monument in the wood of *St. Germain,* at the distance of a few leagues from *Paris,* with the words
CHARLES LINNE, engraved upon it. Most of the members, who were
present at the meeting when this resolution was taken, went on a Sun-
day to *St. Germain.* A short time before, some troubles had broken out
there between the inhabitants and the national guards; and whenever three
or four individuals were seen together in any place, the people always
thought that some plot was going forward. The members of the society, about forty in number, heedless of the troubles and ferment, fully
experienced this disposition of the people on their arrival. The populace manifested their suspicions at the meeting of so numerous a
society by the bitterest invectives, and declared the good and innocent
LINNÆANS to be a horde of aristocrats, meditating some dangerous
plot. At this serious juncture the matter was on the point of being terminated by fighting and bloodshed, as some members, conscious of their
innocence, and fired with their enthusiastic resolution of erecting the
monument, attempted to aggravate the fury of the enraged multitude by
warm and spirited remonstrances.

What roused and fostered most the suspicions of the populace, were
the tin-boxes which some of the members bore across their shoulder, fas-
tened with a broad ribband. They had brought those cases to put in them
such plants as they might collect on their way. It fortunately, however, so
happened,

happened, that some eminent persons from *Paris* were present with the members, who had a certain acquaintance among the inhabitants of *St. Germain.* Meanwhile, several members had returned home at the commencement of the dispute. Those who still remained, also thought it adviseable to wait quieter times, a quieter place, and the assembling of an undisturbed and solemn society. Thus the revolutionary spirit prevented for this time the raising of the monument.

A few days after the LINNÆAN Society made a formal application to the NATIONAL ASSEMBLY, to obtain permission to erect the projected monument in the royal botanical garden, under the highest cedar of Mount *Lebanon.* The Assembly, without the least difficulty, decreed that the request of the society be granted.

In the evening of the 23d of August 1790, the bust of LINNÆUS, which was only made of stucco, imitating bronze, and standing upon a stone-pedestal painted in colours imitating porphyry, was solemnly inaugurated by the light of torches, and the names of all the LINNÆANS present, were buried in a vase at the foot of the monument.

Between this period and the close of the year 1790, the number of the members had so considerably increased, that the society found it necessary to hold their meetings in the great amphitheatre of the royal botanical garden. It then resembled one of those clubs which began at that period to become so numerous at *Paris.* Many of the members had not the smallest knowledge of natural history, and curiosity was the only motive from which they resorted to the meetings of the society.

Under those circumstances, it was resolved to give to the society a proper constitution, to enact laws and statutes, and thereby to ensure to it duration and greater utility. Between twenty and thirty of the mem-

bers

bers united together, hired a place to hold their meetings, made statutes, elected a president, who is chosen every three months from among
the members; a secretary, whose trust is renewed quarterly; changed,
from motives of policy, the original name of *Société Linnéenne*, for that
of *Société d'Histoire Naturelle*, and appointed ordinary, honorary, and
corresponding members, who are received by ballot. This society has
already published several volumes of its transactions. It was also
this society which petitioned the National Convention to send out some
ships in quest of the celebrated French navigator, Count DE PEYROUSE,
who had not been heard of for many years. Shortly after, in consequence of a decree, an expedition sailed from *Brest* for this purpose,
which had on board three members of the society as naturalists.

In the year 1788, a society of botanists and naturalists collected at
London, under the presidency of Dr. JAMES EDW. SMITH, and in
honour of our great luminary, assumed the name of the LINNÆAN
SOCIETY. The first volume of the transactions of this patriotic literary
body appeared at *London* in 1792. It is published in quarto by Messrs.
WHITE, and contains twenty-seven treatises in English, Latin and
French, making altogether two hundred and fifty-seven pages. The
presidency of this society goes by turns, and Sir JOSEPH BANKS succeeded Dr. SMITH in that honourable function. Several volumes of
the transactions have regularly appeared since, and been translated into
different languages *.

* " The LINNÆAN SOCIETY," says Dr. SMITH, in a letter to the author, " I instituted
" in 1788, having engaged a number of members for it in my travels. We have just pub-
" lished a volume of transactions in quarto with twenty plates; and at the publishers
" (WHITE and SON) you will see a list of the members."

A third

A third LINNÆAN Society was formed at *Leipsic* in the year 1790, under the auspices of Professor LUDWIG, which has twelve students as ordinary members.

Among the many marks of honour and distinction conferred upon LINNÆUS and his system after his death, we ought not to omit here, that the present Prince Royal of *Denmark* had a service of porcelain made, on which the *Flora Danica* is beautifully painted and represented, according to the LINNÆAN system*.

Exclusive of the three medals which have been struck in *Sweden*, to perpetuate the memory of LINNÆUS, his portrait has also been frequently engraved. The first portrait which appeared in *Germany* was published at *Leipsic*, in front of the edition of his *Systema Naturæ*, 1798. The best engravings of LINNÆUS are to be found before the second edition of his *Species Plantarum*, published at *Stockholm* in 1762; and in the sixth edition of his *Genera Plantarum*, which appeared in the same city in 1748. In this latter portrait, LINNÆUS is represented in a loose dress, leaning upon a volume of his *System of Nature*; and holds a branch of the *Linnæa* in his hand. In the former LINNÆUS appears in full dress, decorated with the Swedish order of the polar star, and below it is the following distich, written by CHARLES AURIVILLIUS, the celebrated philologist at *Upsal*, who died in 1786:

> " *Hic ille est, cui regna volens natura reclusit* ;
> " *Quamque ulli dederat, plura videnda dedit.*"

---

* In the dreadful conflagration which destroyed the royal mansion at *Copenhagen*, with the most valuable effects, this superb monument of botanical taste is said to have also perished. TRANSLATOR.

Among

Among the Swedish engravings of LINNÆUS, we ought also to notice one, done by ACKERMANN, in quarto, and another in octavo by SNACK, in form of a medallion.

There is likewise a portrait of LINNÆUS in the first number of SCHWEDERUS's *Collection des Portraits des Swedois celebres,* published at *Stockholm* in 1778.

Representations of LINNÆUS appeared, by the celebrated artist ARCHEVEQUE at *Paris,* on a large medallion in form of an antique; and at *London* by WEDGWOOD and BENTLEY likewise on a valuable medallion. In the latter the profile of LINNÆUS is white on a blue ground, with the *Linnæa* on his breast.—There is farther, a beautiful likeness of LINNÆUS prefixed to MILLE's *Illustration of the* LINNÆAN *System.* One of the finest and most excellent portraits of LINNÆUS is that which has been painted by the celebrated Swedish artist, ROSLIN and engraved by Messrs. FACIUS. LINNÆUS is there represented in the decline of life. This portrait bears the following inscription :

" *CHARLES VON LINNE,*

" BORN ⅔ MAY 1707. DIED JAN. 10, 1778."

Engraved from the original picture in the possession of Sir JOSEPH BANKS, Bart. Published June 24, 1788, by JOHN and JOSIAH BOYDELL, *London.*

From ACKERMANN's original painting, several impressions of LINNÆUS have been formed in plaster of *Paris.* One engraved by ENDNER at *Leipsic,* is particularly remarkable. But were we to mention the different portraits of LINNÆUS, prefixed to the many editions

editions of his works, it would take up both too much time and space in the present work.

The scientific inheritance left by LINNÆUS, his excellent collections of natural history, his herbarium, manuscripts and letters, remained in the possession of his family till the death of his son in 1783. A British naturalist of considerable property, but whose great talents far outshine his fortune, and whose love of nature is of the most ardent kind, Dr. JAMES EDWARD SMITH of *London*, obtained those treasures. He agreed to purchase them of the widow of LINNÆUS for the sum of *one thousand guineas*; infinitely glad at his being able to carry that golden fleece to *England* for so trifling a consideration. How much must *Sweden* regret, that the treasures of her immortal genius, should have fallen to the share of a foreign land! It is, however, a consolatory reflection, that they fell into excellent hands, and that their present proprietor will use them in the best manner, for the benefit of natural history. Dr. SMITH has already published several of the unknown productions of LINNÆUS, and the scientific world may expect to reap many more advantages from his penetrating knowledge and unremitting diligence.

At first, no person at *Upsal* could in the least imagine, that the invaluable learned remains of the prince of botany would ever be exported to a foreign country. A patriotic Swede and zealous promoter of natural science, of the name of MAUHLE, who was at that time in *China*, upon business concerning the Swedish *East India* Company, is said to have endeavoured to get them into his possession*, by giving directions

to

---

* Crinum Africanum;—novum genus constitui et MAUHLIAM in honorem nobilissimi Dom. Jo. MAUHLE nominavi, qui solus pecuniam mihi suppeditaverat ad servandum in patria Mu-
L l   seum

to Dr. DAHL, a pupil of LINNÆUS, to purchase the whole, and ordering the sum necessary for that purchase to be paid to him. Dr.
DAHL is even stated to have agreed for them at two thousand ducats;
but he did not succeed, and Dr. SMITH had the preference. We can
give the following additional particulars respecting the disposal of the
learned productions left by LINNÆUS:

" The collection," writes a Swedish literatus, in a letter to an eminent German botanist, dated March 3d, 1784, " are still in the same
" state which they were in at the death of the younger LINNÆUS. An
" Englisman of the name of SMITH has offered one thousand guineas
" for them, but he wants all the books and manuscripts. M. ALSTROE-
" MER lays a claim to the *Herbarium*, which the younger LINNÆUS col-
" lected in his youth; this separation, though not in the least prejudicial
" to the whole, makes, perhaps, such an impression upon the purchasers,
" that they will not give the whole sum of two thousand ducats. In
" striking a bargain of such importance, it may be considered as an un-
" fortunate circumstance, to have to deal with so many heirs; the one
" will not always consent to do what the other will. If I can pre-
" vent the letters from being sold, it would be a good thing to have
" them printed in *Germany* for the benefit of the heirs; and should this
" be the case, I will take the liberty of addressing myself to you."

DAHL himself, in a letter to a German friend, dated November 30th, 1784, expresses himself thus: " I agreed with Mr. ****,
" who disposes of the property of LINNÆUS, for the library and

seum immortalium a LINNE; quod tamen, numerata licet eadem pecuniarum summa nescio
quo fato exteris cessit. See ANDR. DAHL *Observationes Botanicæ Circa Systema Vegetab.
Divi a LINNE. Goetting.* 1784. Editum, &c. *Havniæ* 1787.

2

" the collections at the sum of two thousand ducats. But while he endea-
" voured to amuse me with his promises, he profited by the interval to
" convey them out of the kingdom. I was obliged to apply to the King, to
" obtain an order for stopping them, but I applied too late. This circum-
" stance obliged me to reside at *Stockholm* for some months *."

Those who wish for the best and most authentic information, not only
about the remarkable circumstances which attended the sale of the LIN-
NÆAN collections, but also respecting their contents and quality, will
find it among the supplements to this biography, in an ample letter from
Dr. J. E. SMITH to the author.

LINNÆUS was the father of six children, two sons and four
daughters. Of the eldest son, CHARLES LINNÆUS, who succeeded
his father in his professorship, we shall give a particular account in the
course of this work. The youngest, whose name was JOHN, died
while an infant. ELISABETH CHRISTINA, the eldest Miss LINNÆUS,
married in 1761 one BERGENCRANTZ, a captain of cavalry in the
service of *Sweden*, and has been dead these many years. The fruit of
her marriage was a daughter, born in 1764. The three other daughters of LINNÆUS are the only surviving branches of that great man's
family. Misses LOUISA and SARAH CHRISTINA, the two eldest, remain in a state of celibacy with their mother at the villa of *Hammarby*, one league from *Upsal*. And Miss SOPHIA, her youngest, has

---

* " Jag hadde accorderat mede . . . . . , som disponerade om LINNÉERNAS egendom, om
" eras Samlingar och Bibliotheque, mot en summa stor 2000 ducater; men under dät han
" uppeholt mig met löften, behagade han, lurendrega dem ur Riket. Jag var nösakad, at
" vända mig till Konunger, och begära sequester men köm for sent. Dä te har giort, at jag
" most vistas par monander *Stockholm*."

sealed

sealed the conjugal bond with SAMUEL DUSE, procurator of the senate of the university of *Upsal* *.

It was this daughter whom LINNÆUS cherished as the darling of his
family; and the following extraordinary occurrence will account for
this predilection.   She was—all appearances at least bespoke her to
be—still-born.   " No !" said LINNÆUS, " she must not, she shall not
" die !"   He pressed her to his bosom, emitting his breath from his
mouth into her's,—and behold ! She revived and lived †.

The brother of our luminary, who holds the rectory of *Stenbrohult*
is still alive, but without any male issue.

ELIZABETH CHRISTINA, the eldest daughter of LINNÆUS, acquired
a learned reputation in the literary annals of *Sweden*.   The knowledge
which she had of natural history was considerable, and even rare for a
person of her sex‡.   In the year 1762 she first discovered that the
herb *Tropæolum* emitted sparks of fire like an electrical machine. This
happened at the fall of day, and ceased when it became quite dark.
The discovery of this remarkable and interesting phenomenon was in

---

* I have for the most part extracted this new and interesting information from a letter.
addressed to me by a friend, dated *Upsal*, August 12th, 1791, who thus expresses himself:
" Prædia *Hammarby* et *Soefja*, uno milliari ab *Upsalia* distantia, possidet vidua LINNÆI,
" adhuc in vivis superstes. Filiarum ejus natu maxima nupsit nobili viro BERGEN-
" CRANTZ, magistro equitum, ante plures vero jam annos mortua est. Natu minima ma-
" trimonio duxit virum nobil. SAM. DUSE, litium academiæ curatorem et habitat *Upsaliæ*.
" Duæ reliquæ cum matre in prædio *Hammarby* vivunt. Filium etiam habuit LINNÆUS Jo-
" HANNEM, in prima pueritia mortuum. Frater ejus, qui de apibus scripsit, vita adhuc.
" fruitur."

† Communicated to the author by a most intimate friend of LINNÆUS in *Germany*.

‡ Several erroneous and hyperbolic statements have been made in this respect.   In a work
entituled, " *Voyage en Suede, par un Officier Hollandis*, 1789," it is alledged that she excelled LINNÆUS, jun. in every sort of knowledge, and had written many excellent works on
botany.   It is however well known that LINNÆUS jun. was not alive at that time.

honour

honour of her, described and recorded in the transactions of the Royal Academy of Sciences of *Stockholm*, (tom. xxiii. 1762).

The stature of LINNÆUS was a little below the common size, though neither lusty nor lean, yet the structure of his frame was strong and solid. He rather stooped a little when walking, and had contracted this habit from the frequent examination of plants, and from his constant search after vegetable or other natural productions. From his infancy his veins had much swelled with blood. His head was large, somewhat elevated backwards, and a traverse line separated the fore-part from the hind. His eyes were brown and fiery, his sight was very sharp, and his ear extremely quick in catching every sound, except music. It is rather singular, that the man, who was all alive to joy and social harmony, should have felt an antipathy, as it were, for that art which best expresses those affections, and has mostly been the delight of great men. Even the grave and serious BOERHAAVE found his chief comfort and recreation in music*. Another circumstance to be noticed as a peculiarity in LINNÆUS was, that his memory, so excellent and uncommonly vigorous in his youth and in the flower of his age,—that memory which encompassed whatever was remarkable in nature,—became at last as weak as it formerly had been strong, and began already to fall off very considerably after he had completed his fiftieth year. To the too violent exertion and overburdening of his memory, its early decay ought, therefore, to be attributed.

His memory, like all his talents and endowments was, in point of science, solely devoted to natural history. He loved the *Belles Lettres*,

---

* Fessus—writes BOERHAAVE of himself in his diary—testudinis concentu solabatur lassitudinem; musices amantissimus.

and even when old age had chilled the brilliancy of his imagination, would frequently read OVID and VIRGIL, and rehearse with ease and pleasure, several passages from the works of those poets. He was not fond of what is properly called the philology of words. While at college, he had already but too much evinced his aversion to the learning of languages. In the foreign countries which he had visited, in *England*, *Holland*, and *France*, the Latin language became mostly his aid in his intercourse, which was almost entirely confined to the learned. In this language, with the assistance of the Greek, of which he had a competent knowledge ·for his profession, he expressed himself in describing objects of natural history, with ·ease, fluency, masterly conciseness, perspicuity, and precision. Simplicity, the predominant feature of his whole character, was also remarkable in the language of his science, which derived from him so many reforms and perfections. The diction of a technical man could not surely be that of a CICERO. The object of which he complained, appeared more important to him than the vesture which he threw about it.。 His descriptions and his letters please, though one ought not to search for elegance of latinity in them. Owing to the quickness with which he wrote, he would sometimes commit errors even against the grammatical accuracy of the vernacular tongue of the Romans, and some of his letters which we had occasion to insert in this work, will furnish ample proof of the truth of this assertion. The greatness of LINNÆUS becomes an inducement even to mention the most trifling particulars. He frequently used to say to his friends :—" I WOULD RATHER HAVE THREE " SLAPS FROM PRISCIAN, THAN ONE FROM NATURE.—*Malo tres*
" *alapas*

" *alapas a* Prisciano, *quam unam a Natura*.*" When he was chosen
member of the French Royal Academy of Sciences at *Paris* in 1763,
he composed his letter of thanks to that learned body in Swedish, and
had it translated into Latin by his friend the late Swedish librarian
Frondin. In other respects, it cannot be denied, that a more extensive knowledge of languages, especially of the modern ones, would
have proved highly useful to Linnæus. The complaints of his not
having profited wit hutility by the works of foreigners, would then have
been less numerous, if not entirely removed. He was tolerably well
versed in the German, but spoke it very rarely. " I had however
" the pleasure,"—says the celebrated botanist Ehrhard at *Hanover* †,
" of his once conversing with me in *Germany* for a whole afternoon
" in the spring of 1773."

His activity was as great as his thirst for truth, and for the more
profound and more extensive knowledge of his science was unquench-
able. The strictest order, the most punctual regularity distinguished
all his actions. In summer he usually slept five hours, from ten at
night till three o'clock in the morning; in winter his rest lasted nine
hours, namely, from nine in the evening till six in the morning. He
proportioned the length and duration of his sleep to the season of the
year; and the time for study and occupation he always limited by the
natural flow of his spirits. Whenever he felt himself fatigued, he laid
by his work; at night he used to be very fond of good company, displayed much mirth and jollity, joked, and would often set whole
circles in a roar in which he most heartily joined them. Owing to his

* From a Letter of one of his most intimate friends at *Stockholm.*

† In a Letter to the Author.

sanguine

sanguine temper he became very susceptible to transitions from joy to sadness, and from these to anger. His heart was downright probity itself, and from his lips streamed candor, truth and virtue. Faithful and affectionate to his friends, he never even retaliated upon his enemies their malice and enmity; he was not apt to forget an offence easily, and used to say: " I will not suffer myself to be deceived a " second time."—All the concerns of house-keeping and domestic œconomy he entrusted to the care of his spouse, who ruled the family. He was a true and tender husband, and his fondness as a father was not less remarkable than his other good qualifications.

His mansion was neat and filled with handsome furniture, he never disliked feasting his friends; but the poverty which had once oppressed him in his youth, would not permit him to be lavish of expence. In all that related to his science, to natural curiosities, books, correspondence; or if he saw a person that really needed relief, for instance, a widowed mother with infant orphans, nothing could then restrain his liberality and beneficence. The excellent collections of literary and natural treasures which he left behind him, prove what considerable expence he was at, as a literatus and a friend of nature. We will illustrate this assertion by the following comparatively speaking diminutive instance:—In 1764 he wrote thus to the celebrated Austrian naturalist J. A. Scopoli, who was at that time a physician at *Istria* in *Carinthia*, and became afterwards professor of chemistry and botany at *Pavia*, where he terminated his meritorious life May 3, 1788: " After many " vain endeavours, I have at last received your *Description* of the *Carin-* " *thian insects* from *Holland*. The postage alone stands me in about " three ducats, but I do not grudge the expence. That work has af-

3

" forded

" forded me more pleasure than an hundred ducats would have done.
" I am astonished at your boundless industry in collecting, classing,
" and describing your work.   None but him who had a share in such
" labour can form himself an adequate idea of it *."

To the poor—and even to the rich, foreign students, who resided at *Upsal* entirely on his account, he left the whole of the perquisites, which they must otherwise have paid him for his lectures.   To the former he remitted that money from pure motives of beneficence, and from the latter he would not receive it, that he might convince them how nobly proud he was of his science.   Besides the testimony which professor FABRICIUS gives in this particular with regard to ZOEGA and himself, we will communicate here the following farther illustrations of the generosity of LINNÆUS.

When Dr. GIESEKE took his leave of our luminary in autumn of 1771, he presented to him a Swedish bank note as an acknowledgment for the pains he had taken to instruct him, but he absolutely declined acceptance.   After reiterated intreaties he asked GIESEKE:—" Pray,
" tell me candidly, are you rich, and can you afford it—can you well
" spare this money on your return to *Germany* ?——If you can, give
" the bank note to my wife.   But should you be poor, so help me
" God, 1 would not take a single farthing from you. †."

* Post varia frustranea tentamina tandem accepi tuam *Entomologiam Carniolicam* exhibentem insectæ Carnioliæ indigenæ, *Vindob* 1763, 8vo, maj.) eamque ex Belgio et quidem sumptibus trium fere ducatorum aureorum pro solo tabellario adducente; neque hoc doleo, quum ex ea plus oblectamenti hauserim, quam ex centum ducatis.   Obstupesco ad infinitum laborem, in colligendo describendo et disponendo, quem nullus alius intelligere usquam potest, nisi qui ipse manum labori admovit.

† Nam si pauper esses—ita me Deus!—(this was the usual form of oath of LINNÆUS) ne obolum a te acciperem.

" To the praise of LINNÆUS I must farther own," says Mr. EHR-
HART, the celebrated botanist at *Hanover**,—" that notwithstanding
" his parsimony, he neither did nor would accept a single penny as an
" honorary for the lectures which he gave me."—" You are a Swiss,"
said he once to me, " and the only Swiss that visits me. I shall take
" no money of you, but feel a pleasure, in telling you all I know
" *gratis*."

Notwithstanding those liberal sentiments, gold, the noblest of metals,
did not a little recreate his sight, and inspire him with fondness. " And
" why," says Dean BÆCK, " should gold not have been amassed by
" him, who hoarded up all that was precious or beautiful in the lap
" of nature."

In the common social intercourse he was fond of conversation,
kind and condescending towards his inferiors,—and at the same time,
a prepossessed and enthusiastic friend of reputation and honour. His
coat of arms bore for its motto the words, with which ANCHISES
spirits up ÆNEAS, and PALLAS invokes HERCULES: " FAMAM EX-
" TENDERE FACTIS."—" TO SPREAD FAME BY DEEDS†". The
truth of this motto he fully realized. Honour was in him like in other
eminent men, the source of his greatness. The liberal will in other respects hardly deem it necessary to gloss over by apologies that manifes-
tation of self-love, which is generally inseparable from true honour‡.

.

                                                    LINNÆUS

---

* In a Letter to the Author.

† " Et dubitamus adhuc virtutem extendere factis !"—VIRGIL. Æn. Lib. VI. Vers. 809.
    ——" Sed famam extendere factis
    ——" Hoc Virtutis opus."———VIRGIL, Æn. Lib. X. Vers. 468 and 469.

‡ The late celebrated Chevalier PETER WARGENTIN, Secretary of the Royal Academy
at *Stockholm*, gives the following opinion in a Letter dated *Stockholm*, July 23, 1751.
                                                    " Apud

" Linnæus is censured," says Dean Bäck, " for having aspired at
" universal dominion in botany, and for having been angry with those
" who strove like him to acquire eminence in that science. Jealousy
" is almost constantly found to operate upon great men. And the re-
" public of science has neither Pompeys nor Cæsars. Exclusive do-
" mination in the regions of literary eminence belongs to him alone
" who has truth on his side; nature confirms the truth, while time on
" the other hand, destroys presumption and caprices. And who had
" more virtue and more merit on his side than Linnæus ? Who could
" with greater right raise himself the monarch of natural science ?
" Hence how generally and voluntarily have his laws been adopted."

We will readily allow that Linnæus wished to acquire honour by
his labours. But he did not neglect, as his pupils can prove, to pay
proper homage to the discoveries of other men. He mentioned with
gratitude all those, who showed or sent him the least curiosities of
nature. He thought it was his prerogative, to see and describe those
plants, which his disciples procured by resources of their own. He acknowledged their confidence as a strong mark of politeness; but when
they lost sight of this confidence, he could not forbear expressing
his displeasure. In other respects he did not like to speak publicly of
things which he had not seen himself.

The arms of Linnæus were perhaps the most expressive of any
learned man of the age; at the top above the helmet was the plant
which bears his name, and whose leaves hung down on both sides, in

" Apud nos in Linnæo ipsiusque discipulis Academiæ Upsaliæ fere unica spes, quoniam alii,
" quamvis in Chemicis, Medicis peritissimi, raro sua inventa communicant. Ne itaque mi-
" reris, quod quandoque Linnæum impensius laudemus. Hæc ipsius unica est merces pro
" tot laboribus."

M m 2   the

the centre of the divisions was an egg,—an allusion to the principle of HARVEY: " *Omne animal ex ovo*,"—and to the basis of his sexual system: " *Omnis planta e Semine* ;"—at the top was a crown, and on each side another, signifying the three reigns of nature, and borrowed from the medal which Count TESSIN had ordered to be struck in honour of him ; from below appeared the order of the *Polar* Star, encompassed by his motto : *Famam Extendere Factis*.

The hand which LINNÆUS wrote, was upon the whole of a diminutive size, but remarkably plain and well formed for a literatus. In the earlier part of his life it must even have been remarked as a fine hand *.

One of the most distinguished attributes of the mind of LINNÆUS were his religious sentiments, and his profound adoration of the Divinity.   He resembled in this respect, NEWTON, HALLER, LOCKE, EULER and others, whose respect of religion rendered their knowledge still more estimable.   The deeper he penetrated into the secrets of nature, the more he admired the wisdom of her creator. He praised this wisdom in his works, recommended it by his speeches, and honoured it in his actions.   Whenever he found an opportunity of expatiating on the greatness, the providence, and omnipotence of GOD, which frequently happened in his lectures and botanical excursions, his heart glowed with a celestial fire, and his mouth poured forth torrents of admirable eloquence.   This made him one of the best inculcators of morality ; he instilled by so doing a similar spirit of religion into the breast of his pupils.   He kept, as we already observed, a diary

* This assertion is proved by some Letters of LINNÆUS, which the Author himself has seen.

like

like HALLER, in which he recorded the principal occurrences of his life. Besides this, he had began to write a little work in 1733, which he called NEMESIS DIVINA; and in which he recorded as it were, for his own warning, the punishments inflicted by Providence, and those catastrophes and adversities which befel others, and which from long experience, he had either foreseen or had a presentiment of. Over the door of the hall, in which he gave his lectures, was the following inscription: " INNOCUI VIVITE! NUMEN ADEST!"—" *Live guilt-* " *less ! God observes you !*"--He could never think on the wonderful paths on which the Almighty had guided him without being moved, and without thanking his Providence for all the proofs of his grace and mercy. He concluded the tract which contains the occurrences of his life with these words : " *The Lord was with thee, where ever thou* " *didst go,. &c. &c.*.

One of his celebrated pupils, the late Chevalier MURRAY of *Goettingen,* when publicly announcing the death of his great teacher in 1778, added the following illustration of his character*.—" Every can- " did and impartial mind cannot but acknowledge how much natural " history stands indebted to LINNÆUS for his writings, for his lectures, " for his correspondence, for his most active zeal, and for sending the " ablest pupils to all quarters of the globe ; and with regard to medicine, " for fixing the solid basis of a successful practice, and ascertaining the " remedies. By the order, truth, precision and perfection, and the im- " mediate application of theory to practical use, which he introduced in " his favourite science, he not only weaned his countrymen from a whim-

* See J. A. MURRAY's Medico-practical Library, Vol. III, Part I. *Goettingen* 1778, Page 15.

" sical

" sical and pretended study of antiquities, but kindled in all *Europe* and
" in other enlightened parts of the world, an enthusiastic love of natural
" history, which even captivated monarchs. As long as the world shall
" exist, there will be opportunities of making alterations, additions, and
" commentaries in certain learned productions; but what is all this, if
" compared to the merits of an original creator. His mind was too ele-
" vated and too noble to have ever suffered him to abuse or vex even
" those who had cowardly and morosely attacked him. Not a line of such
" a tendency obscures his splendid literary career. The Swedish court ex-
" pressed the esteem which it felt for him, not only by promoting and
" facilitating the progress of his science, but also by conferring upon
" him personal rewards; he graced the presence of his King; in the
" temple which is consecrated to nature at *Drottningholm*, a medallion
" representing him i suspended amidst the most illustrious *Swedes*, and
" a superb mansoleum has been erected to him after his death.—Many of
" his countrymen, heedless of the dangers which abound on the stormy
" seas and in wildernesses, the repairs of ferocious beasts, exposed
" themselves, merely to gratify their venerable professor by natural col-
" lections. One of them sent him a service of porcelain from *China*,
" purposely manufactured for him and bearing a representation of the
" LINNÆA BOREALIS on the outside. Others attempted by their
" pencil, or CHISEL, to render imperishable their name by publishing
" his portrait. As long as LINNÆUS preserved the faculty of thinking,
" he constantly had in his mind his darling motto: *Famam Extendere*
" *Factis*.—It raised him from the humblest obscurity to the summit of
" permanent fame."

1

" Tender

" Tender to his friends," says Condorcet in his panegyric, delivered before the Royal Academy of sciences at *Paris**, " amiable " and blithsome in familiar converse, noble with the great, plain and " good-natured to his inferiors, Linnæus never purchased by base- " ness the privilege of making others feel the humiliating weight of " pride; and was the less jealous of affecting a precarious prero- " gative than he was confident of his real greatness. Rich by the " munificence of his court, he never deviated from that simplicity of " life, from which no man can stray without being punished by ridicule " and loneliness."—A short time after he had suffered an apopletic stroke, he composed a brief account of his life, and sent it to this Academy to furnish materials for his panegyric. In this production he speaks with as much candor of his labours and discoveries as he does of his faults.—" He owns that he might · :rhaps be too easily

* Sensible avec ses amis, aimable et gai dans la Societé intime; nobles avec les grands, simple et bon avec ses inferieurs, on ne le vit jamais acheter par des bassesses le droit de faire eprouver des hauteurs, d'autant moins jaloux d'affecter une superiorité precaire, qu'il etoit plus sûr d'en avoir une rééle. Riche des bienfaits de la Cour, il ne quitta jamais, cette simplicité de vie, dont on ne peut s'ecarter, sans en etre puni par le ridicule et par l'ennui.— Très peu de temps apres son attaque d'apoplexie, il dressa lui même une courte notice de sa vie, et il voulut qu'elle fit envoyée à l'academie pour servir de materiaux pour son eloge. Cette avec une égale simplicité qu'il y parle de ses travaux, de ses deconvertes, ou qu'il convient de ses defauts. Il avoue qu'il fut peut être trop facile à s'emouvoir, ou à s'irriter; que lent à embrasser une opinion, il tenoit peut-être avec trop d'opiniatrete à celles, qu'il avoit une fois adopté; qu'il ne souffrit avec assez de moderation ni les critiques, qni s'eleverent contre lui, ni les contradictions, qu'il eprouva de la part de ses rivaux. Ces aveux provent seulement, que M. de Linné eut pour la gloire passion veritable, et que cette passion à comme toutes les autres ses excès et ses faiblesses; mais combien peu d'hommes ont comme lui le courage d'avouer ces faiblesses!—
Ainsi ce soin de s'occuper de son éloge, qui dans un autre eut été peut être l'effet d'un vain amour propre, ne fut chez lui, qu'une nouvelle marque de son amour pour la verité. Apres avoir combattu toute sa vie les erreurs il ne vouloit pas laisser subsister celles, que l'admiration ou l'envie auroit pu accrediter, pour et contre lui. *Eloge de M. de Linné*, p. 80.

" moved

" moved or irritated; that he is but slow in adopting opinions, and
" perseveres perhaps with too much obstinacy in those which he had
" once received; that he was not possessed of moderation sufficient to
" resist the censure and the contradictions of his rivals.—Such avowals
" only prove, that LINNÆUS was passionately fond of fame, and that
" this passion like all others is subject to frailties and excesses. But
" how small is the number of men who have that courage which he
" had to own their frailties."

    " Thus the care which he took of his eulogium, and which in another
" man might perhaps have been the mere impulse of vanity, was in him
" but a fresh proof of his love of truth. After having combated errors
" all his life time, he would not palliate those which admiration or envy
" might have urged for or against him."

    The extraordinary laconism in the works of LINNÆUS, and per-
haps the too frequent use of systematic description, render the perusal
of them difficult ; they require more being studied than read; but
afford afterwards a rich compensation in the precision of his ideas,
and in the advantage of presenting, all at once, a multiplicity of results.
LINNÆUS was well aware that naked truth possessed the most captivat-
ing charms, and that those ornaments which are used to set her off, serve
only to mask her. He was more eager to form naturalists and to instruct
students than to entertain amateurs. The powers of eloquence which
allure the latter and please the idle fancy, were a gift which he never
desired to make his own. His countrymen, at the same time, found in
the works which he wrote in his mother-tongue, an elegant and pleasant
diction, and that kind of eloquence, which among all others, is the
most enrapturing, and perhaps the only one peculiarly adapted to phi-

losophical works, I mean, that eloquence which comprises many thoughts in a few words, and expresses new and important truths, in a noble and artless language.

In all the works of LINNÆUS, there reigns a profound adoration of Providence, a lively admiration of the greatness and wisdom of his ways, and a tender gratitude for his benefits. He believed in Providence, because his daily observations upon nature furnished him with fresh proofs of her sublime immensity, and he daily saw instances of it before his eyes.

All authentic particulars, which can contribute to a stricter knowledge of the life, character and peculiarities of a man, who has rendered himself as eminent and as immortal as LINNÆUS, cannot fail to prove agreeable and interesting. We shall therefore subjoin here those anecdotes which Professor FABRICIUS of *Kiel,* one of his most celebrated pupils, has collected respecting him.

" For two whole years," relates FABRICIUS †, namely from 1762 till 1764, " have I been so fortunate as to enjoy his instruction, his gui-
" dance and his confidential friendship. Not a day elapsed, on which I
" did not see him, on which I was not either present at his lectures, or,
" as it frequently happened, spent several hours with him in familiar con-
" versation. In summer we followed him into the country. We were
" three, KUHN*, ZOEGA †, and I, all foreigners. In winter we lived
" directly facing his house, and he came to us almost every day, in his

* See *Deutsches Museum,* No. V. *Lips.* 1780, p. 431.

† KUHN was an American, born at *Philadelphia.*

‡ ZOEGA died as a Coonsellor of State to the King of *Denmark* at *Copenhagen,* December 29, 1788. He was born October 7, 1742.

" short red *robe de chambre*, with a green fur-cap on his head and a pipe
" in his hand. He came for half an hour but stopped a whole one;
" and many times two. His conversation on these occasions was ex-
" tremely sprightly and pleasant. It either consisted in anecdotes rela-
" tive to the learned in his profession, with whom he got acquainted in
" foreign countries, or in clearing up our doubts, or giving us other
" kinds of instruction. He used to laugh then most heartily, and dis-
" played a serenity and an openness of countenance, which proved how
" much his soul was susceptible of amity and good fellowship.

" Our life was much happier when we resided in the country. Our
" habitation was about half a quarter of a league distant from his house
" at *Hammarby*—in a farm where we kept our own furniture and other
" requisites for hou~ keeping. He rose very early in summer, and
" mostly about fou. clock. At six he came to us because his house
" was then building; breakfasted with us, and gave lectures upon the
" natural orders of plants *(ordines naturales plantarum *),* as long as he
" pleased, and generally till about ten o'clock. We then wandered
" about till twelve upon the adjacent rocks, the productions of which
" afforded us plenty of entertainment. In the afternoon we repaired to
" his garden, and in the evening we mostly played at the Swedish game
" of *trissett,* in company with his spouse.

" On Sundays the whole family usually came to spend the day with
" us. We sent for a peasant who played on an instrument resembling a
" violin, at the sound of which we danced in the barn of our farm-
" house. Our balls were certainly not very splendid, the company but

* The publication of those lectures by Dr. GISEKE, is to be found in the List of the
Works of LINNÆUS.

" small,

" small, the music superlatively rustic, and no change in the dances,
" which were constantly either minuets or Polish; but regardless of
" these wants we passed our time very merrily. While we were
" dancing, the OLD MAN, who smoaked his pipe with ZOEGA, who
" was deformed by nature, and emaciated, became a spectator of
" our amusement, and sometimes, though very rarely, danced a Polish
" dance, in which he excelled every one of us young men. He was
" extremely delighted whenever he saw us in high glee, nay, if we even
" became very noisy; had he not always found us so, he would have
" manifested his apprehensions lest we should not be sufficiently en-
" tertained.—Those days, those hours shall never be erased from my
" memory, and every remembrance of them is grateful to my heart!

" What made him so excessively kind toward' us was, because we
" were foreigners, and besides some Russians w   uld not bestow great
" pains upon their studies, we also were those no alone adhered to
" him, who alone heard and attended him, and remained at *Upsal* en-
" tirely on his account. He found that we loved his science, and that
" we proved this love by a most zealous application to its different
" pursuits. He felt therefore, great pleasure in convincing his own
" countrymen, that his science would be esteemed abroad, even when
" it should begin to decline in *Sweden*. He was also fond of conversa-
" tion on all subjects relative to natural history, for which he had but too
" little opportunity at *Upsal*. That science almost entirely engrossed his
" speech, and every thought of his mind; and being the only natu-
" ralist then at that university, such a privation must have occasioned to
" him a great deal of irksomeness.

N n 2   " When

" When I got acquainted with Sir Charles Linnæus, who was
" then in his fifty-sixth year, increasing age had already furrowed his
" front with wrinkles. His countenance was open, almost constantly
" serene, and bore great resemblance to his portrait in the *Species Plan-*
" *tarum*. But his eyes,—of all the eyes I ever saw,—were the most
" beautiful. They certainly were but little, but darted a refulgent
" splendor and a penetration of aspect which I never observed before
" in any other man. It sometimes appeared to me, as if his looks would
" penetrate through the very innermost recesses of the heart.

" His mind was remarkably noble and elevated, though I well know
" that some persons accused him of several faults ; the acuteness and
" energy of his mental faculties, even shone through his eyes. But his
" greatest excellence consisted in the systematical order, by which his
" thoughts succeeded each other. Whatever he said or did was faithful
" to order, to truth, and to regularity. In his youth his memory was
" uncommonly vigorous, but it began to sink early into decay. Even
" when I was with him, he could not sometimes remember the names
" of his dearest friends and relatives. I still recollect to have seen him
" once very much embarrassed, when, after writing a letter to Moræus,
" his father-in-law at *Fahlun*, he almost found it impossible to recollect
" his name.

" His passions were strong and violent. His heart was open to every
" impression of joy ; and he loved jocularity, conviviality and good
" living. He was an excellent companion, pleasant in conversation,
" full of strong hits of fancy and seasonable and entertaining stories ;
" but at the same time, suddenly roused to anger and boisterous ; the
" sudden effervescence of this fiery passion subsides however, almost

" as

" at the very moment of its birth, and he immediately became all plain
" good-nature again. His friendship was sure and invariable. Science
" was generally its basis; and every one who knew him must own
" what concern he always manifested for his pupils, and with how much
" zeal they returned his friendship, and frequently became his defenders.
" He was so fortunate as to find among his favourites none that were
" ungrateful; even ROLANDER deserved more to be pitied than
" blamed.

" The ambition of LINNÆUS knew no bounds; and his motto, *Fa-*
" *mam Extendere Faëlis,* was the real mirror of his soul *. But this am-
" bition never extended beyond the regions of his science, and it never
" degenerated into surly and offensive pride. He certainly did not
" care much for the opinion of his cotemporaries, and only heeded that
" which proceeded from those, who were men of genuine literary merit.
" His way of living was moderate and parsimonious, his d.   plain,
" and oftentimes even shabby. The high rank to which his King had
" raised him, pleased him only as far as he considered it as a proof
" of his scientific greatness.

" In the pursuits of his studies he could but ill brook contradiction
" and opposition. He corrected his works agreeable to the just re-
" marks of his friends, whose hints he received with gratitude;—but
" the attacks of his opponents he despised, and instead of answering he

* LINNÆUS commonly wrote this motto in the memorial-books presented to him by his
continental friends; the late celebrated Chevalier IHRE, who, though a sincere friend of
LINNÆUS, disliked nevertheless all ostentation, inserted frequently opposite the writing of
LINNÆUS these words " *Non magna sunt, quæ tument.*"—The Author has verified this
from several originals.

" consigned.

" consigned them to that obscurity and oblivion in which they have
" long ago been buried. Notwithstanding this, he could not easily for-
" give aggressions, and strained every nerve to erase them from the
" annals of literature. He was liberal in dispensing praise, because
" he was fond of being flattered; and this, indeed, may be consi-
" dered as his greatest foible. At the same time, his ambition was
" founded upon the consciousness of his own greatness, and upon the
" merits which he acquired in a science, over which he had for
" so many years wielded the sceptre of sovereignty. TOURNEFORT,
" as he often told me, was his pattern in his youth; he did all he could
" to equal him, and found at last, that he had left TOURNEFORT at a
" great distance beneath him.

" LINNÆUS has been particularly charged with avarice. It cannot be
" denied, that his way   'iving, considering his good circumstances, was
" very oderate, and that he surely did not despise gold. But if I weigh
" in my mind, those extremes of poverty, which so long and so heavily
" overwhelmed him, I can easily account for this parsimony. But I
" could not say, that his frugality ever degenerated into sordid avarice.
" I can even prove quite the contrary by my own experience. After hav-
" ing given us lectures all the summer round, we were not only obliged
" to urge him to receive the fee due for these lectures, but even
" to leave the money slyly upon his chest, as he had signified his
" resolution not to take it, in a final and peremptory manner.

" He was not quite happy and comfortable in his own family. His
" wife was tall, robust, domineering, selfish, and destitute of every ad-
" vantage of a good education. She frequently robbed us of the joys
" which gilded our social moments. Unable to hold any conversa-

2   " tion

" tion in decent company, she consequently was never much fond of it
" herself.

" Under those disadvantages, the education of the children of L I N-
" N Æ U s could not but be of an inferior description. The young ladies,
" his daughters, are all good-tempered, but rough children of nature,
" and deprived of those external accomplishments which they might
" have derived from a better education. The younger L I N N Æ U s, who
" succeeded his father in his professorship at *Upsal*, is certainly not en-
" dowed with the same vivacity; but the great knowledge which he
" acquired by a constant practice of botany, and by the many and ex-
" cellent observations of his parent which he found in his manuscripts,
" must have rendered him a very useful man there. The eldest daugh-
" ter, who married Captain V O N B E R G E N C R A N Z, returned afterwards
" to her parents, and lived constantly in their use.

" The merits of L I N N Æ U s in the sciences are uncommonly great.
" He not only enriched them considerably himself, but formed also a
" great number of pupils of the greatest scientific eminence. He
" found means, partly by the charming method of delivering his lectures,
" partly by his excursions and friendly demeanour, to inspire them
" with a love of natural history, which they always preserved after-
" wards, and which induced them to undertake long and important tra-
" vels and voyages, and to enrich their science at home by valuable
" tracts and observations. But few were those teachers, who had
" the good fortune to form so great a number of disciples, who all con-
" tributed in some measure, to extend the limits of their science; and
" there is no country but *Sweden*, which ever sent out so many travellers
" to make discoveries in natural history.—L I N N Æ U s was also my
" teacher,

" teacher, and I acknowledge with emotion, how greatly indebted I am
" to him for his lessons and his friendship.

" Besides the labour which he bestowed upon medicine, especially
" upon the *Materia Medica* and Pathology, nature was his principal oc-
" cupation, and proclaimed him also as the first darling of his time.
" Great was he in discerning and arranging the immensity of beings
" which cover the globe; and perhaps greater still in the extraordi-
" nary number of observations, and in the *hypotheses* which are founded
" upon them, and gradually became theoretical truths. The *hypotheses* of
" LINNÆUS indicate most particularly the brilliancy of his imagination,
" and at the same time, the strength of his judgment. Some of them
" appear extremely bold and venturesome at first; but upon closer
" inspection, we find the observations in nature on which they are
" founded, and must acknowledge them afterwards if not as true, at
" least as probable and as deserving of a more minute enquiry.

" Among his manuscripts there must certainly have been found
" many important remarks; I should have been very desirous of see-
" ing those which relate to the general arrangement of nature. He must
" have collected the most interesting observations on this head. He
" contemplated nature with the greatest accuracy, and with so much
" knowledge and judicious skill, as to have penetrated into her most
" secret mysteries. But he dared not, as he himself assured me, publish
" those observations during his life, because he was afraid of the exces-
" sive violence of the Swedish divines, who, frequently too faithful
" and too bigotted to their own arguments, do not consider, that na-
" ture as well as revelation proclaim in unison of .inciple, the hands
" of that GREAT MASTER, who formed both. LINNÆUS had the ex-
                                                        " ample

" ample of his pupil Forskal before his eyes, who immediately after
" his return from *Goettingen*, saw himself involved in so many theolo-
" gical disputes, as would, perhaps, have been carried too far, had he
" not left the field of litigation, by setting out on his voyage to
" *Arabia*.

" Linnæus knew how to secure to himself, even in his earlier days,
" that dominion over the three reigns of nature, which he preserved
" till death.

" In mineralogy his very countrymen entered the lists of contention
" against him. He certainly was often attacked and censured with in-
" justice; and the little inaccuracies, which will never fail to exist in
" works of that importance, ought to have been palliated and over-
" looked, on account of the other great merits of their author. It is,
" however, an incontrovertible fact, that he first introduced systematic
" regularity in the mineral reign. He formed the classes, and deter-
" mined the genera and species by regular distinctive marks, which he
" derived from the external appearance. Thus mineralogy became a
" regular science, after it had formerly been but a chaos created by the
" miners, who used to discriminate the minerals partly by practice and
" partly by fire. Linnæus having once left the mines, having no la-
" boratory, and being over-burdened by a multiplicity of other occu-
" pations, discontinued to exert himself so much in mineralogy. His
" system is however excellent, his hypothesis the fruit of the ripest
" reflection, his description of the species are excellent, and his obser-
" vations truly important. In spite of all attacks, his name will like-
" wise be handed down in this science to the latest posterity.

o o   " The

" The vegetable reign possessed the greatest charms for LINNÆUS;
" he bestowed upon it the best share of his time and abilities. When
" he first appeared in the field of science in 1732, TOURNEFORT's system
" of botany derived from the structure of the inward cover of the
" flower, was every where popular and universally accepted. But during
" the latter part of its most flourishing epoch, a kind of barbarism was
" perceived in that system. A great number of new plants having been
" discovered, it so happened that the characters of the inward cover of
" the flower proved insufficient to distinguish one from another with
" plainness and regularity. Botanists began, therefore, to have recourse
" to the outward appearance, and to copper-plates, not without preju-
" dice to the certainty of the real system.

    " LINNÆ J soon perceived the error and its real foundation, in the
" want of sufficient and solid characters, which the inward cover of the
" flower could never have procured. He sought, therefore, a safer
" basis for his system, and took at first the outward cover of the flower
" to effect his purpose. But he found it equally insufficient. He ulti-
" mately examined the SEX of the PLANTS, which had in some mea-
" sure been already known before him, though never used as a system.
" Upon these enquiries he built his SEXUAL SYSTEM, which soon
" met with universal approbation and spread itself throughout Europe.
" That he might render it the more firm and imperishable, he intro-
" duced the natural characters of the genera, which he took from all
" the parts of fructification, and from which he obtained a great num-
" ber of distinctive marks, which will never fail accurately to point
" out the genera. He demonstrated the true principles of a botanical
" system, introduced a solid, certain and definitive technology, and

                              3   " demon-

" demonstrated the various errors of his predecessors, which had made
" their systems totter, and rendered uncertain the definition of the
" plants. This laid the foundation of his authority in the science
" of botany, which he extended still farther in a most extraordinary
" manner, by the excellent, concise and plain DIFFENTIÆ SPECI-
" FICÆ, by the trivial names, and a solid and precise synonimy. After
" the entire arrangement and completion of his system, when the de-
" nomination and definition of plants could no longer embarrass its
" progress, he began to give a great number of the descriptions of the
" new species, which are all real master pieces, and the knowledge of
" which he partly owed to his travels, partly to his pupils, and from
" which the many editions and the important emendations of his sys-
" tem have originated. He was, at the same time, extremely cautious
" in not mentioning any plant as a species or as a genus, of which he
" either did not well know the characters, or did not find n suf-
" ficiently clear to his understanding. He acted thus, merely that he
" might not prejudice the solidity of his system.

" The number of his new and important observations in botany is
" very great. They are for the most part to be found in the collection
" of his academical dissertations. He also took uncommon pains to
" finish his ORDINES NATURALES, or the natural affinity which sub-
" sists among the plants; but notwithstanding the great extent of his
" exertions, those productions only remained fragments, and many
" plants still are left, to which he could not assign a place in their
" natural order. I wished at the same time to get better acquainted
" with the distinc ve marks of his natural classes and with his obser-
" vations upon them. He subjoined them finally, though with too

" much

"' much laconism, to the last edition of his GENERA PLANTARUM,
" which was the result of some lectures he gave us in summer, in the
" country, upon the NATURAL ORDERS.

" These are his merits in botany, to which he gave a quite new ap-
" pearance, and enriched with many valuable remarks*."—" If we
" make conjecture of the value of the LINNÆAN method," says the
celebrated HILL in his *Vegetable System*, " it will live, even when a
" natural method shall be found, as long as there is science."

" LINNÆUS manifested the same spirit of systematical order in the
" animal reign. He found it a real chaos, in which the infinite number
" of animals were confounded without characteristic distinction and
" without order. There had hardly been any regular and fixed classes
" introduced, at least not among the smaller kinds of animals. But he
" made it a regular science He limited the various classes by plain dis-
" tinctive marks, introduced the solid genera, determined the species,
" and took pains to lessen the great number of variations. I must
" freely own, that LINNÆUS himself was very sensible, that his system
" of the animal reign was not built upon so safe a foundation as his
" botany, and that his generical characters were far more tottering and
" more undefined. It is, however, the only system which comprises the
" whole animal reign, which is certainly a great prerogative, if we only
" consider the circumstances in which LINNÆUS found that science.
" It remained almost entirely uncultivated, consisted only of a few de-
" scriptions which were extremely deficient, and of a small number of
" copper-plates so badly executed as hardly to be discernible. In

* See a special sketch of the Botanical Reform of LINNÆUS in the Supplements annexed
to this work.

2   " Ichthyology

" Ichthyology, he alone profited by the labours of his ill-fated friend
" ARTEDI.

" LINNÆUS was likewise the first who separated the worms from the
" insects, defined both classes by real characters, and introduced genera,
" sorts, and orders—a foundation upon which almost all his successors
" built after him. He also augmented all the different parts of the ani-
" mal reign by a very considerable number of new discovered species,
" by exact and more accurate descriptions, and by a great quantity of
" the most important discoveries, which chiefly relate to animal œco-
" nomy.

" LINNÆUS was therefore a great man in all the branches of natural
" history. His name will consequently remain immortal in them all. Pos-
" terity will admire the penetrating spirit, the precision and the energy,
" which shine forth in the works of that original genius, who rendered
" his science the most regular, and was th. boast of his cou: and
" the pride of his age."

BIOGRAPHICAL

BIOGRAPHICAL PARTICULARS

OF

THE LIFE

OF

PROFESSOR CHARLES LINNÆUS, JUNIOR.

BIOGRAPHICAL PARTICULARS, &c.

To the picture of the FATHER, we shall also add here, as a like piece, the portrait of his SON, Professor CHARLES LINNÆUS, who was the heir of his academical office, of his knowledge and his celebrity:—but who was too prematurely snatched away from his career, even before able to attain that greatness, which was his aim, the expectation of his citizens, and the hope of the literary world.

CHARLES LINNÆUS, as we have already mentioned in the seventh section of this work, was born January 20, 1741, in the house of his grandfather, at *Fahlun*, the capital of *Dalecarlia*. His future destination was soon decided, and left no room to hesitate. The natural inclination and the science of the parent were also to devolve to the share of his son. There was no study in which the latter could find a better opportunity of becoming eminent, than that which had already gained immortality to his sire. From his earliest infancy his education had been planned to make him a naturalist; and what had once been found reprehensible in his father, was now deemed praise-worthy in him.

P p   He

He was encouraged in culling flowers, examining plants, &c. &c. And these occupations proved both grateful and pleasant to the juvenile student.

In order to regulate his occupations, to form his mind, and his natural capacities, he was early put under the care of private tutors. His father chose for this purpose, the most hopeful young men who then studied at *Upsal.* These were LOEFLING, FALK, and RO-LANDER, whom LINNÆUS afterwards recommended to go out on ·c~ages of discovery, and some of whom made a most fatal exit. They · re chiefly ·-·· :d to impart to their pupil the knowledge of the language of the learned world, and of the technical terms of the science ~·· ch he studied. From the habitual practice of conversing in Latin, he soon learned to talk that language with much fluency, and all his discourses be·ng constantly directed to objects of natural history, he c :ourse, could not but acquire a great knowledge of natural productions*. Already in the tenth year of his age he knew most of the plants in the botanical garden at *Upsal,* and assigned to them their right names.

His early distinction, and the authority and influence of his father, procured him likewise early honours and dignities. He already ascended the first step of literary greatness in his eighteenth year, being appointed demonstrator in the botanical garden at *Upsal.* Before him, no such academical charge existed in that University. At twenty-one he appeared as an author, by publishing the beginning of his descrip-

---

* In his epistolary style, and on other occasions, when he expressed himself with quickness, his Latin was as incorrect as his father's. The hand which he wrote was somewhat larger, but resembled much in other respects that which his father wrote. His coat of arms did not bear the motto: *Famam Extendere Factis.*

tion

tion of the rarest and most remarkable plants in the botanical garden of that University,—a work, which he continued afterwards*. His father had given him instructions how to complete this production, and it became the means of totally securing his subsequent fortune. On the 19th of March 1763, in the twenty-second year of his age, he was nominated adjunct professor of botany, with the extraordinay promise, that after the death of his father, he should succeed him in all his academical functions;—a distinction, a rapidity of preferment which excited in no small degree the envy of his young colleagues. In order to qualify himself in a proper manner, for the future exercise of all his dignities, he took his degree of Doctor of Medicine in 1765, under the presidency of SAMUEL AURIVILLIUS.

Young LINNÆUS, as a public man, was now as happy as possible, but not so in the circle of his relations, where he ought to have experienced the greatest pleasure. He began to give lectures; but his diligent exertions for the benefit of the learned world, and the fondness for his science, received a check, and degenerated into displeasure and splenetic disgust.

The occasion of this disgust was as sad as the thing in itself was extraordinary, and an unnatural oddity. The son had the misfortune, instead of being the delight of his mother, to become the object of her hatred. Considering him as the only son,—as a son, who distinguished himself so much, it appears to be a singular phenomenon, the more so, as her antipathy continued to last without the least abatement. The

* CAROLI LINNÆI, Filii, Decas Prima Plantarum Rariorum Horti Upsaliensis, sistens descriptiones et figuras plantarum minus cognitarum, Stock. 1762. fol. Decas Secunda, ibid. 1763. Fasciculus primus Plantarum Rariorum Horti Upsaliensis. He discontinued the publication of the Fasciculi.

causes

causes and motives of this maternal ill-will are of such a nature, as may well remain unnoticed by us.

"It was singular," "says professor FABRICIUS, who speaks as an ocular witness, "that the lady of LINNÆUS should have had so "particular an aversion to her son. He could not have had a greater "enemy in the world than his own mother. The father was obliged "to send him out of the house, and when he was at liberty to appoint "a person to be his successor, she forced him to pass by his own son, "and to choose Doctor SOLANDER, who she thought would marry her "elde   ughter: but as SOLANDER refused to leave *England*, he "ultimately fixed his choice upon his son, though still very much "against the will of his wife. After the father's death she forced him "to purchase every article of her, even the herbarium."

The truth and impartiality of this account is confirmed by the una-nimity of all other collateral testimonies. The strongest and most nu-merous proofs might be adduced on this subject. Were it compatible with the duty of veracity, which is incumbent on every historian, how chearfully would we pass in silence all particulars of this kind. We will therefore entirely confine ourselves to add the following account, by way of appendage to that given by FABRICIUS. It is extracted from a letter of a celebrated man, who had long been in an habit of the greatest intimacy with LINNÆUS and his son.

"The lady of LINNÆUS was a good housewife, but in no respect a "pattern of a sweet and mild mother, or of a tender spouse. Her only "son lived under the most slavish restraint and in continual fear of her. "Even when he had attained the age of manhood, and bore an acade-"mical dignity, she compelled him to SWEEP HIS OWN ROOM.

2   "One

" One of his kinsmen once made him a present of a great coat;—she
" also envied him this gift, and when it was worn out— HE CLANDES-
" TINELY WENT INTO THE GARDEN, AND THERE TURNED IT HIM-
" SELF. Thus was the son, notwithstanding the affluence of his pa-
" rents, reduced by the singular inextinguishable antipathy of his
" mother, to circumstances and offices as low as those to which ne-
" cessity had once driven his father."

Galled by these shackles of slavery and constraint, the flower of his
mind faded, and he lost that eagerness of zeal which he formerly manifested in his studies. His disgust lessened also the affection of his
father. One of his German friends took leave of him, after he had
completed his thirtieth year, previous to his departure from *Upsal*.
—" AH! HOW I ENVY YOU AND YOUR GOOD FORTUNE!" said he,
penetrated with sentiments of friendship, blended with melancholy discontent.—" YOU ARE AT FULL LIBERTY; YOU RETURN NOW TO
" YOUR COUNTRY TO ENJOY PROSPERITY AND CONTENTMENT. —
" How much more do I envy you," replied his friend, " your fortune
" is made, and I must first go in quest of one; YOU ARE YOUR
" FATHER'S SUCCESSOR."———" POH! MY FATHER'S SUCCESSOR,"
replied he; " I WOULD RATHER BE ANY THING ELSE; I WOULD
" EVEN PREFER BEING A SOLDIER*!"

This lowness of spirits and depression of mind was fortunately removed some time after. He was quite overjoyed when his father
made him a present of all the duplicates of plants which his herbarium
contained. He received also many encouragements from other quarters;—and, all on a sudden, his soul was roused from its lethargy,

---

* Communicated by the person to whom he said these words.

and

and shook off those ties which had so long warped his faculties. From this moment, he continued to show himself the most zealous lover and promoter of his science.

In the beginning of the year 1778 ensued the death, which was so heavy a loss to the sciences and to the Universities of *Upsal,* and a loss still heavier to him as a son. He was so fortunate as to inherit an illustrious name; but how arduous was the task of preserving the lustre of that name, and of compensating as much as possible for the loss of him, whose successor he had been appointed fifteen years before.

Meanwhile he entered, with revived courage and energy, the career assigned to him, and accumulated both honour and merit in his functions as a professor. The sphere left for his activity to exert itself in, was equally vast and important. The arrangement of the manuscript collections of his fathe , and the superintending of the new editions of several of his works, required both great industry and attention.

A paternal manuscript became the first among the collection, which he was induced, agreeable to the wish formerly expressed by his father, to communicate to the learned world. This was the SUPPLEMENT to his SYSTEM of the VEGETABLE REIGN: *Supplementum Plantarum Systematis Vegetabilium. Brunswig,* 1781, in octavo.—Several erroneous reports have been circulated respecting the publication of this supplement. We, therefore communicate here the following authentic account, in the words of the celebrated man, to whose care its publication had been entrusted.

" About three months before my departure from *Sweden,*" says the great botanist, EHRHART, in a letter to the author, " in 1776, the vene-
" rable LINNÆUS asked me, if I chose to take the *Supplementum Plan-*

1   " *tarum*

" *tarum* with me to *Germany*, and to get it printed there. I promised him
" I would. A little before my departure, I put him in mind of the proposal
" he had made; but he then told me, that he would wait THUNBERG's
" return from his travels, to publish the discoveries of the latter in the
" Supplement, and to send me the manuscript, as soon as every thing
" should have been inserted in its proper place. But THUNBERG did
" not return till after the death of LINNÆUS. He arrived, and com-
" municated his new plants and their characters to the son of his great
" master, who arranged them in their right order, and sent me the ma-
" nuscripts in the autumn of 1779, to be printed. I perused it, set down
" my doubts and observations, and sent them to LINNÆUS. A corres-
" pondence then began between us, which lasted almost the whole of
" the ensuing winter. After this, I had copied it afresh, and began to
" get it quite ready for the press; I was however, prevented, by the
" botanical tour through the electorate of *Hanover*, with which his BRI-
" TANNIC MAJESTY had expressly charged me. I got it ready at-last, in
" the winter between 1780 and 1781. The work was to be printed at
" *Hanover*, under my immediate inspection; but it did not take place.
" I agreed afterwards for the printing of the work at *Brunswick*, in the
" asylum. The principals of the Orphan Asylum procured new types
" for this purpose, printed it off in the summer of 1781, and paid an
" honorary of two ducats per sheet, which I sent to LINNÆUS after
" his return from *England*. Messrs. DU ROI and POTT at *Brunswick*,
" were so kind, while I travelled about, to take care of the correspon-
" dence."

Thus, after so many obstacles, the liberal and unremitting efforts
of a German friend of LINNÆUS, effected the publication of a work,
the

the possession of which was coveted by many. It was originally projected to enrich it with a most valuable addition; this was the *Genera
Muscorum* of the celebrated EHRHART. But this insertion was not
made; either because LINNÆUS found it too laborious a business to
attend to it, as he designed to get an edition of the *Supplementum Plantarum* printed at *London*; or, what appears more probable, because the
English persuaded him to omit the *Genera Muscorum*, as they could not
at that time see the merits of the discoveries of Mr. EHRHART, in their
proper light.

The *Supplementum* contained and described ninety-three genera and one
thousand three hundred and three species of plants. The son imitated the
father, in not adopting, as his own, the supposed definitions and descriptions of others; and in not describing as new any plants which he had
not seen himself, and in a more particular manner got acquainted with.
He also honoured the memory of several of his countrymen, a FALK,
a TERNSTROEM, a MONTIN, a RETZIUS, an ECKEBERG, a SPARR-
MANN, and a THUNBERG, either by naming plants after them, or by
adopting those names, which had already been assigned to them by
others.

Besides his lectures, he also gave other proofs of his literary activity
in different dissertations, which were defended under his auspices. He
described some new *genera* of *grasses*, and published a treatise upon the
lavenders, and some new elucidations respecting the fructification of the
mosses *.

Long

* Dissertatio illustrans Nova Graminum Genera; Resp. D. E. NÆZEN; *Upsal*, 1779.—
Dissert. de Lavandula, Respond.   J. D. LUNDMARK, *Upsal*, 1780.—Methodus Muscorum
Illustrata, Resp. Ol. SCHWARZ, *Upsal*, 1781.—These dissertations may be seen in the *Amœ-
nitat.*

Long before he succeeded his father in his office, it had been his chief wish to travel. But as long as he laboured under so many constraints in his father's house, he found it impossible to realize that wish. No sooner had he become his own master, than he burnt with a desire of accomplishing it. He intended to publish a new edition of the principal work of his father—the *System of Nature*,—and for this reason wished the more anxiously to see foreign herbals, especially the natural productions collected in the countries lately discovered in the South Seas.

Money, which is always required in travelling, had long been the principal obstacle to his departure. A patriotic friend at last offered Linnæus the sum requisite for defraying his travelling expences. This was Baron Nicholas Alstroemer, Commander of the Order of *Vasa*, at *Gothenburgh* *. This temporay suspension from his academical office created no kind of inconvenience. Thunberg had been appointed demonstrator of botany after his return to *Sweden*. Government, therefore, gave Linnæus leave to travel. The celebrity of father's name promised him a good reception abroad, and he found it accordingly.

The first country, which, from his thirst after knowledge he longed to see, was *England*. In the spring of 1781 he embarked, and reached *London* in the course of May. The most interesting person with whom he wished to get acquainted there, was Sir John Banks, President of

nitat. *Acad.* Edit Schreberi, *Erlang*, 1790, vol. x.—Cui accedunt Dissertationes Botanicæ, C. A Linne, Filii. See also *Acta Medicorum, Suecicorum*, seu Sylloge observationum et casuum rariorum, præsertim in Historia Naturali, Praxi Medica, &c. tom. i. *Ups.* 1783. 8vo.

* Linnæus designed him for the heir of the Herbarium which he had collected during his father's life. Alstroemer received it accordingly, but not the duplicates of plants, which Linnæus had collected on his travels.

the

the Royal Society of *London*, that great lover of nature, who so much distinguished himself, and acquired such transcendent merit as a promoter of natural history, by the great sums which he expends upon natural curiosities, by his own enthusiasm for that science, and by his participating in Captain Cook's second voyage round the world. The manner in which Sir Hans Sloane had received the father, and the reception which the son now met with, formed a most striking contrast. Sir Joseph was an ancient correspondent and friend of his father's, and received the younger Linnæus, whose countryman and colleague Dr. Solander had accompanied him on his voyage round the world, and was now his intimate friend and assistant, with all that warmth of friendship and kindness, which, under similar circumstances, can possibly be expressed by the noblest and most elevated mind.

Sir Joseph made Linnæus welcome to make his house his own during his stay in *England*, and the latter found in it the most select company. The rare collection of natural treasures brought together from all parts of the world, especially those from the new discovered countries in the South Seas, which he saw at Sir Joseph's, was the greatest treat for his curiosity and his love of knowledge. This collection, on account of the copiousness, the rarity, and value of its contents, is the first of which any private individual could ever boast in *Europe*. Linnæus viewed, and examined article by article, and saw more curiosities here than he would have observed, had he travelled himself for a long series of years in the remotest quarters of the globe. Sir Joseph, with his wonted liberality, enriched his visitor with a number of duplicate-plants and other natural curiosities. The British Museum, that great repository of natural science and art, whose immense treasures were then principally

2   under

under the care of Dr. SOLANDER, was constantly open for his inspection, with all its herbals and collections.

The public and private botanical gardens, the royal botanical garden at *Kew*, that at *Chelsea*, and that of the Marquis of ROCKINGHAM at *Wimbledon*, became particular objects of his attention. He also visited the principal museums of natural history, the libraries and menageries, &c. belonging to private persons both in and about *London*; amongst others, those of the Dutchess of PORTLAND, of Dr. WILLIAM HUNTER, Sir ASHTON LEVER, Dr. FORDYCE, Dr. FOTHERGILL, Dr. PITCAIRN, Dr. LETTSOM, Messrs. GORDON, YEATES, LEE, MALCOLM, &c. &c.

Wherever he could find an opportunity of gratifying his scientific curiosity, he eagerly sought after it; and the enthusiastic love of botany and natural history which then prevailed in *England*, afforded him every where the most cordial reception, and the profoundest respect for that name which his father had rendered so celebrated.

Among the men, who first made known the LINNÆAN system of botany in *England*, was the celebrated Dutch naturalist, PETER CAMPER*. He had recommended it in the most particular manner during his first residence in this country, from 1748 till the summer of 1749. He found an opportunity in his intercourse with Sir HANS SLOANE, Dr. SMELLIE, Dr. HILL, COLLINSON, CATESBY, &c. &c. to show to the British naturalists and botanists, how plants were to be examined according to the method of LINNÆUS. His demonstrations excited admiration and roused to and fro a spirit of investigation.

* Born at *Leyden*, May 11th, 1722, and died April 7th, 1789. This account comes from a person who was personally acquainted with LINNÆUS, CAMPER and SOLANDER. See *Levechez Van Camper*, by his son, A. G. CAMPER. *Luewarden*, 1791.

But

But it wanted a real adept to remove the difficulties which obstructed the progress of the LINNÆAN system in *England*. The Britons, who felt so little relish at that time for foreign literature, became afterwards the most zealous admirers and votaries of LINNÆUS; and Dr. SOLANDER contributed a great deal to this favourable change in the general disposition of the British literati.

When Dr. SOLANDER left *Sweden* to go to *England*, LINNÆUS gave him a letter to ELLIS, in which he recommended him as strongly as if he had been his own son. The incidental qualification of being a pupil of LINNÆUS, soon endeared him to almost every lover of natural history at *London*. His own prepossessing and amiable qualities served still farther to foster this favourable disposition on their part. He was so generally beloved, that every body owned that SOLANDER had not a single enemy. When he was appointed inspector of the British Museum, there was only an incomplete and useless catalogue of its treasures; he was therefore charged with making a new one. He wrote seven large quarto volumes, and laboured from an early hour in the morning till two or three o'clock in the afternoon. At that time he adjourned his exertions according to the *London* custom till next day. When he made the voyage round the world with Captain COOK, and in company with Sir JOSEPH BANKS, his annual salary, as inspector of the British Museum, was doubled. In 1771, the father of LINNÆUS complained that he had not heard of SOLANDER for several years, yet he had done as much for him as for any one of his pupils. He rejoiced, however, at seeing the new edition of ELLIS's *Essay on Corallines*, published under the auspices of SOLANDER, who sent him some of the proof-plates. SOLANDER was the oracle of natural history in *England*, and

consulted

consulted whenever any new natural production was to be described, defined or named. · What proves his indefatigable diligence, are the collections of plants of Sir HANS SLOANE, and those of RAY, PETIVER, PLUKENET and others, which Sir HANS purchased after the death of their proprietors. Dr. SOLANDER added to each of those plants, by the side of which the names given to them by the original collector were written, the LINNÆAN name ; or, if they were new, he gave them a name of his own choosing.

The younger LINNÆUS had come into a new world of curiosities. and never seen happier days than in the metropolis of *Great Britain*. But this happiness did not remain undisturbed by unpleasant occurrences. Fate had reserved for him the saddest and most melancholy doom of witnessing the death of his friend, Dr. SOLANDER, who was suddenly carried off by an apoplectic stroke. To honour his memory he called a new plant *Sciandra*, the description of which he prepared for insertion in the transactions of the Royal Academy of Sciences at *Copenhagen*. He had already paid the tribute of his gratitude to his kind patron, Sir JOSEPH BANKS, and given a public testimony of respect to his merits, by describing in the *Supplementum* a genus of plants from *New Holland* by the name of *Banksia*. It was also an unfortunate circumstance, that almost half the time of his residence in *England* should have been lost to him. He fell ill of the jaundice, under which he laboured for near two month. After his recovery he continued his travels, by setting out for *France* at the latter end of August, 1781, having sojourned four months and an half in *England*.

On his way to *Paris*, he was accompanied by the French naturalist, M. BROUSSONET, lately a member of the second National Assembly,

1   with

with whom he had got acquainted at *London,* where he had resided a considerable time longer than LINNÆUS, to study ichthyology, in which he almost rivalled the greatness of the ill-fated ARTEDI.—The habit of intimacy which he had contracted with M. BROUSSONET, the letters of recommendation from his acquaintance at *London,* and much more the celebrity and veneration of his father's name, also ensured to him the most hearty and most cordial reception there, on the part of all those persons who felt it an interest to converse with him, and especially on the part of all the lovers of botany, and of the proprietors of natural collections.

Among these were the Duke D'ENGHIEN, the Duke DE CHAULNES, the Duke DE NOAILLES, Marshal of *France,* Messrs. D'AUBENTON, BRISSON, DESFONTAINES, GEOFFROI, GUETTARD, L'HERITIER, the younger DE JUSSIEU, DE LA MARQUE, MALESHERBES, MAUDUIT, LE MONNIER, THOUIN, &c. &c.

LOUIS XVI. the late King of *France,* thought it worthy of his greatness to give him a proof of his royal munificence. He made LINNÆUS a present of the splendid collection of plants engraved at his MAJESTY's own expence (RECUEIL DES PLANTES, GRAVÉES PAR ORDRE DU ROI), consisting of three large folios, with 500 copper-plates. He had the satisfaction of first learning personally the greatness of the celebrity of his deceased parent, by the universal respect paid to him by foreigners.

LINNÆUS having spent the winter at *Paris,* amidst a circle of the most select acquaintance, took his departure in the spring of 1782, for *Holland,*—the country where his father had first founded his reputation. He visited CLIFFORT's botanical garden at *Hartecamp,* not without the

greatest

greatest emotion, nor without the liveliest renewal of his father's remembrance. At the *Hague* he saw every thing which could interest a
man of his profession, especially the cabinet of natural history of the
HEREDITARY PRINCE STADTHOLDER, the botanical garden of Professor SCHWENKE, the collection of shells of M. LYONETT, &c. At
Leyden he likewise took a view of all that deserved his notice, and
having met with the kindest and most friendly treatment on the part of
Professors VAN ROYEN and ALLAMAND, he repaired to *Amsterdam*.
Here he found an old personal acquaintance and fellow-student in Professor BURMANN, who did every thing to render his stay pleasant, and
introduced him to all the lovers and collectors of natural curiosities,
especially to HOUTTYN, VANDER MEULEN, &c. &c. LINNÆUS
amassed here, as he had done in *England* and *France*, considerable
treasures for his herbarium.

Having thus gratified his ardent love and desire of knowledge, he
set out by *Utrecht* through *Westphalia* and *Lower Saxony*, on his return
to *Sweden*. The first German city in which he stopped after having
left *Holland*, was *Hamburgh*. Here he found Dr. GIESEKE, Dr.
GRUNO, and many other personal friends and acquaintance; he saw the
principal museums, the collection of shells of Dr. BOLTEN and many
others. He also made acquaintance with several celebrated literati,
amongst others, with Dr. REIMARUS and professor SCHUTZ. After
having spent about eighteen days at *Hamburgh* in a very pleasant manner, he continued his route to STOCKHOLM. He particularly directed
his way to KIEL, that he might pay a visit to his celebrated friend,
professor FABRICIUS, whom he had the pleasure of meeting with in the
preceding year at *London*. In the house of the greatest entomologist,

he

he found also the greatest and finest collection of insects which he had ever seen. He likewise saw there, the herbarium of his unfortunate countryman FORSKAL. He had now come to *Copenhagen*, the last city where he was to stay, in order to view and examine natural curiosities*. This capital was as eager as other great cities to receive him in the most friendly and most distinguished manner. He saw the Royal Museum of productions of nature and art, the cabinet of natural history of COUNT MOLTKE, Privy Counsellor HOLMSKIOLD, Counsellor FRUS ROTTBOELL, Professor BRUNICH, Counsellor MULLER, and of Messrs. SPENGLER, CHEMNITZ, and CAPPEL. The Danes honoured his knowledge and merits in the same manner as the English and French had done. He had been chosen a Member of the Royal Society at *London*, of the Academy of Sciences at *Montpellier*, of the Medical Society at *Paris*, and also of the Royal Society at *Copenhagen*.

In the month of January 1783, he left that city and went to *Gothenburgh*, whither his friendship and gratitude towards the beneficent promoter of his studies, BARON NICHOLAS ALSTROEMER, had impelled him to go. Finally, after an absence of two years he returned again to *Upsal* from his travels in the month of February, after having been through the same countries which had formerly been visited by his father.

---

* He was already at *Copenhagen* in the summer of 1771. He travelled for the recovery of his health which had been much impaired by the hypochondry, through the Southern provinces of *Sweden*, crossed the Sound, and not having leave to go farther, remained two days at *Copenhagen*. He owned afterwards to a friend, that he then felt a strong temptation to range all over the world, had the love which he bore to his father not induced him to go back.

No traveller could have accomplished the proposed end of his travels more perfectly and more auspiciously than LINNÆUS. His peregrination now promised to yield the richest fruits. He had augmented his knowledge and experience in the most extraordinary manner, established extensive connexions, which promised in course of time to afford him great satisfaction and advantage, and collected a vast quantity of natural treasures, the produce of all quarters of the globe. Exclusive of the knowledge of his late father, how many new elucidations and enlargements in natural history could not be expected from a man who was so enthusiastically fond of his study, and so zealously striving for celebrity as LINNÆUS at the present period! He was occupied with the execution of many useful plans and labours. He had projected fresh treatises upon the plants of the palm and lily kind, finished a work upon the sucking-animals, and intended to publish new editions of his father's SYSTEM of NATURE, besides his MATERIA MEDICA, the PHILOSOPHIA BOTANICA, the GENERA PLANTARUM and the FLORA SUECICA. The moment was just come for him to open his career with splendor, but the hand of fate suddenly arrested his progress.

In the month of August he made a journey to *Stockholm*. He there had the misfortune to be taken ill of a bilious fever. This distemper abated in a short time so much, that he found himself able to return to *Upsal*. But as his recovery had not been quite complete, he had a relapse. Soon after his illness seemed to diminish, but owing to his impatient and inalterable love of nature, it gained a third time upon him, because he viewed too early, and too long, his natural collections, which were kept in a damp and cold apartment. The fever renewed its attacks with in-

R r   creased

creased violence, and he fell in a profound and lethargic slumber, which soon changed into the sleep of death. In the afternoon on the first of November 1783, an apoplectic stroke put a period to his existence, in the full prime of life, and in the forty-second year of his age.

His death eclipsed totally many fine and brilliant hopes. Great men are rare phenomena, and it is a still rarer case for their greatness to be transplanted among their descendants in direct line. NEWTON died single; and so did POPE, LEIBNITZ and VOLTAIRE. BARON EMANUEL HALLER followed his father early to the tomb, and the younger LINNÆUS earlier still. He died in a state of celibacy. The domestic circumstances under which he attained the age of manhood, had not permitted him to choose a partner of his life.

The same domestic circumstances had also a great influence upon the harmony of his mind, and the formation of his character. In a strong and fine body he possessed a noble and excellent heart. He strictly resembled his father by his keen and penetrating eyes, in temper and activity of mind; but he was neither endowed with the enterprising resoluteness and energy of his character, nor with his assurance, his candour, his consciousness of superiority, his love of adulation, and the grandeur of his outward appearance. Fond of praise and honour, he never sought after eulogiums, nor was he forward or ostentatious with regard to his learning and merits. Steadily bent upon the execution of all his undertakings and resolutions, he attended gratefully to the hints and remarks of others, whenever they bore conviction with them. He was the delight of his friends, an honour to the University of *Upsal*, and an

2   object

object of still greater and brighter hopes to his fellow citizens, though they never came to maturity.

Attended by a great number of mourners, his corpse was solemnly deposited on the 30th of November 1783, in the cathedral at *Upsal*, close to his father's remains. M. VON SCHULZENHEIM honoured his memory by publicly delivering a funeral oration. The male branch of the ennobled family of LINNÆUS having become extinct by this death, his coat of arms, according to the Swedish custom, was broke in pieces, and the gardener of the University strewed flowers over a tomb which contains the ashes of a generation, that will remain great and imperishable as long as the earth, and nature and her science shall exist.

REMARKABLE

SUPPLEMENTS.

REMARKABLE HISTORY

OF THE

SALE OF THE LINNÆAN COLLECTIONS.

´ FROM A LETTER OF JAMES EDWARD SMITH, M. D. F. R; S. PRESIDENT OF THE LINNÆAN SOCIETY OF LONDON, AND PROPRIETOR OF THE LINNÆAN COL-LECTIONS, TO THE AUTHOR.

" *London*, November 21, 1791.

" IN the first place I shall give you, Sir, an historical account of the
" sale of the LINNÆAN collections with as much accuracy as I can.

" On the death of the younger LINNÆUS, in the autumn of 1783,
" his Majesty the King of *Sweden* was, I believe, in *France**. The

* The late King of *Sweden* left *Stockholm* in the month of September, 1783, and travelled
by the title of COUNT of HAGA, through *Germany* to *Italy*, went to *Florence*, *Pisa*, and
Rome, and left the latter place April 19, 1784, to go to *Paris*, where he remained till the
19th of July following, after which he returned with the utmost dispatch to *Stockholm*, which
he reached in the beginning of August.

" mother

" mother and sisters of the deceased were anxious to make as large a
" profit as they could of his museum, and therefore within a few weeks
" after his death employed Dr. JOHN GUSTAVUS ACREL, Professor of
" Medicine at *Upsal*, to offer the whole collection of books, manu-
" scripts and natural history, to SIR JOSEPH BANKS, for the sum of
" 1000 guineas (1050 pounds sterling).

" Dr. ACREL wrote to Dr. ENGELHART the younger, now Professor
" at *Gottenburgh*, and who was then in *London*, to make this offer to
" Sir JOSEPH BANKS. It happened, that I breakfasted at Sir JOSEPH's
" that very day, which was December 23, 1783, and he told me of the
" offer he had, saying he should decline it, and advising me strongly
" to make the purchase, as a thing suitable to my taste, and which
" would do me honour.

" At that time we knew very little of what the collections consisted.
" When the catalogue of the books and other particulars were after-
" wards sent, they proved much richer than either Sir JOSEPH BANKS
" or myself had any idea of; but I ought not to omit, that Sir JOSEPH
" acted throughout the affair with the utmost honour and liberality,
" (for which indeed he is very remarkable) always encouraging me in
" every difficulty with his advice and assistance. On the 23d of
" December I made my desire known to my friend, Dr. ENGEL-
" HART, with whom I had been intimately acquainted at *Edinburgh*,
" and we both wrote the same day to Professor ACREL, desiring a cata-
" logue of the whole, and saying, that if it answered my expectations, I
" would be the purchaser at the price fixed.

" In this affair I trusted to the honour of Professor ACREL alone, nor
" did I apply to any body else, to take care of my interest in the mat-
" ter.

" ter. I never was in *Sweden* at any time of my life.—In due time the
" Professor sent an accurate catalogue of books, and a general account
" of the other articles. But by this time the mother and sisters of Lin-
" næus began to think, they had been too precipitate. They had
" been in great haste to sell the collection before the return of the
" King of *Sweden*, perhaps lest she might be obliged to sell it to the
" University of *Upsal*, at a cheap rate ; and they had pitched upon Sir
" Joseph Banks, as the most opulent and zealous naturalist in *Europe*,
" thinking he would give more for it than any body else, and at the
" same time they fixed 1000 guineas as probably the largest sum that
" could be thought of..

" But while they were in treaty with me, enquiries were made;
" which gave them an higher idea of the value of the collection, and
" they had *unlimited offers from Russia.* They therefore wanted to
" break off their negotiation with me ; but Professor Acrel would not
" consent to that, and insisted on their waiting for my refusal. For
" this honourable conduct he has unfortunately incurred their censure,
" and all sorts of false reports have been raised against him, such as,
" that I had bribed him with 100 guineas, which however is so far
" from being the case, that he never had a present from me, except a few
" English books out of the Linnæan library, (worth about six or eight
" guineas) which he desired to purchase of me, as he could not get
" them in *Sweden*, and which I prevailed on him with some difficulty
" to accept. I thought this a very small and inadequate return for the
" trouble he had on my account, and it surely could not be con-
" sidered as a bribe.

s s   " At

" At this time Baron ALSTROEMER, claimed of the heirs of LIN-
" NÆUS a debt, which the younger LINNÆUS owed him, and for which
" they agreed to give him a small herbarium, made by the said LIN-
" NÆUS during his father's life, containing only duplicates of the great
" collection, and not any of the plants he afterwards collected in his
" travels.   On consideration of this they agreed to abate one hundred
" guineas of my purchase money.   To all this I consented.   I paid
" half the money down, and the rest in three months,—-and in October,
" 1784, received the collection in *twenty-six great boxes*, perfectly safe.

" I paid eighty guineas to the captain for freight, which was too much
" by half; but I was careful to avoid all delay. *For the ship had just sailed*
" *when the KING of Sweden returned, and hearing the story, he sent a vessel*
" *after the ship, to bring it back; but happily for me, it was too late.*   The
" English government, in consequence of the application of my friend,
" Sir JOHN JERVIS, was very indulgent to me, in suffering the whole
" collection to pass the custom-house without any examination or ex-
" pence, except a slight duty on the books.

" This is a true statement of the purchase.   As to what Dr. DAHL
" has mentioned in his *Observationes Botanicæ* about a Mr. MAURLE.
" I have authority to say, it is *altogether false*; and if it had been true, it
" could not have prevented the collection coming away, unless the heirs
" had acted dishonourably towards me.   I do not wonder the Swedes
" are angry at losing *such a treasure*; but they ought to stick to truth;
" and I can at any time justify Dr. ACREL and myself by publishing
" our whole correspondence.   I have endeavoured, to do him some
" justice in the dedication of my *Reliquiæ Rudbeckianæ.*

"The

" The collection consists of every thing possessed by the two Lin-
" næi, relating to natural history or medicine. The library may con-
" tain about 2500 volumes, or many more, if all the dissertations were
" reckoned separately. The old Herbarium of Linnæus contains all
" the plants described in the *Species Plantarum*, except, perhaps, about
" five hundred species, (*Fungi* and *Palmæ* excepted) and it has perhaps
" more than 500 undescribed. The herbarium of young Linnæus
" is more splendid and on better paper. It contains most of the plants
" of his *Supplementum*, except what are in his father's Herbarium, and
" has besides about 1500 very fine specimens from Commerson's
" collection, most of them new; besides vast collections from Dom-
" bey, La Mark, Pourret, Guan, Smeathman, Masson, &c.
" and above all, a prodigious quantity from Sir Joseph Banks, who
" gave him duplicates of almost every one of Aublet's specimens,
" as well as of his own West Indian plants, with a few of those col-
" lected in his own voyages round the world, of which last, however,
" he has not yet given many away to any body.

" Young Linnæus also made ample collections from the gardens of
" *Holland*, *France* and *England*; he made his collection a duplicate one,
" independent of his father's and separate from it, as I still keep it, and
" have added many things to it collected by myself in *England*, *France*,
" *Italy* and the *Alps*. I am also enriching it daily by the kindness of
" my friends, and have lately had a fine addition from the *East Indies*.

" The insects are not so numerous; but they consist of most of those
" that are described by Linnæus, and many new ones. The *shells* are
" about thrice as many as are mentioned in *Systema Naturæ*, and many
" of them very valuable, as young Linnæus had increased that part

" of

" of the collection very much. The *fossils* are numerous, but mostly
" bad specimens and in a bad condition. I have also many birds from
" the *South Seas*, with some Indian dresses and weapons, a number of
" dried fish, particularly all those sent by Dr. GARDEN from *Carolina*,
" some seeds of plants, and an *Herbarium Surinamense* in spirits of wine,
" and several other things.

" The *manuscripts* are very numerous. All his own works are inter-
" leaved, with abundance of notes, especially the *Systema Naturæ*,
" *Species Plantarum, Materia Medica, Philosophica Botanicæ, Clavis*
" *Medicinæ*, &c. &c. I have not yet found the *Nemesis Divina*; but I
" have a vast number of papers I have not yet perused. I have *Iter*
" *Laponicum, Iter Dalecarlicum*, and some others; also a *Diary of the*
" *Life of* LINNÆUS, in his own hand, for about the thirty first years of
" his life. I have also *Descriptiones Liliorum et Palmarum* and *Systema*
" *Mammalium*, by LINNÆUS the son, the first of which I shall probably
" publish soon. The *letters to* LINNÆUS are about three thousand.
" Young LINNÆUS left all his things in such disorder, that I have the
" utmost difficulty in arranging them, and I every day discover some-
" thing I did not before know."

A LIST

A

L I S T

OF THE

WORKS OF LINNÆUS.

LIST

OF

THE WORKS OF LINNÆUS,

*THEIR EDITIONS, COMMENTARIES, EXTRACTS, TRANS-
LATIONS, CRITICISMS AND NOMENCLATURES.*

[N. B. *Those Works which are written by* LINNÆUS *himself, and those
Editions which were published under his immediate care, are marked
with Roman Cyphers.*]

^] HORTUS UPLANDICUS, sive enumeratio Plantarum exoticarum, Uplandiæ, quæ in hortis vel agris coluntur, imprimis autem in
horto academico Upsaliensi. *Upsal,* 1731, page 160, in 8vo*.

No. I.

* This was the first production of LINNÆUS, the first display and observance of the
Sexual System. Neither HALLER nor any other Literatus mentions it. The *Florula Lapponica* is generally alledged to be the first work of LINNÆUS. But LINNÆUS himself
mentions

No. I.

Florula Lapponica, quæ continet catalogum plantarum, quas per provincias Lapponicas Westrobotnienses observavit.

This work was written in the year 1732; and inserted in the *Acta Litteraria Sueciæ* of the same year *.

Florulæ Lapponicæ, Pars Secunda.

His second part of the Flora of *Lapland* is also inserted in the Swedish Literary Transactions for the year 1735.

mentions the *Hortus Uplandicus,* even the month of its publication, and some words extracted from the preface. See upon this subject, the following document in a German work published at *Hamburgh* by Dr. KOHL, with whom LINNÆUS kept a correspondence, and lived afterwards in personal friendship; this work is entituled *Hamburgische Berichten,* and Dr. KOHL asks LINNÆUS in a letter, "Is the printing of the *Hortus Uplandicus* "finished?" LINNÆUS in his answer, points out the publication as mentioned above.

* BARON HALLER in his *Bibliotheca Botanica,* tom. ii. Turici, 1772, in 4to. p. 244, begins the LINNÆAN epoch in botany, with the following criticism: Anno 1732, primum CAROLI LINNÆI opusculum prodiit, viri, qui *maximam* in universa re herbaria *conversionem* molitus est, et qui *omnino pene integre suo fine est positus. A natura ardente animo instructus, acerrima imaginatione, ingenio systematico,* opportunitatibus imprimis posteriori suæ vitæ parte usus copiosissimis, cum ex universo orbe undique ad eum certatim naturales thesauri confluerunt, omnibus sui animi viribus, *quas possidet maximas,* in novam rei herbariæ constitutionem incubuit; seque vivente et superstite placita sua a plerisque suis coætaneis recepta vidit. *Neque dissimulari potest; multo accuratius, quam prius solebat, ab eo singulas plantæ partes definitas esse,* multoque magis naturam experimere, quæ nunc dantur descriptiones, etsi novam fere linguam ed *eam rem excogitatam* fuisse fatendem est.—In *Flora Lapponica* primum videas classes superiores a *staminibus* sumtas, inferiores a *tubis,* utrasque a numero, situ et aliquando a proportione, quam nunc methodum sexualem vocant.—

Several separate essays and opinions upon LINNÆUS in the beginning of his literary career, are still to be found in:

Respublica Eruditorum.
1735. November p. 556.
1737. August. p. 73. 87.

Tidender an Lärde og Curieuxe
1734. October 14, No. 41.

No. II.

No. II.

CAROLI LINNÆI Epistola de Itinere suo Lapponico.

This Letter is subjoined in the Supplements, also in the *Commercia Litteraria Norimbergensia ad rei Medicæ et Scientiæ Naturalis incrementa*, Vol. iii. 4to. p. 73 and 74 : and *Hebdom.* 5. No. ii. p. 34.

No. III.

Systema Naturæ, sive Regna tria Naturæ, systematice proposita, per classes, ordines, genera et species, *Lugd. Batav.* apud HAAK, 1735. 14 pages folio *. First edition.

No. IV.

The *Second Edition—Stockholm*, ap. KIESEWETTER, 1740, in octavo, 80 pages.

Revised and augmented by LINNÆUS, with the characters of the genera and the names of the animals.

The *Third Edition—Halle*, by GEBAUER, 1740, seventy quarto pages, published with a preface by J. J. LANGE; to which are added the German terms.—This is a mere copy of the Dutch edition.

The *Fourth Edition.—Paris*, 1744, one hundred and eight octavo pages, properly speaking, published under the care of Dr. AB. BÆCK, who was then at *Paris*, but augmented with the French terms by BERNARD DE JUSSIEU; is in other respects a copy of the second edition, printed at *Stockholm*.

* Summa labore—*in Systemate*—genera constituta esse et characteres redintegratos, palam, est. Ipse ordo a natura certe longissime recedit, qui naturales classes divellat et plantas dissimillimas colliget, separet simillimas. HALLER in Bibliotheca Botanica, tom. ii. p. 244.

The

The *Fifth Edition.—Halle*, 1747, eighty-eight octavo pages, by M. G. AGNETHLER, containing the German terms:—likewise a copy of the second edition, published at *Stockholm.*

No. V.

The *Sixth Edition.—Stockholm*, 1748, in two hundred and thirty-two octavo pages, with eight plates, with the portrait of LINNÆUS, and augmented by him with the distinctive marks of the genera of plants, and a description of the species in the animal and mineral reigns.

The *Seventh Edition,—Leipsic*, 1748, two hundred and thirty-two octavo pages, with eight plates, a mere copy of the preceding edition, to which are superadded the German terms.

The *Eighth Edition—Stockholm*, 1753, one hundred and thirty-six octavo pages, in Swedish; the Vegetable System, by J. J. HARTMANN; the Mineral System, by Mr. MOELLER.

The *Ninth Edition—Leyden*, 1756, two hundred and twenty-eight octavo pages, published by GRONOV, junior, with some botanical and entomological additions, after DE GEER and REAUMUR, in other respects perfectly like the sixth edition.

The *Tenth Edition.—Lucca*, 1758, under the title of:

CAROLI LINNÆI Opera Varia, in quibus continentur Fundamenta Botanices, Sponsalia Plantarum et Systema Naturæ, ex typ. Juncti-niana; merely a copy of the preceding edition with the French names.

No. VI.

The *Eleventh Edition.*—LINNÆUS reckons this as the *Tenth,—Stockholm*, by SALVIUS, 1758 and 1759, two volumes. The first

.1   volume

volume contains the animals, with the synonyms in eight hundred and twenty-one pages ; the second contains the minerals in five hundred and sixty pages ; this edition is considerably augmented, the following three are copied :

The *Twelfth Edition.—Halle,* 1760, by J. J. CURT, in two volumes octavo, with a preface of J. J. LANGE.

The *Thirteenth Edition.—Leipsic,* 1762, two volumes in octavo ; a mere speculation of a greedy bookseller, without additions, and abounding with errors. LINNÆUS reckoned this as the eleventh edition.

The *Fourteenth Edition.*—Tomi ii. Pars. i. et iii. Pars. i. *Hague,* 1765 folio ; as bad as the preceding, with ten very inaccurate plates on the three first Classes of the System *.

No. VII.

The *Fifteenth Edition.*—(According to LINNÆUS the *Twelfth)*— The last which was published under his own care and inspection ; it bears the following title :

Systema Naturæ per Regna tria Naturæ, secundum classes, ordines, genera et species, cum characteribus, differentiis, synonymis, locis, Holm, apud SALVIUM, 1766-68, three volumes in octavo, the first of which contains the Animal System, in one thousand three hundred and twenty-seven pages ; the second the Botanical System, in seven hundred and thirty-six pages, and the third the Minerals in two hundred and thirty-six pages. The third volume was separately printed at *Halle,* in 1770, with plates.

* Anglice, Gallice et Belgicæ, vera fraus bibliopolarum—cum nominibus alienissimis et tanta inscitia, quantam hoc nostro ævo nunquam exspectassem. HALLER, BIBL. Bot. Tom. ii. p. 552.

Sixteenth Edition.—A copy of the preceding *Stockholm* edition, *Vienna* at *Trattner's*, 3 vol. 1767, 1770.

Seventeenth Edition.—(According to LINNÆUS the thirteenth, called in the title the *Eleventh*)—aucta, reformata, cura J. F. GMELIN, *Leips*, 1788, the six volumes of the first part in large octavo, comprising altogether three thousand nine hundred and nine pages. The first part, which contains the Animal reign, is completed in the six vols.

And Tom. ii. Pars *Prima et Secunda, Lips.* 1792. The first part of eight hundred and eighty-four pages in octavo, comprises with new genera and species of near one hundred botanists, the twelve first Classes of the LINNÆAN System.

No nation can produce so complete a repertory of Natural History as the above. With infinite labour, exertion and judgment, all the recent discoveries and observations in all the branches of Natural Science, have been united in it.

In the Animal reign, the works of SCHREBER, PENNANT, FABRICIUS, GOETZ, SCHROETER, MULLER, CRONSTEDT, VON VELTHEIM, BERGMANN, KIRWAN, BLOCH, HERBST, STOLL, VOIGT, FUESSLI, SESTINI, BUFFON, ADANSON, CAMPER, and the Travels of PALLAS, SONNERAT, LESKE, LEPECHIN, GULDENSTÆDT, PEYROUSE, RASUMOWSKY and of an infinite number of other learned men have been consulted.

Had LINNÆUS even enjoyed a longer life, no such enlargement and perfection of his code of nature could have been expected from him in the North *.

* LINNÆUS himself wrote to Professor GIESEKE, on the 20th of December 1774, as follows: " Naturæ Scientia in dies augetur tot novis inventis, ut vix ea comprehendere valeam.

2   If

If we reckon the great number of editions copied in distant climes from the System of Nature of LINNÆUS, their number must probably amount to between twenty and thirty.

Even at *Batavia*, a society of literati resident there, caused an extract of the LINNÆAN System to be published in quarto, with the names in the *Malay* language added to it †.

For GILIBERT's edition see farther below, under the head of the *Species Plantarum.*

Sir CHARLES LINNÆUS's System of Nature, published after the thirteenth edition of GMELIN by Dr. G. W. S. PANZER, vol. i.; the Sucking Animals. *Berlin*, 1791, large octavo, with plates.

---

† Libri LINNÆI pauci extra Europam impressi sunt; sed tamen ex systemate ejus extractum quoddam impressum fuit *Batavia,,* in insula *Java,* cura societatis litterariæ, cum adjectis nominibus Malaicis, in quarto ——From a letter of the Chevalier THUNBERG to the Author.

CRITICAL WRITINGS

ON

SOME SEPARATE PARTS

OF THE

LINNÆAN SYSTEM OF NATURE.

C. G. Ludwig Observationes in Methodum Sexalem Linnæi, Progr. *Lips.* 1739, in eight quarto pages. Reprinted in J. J. Reichard's Sylloge Opusculorum Botanicorum, part i. *Frankfort,* 1742, octavo.

C. A. a Bergen, utri Systematum, an Tournefortiano, an Linnæano potiores partes deferendæ, Progr. *Frankofurt ad Viadr,* 1742, eight pages, quarto.

J. Th. Klein Summa dubiorum Circa Classes Quadrupedum et Amphibiorum in Carol. Linnæi Systemate Naturæ, &c. *Lips.* 1743, fifty-six pages, quarto.

J. S. Poppowitz, professor of the German language at *Vienna,* Demonstration that the Linnæan system is useless. See his researches

respecting

respecting the Sea, &c. *Frankfort* and *Leipsic*, 1750, quarto, in German.

CAROL. ALSTON, Animadversiones in Sexum Plantarum et Systema LINNÆI. In the Essays and Observations Physical and Literary, *Edinburgh*, vol. i. 1754. Also in the *Gentleman's Magazine*, vol. xxiv, page 463.

C. G. FISCHER: Whether a Cabinet of Natural History can be arranged according to the LINNÆAN System, in the New Social Narratives for the Lovers of Natural History, &c. *Lips.* 1758, part i. page 163. German.

J. QUER, Flora Espannola, o Historia C. las Plantas, que se crien en Espanna. *Madrid*, 1762, two vols. quarto.

Both volumes contain many criticisms against the Sexual System of LINNÆUS. QUER died in 1764. This FLORA has been continued and completed afterwards by Dr. CASIMIR GOMETZ, from 1762 to 1784, in four volumes.

C. C. KROYGER, Dissertatio de Sexualitate Plantarum, ante LINNÆUM cognita. *Hafnia*, 1761, quarto.

H. J. V. CRANZ, Institutiones rei Herbariæ, juxta nutum Naturæ digestæ ex habitu. *Vienna*, 1754, in two volumes.

This work, like the other numerous productions of Professor CRANZ, abounds with censure and obloquy against LINNÆUS.

De Pediculari Comosa; Leipsic, 1791, five pages and an half in octavo, by Dr. STEPHAN, dedicated to the LINNÆAN Society at *Leipsic*, contains a vindication of LINNÆUS against the assertions which CRANZ had made respecting this plant.

De

De Botanicis CAROLI LINNÆI *Institutionibus,* was left behind in manuscript with other censorious productions against LINNÆUS, by Professor JULIUS PONTEDERA, who died at *Padua,* September 3, 1757. The publication of all these manuscripts was advertised at *Padua* in 1790, in two quarto volumes.

J. P. SHIMERT, Dissertation de Systemate Sexuali. *Tyrnaviæ,* 1776, octavo, twenty-four pages.

S. AUGUSTIN, Prolegomena in Systema Sexuale, tabulis æneis ad facilius intelligendos terminos illustrata, *Vienna,* 1777, octavo, eighty-four pages.

LINNÆUS's System of Botany, so far as relates to his Classes and Orders of Plants, &c. by W. CURTIS, *London,* 1777, in quarto, nineteen pages, with four plates.

Some Illustrations of the System of Nature, in J. S. SCHOETER's Journal for the Lovers of the Mineral Reign, vol. vi. *Wiemar,* 1780, German, in octavo. From page 315 to 349 it contains an index of the alterations in the twelfth edition of the LINNÆAN System compared with the tenth.

Emendations by the same author, in his Introduction to the Knowledge of Shells, according to the LINNÆAN Method. Vol. i. *Halle,* 1783.

Criticisms on the LINNÆAN System, in the Miscellanies by the Hon. Dr. BARRINGTON. *London,* 178:, quarto, 226 pages.

J. A. SCOPOLI Annus Historico-Naturalis, vol. iv. 1770, octavo—contains several critical illustrations respecting the LINNÆAN Classification of Plants.

Consideration

Consideration of the Linnæan System of Entomology, and of my own; by J. C. Fabricius. Vol. ii. of the Writings of the Friends of Natural History. *Berlin*, 1781, in German.

Objections against Linnæus respecting the Propagation of Mosses, by V. J. De Necker. *Manheim*, in the *Acta Academiæ Theodoræ Palatinæ*—in German.

J. W. Roth's List of Plants, which are not comprised in the proper Orders of the Linnæan System, by the number and quality of their generical parts, with an Introduction. *Altenburg*, 1781, large octavo, in German.

F. C. Medicus's Observations on the Linnæan Genera, in his Botanical Remarks for the year 1783. *Manheim*, 1783, vol. ii. German.

Explication du Système Botanique du Chevalier Von Linné, pour servir d'introduction à la Botanique, par M. Gouan, Conseiller, Professeur, &c. à *Montpellier*, 1787. Large octavo, seventy-two pages.

Methodi Linnæi Botanicæ delineatio; Auctore J. E. Gilibert, *Colon.* 1789, octavo.—A Critique of the Linnæan System by Rector Lichtenstein at *Hamburgh*, in W. Smellie's Philosophy of Natural History, from the English, with additions by the same; and with illustrations by Dr. E. A. W. Zimmermann. *Berlin*, 1791, octavo, vol. i. page 329 *et seq.*

D. Cyrilli Tabulæ Botanicæ elementares quatuor priores, sive icones partium, quæ in fundamentis describuntur. *Neapol.* 1790. In five folio sheets, with unjust, bitter and morose reflections upon Linnæus in the preface.

O N

THE ANIMAL REIGN.

ANIMALIUM Specierum in Classes, Ordines, Genera, Species methodica dispositio, additis Chara&eribus, differentiis atque Synonymis, accomodata ad Systematis Naturæ decimam Holmiensem editionem in formam Enchiridii reda&um. *Lugd. Batav.* 1759; in o&avo.

PETR. CODDAERT Kort Begriep van het Zamenstel der Natur van den Heer C. LINNÆUS, med zeer veele zorten vermedert. Two numbers; *Utrecht,* 1773 and 1774.

D. MARCI (HOUTTYN) Natuurlyke Historie af uitvoerige beschryving der Dieren Planten, en Mineralien, volgens het zamenstel van den Heer LINNÆUS.—*Amsterdam,* first division, thirteen parts, from 1774 to 1780, in o&avo—Dutch.

The Complete System of Nature of Sir CHARLES LINNÆUS, according to the twelfth edition, and the method of HOUTTYN's Work, with a full Illustration by PH. L. ST. MULLER. *Nuremberg,* at RASPE's, 1776; seven parts, in o&avo. German.

The first part of the above work contains the sucking animals, with thirty-two plates.

The second, the Birds with twenty-eight plates.

The

The third, the Amphibious Animals with twelve plates.

The fourth, the Fishes, with eleven plates.

The fifth, the Insects, with thirty-six plates.

The sixth, the Worms, with thirty-seven plates.

The seventh, the Supplements and an Index, with three plates. The price of this work is eighteen rix-dollars.

Compendium of the System of Nature of CHARLES LINNÆUS, as far as it relates to the Animal Reign, with a complete display of MULLER's edition. *Nuremberg*, 1781, and 1782 ; 2. vol. with thirty-nine coloured plates; price eight rix-dollars.—German.

· Systeme Naturel du Règne Animal par classes, familles, genres et especes, avec une notice de tous les animaux, les noms Grecs, Latins et vulgares, suivant la méthode de M. LINNÆUS. a *Paris*, 1754. Vol. ii. 8vo. with plates.

Entomological Supplements to the twelfth edition of LINNÆUS's System of Nature, by J. A. E. GOETZE. *Leipsic*, 1777, to 1781, three volumes in octavo, the last of which consists of three parts. German.

C. A LINNÆI Entomologia Fauniæ Sueciæ descriptionibus aucta, curante et augente Car. DE VILLERS, four volumes. *Lugd. Batav.* 1785—9.

Institutions of Entomology, being a translation of LINNÆUS's *Ordines et Genera Insectorum*; or a systematic arrangement of insects, collated with the different systems of GEOFFROI, SCHAFFER, and SCOPOLI, together with observations of the translator; by THOMAS YATES. *London*, 1773, in octavo.

The *Genera Insectorum* of LINNÆUS exemplified by various specimens of English insects, drawn from nature, by JAMES BARBUT. *London*, 1784, in quarto.

The

The *Genera Vermium* of LINNÆUS exemplified by several of the rareft and most elegant subjects, in the orders of *Testacea, Lithophota* and *Zoophyta*, by JAMES BARBUT, *London*. 2 vol. in quarto with coloured plates.

J. J. ROMER's *Genera Insectorum* LINNÆI et FABRICII, iconibus illustrata, *Turici*, 1790.

Dictionario dos termos technicos de historia natural, extrahidos das obras de LINNÆU, com sua explicacâo e estampas, para facilitar a intelligencia dos mesmos; pelo DR. DOMINGOS VANDELLI. *Coimbra,* 1788, quarto—*Portuguese.*

Systematical Compendium of the Three Reigns of Nature, for the use of teachers and authors instructing young people. *Nuremberg,* 1777, and 1778, 2 vol. with plates—*German.*

The above work is an extract from the German translation of the System of Nature.

Systema Naturæ, ex editione xii. in epitome redactum et prælectionibus academicis accomodatum, a Jo. BECKMANN. *Goetting.* 1772, in 2 vol.

C. a LINNÆI Terminologia Conchyliogica, edit. a Jo. BECKMANN. *Goetting,* 1780, small octavo.

Synonima LINNÆANA, by the same, a corrected edition at G. REYGER's, *Dantzic,* 1760, quarto—Also in the first number of the *German Naturalist,* publifhed in German. *Halle,* 1774.

CAROLI LINNÆI Nomina Insectorum in usum auditorum edita a SAM. GUST. WILCKE. *Gryphiswald,* 1763—32 pages in quarto.

Sir CHARLES LINNÆUS's Termini Conchyologici, or technical terms for shells, in Latin and German, by J. J. SCHROETER.—*Weimar,* 1782, octavo, pages 45.

1   The

The above work is strictly speaking the following dissertation of LINNÆUS: Fundamenta Testaceologiæ, resp. AD. MURRAY, in the Amœnitat. Acad. vol. 8.

Doctoris J. F. BOLTEN ad LINNÆUM Epistola de novo quodam Zoophytorum genere; *Hamb.* 1771. quarto, 12 pages *.

F. A. DONNDORF's Zoological Supplements to the 13th edition of the Linnæan System of Nature. 3 vol. large octavo, *Leipsic*, 1792.

Commentatio Philologica de Simiarum, quotquot veteribus inno-tuerunt formis earumque nominibus, pro specimine methodi, qua historia naturalis veterum ad Systema Naturæ Linnæanum exigenda atque adornanda, ab auctore M. A. A. H. LICHTENSTEIN, Johann, Hamb. Rectore. *Hamb.* 1791, 80 pages octavo.

ON

THE VEGETABLE REIGN.

No. VIII.

Supplementum Plantarum Systemat. Veget. bil. xiii. Generum edit. vi. et Specierum edit. ii. *Brunovici*, 1781. 30 sheets, in octavo. Respect-ing this work, see the Life of the YOUNGER LINNÆUS.

* Thofe writings which were published *ad motum et methodum* LINNÆI, are not placed here. Their titles alone would be fufficient to fill a volume.

The

The Younger LINNÆUS's Supplement to the sixth edition of the *Genera Plantarum* and the first and second *Mantissa*, translated from the Latin into *German*, by J. J. PLANER. *Gotha,* 1785, 112 pages octavo.

FRANCIS EHRHART's Supplement to the LINNÆAN *Supplementum Plantarum. Hanover,* 1787---8, vol. 1, from page 174 to 194.

No. IX.

Systema Vegetabile, secundum illustris auctoris observationes emendationes novissimas, editum a J. A. MURRAY. *Goetting,* 1774. This was the 13th edition of this part of the system.

The *fourteenth edition;* præcedente longe auctior et correctior, by the same. *Goetting,* 1784---987 pages, in large octavo.

Observationes Botanicæ circa Systema Vegetabilium Divi A LINNÉ, *Goetting.* 1784, editum &c. auctore ANDR. DAHL, Westgothia— Succo. *Havaniæ,* 1787, *Zurich,* 1788.

The System of Plants of CHARLES VON LINNÉ; the fourteenth edition by J. A. MURRAY. *Vienna,* 1786.-- *German.* The same republished. by G. A. WEIZENBECK, 2 volumes. *Munich,* 1786---7.

OL. SCHWARZ Observationes Botanicæ, quibus plantæ Indiæ Occi-. dentalis aliæque Systematis Vegetabilis, edit. xiv. illustrantur, carumque characteres passim emendantur, cum tab. æn. *Erlang.* octavo, 1791.

Additions and emendations to the 14th edition, in A. J. RETZII Observat. Botanicæ, fascicul. v. *Lips.* 1789, in fol.

CAROLI LINNÆI Systema Vegetabilum secundum classes, ordines et genera cum characteribus et differentiis juxta edit xiv. a Clar. J. A. MUR-

Murray; edit. xv. curante J. Scannagata, Custod. Hort. Reg. Ticinens. *Ticini*, 1789, 288 pages in octavo, an abridgment.

A *fifteenth edition* of the *Systema Vegetabilium* will be published in course of time, by Dr. J. E. Smith of *London* *.

In the year 1791, an edition of the Vegetable System was advertised for publication in *Portugal*.

Linnæi Regnum Vegetabile, juxta Systema Naturæ in classes, ordines et genera constitutum, ex ejus operibus redactum, nec non e Philosophia Botanica. ejusdem, aliorumque operibus locupletatum, præmissis definitionibus, curante Xaver. Manetti. *Florent*. 1756, octavo, with two plates.

Casim Bianchi Vademecum Botanico, continente gli caratteri della, 10th edit. del *Linnæo*, &c. *Firenze*, 1763.

Philip Miller's Short Introduction to the Knowledge of the science of Botany, explaining the terms of art made use of in the Linnæan System. *London*, 1760, octavo.

C. F. Arendorf Comparatio nominum officinalium plantarum cum nominibus botanicis Linnæi et Tournefortii, Lat et Germ. *Berolin*, 1762, octavo.

J. G. Berwald of the Sexes and the Fructification of Plants. *Hamb*. 1778, octavo—German.

Jo. Berkenhout Clavis Anglicæ Linguæ Botanicæ Linnæi. *London*, 1764, octavo, and 1766.

* Dr. Smith's Edition of the Systema Vegetabilium promises to be a most valu-able one.—I am also preparing fa.s he, in a Letter to the Author, a new Edition of *Systema Vegetabilium*; but this must be a work of time, as I mean to examine every plant with my own eyes, and not be a mere copier like my predecessors. The work will be accompanied with a volume of *Observationes Botanicæ*, in which I shall give my reasons for all the changes I make, and descriptions of all my new plants.

D. W.

D. W. WITHERING's of *Birmingham*, botanical arrangement of all the vegetables growing in *Great-Britain*, according to the Linnæan System. *London*, 1789.

F. J. LIPII Enchiridion Botanicum, sistens delineationem plantæ C. VON LINNÉ definitam, exemplis et figuris illustratam. *Vienn.* 1766, octavo, five sheets and an half.

The Vegetable Reign, after the most Modern System of Nature, of SIR CHARLES VON LINNÉ, 2 vol. *Erfurt*, 1770; by C. F. DIETRICH.—*German.* His Elements of Botanical knowledge, by the same author; *Erfurt*, 1771, octavo, three hundred and fifty-eight pages, and 1785, with plates.—*German.*

G. C. OEDEX, *Index Plantarum* in LINNÆI Systemate, Nat. edit. x. recensarum. *Havn.* 1761, in *twelves.*

Index Regni Vegetabilis, qui continet plantes omnes, quæ habentur in LINNÆANI Systematis, edit. xii. auctor, N. J. JACQUIN. *Vindob.* quarto 1770.

Index Plantarum, quæ continentur in LINNÆI Systemat. edit. xiv. edit. novissima by the same.----*Viennæ* apud WAPPLER, 1785, quarto, one hundred and seventy-six pages. This work contains 10271 plants.

Nomenclator Botanicus enumerans plantas omnes in Systemate Naturæ, Speciebus Plantarum, edit. ii. et mantissi binis, 8vo. *Lips.* 1772.

Catalogus Plantarum omnium juxta Systema Vegetab. LINNÆI ad edit. xiii. in usum Horti Pragensis, auct. J. MICKAU. *Praga*, 1776, twenty-six sheets, in octavo.

Index LINNÆUS, in Plukeneti Opera, &c. et Index LINNÆNUS in Dillenii Historiam Muscorum, auct. DR. P. D. GISEKE. *Hamb.* 1779,

large

large quarto---39 pages. LINNÆUS himself has revised this work in manuscript.

DOMINICI VANDELLI Viridarium Grisley Lusitanicum, LIN-NÆANIS nominibus illustratum jussu academiæ in lucem editum. *Co-nimbricæ*, 1789, octavo.

Directions for beginners to collect plants with utility and pleasure, and to define and fix them according to the Linnæan system; by A. W. ROTH, GOTHA, 1778, octavo.—German.

Compendio de Botanica, ou Nocoes elementares dessa sciencia, segundo os melhores escritores modernos, (especially according to LINNÆUS,) *ex-postas na lingua Portugueza;* por FELIX AVELLAR. BORTERO. Lisbon, 1778.---vol. ii. large octavo.

Compendium Botanices, Systematis LINNÆANI conspectum ejus-dem-que explicationem ad selectiora plantarum Germaniæ indigenarum genera, earumque species continens, auctore, C. F. Reuss, edit. prima. *Ulmæ,* 1774. Edit. secunda, *ibid.* 1785.

Hr. Arch. och. *Ridd,* C. VON LINNÉ *Inledning* i ort. Riket, efter Systema Naturæ, *pa Suenska öfversatt* of J. J. HARTMANN. Edit. ii. *Westeras,* 1777; eleven sheets, in octavo, with three plates. Swedish.

C. a LINNÉ *Systema Plantarum,* secundum classes, ordines, genera, species, cum characteribus, differentiis, nominibus trivialibus synony-mis selectis et locis natalibus, a J. J. REICHARD. *Francof.* ad *Moen.* Vol. iv. 1779,—1781.

Institutiones Botanicæ, auct. Petagna; Neapol. Vol. v. The last was published in 1787. This work consists of commentaries on the LINNÆAN System.

CHARLES

CHARLES VON LINNÉ's Vegetable System reduced to a tabular form, by G. A. WEIZEMBACH. *Munich;* large octavo, 1785. *German.*

Epitome of the Linnæan Vegetable System, for the use of the lovers of œconomy, manufactures and commerce. Vol. i. with plates; large octavo. *Nuremberg,* 1791. German.

C. VON LINNÉ's description of all the plants of the bulbous kind, with plates, 1784. German.—also at *Nuremberg.*

Methodi Linnæanæ Botanicæ delineatio, exhibens charaﬅeres essentiales generum, nec non specierum, quæ in demonﬅrationibus botanicis describuntur &c. opus, herbationibus accommodatum, curante, J. C. GILIBERT. *Lyon,* 1790; four hundred and eighty-two pages, octavo.

Plantæ Cryptogamæ LINNÆI, Auﬅ. FR. EHRHART. *Hannov.* 1785, folio.

GUIL. DRESKY de Valeriana officinali LINNÆI. *Erlang.* Quarto, 1776.

Dr. G. A. SUCKOW's Diagnosis of the genera of plants, according to the newest and eighth edition of the Linnæan sexual method. *Lips.* 1792, large octavo. German.

N. E. PEEREBOM Materia Vegetabilis, Systemati Plantarum, præsertim *Philisophiæ Botanicæ* inserviens, charaﬅeribus quoscunque LINNÆUS indicavit, delineatis, Decas ii. cum fig. *Lugd. Batav.* quarto, 1787.

THOMAS MARTYN, thirty-eight plates, drawn and engraved by Os. NODDER, with explanations to illustrate LINNÆUS's System of Vegetables. *Lond.* 1788, octavo.

C. a LINNÉ Systema, Genera et Species Plantarum Europæ, cura J. E. GILIBERT, cum fig.—viii. volumes the last publifhed in 1788, octavo.

Illustratio Systematis Sexualis. An Illustration of the Sexual System of LINNÆUS, by JOHN MILLER, Lat. and English. *London,* 1777, large folio.

This work appeared from 1770, to 1777, in fifteen nuumbers, containing altogether two hundred and fourteen copper-plates and one hundred and eleven leaves of letter-press. In front of the splendid title is prefixed the Portrait of LINNÆUS. This is the most sumptuous and valuable work of its kind which ever appeared. The Author was a native of *Wurtemberg* in *Germany,* and presented a copy of it to the University of *Goettingen.* The price is twenty guineas. .

JOHANNI MILLLERI Illustratio Systematis Sexualis Linnæi. *Francfort,* 1789, in octavo, with coloured plates, Price four ducats; common, six rix-dollars.

Plantarum Icones, hactenus ineditæ, plerumque ad plantas in Herbario Linnæano conservatus delincatæ, auct. JACOBO EDUARDO SMITH, M D. Societatis Regiæ Londinensis, Ulyssip. Agron. Paris. Socio; Societatis LINNÆANÆ Londinensis Præside. *Lond.* 1789. Fascicul. ii. fourteen sheets and an half, and twelve plates.—Fascicul. ii. 1791. Fascicul. iii. 1791.

Ejusdem Icones pictæ plantarum rariorum, *Lond.* 1790-2. ii Fasc. and Spicilegium Botanicum, *Lond.* 1790-2. Fascicul. ii. fol. Lat. et Angl.

Collection.

Colleftion of dried plants, named on the authority of the LIN-
NÆAN Herbarium, &c. by JAMES DICKSON. *Lond.* 1789-90. Fascicul. ii. fol.

In 1792, appeared at London, the second volume of the oftavo
edition of JOHN MILLER's Illustration of the Sexual System of LIN-
NÆUS, containing the Termini Botanici, illustrated with fix-hundred
and seventy-five figures; delineated from such plants as have the cha-
rafter of each term.

TOURNEFORTII et LINNÆI Institutiones rei herbariæ, edit. nova
aufta et correftior, cum icon. 4 tom. oftavo *Lugd.* (properly speaking at *Lyons*) apud DE LA MOLLIERE, 1792.   -

Jo. ELLIS's Dionæa, de muscipula planta, irritabili nuper deteƈta;
Epistola ad C. a LINNÉ. *Lond.* 1769, quarto.

Icones Plantarum Indigenarum et Exoticorum; or a Colleftion of
Figures of Indigenous and Exotic Plants, drawn from nature, and described in the last edition of MURRAY's LINNÆAN System of Plants,
by a Society of Botanists, in fix Numbers. *Vienna,* 1791, 5th year,
large oftavo edition, in German. This whole work which consists of
thirty numbers, may be had for thirty rix-dollars, or about six guineas
and an half English money.   •

Of the PRACTICA BOTANICA del CAVALLERO CARLOS LINNÆUS,.
appeared at *Madrid,* in 1788, the 7th vol. in large oftavo, containing two hundred and twenty-seven pages. It comprises from the 21ft
to the 24th class.

NUEVOS REMEDIOS, que ha puesto in Praftia DON ANTONIO CAR-
DEVILA deducidos del metodo Botànico de LINNEO; en *Madrid*
1779. Spanifh.   •

                                                            Separate

Separate remarks and allegations upon the LINNÆAN System. See ROEMER and USTERI's Botanical Magazine, *Zurich*, octavo, 1787 to 1791. German.

No. X.

LINNÆI Epistola ad BALDINGERUM de Filicibus, *Jenæ* 1771.

ON . .

THE MINERAL REIGN.

SIR CHARLES LINNÆUS's complete Natural System of the Mineral Reign, according to its twelfth edition; a free translation with additions, by J. F. GMELIN. *Nurembergh*, 1778 to 1779, in four large octavo volumes, with fifty-six plates. .

No. XI.

Hypothesis Nova de Febrium Intermittentium Causa. *Harderovici*, 1735 in quarto. This Dissertation of LINNÆUS was composed when he first took his degree as Doctor of Medicine at *Harderwyk* in *Holland*. It is copied in SCHREBER's edition of the *Amœnitat. Acad.* vol. x. *Erlang.* 1750.

No. XII.

The *First Edition.*—*Fundamenta Botanica*, quæ majorum operum prodromi instar, theoriam scientiæ Botanicæ per breves aphorismos tradunt. *Amstelod.* apud Sсноυτεν, 1736.   Thirty-six pages in twelves.

No. XIII.

The *Second Edition.*—Auβior a LINNæo, *Stockholm,* 1740, thirty-
two pages oβavo.

The *Third Edition.*—Abo, 1740, thirty-two pages, quarto.

The *Fourth Edition.*—*Leyden,* 1741, fifty-one pages, oβavo.

The *Fifth Edition.*—*Paris,* 1744, twenty-six pages oβavo.

The *Sixth Edition.*—*Halle,* accedit Dissertatio J. GESNERI de Vegetabilibus, apud BIERWIRTH, 1747, p. 78, oβavo.

Seventh Edition.—*Lucca,* 1758, in oβavo.

The *Eighth Edition.*—*Paris,* 1774, oβavo.

David De GORTER (Jон. fil.) Elementa Botanica, methodo LINNæI
accommodata, ac in usum auditorum evulgata, *Harderovici,* 1749,
ninety oβavo pages, with eleven plates.—This work is a commentary
on LINNæUS's *Fundamenta,* from page seventy-eight to two hundred
and nine.

LINNæI Elementa Botanica, per DAN. SOLANDER. *Ups.* 1756, containing sixty-four oβavo pages.

No. XIV.

The *First Edition.*—*Bibliotheca Botanica**, recensens Libros plus
mille de plantis, huc usque editos, secundum systema auβorum na-

* Etsi parum plena est, neque subito potuit plena enasci, ingenii tamen sui auβoris vestigia
fert in tabulis inque tota dispositione. HALLERUS in Biblioth. tom. ii. p. 245.

3   turale,

turale, in classes, ordines, genera et species dispositos, additis editionis loco, tempore, forma, lingua. *Amstel.* apud SCHOUTEN, 1736, one hundred and thirty-six pages in twelves. The *Second Edition.*—Correctior præcedente. *Hallæ,* apud BIER-WIRTH, 1747, one hundred and twenty-four pages in octavo. The *Third Edition.*—*Amstelod.* 1751, two hundred and twenty pages, in octavo.

●

No. XV.

MUSA CLIFFORTIANA, Florens *Hartecampi* prope *Harlemum,* 1736, *Lugd. Batav.* forty pages in quarto*.

No. XVI.

The *First edition.*—*Genera Plantarum* earumque characteres naturales, secundum numerum, figuram, situm et proportionem omnium fructificationis partium. *Lugd. Batav.* apud WISHOF, three hundred and eighty-four octavo pages. It contains nine hundred and thirty-five genera†. The *Second Edition.*—Aucta et emendata *ibid.* apud eundem, 1742, five hundred and sixty-nine pages in octavo, with one copper-plate. Contains one thousand and twenty-one genera.

* Plena historia plantæ et character expeditus, etsi alii Clariss. Viri paulo aliter florem se habere repererunt, difficilis enim et paradoxa planta est. HALER, in Biblioth. tom. ii, p. 245.

† HALLER judges thus of this work : Characteres hiulcos TOURNEFORTII, laxos RAII, nimis partiales RIVINI, non semper fideles MAGNOLII, ita uberrimos, ita ex ipsa natura erutos reddidit, ut perinde cuivis systemati condendo fidi sunt duces futuri.

The

The *Third Edition.*—*Paris,* 1743, four hundred and thirteen pages, in octavo, with the French terms:—a mere copy of the preceding edi.ion replete with errors.

The *Fourth Edition.*—Genera Plantarum, &c. quæ novis lxx. generibus auctoris, sparsim editis locupletata, in usum auditorii recudenda curavit C. C. STRUMPF, Botan. Prof. *Halæ* apud KÜMMEL, 1752, four hundred and seventy-three pages in octavo. Contains one thousand and ninety genera.

No. XVII.

The *Fifth Edition.*—A LINNÆO reformata et aucta. *Holm.* apud SALVIUM, 1754, thirty six sheets in octavo. Contains one thousand one hundred and five genera.

No. XVIII.

The *Sixth Edition.*—Also by LINNÆUS; it was the last which he published, *Holm,* 1764, five hundred and eighty pages in octavo. It contains one thousand two hundred and thirty-nine genera.

The *Seventh Edition.*—*Vienna,* 1764, by TRATTNER.

The *Eighth Edition.*—*Vienna,* 1767, by the same.

The *Ninth Edition.*—Novis genertibus ac emendationibus, ab ipso auctore sparsim evulgata et aucta, cura J. F. REICHARD. *Francfort,* 1778, in octavo ; contains one thousand three hundred and forty-three genera.

The *Tenth Edition.*—Prioribus editionibus longe auctior atque emendatior, curante J. C. D. SCHREBER, who reckons it for the eighth edition. *Francfort,* 1790, and 1791, two vols. octavo.

The *Eleventh Edition.*—Præcedentibus longe auctior, curante THAD. HANKE, 2 vol. *Vindob.* 1791, octavo.

.SUPPLEMENTS,

·SUPPLEMENTS

ADDED TO

THE ABOVE WORKS

BY LINNÆUS HIMSELF.

––––––––––

No. XIX.

CAROLI LINNÆI Corollarium Generum Plantarum; cui accedit Methodus Sexualis. *Lvgd. Batav.* 1737, octavo.

No. XX.

CAROLI LINNÆI Decem Plantarum Genera et additamenta ad Generum editionem secundam, in the *Acta Societ. Scient. Upsal,* 1741, pages seventy-eight.

XXI.

Mantissa Plantarum, Generum editionis sextæ et epecierum Editionis secundæ. *Holm.* 1767, one hundred and forty-two pages in octavo.

XXII.

Mantissa Plantarum altera. Holm. 1771, five hundred and fifty-eight pages in octavo.

Essay

Essay of a German Nomenclature of the Genera of LINNÆUS, by J. PLANER. *Erfurt*, 1771, two hundred and twenty-four pages in octavo. German.

CHARLES VON LINNÉ's Genera of Plants and their natural distinctive marks, from the number, form, situation and proportion of all the parts of the flower; translated according to the sixth edition, and the first and second *Mantissa*, by J. J. PLANER. *Gotha*, 1775, two volumes in octavo. German.

Traducion de las Generos de las Plantas DE LINNEO, per D. ANTONIO CAPDEVILA, Medico in esta Corte, Professor Real de Botanica, Socio de la Real Sociedad de las Ciencias de *Gottingen*, &c. en *Madrid*, 1774. Spanish.

Het. xix. *Classe* van de *Genera Plantarum* van de Heer LINNÆUS, *Syngenesia* genaamt; opgehcldert en vermeedert &c. door DAVID MEESE, te *Leuwarden*, 1761, large octavo, Dutch.

A. C. ERNSTING's historical and physical description of the genera of plants, to which has been added LINNÆUS's systematic list of the genera of plants. *Lemgo*, 1762, two volumes in quarto ; German.

On some artificial *Genera* of the family of the *Malvæ*, also of the classes of the Monadelphios, to which is added an opinion upon the LINNNÆAN Genera and their classification, &c. by F. C. MEDICUS. *Manheim*, 1787, one hundred and fifty-eight pages in octavo. German.

No. XXIII.

Viridarium CLIFFORTIANUM. *Amstel.* apud SCHOUTEN, 1737, octavo.

No. XXIV.

No. XXIV.

Hortus Cliffortianus, plantas exhibens, quas in hortis tam vivis, quam siccis, *Hartecampi* in Hollandia coluit Vir nobil. et gener. Georgius Clifport, J. V. D. reductis varietatibus ad species, speciebus ad genera, generibus ad classes, adjectis locis plantarum natalibus, differentiisque specierum. *Amstel.* 1737, five hundred and two pages in folio, with thirty-two copper-plates*.

No. XXV.

The *First Edition.*—*Flora Lapponica,* exhibens plantas, per Lapponiam crescentes, secundum Systema Sexuale, collectas itinere impensis Societ. Reg. Litterar. Scientiar. Sueciæ, anno 1732 instituta, additis synonymis et locis natalibus omnium, descriptionibus et figuris rariorum, viribus medicatis et œconomicis plurimarum *Amstel.* ap. Schouten, 1737, three hundred and seventy-two pages, in octavo, with plates. The *Second Edition.*—Aucta et correcta, auct. J. E. Smithi, *London,* 1792 †.

No. XXVI.

The *First Edition.*—*Critica Botanica,* in qua nomina plantarum generica, specifica et variantia examini subjiciuntur, selectiora confirmantur, indigna rejiciuntur, simulque doctrina circa denominationem planta-

---

* Hic incepit (ut in Flora Lapponica) vir Cl. species generibus subjicere et synonyma, in plantis fere peregrinis et hortensibus, quarum multæ raræ et novæ. Haller in Bibl. Bot. T. II. p. 246.

† I am also printing a new edition of Linnæus's *Flora Lapponica,* enlarged and corrected, which will be out in two or three months.—In a Letter from Dr. Smith to the Author, written in November, 1791.

rum

rum traditur; cui accedit BROWALLII Discursus de introducenda in scholas Historiæ Naturalis lectione.   *Lugd..Batav.* apud WISHOF, 1737, two hundred and twenty pages in octavo *.

The *Second Edition*—Critica Botanica LINNÆI, cum dissertatione de vita et scriptis auctoris. edit. a J. E. GILIBERT, *Colon.* 1788.

No. XXVII.

The *First Edition*—*Classes Plantarum*, seu Systema Plantarum; omnia, a fructificatione desumta, quorum sexdecim universalia et tredecim particularia, compendiose proposita secundum classes, ordines et nomina generica, cum clave cujusvis methodi et synonymis genericis.   *Lugd. Batav.* apud WISHOF, 1738, six hundred and fifty-six pages in octavo.

The *Second Edition.*—*Halæ*, apud BIRWIRTH, 1747, in octavo.

Supplements and Continuations of the LINNÆAN Collection of Botanical Systems, are to be found in the Botanical Magazine of ROEMER and UTERI, published at *Zurich.*   No. I. 1787, begins with the System of Prof. ALLIONI at *Turin.* German.

No. XXVIII.

The *First Edition*—PETRI ARTEDI, Sueci Medici, Ichthyologia, sive opera omnia de piscibus; scilicet Bibliotheca Ichthyologica; Genera

---

* Partem quartam Fundamentorum Botanicorum hic uberius deducit, quæ agit de nominibus plantarum.   Generum nomina vult sibi stare, neque ab alia similitudine deduci, neque barbariem sapere. Nomina Cl. virorum in plantis suadet dedicari, rectius quam VAILLANTIUS. Nomina specierum jubet definitionem exprimere suæ plantæ; ideoque RIVINIANA et BAUHINIANA rejicit. *Idem* tam in posterioribus operibus præter nomina erudita, trivialia introduxit, quorum vulgo usus esset; et *quæ ipsa sunt Rivini nomina. Multum hoc opere sibi conflavit invidiæ Auctor,* quo, *ut puto,* voluit rationem reddere, cur nomina in recepta undique rejecerit. HALLER in *Biblioth. Botan.* tom. ii. p. 246.

Piscium

Piscium; Synonyma Specierum et Descriptiones; omnia in hoc genere perfectiora quam antea ulla. Posthuma vindicavit, recognovit,
coaptavit et edidit. CAROLUS LINNÆUS. *Lugd. Batav.* apud WISHOF,
1738, in octavo, five hundred and fifty-six pages.
The *Second Edition—*Aucta et Emendata. A J. J. WALBAUM,
Gryphishw, 1788 and 1791, three volumes in quarto.

PETRI ARTEDI, Synonyma Piscium Græca et Latina, emendata,
illustrata atque aucta; seu Specimen Historiæ Literariæ Piscium; cum
Hippopotami Veterum Historia Critica. Auctore J. GOTTL. SCHNEI-
DER, *Leips.* 1789.

ORATIONS OF LINNÆUS.

No. XXIX.

THE *First Edition—Tal om. Merkwaerdigheten uti Insetlerne.* Stock-
holm, 1739, octavo.—This oration was made by LINNÆUS in the
Swedish language, when he resigned his office as President of the
Royal Academy of Sciences at *Stockholm.*

The *Second Edition*—Translated into Dutch. *Leyden,* 1741, in octavo.

The

The *Third Edition*—Oratio de memorabilibus in Insectis; Latine vertit. ABRAH. BÄCK. *Paris,* 1743. Inserted in the *Amoenitat. Acad.* vol. vi.

The *Fourth Edition*—Reprinted in Swedish. *Stockholm,* 1747, in octavo.

The *Fifth Edition*.—*Stockholm,* 1752, in octavo, with the insects numbered as in *Fauna Suecica.*

The *Sixth Edition*—Translated into German in the Universal Repository of Nature, Art and Science. *Leips.* 1754, vol. ii. page three hundred *et seq*—German.

The *Seventh Edition*—Also in German, translated from the last Swedish edition, by C. H. GROENING. *Schwerin,* 1784, octavo.

No. XXX.

The *First Edition*—*Oratio de Peregrinationum intra Patriam Necessitate.* *Upsal,* 1742, quarto; delivered when LINNÆUS assumed his professorial functions.

Second Edition—Eadem Oratio—accedit Elenchus Animalium Suecæ; BROWALLII Examen Epicriscos SIEGESBECKIANÆ et GESNERI Dissertatio de Vegetabilibus. *Lugd. Batav.* apud HAAK, 1743, octavo.

The *Third Edition*—Inserted in the *Amoenitat. Acad.* vol. ii.

No. XXXI.

The *First Edition*—*Orbis Eruditi Judicium de* CAR. LINNÆI, M. D. *Scriptis.* *Upsal,* 1741, one small octavo sheet.

LINNÆUS published the above pamphlet in an anonymous manner, chiefly to vindicate himself against the attacks of WALLERIUS.

2

The

The *Second Edition*—In the *Collectio Ep'stolarum* CAROLI A LINNÉ; accedunt opuscula pro et contra LINNÉ scripta extra Sueciam rarissima; edid. D. H. STOEVER. *Hamburg*, apud HOFFMANN, 1792, octavo.

No. XXXII.

The *First Edition*.—Oratio de telluris habitabilis incremento. *Upsal,* 1743, quarto.

The Second *Edition*—una cum ANDR. CELSII oratione de mutationibus generalibus, quæ in superficie corporum cœlestium contingunt. *Lugd. Batav.* 1744, one hundred and four pages in octavo.

The *Third Edition*—Reprinted in the *Amoenitat. Acad.* vol. vi.

The *Fourth Edition*—Translated into German in the Universal Magazine of Nature, Art and Sciences. *Leipsic*, vol. vii. page 37, *et seq.*

The *Fifth Edition*—Translated into Swedish by the title: Tal om Jordens tilväxt. *Stockholm,* 1776, in octavo.

Thoughts on the Opinion of LINNÆUS on the Increase of the Habitable Earth. *Dantzic,* 1767.

No. XXXIII.

The *First Edition*—*Oratio Regia, coram Rege Reginaque habita.* 1759, in folio—Swedish.

The *Second Edition*—Translated into Latin in the *Amœnitat. Acad.* *Edit.* SCHREBER, vol. x. *Erlang,* 1790.

No. XXXIV.

The *First Edition*—*Deliciæ Naturæ*, oratio habita, 1772.

The

The *Second Edition*—Translated into Swedish by LINNÆUS himself, at the request of the students from the different Swedish provinces, under the title of CAROLI VON LINNÉ *Deliciæ Naturæ*; *Tal, hallit Upsala Domkyrka, ar 1772, den 14 Dec. vid Rectoratets nedlaggande.* *Stock.* 1773, two sheets octavo.

The *Third Edition*—In Latin, in the *Amoenitat. Acad.* SCHREBER. vol. x. 1790.

NARRATIVES

OF

THE TRAVELS OF LINNÆUS.

No. XXXV.

OELÄNDSKA *och Gothlänska Resa. Stockh. och Upsal,* 1745, three hundred and forty four pages, in octavo, with two plates—Swedish.

CHARLES VON LINNÉ's Travel's through *Oëland* and *Gothland*, translated into German by J. C. S. SCHREBER. *Halle,* sold by J. J. CURT, 1763; four hundred and thirty-two pages, large octavo, with five plates —German.

No.

No. XXXVI.

Wästgötha Resa; af Ricksens Ständers befalning förättad. *Stockholm,* 1747; two hundred and twenty-four pages in octavo, with five plates— Swedish.

CHARLES VON LINNÉ's Travels in *West Gothland,* translated by J. C. D. SCHREBER. *Halle,* 1765; large octavo—German.

No. XXXVII.

Skänska Resa, Förrättad a 1749. *Stockholm,* by SALVIUS, 1749; four hundred and thirty-four pages in octavo, with six plates.

CHARLES LINNÆUS's Travels in the Kingdom of *Sweden,* undertaken by command of the Swedish Government, for the benefit of Natural History, Œconomy and Medicine. Translated from the Swedish by C. E. KLEIN. *Stockholm* and *Leipsic,* vol. i. with three plates—German.

No second volume of the above work has ever appeared.

VOYAGES AND TRAVELS

OF THE

PUPILS OF LINNÆUS,

PUBLISHED BY HIMSELF.

No. XXVIII.

FREDERICI HASSELQUIST, *Iter Palestinum;* Eller Resa til Heliga Landet. *Holm.* 1757, octavo—Swedish and Latin.

FREDERICK HASSELQUIST's Travels in *Palestine,* from the year 1749 till 1752; published by command of the Queen of *Sweden,* by CHARLES LINNÆUS. Translated into German by TH. H. GADEBUSCH. *Rostock,* 1762, octavo.

Translated into French. *Paris,* 1769, twelves.

———— into English. *London,* 1771, octavo.

No. XXXIX.

PETRI LŒFLINGII Iter Hispanicum; Ella Resa til Spanksa Länderna, uti *Europa* och *America,* förrättad ifran 1751 til 1756; med beskrifninger och rön öfver de märkwärdigeste wäxter. *Stockholm,* 1758; large octavo. Swedish.

PETER

PETER LŒFLING's Travels in the Spanish Territories in *Europe* and *America*. Translated from the Swedish by A. B. KOELPIN. *Berlin,* 1766; large octavo, with plates. Reprinted in 1776, in octavo. German. Translated into English by J. R. and J. FORSTER. *London,* 1771. [Compare here the article in the Biography, which treats of the travelling Pupils of LINNÆUS.]

No. XL.

The *First Edition—Flora Suecica,* exhibens Plantas, per Regnum Sueciæ crescentes, systematice cum differentiis specierum, synonymis auctorum, nominibus incolarum, solo locorum, usu Pharmacopæorum. *Lugd. Batav.* apud WISHOF, 1745; three hundred and ninety-two pages in octavo; contains one thousand one hundred and forty plants *.

No. XLI.

The *Second Edition—*Aucta et Emendata. *Stockholm,* apud SALVIUM, 1755. Thirty-four sheets and an half in octavo; with one hundred and fifty-six plants, augmented with the trivial names †.

No. XLII.

The *First Edition—Fauna Sueciæ* regni, mammalia, aves, amphibia, pisces, insecta, vermes; distributa per classes, ordines, genera et species.

---

* Multas ubique veras meridionalium regionum species pro varietatibus habuit, quas ipse non legisset. Nonnunquam in alios scriptores asperius animadvertit. HALLER. in *Biblioth. Botanica,* tom. ii. page 247.

* The younger LINNÆUS had prepared and got quite ready for the press, a third and much enlarged edition of the *Flora Suecica.* On account of his sudden death it did not appear in *Sweden.* The manuscript, with his additions and emendations is in the possession of Dr. JAMES EDWARD SMITH, who has since published this new edition.

Holmiæ,

Holmiæ, apud SALVIUM, 1746; four hundred and eleven pages in octavo, with two plates.

Dissertatio Entomologica, sistens Insecta *Suecica.* *Upsal,* 1790 and
1791; in quarto; Auctore BECKHIN; contains additions.

No. XLIII.

The *Second Edition*—Augmented with additions and the trivial
names. *Holm.* 1761, apud SALVIUM; five hundred and fifty-nine
pages, octavo, with two plates; contains one thousand two hundred and
sixty-nine indigenous plants.

Dr. AFZELIUS has increased the number of the Swedish indigenous plants with eighteen more, which were inserted in 1787 in the
Transactions of the Swedish Royal Academy of Sciences.

No. XLIV.

The *First Edition*—*Flora Zeylanica,* sistens plantas Indicas Zeylonae
insulae, quae olim 1670—1677 lectae fuere a PAULO HERMANNO, Profess. Botan. *Leydensi;* demum post 70 annos ab A. GÜNTHERO orbi
redditæ. *Holm.* 1747; two hundred and fifty-four pages in octavo,
with four plates.

The *Second Edition*—Copied from the former. *Leipsic,* 1748.

No. XLV.

Hortus Upsaliensis, exhibens plantas exoticas, horto Upsaliensis Academiæ a CAR. LINNÆO illatas ab anno 1742, in annum 1748, additis

* *Opus magni momenti et multi laboris,* cujus fructus in breves aphorismos collecti hic
habentur. Multa et pulchra de floribus plenis, &c. HALLER in *Bib. Bot.* tom. ii. page 250.

differentiis,

differentiis, synonymis, habitationibus, hospitiis, rariorumque descriptionibus, in gratiam studiosæ juventutis. *Holm.* 1748; three hundred and six pages in octavo, with three plates.

No. XLVI.

The *First Edition—Philosophia Botanica*, in qua explicantur Fundamenta Botanica, cum definitionibus partium, exemplis terminorum, observationibus rariorum, adjectis figuris. *Holm.* apud KIESEWETTER;
three hundred and sixty-two pages in octavo, with nine plates.

The *Second Edition—Vienna*, 1755; octavo.

The *Third Edition—Vienna*, 1763; octavo.

The *Fourth Edition—London*, 1765—English.

The *Fifth Edition—Vienna*, by TRATTNER, 1770; octavo.'

The *Sixth Edition—Berlin*, 1780; revisa et emendata curante J. G.
GLEDITSCH. Is like the second edition, except the additions.

The *Seventh Edition—Colon.* 1787; curante J. E. GILIBERT; large
octavo; called in the title *Editio Quarta*.

HUGH ROSE's Elements of Botany, being a translation of the *Philosophia Botanica* and other Treatises of LINNÆUS. *London*, 1775, 8vo.

LINNÆI *Institutiones Botanicæ*, translated, with a view of the ancient
and present state of Botany, and a Synopsis, exhibiting the essential
or striking characters which serve to discriminate the genera of the
same class and order. By C. MILNE, two volumes; *London*, 1772,
with a Supplement, 1772; in quarto.

Traduccion de la *Filosofia Botanica* del celebro CARLOS LINNÉ,
por D. ANTONIO CAPDEVILA, Medico, Prof. Real, &c. en *Madrid*,
1771; octavo.

2　　　　　　　　　　　　　　　　　　　　　There

'There is another translation in Spanish with notes, by Don ANTONIO PALAN Y VEDERA, Professor of Botany at *Madrid* *.

N. J. DE NECKER Elementa Botanica, &c. cum tabulis; accedit Corollarium ad Philosophiam Botanicam LINNÆI speƐtans, &c. 3 vol. *Argentorati*, 1791, 8vo. Also with a separate Corollarium. *Neowedæ*, 1791.

Additions and Illustrations relative to the Philosophia Botanica, in J. A. SCOLOPI Fundamenta Botanica. *Paviæ*, 1783 and 1786; one hundred and forty-seven pages, oƐtavo. Italian

Epitome of the Philosophy of Plants, according to the LINNÆAN system. *Augsburg*, 1787, ninety-three pages, oƐtavo.

No. XLVII.

The *First Edition—Species Plantarum*, exhibens plantas, rite cognitas, ad genera relatas, cum differentiis specificis, nominibus trivialibus, synonymis seleƐtis, locis natalibus, secundum systema sexuale digestas *Holm*. apud SALVIUM two volumes in oƐtavo, 1753, one hundred and twenty pages *.

No. XLVIII.

The *Second Edition—*AuƐta ab auƐtore, 1762—: vol. sixteen hundred and eighty-four pages, in oƐtavo.

---

* See CAVANILLES on the Present State of *Spain. Berlin*, 1785; page 74. German.

✦ Primum adnotasse oportet, solas hic plantas recenseri, quas auƐtor coram habuerit, numerossissimas adeo, etiam Europæas omitti, quoties viri oculos fugerunt. Deinde, copiosissimum tamen esse catalogum, cum undique per difcipulos, amicos, etiam incognitos, plantæ rarissimæ ad Cl. virum confluxerint. Passim priora sua placita emendavit, et qua, varietates dixerat, inter species recensuit. Rariores passim deseruit.—*Editio fecunda* potissimum indicis et peregrinis plantis ditior. Studium idem. Iterum passim aliquas species recepit, quibus fidem negaverat, et tamen in plusculis pergit in sententia, quam nuper demum deseruit, ut plerasque nunc pro speciebus adgnoscat, quas inter varietates relegaverat. *Maximum opus, et æternum, plenius futurum, si aliis, etiam plantarum gnaris viris, fidem habuisset, qui in regione magis australi plantas, Septentrioni a natura negatas, recentes et florentes viderunt.* HALLER, in *Bibl. Bot.* t. ii. p. 252.

The

The *Third Edition—Vindob.* by TRATTNER, 1764, two volumes.

CAROLI A LINNÉ systema, genera et species plantarum Europæ, cura J. E. GILIBERT, tomi xii. cum fig. large octavo. *Colon. Allobrog.* 1764.

A new edition of the Species Plantarum may be expected in course of time of Dr. J. E. SMITH, at *London**.

J. H. H. LUDER, on the Botanical definition of some culinary plants which are not described with sufficient accuracy in the third edition of LINNÆUS's species of plants. Inserted in a German work entitled: " The most Modern Varieties ;" Third Year. *Berlin,* 1780, large octavo.—German.

Two hundred Botanical Remarks upon the *Species Plantarum* of LINNÆUS, by B. P. SCHRANK, in the *Acta Academica Electoralia Moguntina, Erfurt.* ad anno 1780-1.—German.

LINNÆUS's *Mantissæ* to the second edition of this work, of 1767 and 1771, may be seen above, under the head of *Genera Plantarum*†.

The following work, which lately made its appearance in Germany, ought also to be mentioned here as an effort of LINNÆUS.

CAROLI A LINNÉ Prælectiones in *Ordines Naturales* plantarum, ex manuscripto proprio et Jo. CHRIST. FABRICII, edid. Dr. P. D. GIESEKE, accedit palmarum, &c. uberior expositio. *Hamburg.* apud HOFFMANN, 1792, octavo, cum figuris.

---

* The *Icones omnium Specierum Plantarum* LINNÆI Equitis, which was prepared for the public at an immense expence, by the late CAROLINA LOUISA, Margravine of *Baden,* has not yet made its appearance.

† " There are an infinite number of errors in the *Species Plantarum,*" says Dr. SMITH, " which can only be corrected from the LINNÆAN Herbarium."

No.

No. XLIX.

Museum Tessinianum, opera Comitis C. G. TESSIN, Regis Regnique Senatoris &c. collectum :

HAN's Excellence Rickrodets Heer. Gr. C. G. TESSIN's Naturalie Samling. *Holm.* 1753, Latin and Swedish, ninety pages in folio, with plates.

No. L.

Museum Regis ADOLPHI Succorum, &c. in quo animalia rariora, imprimis exotica, quadrupedia, aves, amphibia, pisces, insecta, vermes describuntur et determinantur. This work is in Latin and Swedish. *Stockholm,* 1754, one hundred and thirty-five pages in folio, with thirty-five plates.

Dr. JAMES EDWARD SMITH has translated the preface to the above work into English, under the following title : " LINNÆUS's Reflections on the Study of Nature." *London,* 1785, octavo.

No. LI.

Museum Reginæ LOUISÆ ULRICÆ in quo animalia rariora exotica, imprimis insecta et conchylia describuntur et determinantur ; et Musei Regis ADOLPHI tomi secundi prodromus. *Holm.* 1764, seven hundred and twenty pages in octavo, and the prodomus one hundred and ten pages, same size.

The QUEEN's Museum contains four hundred and thirty-six insects, and four hundred and thirty conchylia.

No. LII.

No. LII.

Disquisitio quæstionis, ab Acad. Imper. Scientiar. *Petropolitanæ* in annum 1759 pro præmio propositæ: Sexum Plantarum argumentis et experimentis novis, præter adhuc jam cognita vel corroborare vel impugnare, &c. ab eadem Academia die 6 Sept. 1760, in conventu publico præmio ornata. *Petropol.* typ. Acad. 1760, forty pages in quarto.

The *Second Edition.*—Also in the *Nova Commentaria* Academ. Scientiar. Imperial. *Petropolit.* Tom. vii. 1761.

The *Third Edition.*—LINNÆUS's Dissertation on the sexes of plants; translated by J. E. SMITH, M. D. &c. *Lond.* 1786, octavo.

The *Fourth Edition.*—In French, by P. M. A. BROUSSONET, in the *Journal Encyclopedique.* vol. xxii. 1788, August 2, page one hundred and one to one hundred and eight, and Sept. 1, page two hundred and ninety-eight to three hundred and seven, by the title: Remarques concernant la Dissertation de LINNÉ sur le Sexe des Plantes, &c. suivies de la traduction de cette dissertation.

The *Fifth Edition.*—With notes by BROUSSONET in the Amœnitat. Academ. Edit. SCHREBER, Vol. x. *Erlangen,* 1790*.

No. LIII.

Nitraria, planta obscura explicata, in the *Nova Commentaria Petropolit.* tom. viii. p. 315.

---

* "The Dissertation de *Sexu Plantarum* in Amoenitat. Acad. vol. x." says Dr. SMITH, in a Letter to the Author, "is augmented from the French edition;—my English one has "more notes, which BRONSSONET did not choose, because they relate to ADANSON."

No. LIV.

No. LIV.

The *First Edition.*—*Materia Medica* Regni Vegetabilis. *Holm.* 1749, octavo*.

Materia Medica Regni Animal. *Upsal,* 1750.

Materia Medica Regni Lapid. *Upsal,* 1752.

The three above works were published as dissertations, and the two latter are inserted in the Amœnitat. Acad. vol. ii. and iii.

The *Second Edition.*—Published complete, for the first time, by Dr. L. TESSARI. *Venetiæ,* 1762, in octavo; with his Materia Medica Contracta.

The *Third Edition.*—J. C. D. SCHREBER. *Lips.* et *Erlang.* 1772, augmented and published by LINNÆUS's own previous knowledge.

The *Fourth Edition.*—*Vienna,* 1774; reprinted from the preceding Edition.

The *Fifth Edition.*—Auctior, Cura J. C. D. SCHREBER, *Lips.* et *Erlang.* 1787, three hundred and eighteen pages, large octavo.

Mantissa Editionis quartæ Materiæ Medicæ, *Erlang.* 1783, octavo.

The *Sixth Edition,*—By the same, *Lips.* et *Erlang.* 1787, three hundred and eighteen pages, large octavo.

FRANCISCI TAVARES Medicamentorum Sylloge, propriæ pharmacologiæ exempla sistens, in usum academicarum prælectionum. *Conimbricæ,* ex typogr. Academico. *Regia,* 1787, octavo.

* Plantas plurimas et celeberrimas, ob utilitatem medicam, ut tamen verum earum genus ignoraretur, ad sua genera revocavit. Varias etiam plantas ob vires medicatas celebrat, quas officinæ ignorant :—*Sed totum opus legere oportet quod sit inter optima Auctoris.* HALLER, in Bibliotheca Bot. vol. ii. p. 249.

2 The

The LINNÆAN Materia Medica is the basis of this work.

Dr. W. CULLEN's Epitome of Medical Nosology, or a systematic division of diseases, by CULLEN, LINNÆUS, SAUVAGES, VOGEL, and SAGAR. *Lips.* 1786, two volumes, large octavo.

No. LV.

First Edition.—*Genera Morborum. Upsal,* 1763, with a Swedish Nomenclature, first published as a dissertation in the *Amœnitat Acad.*
The *Second Edition.*—In usum auditorum publicata, by J. C. KERSTENS. *Hamb.* et *Gustrow,* 1774.
The *Third Edition.*—*Monspeliæ,* 1787, quarto, by M. GOUAN.

No. LVI.

The *First Edition.*—*Clavis Medicina* duplex, exterior et interior. *Holm.* 1763, twenty-nine pages, in octavo.
The *Second Edition.*—Cum præfatione edidit, Fr. Cr. BALDINGER. *Longosalissæ,* 1767.—Aphyteia & Hypericum. *Upsal,* 1766.—Two Academical Dissertations, the two last productions of LINNÆUS, in the Amœnitat. Acad. Edit. SCHREBER, vol. viii. The former plant has been sent to him in 1774, by THUNBERG, from the *Cape of Good Hope.*

The LINNÆAN Lectures upon the *Clavis Medicinæ,* which Dr. GIESEKE of *Hamburgh* promised to publish ten years ago, will appear in the course of the present year at farthest.

No. LVII.

The *First Edition.—Amoenitates Academicæ,* seu dissertationes variæ physicæ, medicæ, botanicæ; ante hoc seorism editæ, nunc colleQæ et auQæ.

Tomus Primus. Holm. et *Lips.* apud KIESEWETTER, 1749, oQavo, with fifteen plates.

Tomus I. *Lugd. Batav.* apud HAAK, 1749, different from the *Stockholm* Edition. No continuation has since appeared at *Leyden.*

Tomus I. *London,* 1762; English.

Tomus II. to Tom. VII. *Holm.* apud SALVIUM, 1751 to 1769. Contain altogether one hundred and fifty dissertations.

The *Second Edition.*—AuQæ cum tabulis æneis, curante J. C. D. SCHREBER. *Erlang.* 1785 to 1791.

This Edition contains the seven original volumes, besides the latter dissertations of LINNÆUS, and the shorter traQs and writings both of him and his son, augmented to ten volumes*.

SeleQæ ex Amœnitatibus Academicis CAROLI LINNÆI Dissertationes, ad universam historiam naturalem pertinentes, quas edidit et auxit L. B. & S. J. BIWALD, e Societate JESU. *Græcii,* apud LECHNER, 1764 to 1769, three volumes in quarto.

Reprinted in the same place, by ZAUNRITH, in 1786.

SeleQ Dissertations from the *Amœnitates Academicæ* of LINNÆUS, by BRAND, vol. ii. *Lond.* 1781, oQavo.

---

* The younger LINNÆUS intended to publish himself an eighth volume of the Amœnitates Academicæ; but certain obstacles prevented that publication.

SIR

Sir Charles Linnæus's Select Dissertations on subjects relating to Natural History, Natural Philosophy and Medicine; with plates and notes. *Leipsic,* three volumes, large octavo, from 1776 to 1778. German.

This work contains a German translation of the following Dissertations, namely in the first volume.

1. On the Espousals of the Plants.
2. On Coffee.
3. On Tea.
4. On the Utility of Natural History.
5. On Sea-hogs.
6. On the Diet to be observed in drinking Mineral Waters.
7. On Bread.
8. On the change of Corn.
9. A list of Œconomical Plants.
10. On the Sleep of Plants.
11. On the New Discoveries in Natural History.
12. On the Inhabited Earth.
13. On the Virtues of Plants.

VOLUME II.

1. On the Œconomy of Nature.
2. On the Abodes of the Plants.
3. On the Worm *Tænia.*
4. On the Generation of Crystals.
5. On the Drilling of Chocolate.
6. On the Esculent Plants and the trees which grow wild in *Sweden.*

3
7. On

. ˙7. On the Plants of the Sallad-kind.

8. On the transmigration of Birds.

9. On the Odor of Medicines.

10. On the Fig-tree.

11. On Fruit Brandy.

VOLUME III.

1. On the cause of Intermitting Fevers.

2. On Botanical Gardens.

3. On the Tussilago Anandria.

4. On the Corals of the Baltic.

5. On the attention bestowed upon Nature.

6. On the plant Senega.

7. On the Pelovia.

8. On the Betula Nana.

9. On the origin of the Calculus.

10. On the Fodder given to the Swédish Animals.

11. On the Taste of Medicines.

Several dissertations from the Amœnitates Academicæ, are also to be found in a Swedish work entituled *Samling af Rön Uptakter uti Physick*, &c. *Gothenburgh*, 1781.

SEPARATE

SEPARATE DISSERTATIONS

FROM THE

AMOENITATES ACADEMICÆ,

REPRINTED, TRANSLATED OR COMMENTED.

VOLUME I.

3. In French, with notes, by M. A. Millin de Grandmaison, by way of Appendix to the French translation of Dr. Pulteney's Revne Generale des Ecrits de Linné, vol. ii. page two hundred and eleven to two hundred and ninety seven.

III.   *Betula Nana. Upsal,* 1743, resp. L. M. Klase.
In French, by the same, also printed at *Upsal.*

IV.   *Ficus. Upsal,* 1744. Respond. C. Hegardt.—See the same in German, in the Hanoverian Magazine, 1756, page one thousand four hundred and fifty-three.

V.   1. *De Crystallorum generatione. Upsal,* 1747, Respond. M. Kæhler.

2. German; in the Mineralogical Recreations. *Berlin,* vol. i. page three hundred and thirty-one.

3. Also translated from the Latin into German, by M. Kæhler. *Grætz,* 1772, in octavo.

VI.   Flora Œconomica. *Upsal,* 1748, Respond. E. Aspelia.
The same in Swedish, *Stockholm,* 1749, octavo.

VOLUME II.

I.   2. De Tænia. *Upsal,* 1748, Respond. G. Dubois.
The Contents of this Dissertation are repeated in S. S. Bedde's Dissertatio de Verme Tæniæ. *Viennæ,* 1766, thirty-five pages.

II.   1. Pan Suecus. *Upsal,* 1749, Respond. N. Hesselgreen.

2. The

2. The Pan of *Sweden*, or a Treatise on feeding the indigenous animals in *Sweden*; from the Latin; with explanatory notes, by X. J. Lippert. *Vienna*, 1785, large octavo. German.

3. Translated into English, by R. Pulteney, M. D. F. R. S.

4. With additions and emendations, by A. G. Tengmalm in Modeer's *Hushalnings Journal*, Octob. 1779, and Jan. 1780. *Stockholm.* Swedish.

VOLUME III.

I.   *Calendarium Floræ. Upsal*, 1756, Resp. A. M. Berger.
      In English, in the Miscellaneous Tracts, relating to Natural History, Husbandry, and Physic, by B. Stillingfleet. *London*, 1762.

II.   *Vernatio Arborum. Upsal.* 1753, Respondente Henr. Barck.
      2. In German, in the Hanoverian Collections, 1756.
      3. In Forster's German Magazine, vol. vi. page three hundred and nineteen.

III.   *Hospita Insectorum Flora. Upsal*, 1752, Respond. J. G. Forskal.
      In Dutch, in the Uitgezokte Verhandeling uit de Niewestе Werken Van de Societeten der Wetenskapen in Europa, vol. ii. page four hundred and eight. *Amsterdam*, 1765, octavo.

IV.   *Noxa Insectorum. Upsal*, Respond. M. Bäkner.
      Treatise on the Noxiousness of Insects, with the additions of

Professor

Professor BIWALD, from the Latin, with a variety of notes. *Salsburgh*, 1783, octavo.

V.   *Miracula Insectorum. Upsal*, 1752, Respond. G. E. AVELIN.

German, in the General Magazine of Nature, Art and Science. *Leipsic*, vol. ix. page three hundred and twenty-one.

VI.   *Noctiluca Marina. Upsal*, 1752, Respond. C. F. ADLER.

Critical Additions to the above work, in the Gentleman's Magazine, vol. twenty-seven, page two hundred and eight.

VII.   1. *Plantæ Esculentæ Patriæ. Upsal*, 1752. Respond. HIORTH.

2. In Swedish, with additions, by C. G. LOEWENTHIELM.

3. Translated into German, from the Swedish, with a German Nomenclature, in a work called the Stockholm Magazine, vol. iii. page one hundred and ninety-seven.

VIII.   1. *Instructio Musei rerum naturalium. Upsal.* Respond. D. HULTMANN.

2. In German, entitled: A Treatise on Cabinets of Natural History, or an Introduction how to arrange those cabinets, and to class natural treasures, from the Latin, with notes, by C. MURR. *Leipsic*, 1772.

3. In German, in the Hanoverian Supplements, 1759, page fifteen, twenty-two, forty-two, &c.

VOLUME IV.

I.   *Ovis. Upsal*, 1754, Respond. J. PALMÆRUS.

In

In German, in Schreber's New Œconomical writings, vol. x.
Halle, 1768, page one hundred and eighty-two.

II.   *Somnus Plantarum.* *Upsal,* 1755, Respond. P. Bremer.

 2. Observations on the Sleep of Plants, &c. in the Philosophical
 Transactions, vol. l. 1760, part two, page five hundred
 and six.

 3. In the Gentleman's Magazine. *London;* published by Nichols,
 1757, page three hundred and fifteen.

VOLUME V.

I.   *Transmutatio Frumentorum.* *Upsal,* 1757, Resp. B. Horn-
borg

 In German, in Schreber's New Œconomical writings, vol.
 viii. *Halle,* 1767.

VOLUME VI.

I.   *Usus Historiæ Naturalis.* *Upsal,* 1766, Respond, M. Aphonin.
 In German, with notes. *Dresden,* 1774, in octavo.

II.   *Termini Botanici.* *Upsal,* 1762, Respond. J. Elmgreen.

 2. Editio Nova Auctior, by Dr. Schreber. *Lips.* 1767, in octavo.

 3. —— *Edinburghi,* 1764, in octavo.

 4. Termini Botanici, classium methodii Sexalis generumque characteres compendiosi, recudi curavit, primos cum suis definitionibus, interpretatione germanica donatos, a P. D.
 Gieseke. *Hamb.* 1781, two hundred and nineteen pages in
 octavo.

5. Caroli Linné Termini Botanici, Dissertatione academica explicath *Erlang.* 2789, thirty-two pages in octavo.

6. *Termini Botanici* secundum Methodum Caroli Linné, ex variis ejus operibus congesti, v. Jo. Reinh. Forster, Enchiridion historiæ naturali inserviens. *Halæ,* 1788, octavo, page one hundred and sixty-three.

7. F. J. Maerter Fundamenta et Termini Botanici, congest. secund. Method. et ad ductum Caroli Linné, in usum prælectionum. *Bruxel,* 1790.

VOLUME VII.

1. *Fundamenta Entomologiæ. Upsal,* 1767, Resp. A. J. Bladh.

2. Fundamenta Entomologiæ, or an Instruction to the knowledge of Insects, by William Curtis. *Lond.* 1772, with plates.

2. Translated into French, with additions, by M. de Bruguieres. Fundamenta et Termini Entomologiæ, Secundum Methodum et ad ductum C. a Linné.—See Forster's Enchiridion, page ninety-one, et seq.

See in the same work according to the Linnæan method: Fundamenta et Termini Ornithologiæ et Ichthyologiæ.

4. Th. P. Yeates's Institutions of Entomology, being a translation of Linnæus's *Ordines et Genera Insectorum. Lond.* 1773, octavo.

VOLUME VIII.—*Edid.* Schreber.

1. *Fundamenta Testaceolgiæ. Upsal,* 1771, Respond. A. Murray.

1. In

1. In German, in a work called the most Modern Varieties, page three hundred and thirty-seven and three hundred and fifty-three.

2. In Latin, in de Bornii Museo Cæsareo Vindobonensi Testac. *Viennæ*, 1778.

II. *Plantæ Surinamenses. Upsal.* 1775, Respond. J. ALM.
Reprinted, with additions, in C. C. GJONVELLIO Thesauro Suedico—Gothico. vol. i. *Stockholm*, 1781, octavo.

A

L I S T

OF OTHER TREATISES INSERTED BY LINNÆUS IN THE TRANSACTIONS OF THE ACADEMY OF SCIENCES OF UPSAL, EXCLUSIVE OF THE FLORA LAPPONICA.

1. ANIMALIA Regni Sueciæ, 1738.

2. Orchids, iisque affines, 1740.

3. Decem Genera plantarum nova, 1741.

4. Euporista in febribus intermittentibus, 1742.

5. Euporista in Dysenteria, 1745.

6. Pi ..... Œconomicus, 1743.

7. A ..... Œconomicus, 1744.

8. Sexus

8. Sexus Plantarum, 1744.
9. Sexus Plantarum Usus Œconomicus, 1745.
10. Theæ potus, 1746.
11. Scabiosæ novæ speciei Descriptio, 1744.
12. Penthorum, 1744.
13. Cyprini pinnæ ani radiis xi. pinnis albentibus descriptio. 1746.

FARTHER TRACTS AND ESSAYS

WRITTEN BY LINNÆUS, AND INSERTED IN THE TRANS-
ACTIONS OF THE ROYAL ACADEMY OF SCIENCES AT
STOCKHOLM.

In the First VOL.—1739 and 1740.

1. CULTURA Plantarum Naturalis.
2. Gluten Lapponum e perca.
3. Œstrus Rangiferinus.
4. Picus pedibus tridaßylis.

Mr. FORSTER also describes this bird in the Philosophical Trans-
aßions. *Lond.* vol. lxii. page three hundred and eighty-eight.

Also BUFFON, in his Histoire des Oiseaux, vol. vii. page
seventy nine.

5. Mures

5. Mures Alpini Lemures.
6. Passer Nivalis.—

> See BUFFON's Histoire des Oiseaux, vol. iv. page three hundred and twenty-nine.

7. Piscis Aureus Chinensium. [*Cyprinus Auratus.*]
8. Fundamenta Œconomiæ.

VOL. II.—1741.

9. Formicarum Sexus.
10. Officinales Sueciæ Plantæ.
11. Centuria Plantarum in Suecia rariorum.

VOL. III.—1742.

12. Plantæ Tinctoriæ Indigenæ.

> A Treatise which proved the result of a tour to the Island of *Gothland.*

13. Amaryllis formosissma. (*Jacobæa.*)
14. Gramen Sœlting.
15. Fœnum Suecicum. (*Medicago falcata.* Species Plantar. page one thousand and ninety six.)
16. Phaseoli Chinensis species.
17. Epilepsiæ vernensis causa.

VOL. IV.—1743.

18. De Uva ursi seu *Jackas Hapuck* Sinus Hudsonici. (Species Plantar. page five hundred and sixty-six.)

VOL.

VOL. V.—1744.

19. Fagopyrium Sibricum (called afterwards Polygonum Tartaricum by LINNÆUS), Spec. Plantar. page five hundred and twenty-one.

20. Petiveria. Species Plantar. page four hundred and eighty six.

VOL. VI.—1745.

21. Passer Procellarius.—See also BUFFON's Histoire des Oiseaux, vol. ix. page three hundred and seventeen.

VOL. VII.—1746.

22. Limnia—Claytonia Sibirica. Species Plantar. page 194.—De Vermibus Lucentibus ex China. (Cicadæ Species) ibid.
A Plant discovered by STELLER in *Sibiria*.

VOL. X.—1749.

23. Coluber (Chersea) scutis abdominalibus centum quinquaginta, squamis subcaudalibus triginta quatuor.

24. Avis *Sommar Guling* appellata.—BUFFON's Histoire des Oiseaux, vol. iv. page 176.

25. Musca *Frit*; insectum quod grana interius exedit.

The damage which this insect occasions every year in *Sweden* alone, is estimated by LINNÆUS at one hundred thousand ducats, or about fifty thousand pounds sterling. It is known to destroy the tenth part of the barley crops throughout the country.

26. Emberiza Ciris.

VOL.

VOL. XIII.—1752.

27. De Charaḍeribus Anguium.

VOL. XIV.—1753.

28. Novæ duæ Tabaci species. Paniculata et Glutinosa. Spec. Plantar. page 259.

VOL. XV.—1754.

29. De Plantis, quæ Alpium Suecicarum indigenæ fieri possint.—A dissertation, for which LINNÆUS obtained an academical prize.

30. Simiæ, ex Cercopithecorum genere, descriptio. (Simia Diana).

VOL. XVI.—1775.

31. Mirabilis Longifloræ descriptio.

32. Lepidii descriptio. (Cardamines Syst. 199). A new plant, which LŒFLING had sent from *Spain*.

33. Ayeniæ descriptio. (Pusillæ Spec. Plantar. 1354). This plant had been sent him by MILLER.

34. Gauræ descriptio. (Biennis. Species Plantarum, page 493). The seed of this plant was sent him by COLLINSON.

35. LŒFFLINGIA et Minuartia.

VOL. XX.—1759.

36. Entomolithus paradoxus descriptus.

37. Gemma, penna pavonis diḍa.

38. Coccus Uvæ Ursi.

VOL.

XXIII.—1763.

39. De Rubo arctico plantando.

VOL. XXIV.—1764.

40. Observationes ad cerevisiam pertinentes.

VOL. XXIX.—1769.

41. Animalis Brasiliensis descriptio. (Muris Agati, Syst. page 80).
42. Viverræ Naricæ; System. page 64, descriptio.
43. Simia Oedipus.
44. Gordius Medinensis.

VOL. XXXI.—1770.

45. Calceolariæ pinnatæ. Syst. Nat. edit. 13, page 60, descriptio.
  Also some thoughts respecting Tea, in Histoire de l'Academie
  des Sciences, 1763.

A GENEALOGICAL

A

GENEALOGY

OF

THE FAMILY OF

THE LINNÆI.

―――――――

INGEMAR SUENSSON,

A PEASANT AT JOMSBODA, IN THE PARISH OF HWITARYD
IN SMALAND.

OF this man was descended CHARLES TILIANDER, who took his name of a tall linden-tree *(Tilia)*, which stands between *Jomsboda* and *Linnhult.* He studied at *Upsal* in 1660, was appointed preacher at *Lekaryd* in 1678, and died without issue in 1697.

His brother, SUEN TILIANDER, studied at *Upsal* in 1678, lived in the family of Count H. HORN at *Bremen,* as his domestic chaplain, and died rector of *Pjetteryd* in 1712. He was a peculiar lover of gardening and natural history. His sons were, ABEL TILIANDER, who succeeded

him

him in his pastoral office, and was accidentally drowned in a well in
1724; and NICHOLAS TILIANDER, chaplain to a regiment. The
latter left issue CHARLES TILIANDER, born in 1701, who studied at
Lund in 1720; was made adjunct teacher in philosophy therein 1729,
adjunct teacher in divinity in 1730, rector of *Jönköping* in 1741, and at
last a doctor in divinity, and was twice delegated as a representative to the
Swedish diet. He departed life in 1764, leaving behind him two sons,
namely, PETER TILIANDER, adjunct teacher in the college at *Wexico*,
and NICHOLAS TILIANDER, an ensign in a regiment of foot.

ANDERS,

A PEASANT AT JOMSBODA.

His progeny were, AMBERN LINDELIUS, born in 1600, who took
likewise his name from the above mentioned linden-tree; was made
Master of Arts in 1632, two years after adjunct teacher in philosophy,
rector of *Bornorp* in 1638, lecturer in divinity at *Wexico* in 1643, rector
of *Landgaryd* in 1646, and died in 1684. LARS LINDELIUS, his brother died rector of *Jönköping* in 1672.

ERIC AMBERN LINDELIUS, the son of the former, studied at *Upsal*
in 1655, was appointed vicar at *Langaryd* in 1681, and died as preacher
at *Quænberga* in 1715.

LARS LINDELIUS's son was JOHN LINDELIUS, a physician of great
professional repute at *Wexico*, who studied at *Lund* in 1672, at *Upsal* in
1680, and died in 1711.

The male issue of this collateral line of the family of LINNÆUS is
quite extinct.

BENGE

BENGE INGEMARSON,

PEASANT IN THE PARISH OF HWITARYD,

Had issue INGEMAR BENGTSON, born in 1633, farmer of the manor of *Erickstad.*

This INGEMAR BENGTSON was the grandfather of our celebrated LINNÆUS. NILS or NICHOLAS LINNÆUS, his son, took his sirname from the same linden-tree, from which the families of the TILIANDERS and the LINDELIUSES had borrowed theirs. He was born in 1674, assumed his clerical functions in 1704, was made vicar of *Stenbrohult* in 1705, and in 1708 rector of the same place, where he died May 12th, 1748. He had been married to CHRISTINA BRODERSON, the daughter of his predecessor. On the 12th of May, 1707, he had issue of her at *Rashult* in *Smaland,*

CHARLES LINNÆUS,

who went to the school at *Wexico* in 1717, frequented the college there in 1724, studied at *Lund* in 1727, went to the university of *Upsal* in 1728, became lecturer in botany for Dean RUDBECK in 1731, took his degree as Doctor of Medicine at *Harderwyk* in 1735, was elected first President of the Royal Academy of *Stockholm* in 1739, appointed botanist to the King of *Sweden,* and physician to the admiralty in 1740, professor of physic and botany at *Upsal* in 1741, archiater or dean of the university in 1747, created knight of the order of the Polar Star in 1753, ennobled in 1756, and died at *Upsal* January 10th, 7778.

'2   His

His sisters were:

1. ANNA MARIA LINNÆUS, married to GABRIEL HÖK, rector of *Wirestadt.*

2. SOPHIA JULIANA LINNÆUS, married to JOHN COLLIN, rector of *Rysby.*

3. EMERENTIA LINNÆUS, married to the police-officer BRANTNIG.

SAMUEL LINNÆUS, the only brother of our luminary, was born in 1718, studied at *Lund* in 1738, was ordained minister in 1741, took his degree of master of arts in 1745, and succeeded his father in the rectory and prebendary of *Stenbrohult* in 1749. He is still alive, and married to the daughter of NILS OSANDER, prebendary of *Makaryd*, by whom he has several daughters.

CHARLES LINNÆUS married in 1739 SARAH ELISABETH, daughter of Dr. JOHN MORÆUS, physician at *Fahlun*, and had issue—

1. CHARLES LINNÆUS, born at *Fahlun* January 20, 1741; studied at *Upsal* in 1750, was appointed demonstrator of botany in that university in 1759, designed professor in 1763, took his degree as doctor of physic in 1765, succeeded his father as professor of botany in 1778, died in a state of celibacy November 1, 1783. With him the male branch of the family of LINNÆUS became totally extinct.

2. JOHN LINNÆUS died an infant.

3. ELISABETH CHRISTINA LINNÆUS, married to Captain BERGENCRANZ, died several years ago.

LOUISA LINNÆUS, lives unmarried with her mother at *Hammarby.*

5. SARAH CHRISTINA LINNÆUS also lives with her mother at *Hamarby* in a state of celibacy.

6. SOPHIA LINNÆUS was born in 1754, and is married to Mr. DUSE at *Upsal.*

ACCOUNTS

RESPECTING

LINNÆUS,

(GIVEN BY HIMSELF)

DURING THE EARLIEST PART OF HIS LITERARY CAREER,

FROM 1730 TO 1735.

———

" *Upsal*, JANUARY, 1732.

" A Student of medicine and natural history at this University*,
" of the name of CHARLES LINNÆUS, takes great pains to repre-
" sent those two sciences, and botany likewise, in a better light, and
" to render them more flourishing. The foreign herbs and plants
" which are cultivated either in the fields or gardens of *Upland*, have

---

* This first account respecting LINNÆUS, appeared in a German periodical work, published at *Hamburgh*, by Dr. KOHL, entituled *Hamburgische Berichten*, &c. 1732, No.
vi. page 45.

" already

" already been collected by him in a little work, which appeared last
" December, 1771, with the following title :

" Hortus Uplandicus, sive Enumeratio Plantarum Exoticarum Up-
" landiæ quæ in hortis vel agris coluntur, imprimis autem in horto aca-
" demico, *Upsaliensi.*——The author of this work expresses himself
" in the Preface as follows:"—" Secutus sum," says he, " methodum
" propriam et artificialem, *a staminibus et pistillis,* quod sexum vo-
" cant, *desumtam.* Incertas seu classes et sectiones stirpes exoticas,
" in hortis *Uplandiæ* repertas dispescuit, in classibus staminum, in secti-
" onibus pistillorum rationem habet." In other respects, the author
" has also assigned to most of the plants new and particular names, and
" added to each of them their synonyma. He has also found it abso-
" lutely necessary to alter some general denominations. The work
" consists of ten sheets, in octavo."

" *Upsal,* FEBRUARY 15, 1732.

" AN able student of medicine *, Mr. CHARLES LINNÆUS, causes
" a botanical work to be printed here, entituled : FUNDAMENTA BO-
" TANICA, which is to consist of the following twelve parts†. In the
" first part, he relates in a quite novel and masterly manner, the botanical

* See *Hamburgische Berichten,* 1731, No. XII. Page 94.

† The *Fundamento Botanica* did not appear till four years after, namely, in 1736, at
Amsterdam. LINNÆUS sent the manuscript afterwards to *Greifswalde,* but could not find
a person that would undertake to publish it. This shows, how early LINNÆUS prepared
his system, what alterations he made in the *Fundamenta Botanica,*—and at the same time,
how eager he was to make himself known, even by advertising works which still remained
in manuscript.

" books

" books and the history of their respective authors. In the second
" part, he touches upon all the botanical systems and opinions, accord-
" ing to the classes, sections, and general names of the plants; particu-
" larly upon the methods and opinions of Cæsalpinus, Herrmann,
" Knautius, Ray, Rivini, Tournefort, Pontedera, &c. &c.
" besides his own system, to which he intends to add Magnol's as soon
" as he shall have received the valuable work of the latter. In the
" *Methodi Specialiores*, he will observe the generical characters. For
" instance, in the mosses, he will give both the characters of Dil-
" lenius and his own, &c. &c. In the third part of this work he
" treats on the parts of fructification; he explains what they are, how
" they are to be distinguished, and points out in what manner they
" can be regularly ordered and divided. In the fourth, he treats of
" the sex of the plants, and demonstrates it plainly. In the fifth, he
" discriminates the true and general characters from the false ones,
" and teaches how cautiously this must be done, and how not only
" one, but all the parts of fructification ought to be most carefully
" observed, and how the outward form is chiefly to be looked after
" in doubtful cases. He maintains, that the greatest part of the plants may
" be known by their blossom or flower. He ascribes the errors of most
" of the botanists to their ignorance of some of the principal rules. In
" the sixth part, he refutes with sound proofs upwards of seven hundred
" general denominations of plants. In the seventh, he speaks of the
" *Differentiæ Specificæ*, which have been omitted in most of the names,
" merely because the right method to discover them was not known. In
" the eighth, he treats of the variations of plants, and points out how
" they are to be discriminated. In the ninth part, he enumerates the new

" species of plants discovered, according to Tournefort's me-
" thod by several botanists, especially by Rivini, Pontedera,
" Boerhaave, Buxbaum, Vaillant, &c. and reduces the two
" hundred new species of Tournefort to seventy-five. In the tenth,
" he mentions the synonyma, in what manner they are to be used, and
" what is to be observed in each of them. The eleventh, contains in-
" structions how to arrange the description of plants, with suitable ex-
" amples by way of illustration. In the twelfth and last part he con-
" cludes with demonstrating, the great utility of the classes and orders
" as arranged by Nature herself, how manifold they are, and what
" species of plants must be reckoned to each class."

The Author prefixes the following advertisement to his work : " Hæc
" omnia C. CXXX. regulis sive canonibus superstructa, exemplisque
" stabilita sunt. Observationes autem omnes ἀυτοψιᾶ auctoris nituntur.
" Earum in classes distributio a certa corporis parte desumitur, sec-
" tiones, characteres generici prorsus nova methodo instituuntur.
" Nomina specifica nova unicuique tribuuntur, allegatis synonymis."

Upsal, March 15, 1732.

" CHARLES LINNÆUS, the student of medicine, whose name
" has already been several times mentioned in an honourable and flat-
" tering manner, is now occupied with two new works, which have
" never before been the object of the efforts of our learned men, but
                                                                " which,

" which, owing to their rare contents and utility, will probably meet.
" with a good reception."

The first will be entituled: " Methodus Avium Suecicarum, seu Enu-
" meratio Avium CC. in Suecia observatarum.*"

The second.is to bear the title of: " Insecta Uplandica, quorum per
" duas Æstates DCC. collecta sunt †."

" In this latter work, the author will distinguish the insects in a
" quite new manner, by certain classes and sections, and also by gene-
" ral and particular species. He will likewise observe, in the most
" accurate manner, the *Synonyma* & *Differentiæ*, which have not been
" noticed by other authors, and describe every thing that has been.
" left undescribed.respecting those objects.

LINNÆUS'S TOUR THROUGH LAPLAND.

" *Upsal,* JUNE 3, 1732.

" THE Royal Academy of Sciences in this city having resolved to·
" have the most exact researches made in *Lapland,* after every thing·
" which may be considered as remarkable or rare in natural history;
" CHARLES LINNÆUS, who has given public lectures in the garden of
" this University for about two years, has been unanimously chosen
" for that purpose. He will perform the task the more ably, having
" already been occupied several years, in exploring the three reigns of
" nature, and proposed to himself to make the most careful search in

* See *Hamburgische Berichte,* &c. 1732, No. xxii. page 177.
† Both the above works have not appeared with the above title and form.
‡.See *Hamburgische Berichte,* for 1733, No. 64, page 513.

" *Lapland,*.

" *Lapland,* not only for all kinds of fossils and minerals, but also
" for all the trees, herbs, grasses, mosses, plants, animals, birds,
" fishes, worms, &c. and to observe with equal attention the mode of
" living of the inhabitants, its influence upon their health, and every
" thing worth notice. He has already set out on his journey to
" *Lapland* last May, at the expence of the academy, and highly
" pleased wit' ᵃis enterprize."

Upsal, J u n e 24, 1733.

" CHARLES LINNÆUS, our skilful physician and botanist*, has
" returned for some time past, from his travels in *Lapland,* which he
" undertook at the expence of the Royal Academy. He travelled by
" water as well as by land altogether to a distance of six hundred and
" seventy Swedish miles. He remained some time in the mountains of
" *Lapland,* through which he travelled one hundred and fifty Swedish
" miles on foot. When he came under the seventieth degree of polar
" longitude, on the frozen sea, he saw the sun eight whole days without
" setting. Among the principal curiosities which he met with on his
" return, he reckons a flying white squirrel, which he saw near *Tawastia.*
" Since his return, he occupied himself with a *Flora Laponica,* in
" which he gives an account of all the rare and unknown flowers of
" *Lapland.* This work, which is already finished, consists of thirty-six
" sheets, and eighty plates.

* See *Hamburgische Berichte,* for 1733, No. 64, page 523.

He

" He has now another work in hand, to which he gives the name of
" *Lachesis Lapponica.* He will give a proper description in it of the
" œconomy of the Laplanders, of the causes of their longevity, and not
" only contradict Scheffer and other writers on *Lapland,* but make
" plain truth the characteristic of his narrative. Linnæus can boast of
" being the first who travelled in summer through the mountains of *Lap-*
" *land.* He says : that he generally found a very gre' similarity be-
" tween those mountains and the Alps, even with regard to the plants.
" Their summits are generally of so very sandy a nature that no plants
" can grow upon them. He further adds: that in the province of
" *Lapmark,* the soil is every where so very sterile on account of the
" cold northern winds which constantly blow from the monntains,
" that no corn will grow, except on the banks of the rivers, and that
" hardly one hundred inhabitants are to be found in the whole district."
" He observes, however, that he discovered in that province and in
" *Finnemark* a kind of wild corn, which shoots forth from the dry sand,
" and bears the most rigorous cold blasts which prevail in *Lapland,*
" even in summer, without the least prejudice to its growth."

LINNÆUS'S TOUR TO HOLLAND.

LITERARY AND MISCELLANEOUS TRACTS
RESPECTING HIM.

DR. NETTELBLADT writes from *Greifswald**, July, 12, 1734, that he has received the following work: CAROLI LINNÆI Stipend. Wredian. Fundamenta Botanica, quæ majorum operum prodromi instar theoriam Scientiæ Botanicæ per breves aphorismos, sistunt; in quarto; and that an editor is wanted. The work contains two tables: 1. Systema Vegetablium sexuale, &c. staminibus et pistillis construĉtum. 2. Systema Vegetabilium Calycinum: e calycis diversis speciebus compositum.—Doĉtor NETTELBLADT has the manuscript in his own hands, and he who may desire to publish it, is requested to apply to him. LINNÆUS is in other respeĉts a young but very able Swedish botanist, whose exertions will prove very great and serviceable in time, and are already extensive.

CHARLES LINNÆUS, the celebrated Swedish physician and botanist who has frequently been mentioned, travelled a few days ago through *Hambro'* to *Holland*, accompanied by M. SOHLBERG, his pupil. He

* See *Hamburgische Berichte*, 1734. No. 59, 1735, No. 47.

means

means to reside a few years in *Holland*, for the purpose of acquiring
still greater perfection in medicine, natural history and botany, by his
intercourse with the most celebrated scientific Batavians, especially
with BOERHAAVE, with whom he has already carried on a learned correspondence.

LINNÆUS also came to *Holland* to get published, in a manner advantageous to himself, the works which he wrote in   *..en*, especially
three tables in large folio, finished with the most surprising diligence and
ability.   On one of those tables he represented all kinds of flowers
and plants which can be thought of, in a quite new but very plain
manner ; the flowers are reduced to classes by means of the two different sexes, and by the number of the petals or leaves; on the second table
he has collected all the genera of stones in the same manner, and with
such excellent order and classification, that he believes to be able
to give any person in a few hours a general notion both of botany and mineralogy.   He farther intends to publish a work, which
he calls *Flora Lapponica*, and in which he describes and gives plates
of all the unknown plants and flowers which he discovered on his tour
through *Lapland;* also another production to which he gives the title of
Oeconomia Lapponica, and in which he takes notice, in a masterly and
regular style, of all he has seen in his extremely difficult, and in some
instances dangerous peregrination, with regard to œconomy and
natural history, the dresses, dwellings, rearing of cattle, manners,
occupation, diligence and character of the Laplanders.

Whatever this great man thinks and writes is systematical, and he cannot rest till he has brought science, or those defects which he purposes to mend, to that order which is alone congenial to her.   It may

be inferred from this, that he is endowed with the most acute judgment and a large share of natural genius and inventive powers. His se-
dulity, perseverance and diligence are quite uncommon. Few can
equal him in zeal and eagerness to fathom and scrutinize whatever has
hitherto remained a secret to the most prying eye, and whatever
is worthy of any particular attention in the three reigns of nature.
Although he ' ѕ only attained his twenty-eighth year, he has acquired
so much experience by his indefatigableness in reading and making
annotations, that he excels in this respect many eminent men.

   The excellencies of his mind are heightened by the charms of
a most amiable character. Endowed with a softness and sweetness of
temper uncommon among men of letters, he can also boast of a
natural candor, a love of truth and piety, a readiness of rendering service, and a philanthropy free from all envy, asperity and ostentation.

   Among many curiosities he brought with him from *Lapland*, a
Laplander's dress made of rein-deer skins, and a very curious magic
drum.   He will give a circumstantial account of all these things, as he
has been able to enquire into their use, by means of an interpreter
who was his guide through *Lapland*. He needs not therefore to have
recourse, like SCHEFFER, to the spurious accounts of others.

   LINNÆUS even took all possible pains to explore the greatest secrets
of the Laplanders. Among these their famous love of magic may
be reckoned as one of the foremost. He can imitate exactly their
contortions of face and body, and assures us, that those grimaces
are more the effect of gross superstition and a narrowness of imagination, than of a pretended supernatural enchantment, performed by
                                                                the

the aid of the devil. If, for instance, they go out a hunting, and wish to know what game it would be best for them to shoot on that day, or in which district they may meet with it soonest, they take their magic drum, and having laid a little brass ring upon it, beat it with two small sticks, then drop suddenly upon the ground, as it were, in a trance, and utter a kind of howl not unlike that of the dogs*. By the spot on which the ring happens to fall, they prog ♠ ate the good or ill success of their chace.

The second curiosity which he showed us, consisted of an excellent collection of insects, gathered in his two tours through *Lapland* and *Dalecarlia*, and neatly pasted upon paper; their number amounted to one thousand, among which there were sixty-five different species of flies, besides the insect which was known to the ancients by the name of *Oestrum*,—a wasp, of which no modern naturalist had as yet given an accurate description, whose size is considerably large, and not unlike that of the fly, which makes such great havoc among the rein-deer in *Lapland*, as to kill annually several thousands of them. The Swedes would fain give a million of their money for an efficacious remedy to extirpate that vermin.

We have in other respects found an opportunity of obtaining an account of LINNÆUS, written in good Latin by an eminent Swede; also a short description of his last journey through *Dalecarlia*, and of the companions who attended him on that tour, from which we will occasionally give extracts.

* LINNÆUS also informed us, that no *Laplander* could sing, but instead of singing uttered a noise, which resembled the barking of dogs.

We

We have to add by way of conclusion, that LINNÆUS with his travelling companion left this city *(Hamburgh)* with great satisfaction, having had an opportunity of seeing and examining the public library, in which he perused with great eagerness the DANUBIUS MARSILLII, also the principal cabinets of natural history, the botanical gardens and the private libraries, in one of which he was much pleased at finding the ⬤ al work of RAY, which he had so long wished to see. He above all thought himself extremely happy, in obtaining a sight of the seven-headed *Hydra*, which the celebrated SEBA at *Amsterdam* inserted in his *Thesaurus*, as a curiosity at *Hamburgh*. To a naturalist of his experience, who had never seen such a phenomenon, its existence appeared at first an utter impossibility. But having viewed this monster, at the house of a merchant where it laid deposited in a box about an ell and an half long and embalmed in a perfect manner, he could not sufficiently admire and examine it, till after the most scrupulous and minute examination, he finally discovered in the wide gaping mouths of the heads of this Hydra, which had been a little shrivelled and worn by the edge of time, that its teeth bore a strong resemblance to those of the weasels. A person worthy of being depended on, also informed him, that this rare *master-piece* of *nature* had formerly been exhibited on an altar, in a catholic church at *Prague*, whence it had been first removed by the Swedish Count of KOENIGSMARK, after the last capture of that city; that the Count made a present of it to a Nobleman of the name of BIELKEN, whose heirs sent it some years after to be sold at *Hamburgh*. They affixed so high a price to it, that its acquisition was even refused FREDERICK IV. KING of DENMARK, who bid 30,000 rix-dollars, and it is probable that it will after all become the

3   property,

property of a certain great court, whose offer does not exceed 2000 dollars. A plate representing this monster is to be found in the THESAURUS NATURALIUM, published by M. SEBA at *Amsterdam.*

LINNÆUS'S TOUR THROUGH DALECARLIA.

HIS CURIOUS TRAVELLING COMPANIONS.

WE will now give an account * of the scientific tour, which was made last year [1734] all over the Swedish province of *Dalecarlia,* and of which we have received the principal particulars from LINNÆUS, who lately passed through this city on his way to *Leyden.*

Before the latter set out in the summer months on this expedition, undertaken by advice, and at the expence of BARON NICHOLAS REU-THERHOLM, Governor of *Dalecarlia,* several students applied and request-ed to accompany him. He chose seven of the ablest and most zealous of them, that he might proceed on his way with more convenience, and formed in this manner a kind of a caravan of naturalists, and enacted with their assistance certain laws and regulations, for the due observance of which every member made himself answerable. For

* See *Hamburgische Berichte* 1735, Page 586, No. 71.

ECC 2   his

his own part he chose to be their governor, to superintend the whole enterprise, and to take care that every body discharged the functions of the office allotted him.

NÄHEMANN, the first companion, who had made himself known by a good dissertation on the *Darlecarlian* language, *(de Lingua Dalecarlica)* was to act as geographer, to give an accurate description of all the villages, mo𝄆 ⟶ ⟶, lakes, rivers, roads and districts, &c. to say morning and evening prayers, and to preach on Sundays.

CLEWBERG, the second companion, as naturalist, was to make observations on the four elements; such as on the quality of the water, on mineral springs, on sources, on the snow which never melts in the Alps in summer, on the height of the mountains, the weather, the fruitfulness or sterility of soil, &c. &c. He was also charged with digesting, as secretary, the transactions of the society in a proper written form.

FAHLSTEDT, the third companion, as Metallist *(Metallurgus)*, besides collecting stones, minerals, earths, all kind of petrifactions, &c. &c. was further employed as groom, to saddle, water and attend the horses.

STOHLBERG, an able student of physic, as botanist or herbalist was to examine and to preserve as well as possible, all the trees, plants, herbs, grasses, and fungi, which occurred to his view. He was moreover appointed to precede the company as a quarter-master, to procure them good lodgings, and to provide every necessary for their reception.

To EMPORELIUS, the fifth companion was assigned the office of Zoologist, to describe and depict the quadrupeds and all the animals living as well in the water as on the land, such as fishes, birds, worms, &c.

His

His collateral occupation consisted in shooting the game, which was necessary for the support of the company, and in fishing and angling whenever it was deemed expedient.

HEDENSLAD, the sixth companion was commissioned to act as œconomist, to examine the dress of the *Laplanders*, their dwellings, their way of preparing provisions, their matrimonial and funeral rites, their knowledge of medicine, mode of living, diet, &c. & _ ʼd to describe with the pen or the pencil such objects as were most worthy his attention. His additional employment was to communicate to his fellow companions the dispositions and regulations of the president, in the same manner as the adjutant of a regiment announces the orders of the general to his corps, and to call them together whenever it was required, especially in the evening when an account was always given of the transactions of the day; he was also to take care that every companion went to bed and rose again to continue the journey at the proper time appointed.

SANDEL, an American born in *Pensylvania*, as the seventh companion, did the duty of a steward and treasurer; he had the chief care of the fodder, cattle, wood, buying and selling, and discharged the expences of the whole company.

Owing to these excellent regulations and their due observance, the tour was continued and terminated with the greatest ease and convenience. When the president discovered a village, it was not necessary for all the company to ride thither, but the geographer alone was sent to enter it. If some particular stone or fossil was found on the way, the metallist was directed to alight; at the sight of some curious plant or insect, the botanist or zoologist did his duty; they took the respective objects with them, and prepared a description to be inserted at night in

the

the transactions, besides the name of the place where they had been found. The above regulations being thus uniformly observed, the president had nothing to do on the road but remind his companions of what they were to set down in the diary.

At night they all met together, the president then dictated to the secretary the memoranda collected by each companion, in a regular turn from the geography the steward; and if he happened to forget any remark, the companion to whose office that part of the science belonged, refreshed his memory. The president was quite surprised at the readiness and diligence with which his attendants discharged the duties of their respective offices. In the short space of a few weeks, they appeared to him as if they had been accustomed to it for whole years together.

In this manner they travelled through all *East* and *West Dalecarlia,* the *Alps,* a large tract of *Norway,* especially through the parishes of *Binsoas Retwick, Oret, Orsa, Mora, Elfdalen, Seina, Idre, Fielten, Roras, Cranstrand, Lima, Malunos, Iärna, Floda, Gagneahl,* and *Fahlund.*

The transactions or operations of the society are printed on forty-eight written sheets, containing many important observations and discoveries; for instance, in the geographical part is a faithful description and representation of the *Dalelren,* the largest river of *Dalecarlia,* with all its arms and sources; also a geography of the Alpine mountains. In that part which treats of natural philosophy it is stated, that on the highest mountain called *Sterol Sladet,* the clouds which first appeared below, approached the travellers. In mineralogy, there exists a description of one hundred and twenty different curious sorts of minerals and fossils, most of which are to be found in the district of *Rettwick.* In the botanical part is a list of all the plants growing in the whole province, under the title

of

of *Flora Dalecarlica*, with their synonyma and their œconomical and pharmaceutical virtues, written by Baron REUTHERHOLM. In zoology, there is described, among many other curiosities, a magpie never described before, which exists in the Dalecarlian Alps, and whose feet are not armed like those of the other magpies with four claws, but have only three, namely, two from before, and one from behind, which is rather stronger than those in front. In dome· ·medicine, the pleurisy is mentioned as a distemper of an epidemical nature in that country; it is alledged, that it arises from the excess which the inhabitants commit by gorging themselves with a kind of pap made of flour. It is also observed, with regard to the inhabitants of the district of *Orsa*, that they have the misfortune seldom to outlive thirty years of age, and LINNÆUS is of opinion, that the complaint which they labour under is an hectic fever, and arises from the pernicious exhalations of the mines. The tour through *Dalecarlia* also mentions the Dalecarlian dances; how the inhabitants masticate a certain kind of rosin, and dress it in a still more disgusting manner as an aliment; how they bury in the earth a species of rotten fish, which is called *Lunsfisk*, and dig them out again to prepare them for their food. The same transactions describe a kind of bed called *Jullar*, in which the girls amuse themselves with their lovers. In œconomy the work expatiates on the particular prerogatives of *Dalecarlia*, if compared with other Swedish provinces, how these advantages may be farther improved, and all sorts of useful plants cultivated on those Alps.

Härderwyk,

Harderwyk, August 1, 1735.

ON the 23d of June, CHARLES LINNÆUS made his dissertation at this university, for the purpose of obtaining his degree of doctor of medicine. In this dissertation, which is entituled *Hypothesis de febrium inter* ..*ntium causa*, the author founded every thing upon observations and experiments; and having resided in the northern parts of the world, he made his remarks upon what chiefly attracted his notice in those quarters.

This celebrated physician put to press at *Leyden* his *Systema Naturæ*, of which one half is already printed off. It consists only of seven sheets in large folio, and contains an uncommon number of observations.

He founded the system of the mineral reign upon *principia docimastica*. The genera *concretorum et petrificatorum* have been so arranged by him, that it appears impossible to add a single *genus*. He expatiates a great deal on the generation of stones, and states especially, that they are all either primordial like the *glarea* and *argilla*, or produced by time like *humus*, *ochra* and *arena*. He has added the generical characters to all the genera, which has never been done in mineralogy, which science may by this means be easily acquired at the expiration of a few hours study.

He divides the vegetable reign according to a new system, borrowed from the sex of the plants. He has more real genera, inserted in their proper places, than any other systematist ever had. All the general

* See *Hamburgische Berichten. Hamburgh*, 1735, No. 75, page 617.

methods

methods in botany acknowledge the system of CÆSALPINUS as their basis; but the doctrine of LINNÆUS is of a quite different nature. He suppressed the great number of false genera, and reduced every thing to its real genus: he omitted the absurd *nomina generica*, and substituted new ones in their place. He added, by a double theory, the art of getting acquainted with the virtues of the plants. He also first described a great number of new genera of 'ʌnts from the *East* and *West Indies*.

He divided the animal reign into six classes, namely into quadrupeds, birds, amphibious animals, fishes, insects and worms. He added to each the generical characters and the species. No naturalist but himself had ever accurately distinguished the worms from the insects, although in his opinion they are more distinct from each other than the amphibious animals and the birds, or the birds and the quadrupeds. He is of opinion, that the generation of the worms in the bowels of human beings, is not to be attributed to the spawn of the insects.

The *Hygra*, which has been described by the ancients, and denied by some modern writers, he also mentioned as it has been lately found, and is preserved alive in *England*.

A N

ACCOUNT OF LINNÆUS,

THE CELEBRATED MINERALOGIST

E. C. SCHULTZ, AT HAMBURGH.

W HAT occasioned my first literarry correspondence and acquaintance with LINNÆUS, was a prince and a book. I published in 1769
a description of several curiosities of nature, art and antiquity, which
had deservedly attracted the notice and attention of the curious in
MOVER's cabinet of natural history at *Hamburgh**. This cabinet
of

---

* The above work appeared at *Hamburgh* in two volumes, octavo. The reader will not
be displeased with the following brief account respecting the author himself.—Mr. ERNEST
CHRISTOPHER SCHULTZ was born in 1740, at *Koenigsberg* in *Prussia*. He was at the university with Baron JACOBI, the present Prussian minister at the court of *London*. His parents
wanted him to study divinity, but like LINNÆUS, he preferred natural history. In the year
1764 his considerable cabinet of natural treasures, especially a fine collection of ambers, and
a considerable library of natural history, were destroyed at *Koenigsberg*, by the dreadful
conflagration which ravaged that city. He was so affected at this loss, that he resolved to
travel. He afterwards fixed upon *Hamburgh* as the most eligible spot for his general residence, and began to collect another cabinet, and to enrich it, travelled through the principal

having been destined for sale, and my description having been sent to several amateurs in foreign countries, it so happened that it fell into the hands of the Queen of *Sweden,* the sister of FREDERICK the Great, whose love of natural history was so conspicuous. Another copy of my work being at the same time transmitted to the celebrated Count SCHEFFER, governor to the late King, he could not help communicating it likewise to his favourite LINNÆUS.

GUSTAVUS the GREAT, then Prince Royal, went two years after to *France,* accompanied by his governor. The latter introduced me to this Prince during his stay at *Hamburgh,* which lasted from the 23d to the 30th of December of the same year. Several precious stones, very scarce, and partly unknown, amongst others the *Asterias,* whose wonderful appearance I had first discovered shortly before in 1770, and which I illustrated afterwards, besides many other valuable productions of nature, which I had the honour on that occasion to show

---

countries of *Europe.* He made several valuable discoveries, especially that of the rainbow-coloured agate and the *Asterias* of PLINY, which the curious had considered as a nonentity. He composed a treatise upon the *Asterias,* which was read with universal applause at the meeting of the Academy of Sciences at *St. Petersburgh;* and FREDERICK the Great of *Prussia* was so pleased with it, that he sent Mr. SCHULTZ a most flattering note in his own hand writing, in which he thanked him for his discovery. The present King of *Prussia* presented him also with two gold medals, which he received from the hands of Count VON HERZBERG. He first gave the best description of the gem called the *oculus mundi.* It was doubtful whether that gem was the work of nature or of art; but Mr. SCHULTZ proved it to be a natural production, by a treatise which was read in the Royal Academy of Sciences at *Paris* in 1776. Prince FREDERICK of *Brunswick* also complimented him in a letter on the revival of the *Asterias* of PLINY. While he was at *Paris* he bought of an ignorant person a crystal of *Madagascar,* for the sum of three Louis d'ors, which represented in its internal structure the perfect form of a net. The great mineralogist, DELISLE, soon after offered him 4000 livres for it, on the part of the late Queen of *France.*—As a naturalist, his knowledge was of the first rate, and his merits are acknowledged by the first literati of the age.

and

and to explain to the Prince, especially the opal of NONNIUS, and that most rare one, which CRONSTEDT, the Swedish mineralogist, describes to be of a brown and of a blood red colour, made his Highness desire me to give LINNÆUS some account of the above interesting and curious opal.

I obeyed the Prince's command with the greatest pleasure, gave LINNÆUS the desired account, and sent him at the same time some curious gems. He thanked me for my present in a most obliging letter, which I received June 24, 1771 *. Long had I felt a wish of getting acquainted with that great man. My mineralogical tours to the forest *Harzwald*, through *Saxony*, *Holland*, *France*, &c. precluded me however from gratifying that wish. In 1775 I went to *Copenhagen*, where I had formerly passed a few weeks with great utility and delight. On the 20th of September I took my departure from that capital in company of a a Swedish literatus, with whom I made acquaintance at the house of the Swedish ambassador; repaired to *Lund*, where I saw the botanical garden and every thing that was remarkable, and reached *Stockholm* at the end of the same month. During my abode in *Sweden* I visited the villa of *Töresö*, belonging to Count SCHEFFER, who received me with unbounded kindness and cordiality. The late King, to whom I had been presented at *Hamburgh*, while Prince Royal, had ascended the throne, and was just then on a tour through the Swedish provinces. " I had " the pleasure," said Count SCHEFFER, " to introduce you to his Ma-
" jesty as Prince Royal, and you shall not go hence before I shall also
" have introduced you to him as King. Waiting his return, you would

* See the above letter in *Collectio Epistolarm* CAROLI A LINNE, &c. Edidit. D. H. STOEVER, *Hamburg*, 1792.

3

" do

" do well to take a trip to *Upsal*, on a visit to Linnæus."—The Count spoke in terms of the greatest veneration of Linnæus, and I had in other respects long ago resolved in my mind to have an interview with him. I set out accordingly early in the morning of the twenty-fourth of October from *Stockholm*, and reached *Upsal* on the same evening. I had hardly time to rest myself for a few minutes at my lodgings, before the younger Linnæus surprised me with a visit, and invited me to his father's house the next day.

Sir Charles received me with that openness, and that pleasing affability of temper for which he was so strongly remarkable. Although he had then attained the sixty-seventh year of his age, yet he still appeared quite brisk and lively; his stature was short, but his body of a strong and robust make.—" Well !" said he to me in Latin, after we had exchanged the usual compliments, " What new natural curiosity " do you bring me ?"—" Alas !" replied I, " how difficult, how bur- " dering upon impossibility would it be, to bring any thing new to a " Linnæus."—As it happened, I had taken with me, and collected some natural curiosities by the way. I showed him therefore among others, a small crab, which from the characteristic description in his system of nature, appeared to be the *Cancer Hirtellus*. Linnæus re- cognized it to be the same, and asked me, if there was none of a larger size ; he owned, that having never seen them any larger, he had assigned to those little hairy crabs, the Latin diminutive *hirtelli*. I then showed another specimen of the same kind which had not the supposed hair on the back of the shell. He was surprised at seeing on the surface of the back the natural figure of an human face. Cautious and provident as he was in all his researches, he now began to think that art had lent

her

her aid in this singular and striking phenomenon. To remove all
doubts, I took the other crab still covered with the supposed hair, di-
vested it of that cover which nature has laid on the backs of all those
species, and showed him on every one the appearance of an human
face. His attention was still more engrossed, at my making him perceive
through the glass, that those little filaments which sometimes appear
on the back of those crabs and resemble a hairy cover are not hair, if
viewed with the naked eye, but a sort of coraline moss, which sometimes settles upon those crabs, in the same manner as there are among
some sorts of the small shell fish, certain species encrusted with a
madreporous or milleporous sediment.

LINNÆUS convinced himself in the same manner, that the number
of prickles on the back of the *Cancer Hirtellus*, which he had fixed at
ten *(thorace hirto, utrimque quinque dentato)* was not a solid description ;
b t that most of them bore only eight, some nine, and the smallest
number ten. I afterwards gave a separate description and representation of this species.

The elder LINNÆUS, gave no lectures at that time, but I wished
at least for an opportunity to hear his son. The latter just read a lecture in the forenoon upon botany. The time having elapsed with our
conversation upon Zoology, I left his father with the promise according to his request, to come and see him every day during the whole of
my stay at *Upsal*.

The younger LINNÆUS was somewhat taller than his father, but at
that time less corpulent. His delivery was fluent, but mixed with a
certain cold indifference. It appeared as if his exertions were rather
a strict performance of the duties of his station, than a real zeal flow-
ing

ing from a natural fondness of his science : his father, on the contrary betrayed even in his conversation upon subjects relative to natural history an enthusiastic predilection and a most scrutinizing zeal.

The lecture which the younger LINNÆUS gave, was upon the classes of the plants, with five stamina, many living ones were exposed in garden pots in the lecture room, then taken out of the mould, divided into small branches, and distributed among those of the audience, who were the most attentive.

When the lecture hour had expired, the younger LINNÆUS showed me the *Casuar* from *Ceylon*, of which the late Queen Dowager of *Sweden* had made a present to his father: This large bird was uncommonly tame, moved about with a grave strut, and eyed attentively every body that would notice him. He had in his company two English bantams, with their bantlings. The gigantic Casuar showed himself very complaisant and attentive to his little companions, and looked down c 1 the ground at every strut he made; as if he was apprehensive lest he should crush any of his little chucking companions.

At another visit to LINNÆUS I showed him a very rare shell, both halves of which were remarkable for their *cameræ*. As it seemed new and unknown to him, I gave him a specimen, to which I added a still greater curiosity, namely a well-dried original of the *Asteria Columnaris*, so remarkable among the petrifications. He refused at first to accept of these small presents, unless I would take some others in return from his own collections, and proposed to me to take a ride with him to his villa at *Hammarby*.

This excursion however did not take place. At another visit our conversation turned again upon mineralogy. I showed him a rough

and.

and perfectly crystalized ruby, which I had received at *Copenhagen* of Mr. CAPPEL, to whom Dr. KOENIG had sent it from *Ceylon;* its uncommon sexagonous blunted columnar form quite struck him, having never before seen any thing of the kind. I collected afterwards many more species of this class, some of which were still greater curiosities. I stood indebted to a fatal catastrophe for the acquisition of these treasures; namely to the ship of Admiral SIR HYDE PARKER, which was wrecked during the last American war on the coast of the Dutch settlements, and the cargo of which was sold at *Amsterdam.*

I presented to the sight of LINNÆUS a curiosity, still newer and more interesting to him. This was the opal called *Oculus mundi.* He freely owned that he had never seen it, and borrowed the account which is inserted in his system from WALLERIUS's mineralogy. In my opinion, I was the only one at that time, who was positively acquainted with the nature of this stone.—" I envy you," exclaimed the venerable LINNÆUS, " the possession of a gem, which has hitherto " exclusively been preserved in the British Museum*; and I have not " now the least doubt respecting the genuine reality of this extraordi- " nary opal of which you have given me an account some years ago."— Every shadow of doubt was effectually removed, when I showed him the very opal itself, which is the mother of the most beautiful and rarest oculus mundi. His joy and satisfaction was also farther increased, when I laid before him the *rainbow coloured agate* which I also discovered, and the brilliancy of whose colours surpass the most beautiful gems of the East. Enraptured with admiration at the beauty of

* Sir HANS SLOANE gave five hundred pounds for two of those gems, which are not larger than a pea.

this

this stone, LINNÆUS began in a strain of enthusiastic language to expatiate on the magnificence and grandeur of the Creator.—" *Theologia* " *Naturalis,*" exclaimed he, " *est vera Philosophia*: or *Nature best pro-* " *claims a God, &c.*"

Time finally bereft me of the exquisite delight, which I should have experienced, had I been at liberty to enjoy any longer the conversation of this great man. I returned to *Stockholm,* where Count SCHEFFER presented me to the late King. His MAJESTY was graciously pleased to discourse with me upon the *Oculus mundi* which I had discovered, and even to make experiments on the changes of colours.

When I went the next day to take leave of Count SCHEFFER, he presented me, in his MAJESTY's name, with two gold medals. " LINNÆUS," added he, " complains of you to me, for having made " too short a stay at *Upsal.* The opinion which he entertains of you " may be collected from the answer which he returned to the enquiri_s " of two of my friends at *Stockholm**."

My return by the *Baltic* to *Courland* was far from being a pleasant one, as the winter season had then begun to set in. But the remembrance of the happy hours which I passed in *Sweden,* made me forget all the inconvenience of my voyage;—and this remembrance will always continue precious and dear to my reflexion!

---

* These answers were written on two cards ; one of them contained these word· ·
" Dominum E. C. SCHULTZ.
ex professo Curiosum et Mineralogum pulcherrime differentem de lapidibus; cum oblectamento exaudivimus.
CARL VON LINNE.

The second card bore :
Quo, quantoque ardore fervet in scientiam Mineralogicam Clarissimus E. C. SCHULTZ, non latebit quemquam, qui brevi tempore ejus conversatione utitur.
CARL VON LINNE.

BIOGRAPHICAL

BIOGRAPHICAL ANECDOTES,

FROM THE

LIFE OF LINNÆUS,

AS RELATED BY HIMSELF.

[*Extracted from the Latin Diary of* DR. GIESEKE.]

––––––––––

" DABO tibi plantas *Lapponicas*, inter alia mihi. dixit, quum fami-
" liariter aliquando cum ipso colloquerer, Non enim cuivis volupe est;.
" adscendere nives et per pedes iter facere 32 milliarum Suec. ubi
" nullus equus incedere potest, ibique pane et sale ex. solo lacte ran-
" giferino et pisciculo vivere."

Quum in *Lapponia* iter facerem, facies obtegenda erat panno reticu-
lato quem vocant *Flor*, propter,.ingentem culicum copiam ; quod si.
omittis, sub quavis inspiratione aliquot culices tibi sunt exspuendi,.
Lappones faciem et manus pice (liquida?) illinunt, ut ab eorum punc-
turis tuti sint. Ea vero copia ipsorum avibus migratoriis in escam
cedit, illæque iterum *Lapponibus.* Quippe per 12-14 dies ripas fluvii
legi, cujus latitudo quater superavit diametrum urbis *Upsaliæ,* eumque

3.   totum,.

totum, quantum longitudine et latitudine, coopertum anseribus anati-
bus, &c. vidi, adeo, ut non nisi sclopetis opus sit *Lapponibus*, ut per
æstatem partemque hyemis earum carne vivant et recenti et fumigato.

Die XXIV. Junii, (1771) quum me inviseret, narravit
fata sua hoc modo :

" Boerhavius fuit Cliffortii medicus ipsique dixit : nihil ad
" beatam vitam tibi deest, nisi Medicus, qui tecum sit quotidie, quum
" sæpe epuleris et malo hypochondriaco labores, qui diætam tuum ordi-
" net, &c. et si quid majoris momenti accidat, me consulet. Vellem
" quidem, Cliffortius inquit, talem habere si possem, sed ubi in-
" veniam ?—Est hic *Suecus*, quem eo fine tibi commendo, qui Botanicus
" simul, potest horti tui præfectus esse.—Fueram tunc apud Burman-
" num (Jo.) quem a Boerhaavio, salutarum, et tunc rogavit me :
" num vellem plantas videre ? quod prima vice, sub negotiorum præ-
" textu, roganti denegaverat."—" Quasnam videre vis ?"—Multas vellem, ego, quin omnes, sed non novi quales habeas? Porrigit is ali-
quam, et " est rarissima," inquit. Petii unum florem, quem ore emol-
litum examino, et pro Lauri specie declaro. " Non est Laurus, ait
" Burmannus,"—Attamen est Laurus, inquam, et quidem Cinnamomum. " Est Cinnamomum" respondit ; tunc eum auctoribus convici,
esse generis Lauri et sic cum pluribus. Tum ille : " Vis me adjuvare
" in *opera Zeylanico ?* et habitatio tibi parata erit mecum." Hoc ego
accipio et interea Boerhaavius me commendat Cliffortio, ad
quem cum Burmanno *Hartecampum* invitatus, videmus ibi Biblio-
thecam ejus, inque ea Burmannus invenit Tomum II. dum Sloanei
quem nondum conspexerat. Cliffortius : *habeo bis*, dixit, *et dabo
tibi, si mihi* Linnæum *concesseris*. Tandem res meo arbitrio relin-

quitur,

quitur, et ego eligo CLIFFORTIUM qui 1000 *florenos* pro annuo salario cum domo et mensa offert, nec unquam beatior vixi! Quum hortum intravimus, ducor ad hybernaculum, ubi plantæ erant ignotæ, imprimis e Bonæ *Spei*. Has ego post examen partim indico, partim pro novis deblaro, quo CLIFFORTIUS lætatus est.

Dum sic per annum circiter vixi, animum incessit cupido *Angliam* videndi. Propono CLIFORTIO et consentit; convenerat, ut octiduum modo manerem; et uno die iter, itemque uno reditum absolvi posse credidi, sed tantundem (octiduum) in ipso itinere *Roterdamo Londinum* consumsi. Dum MILLERUM, *(Phil.)* cujus præcipue causa veneram, convenio, ostendit is hortum *Chelseanum*, et usque tunc receptis utitur nominibus, v. g. Symphytum, quæ consolida major, &c. Ego sileo. Altero die dixit: *Botanicus ille* CLIFFORTII *ne unicam quidem plantam novit!*—Quod quum rescivi et iterum ipsum adeo, continuat (iisdem nominibus uti;) tum ego: " Non sic appelles, sint nobis certa nomina " brevioraque; sic dicendum est." Tunc irascebatur et morosus dein factus est." Jam ego plantas cupiebam pro horto CLIFFORTII, et quum redii, erat *Londini*, nec nici vespera rediit; bono tum animo fuit, et se daturum promisit quæ rogabam fecitque, quas ego CLIFFORTIO misi et *Oxonium* petii.

Ad DILLENIUM accedens, ibi reperio alium, cui is dixit: *Hic est, qui totam Botanicam confundit.* Hæc quidem verba intellexi, sed non videbaí. Dein per hortum obambulans cum ambobus (erat autem alter ille JACOBUS SHERARD,) video *Antirrhinum minus* quod tunc nondum conspexeram, DILLENIUMQUE rogo: quæ sit?—Hoc tu ignoras? inquit.—Si licet florem sumere, dicam mox, ego.—Sumas;—et dixi. Tertio die, quum viderem, non mutari DILLENIUM, et quum meæ

.opes

opes ad finem vergerent, rogavi, ut vehiculum pro me curaret per servum, crastino die *Londinum* redituro, quum linguam non intelligerem. Misit; et ego: Unicum hunc, inquam, favorem a te peto, explices, cur nuper ea verba dixeris? Negavit explicationem; sed quum instarem, " adscendas mecum" dixit et tunc *Genera Plantarum*, quorum dimidiam partem GRONOVIUS ipse me inscio miserat, promit; in omni fere pagina erat *NB.*—Quid hoc fibi vult?—Tot *falsa genera, quot notæ in tuo libro!*—Ego contendo, non falsa esse, aut si essent, doceret ipse, et mutarem lubenter.—Vide jam in horto, respondit, e prioribus unam, et sumsit *Blitum*, quod stamina tres habere ipse cum aliis dixerat; aperui florem, et reperi unum.—O hoc forte in uno flore aberrat; et plures dum aperiebantur in quibus unum modo. Tum plura genera examinavimus, et semper fuit, uti scripseram. Miratus DILLENIUS dixit; jam tu non abibis, et retinuit per mensem, deditque quascunque plantas optavi vivas pro CLIFFORTIO qui magno cum gaudio me reducem accepit.

Sic vixi, donec Nostalgia me incessit, ideoque discessi a CLIFFORTIO, ut *Galliam* et inde patriam peterem. *Lugdunum Batavorum* quum venissem, obtulit ROYENUS 800 florenos, et ut hortum ex systemate sexuali disponerem voluit, qui hactenus secundum BOERHAAVII methodum erat dispositus; is autem munere botanices se abdicaverat, et ROYENUS in eum valde iratus factus, quod filiam petenti repulsan· dederit. Hoc ego nolui, qui BOERHAAVIO tantum non omnia debebam; seu absolute aliter disponi voluit hortum ROYENUS. Tunc faciamus, inquam, methodum, quæ nec BOERHAAVII nec mea sit, sed tua, et secundum eam plantas disponamus.—Placuit hoc ipsi et *sic orta est methodus* ROYENI, *quam ego scripsi, non ille ; (sed hoc publicari nolo).* Jam vero

1   iratus

iratus CLIFFORTIUS *Lugdunum* venit, et ursit, quod si pretio me reti-
nuissent *Belgæ,* ipse idem solvere potuisset; laboraram autem febre in-
termittente, et vix quum exire potui, Angli invitant, ut secum irem os-
treas comederem; persuasere, ut unicam sumerem et unum cyathum
vini generosi haurirem. Sequenti die Cholera atrocissima correptus,
BOERHAAVIUS exhibit Laudanum, quod non, nisi vitæ periculum in-
stitisset, sumsissem, et intra 24 horas deglutivi drachmas aliquoit ac
restitutus fui. Sed adeo debilis fui, ut quotidie gtt. 1. olei Cinnam.
sumenda erat, alias vacillabam. In eo statu me invenit CLIFFORTIUS
et secum duxit *Hartecampum,* ubi per diem dedit monetam *Batavorum*
auream (ducat) et tectum victumque. Sed post duos menses iterum in-
gruit Nostalgia; et *Galliam* petii. Simulac Brabantiam attigi, eo ipso die
quasi revixi, et onus, quod antea incubuerat, subito evanuit, nec am-
plius oleo cinnamoni opus erat. Postquam parum temporis *Parisiis*
steti, *Rothomago (Rouen), Helsinburgum* petii, et intra quinque dies
appuli.

Jam redux, *Holmiæ* vixi ibidemque amicum sanavi intra quatuorde-
cimo dies a gonorrhoea, quam chiurgus, quo utebatur, intra annum sa-
nare non potuerat; et hinc plures ejus amicorum, qui vinum nullum
assumebant in prandiis, pectus infirmum sibi esse prætexentes. Sanati,
heroice bibebant; mirantur commilitones, et illi dicunt, me posse egregie mederi morbis pectoris. Vocor ad uxorem senatoris, quæ tussi la-
borabat; quam ex acrimonia oriri perspiciens, do *Trochiscos e Tragacan-
tha,* quæ involveret æria, ut semper scatulam secum haberet, iis reple-
tam. Bene ex iis habuit, et cum Regina ULRICA ELEONORA chartis
ludens, etiam sumsit ex iis. Quærit ex illa Regina: cur hoc faciat?—
Narrat, et me commendat ei, quæ et ipsa tussiebat. Idem præscribo,

et

et levatur. Tum Tessino innotui, qui interrogat : Num quid cupe-
rem e Comitiis? quæ tunc erant. Ego, nihil, inquam. Promittit se
effecturum.—Vacat munus medici classici, inquam, sed ego non ob-
tinebo, habebit alius (quem futurum rumor ajebat.) Sed is non habebit, respondit ille ; et post aliquot hebdomades ego accipio diploma.

Ibi vero occasionem habui per quinque annos noscendi morbos et
remedia per observationes et experimenta; dein usa hæc fuere, quum
genera morborum ederem ; quæ riserunt omnes et imprimisis Rosen;
sed aliquot annos post, *prælectiones in eadem habuit.*

ALIO DIE.

" Sed unde tot habes *Arabicas* plantas etiamnum, quum dudum obiit
Forskahl?—ego rogavi. Habeo aliunde, Linnæus respondit, ab
Italis, a Bassio, Monspeliensibus et aliis. Præsertim a Donati, cujus
historia singularis est. Misit eum Rex *Sardiniæ* in Orientem et *Alex-
andriam.* Is vero amatorius capitur ibi pulcherrima puella, quam obti-
nere non potuit, nisi fratrem ejus socium in itinere sibi jungeret. Id
facit, ut sororem obtineat ; ille vero totum mox thesaurum argenti se-
minumque Donati abstulit et aufugit in *Galliam.* Præ timore autem
ne Regi *Sardiniæ* traderetur, ulterius ivit *Byzantium,* postquam *Massilia*
omnia illa *ad me miserat semina,* in quibus aliquot egregia, *quamvis nunquam antea de me audiverat.* Donati autem naufragium faciendo periit
Jul. 11, 1763, natus 1732.

ALIO DIE.

" Certum est, quicquid Tartarum dentium non solvit, nec lithontrip-
" ticum erit. Nam tartarus dentium, tartarus Podagræ, Arthritidis, et
" Calculus sunt una eademque materia. Jam hæc vulgatiora in *Suecia,*

ac

" ac olim fuere; ergo vitium admittitur in diæta quodcunque antea ig-
notum. Sed quale? nondum constat. Forte in purificando Saccha-
" rum Calx admiscetur et hinc oritur."—Non potest, inquam, hæc causa
esse, quum omnis aqua *Goettingæ* calce plena sit et incrustet, calculum
non norunt tamen. Et aqua calcis remedium ad cum sit.—" Novi hoc,
" sed dubitavi, at illud de aqua Goettingensi singulare est."

Ego a juventute inde *multum laboravi tartaro dentium, parum curavi.*
At, a 1750, *malo ischiadico* tam vehementer corripiebar, ut vix possem
domum redire. Per septimi nychthemera somnum non novi præ dolore et fiebat intolerabilis; ergo opium volui assumere, sed impeditus
ab amico, qui accedebat ad octavam vesperis septimi, rogat me uxor:
num *Fraga* edere vellem? tentabo, inquam; erat circa initium temporis
istorum, et sapiebant. Dimidia hora post obdormivi in secundum noctis;
evigilans miror, dolorem non esse tam ferocem; rogo: num dormiis-
s .n? quod asseruere adsidentes vigiles. Num plura adessent Fraga?
—et reliqua comedi. Iterum obdormio in matutinas, et circa malleo-
lum erat dolor. Altero die tantum fragorum comedi, quantum potui,
et secundo mane expergefactus nullum dolorem sentio. Sphacelum
adesse credo, sed pars erat integra et surgere potui, quamvis debilis
essem. Sequenti anno circa idem fere tempus ridiit dolor, et tertio
quoque, sed mitior semper semperque *fragis* superatus est. Et ab eo
tempore liber fui. Non possum autem per hyemem ea servare, nec
ulla successit methodus, quum proximo jam die putrescent.

AN ACCOUNT

AN

ACCOUNT

GIVEN BY LINNÆUS HIMSELF,

OF

HIS TOUR THROUGH LAPLAND

AND

SOME OF HIS FIRST LITERARY LABOURS.

EXCERPTUM ex litteris Domini CAROLI LINNÆI ad Dominum ANDREAM CELSIUM, (qui itinere per *Germaniam* aliasque in posterum terras instituto, tunc *Berolini* versabatur) *Upsaliæ,* die 4 Januarii 1733 datis *.

" Non debui diutius morari, quin te, venerabilis CELSI, itineris meis Laponici, auctoritate et impensis Societatis Regiæ suscepti, paucis in antecessum certiorem faciam.—In tota mea profectione, a mense *Majo* usque ad *Octobrem* præteriti anni (1732) continuata, et *vel sexcentis periculis obnoxia,* 672 *milleari Suecica consumsi. Neque omne iter terra,* d mul tum *per mare et flumina institutum.* In montibus *Lapponicis* 150 *milliaria Suecica pedibus ivi.* Sub elevatione poli 70. grad. in ipso oceano septentrionali huc illuc navigando, per octiduum solem inocciduum vidi.

---

† Vide *Commercium Litterarium,* ad Rei Medicæ et Scientiæ Naturalis incrementum institutum, &c. Annus 1773. Hepdomas x, p. 73 et 74, *Norimberg.* 1733-4.

Per

Per orientale latus Sinus *Bothnici Upsaliam* reversus, in *Tawastia* sciu-rum volantem deprehendi.

Omne reditu meo tempus in conscribendam *Floram Lapponicam* im-pendi. Continebit hæc vegetabilia, in *Lapmarkiis* et jugis montium *Lapponicis* crescentia, novis nominibus et specierum synonymis, novo-rum generum characteribus, rariorum accuratis descriptionibus, planta-rumque nondum descriptarum figuris, una cum usu earundem apud Lappones œconomico et medico, locupletata.

Ante paucos dies hocce opus ad finem perduxi, 36 *plagulis* et 80 *figu-ris* constans. Jam tantum restat ejus in Latinam linguam translatio, quam proximo Paschatis tempore prelo paratam, D. V. promitto. In-terea temporis *ut editorem opusculo meo in Germania, vel alibi, procures, humiliter peto.*

Flora mea absoluta, *Lachesin Lapponicam* elaborandam aggredior. In i... de œconomia *Lapponum* agam, causas sanitatis et longævitatis eorum, simulque prærogativas hujus gentis præ aliis, indigitaturus. Quocirca non SCHEFFERUM, et alios rei *Lapponicæ* scriptores corrigere, sed quæ ipse vidi, fideliter et simpliciter referre lubet.

Probe quidem scio, neminem eorum juga montium. Lapponica æstatis tempore, transivisse. Miram convenientiam inter hosce montes Lapponicos et Alpinos deprehendi; adeo, ut omnes fere plantas, quæ non nisi in Alpibus florent, huc quoque invenerim.

Sane quam plurima, rem botanicam egregie illustrantia, reperiisse mihi videor. Tuo quoque desiderio satisfacturus, rebus œconomicis in itinere meo attendi.

Ipsa

Ipsa montium juga nullo modo vegetabilibus excoli possunt. Lap-markiæ enim omnes, tractibus plerumque arenosis abundantes, terra ni-gra carent. Nullibi idoneus agricolæ locus, nisi circa fluviorum ripas; quamvis id etiam difficillime. Hinc in *Lappmarkiis* vix centum dantur agricolæ, iique paupcrrimi, quia ventic, jugis montium provenientes, fri-gus semper, imo in ipsis diebus canicularibus, afferendo labores eorem non raro irritos reddunt. Speciem tamen segetis in *Lappmarkiis* et *Fin-markia Norwegica* sponte nascentem inveni, quæ in sola arena crescens frigore æstiva difficulter corrumpitur.

Societati Regiæ (Upsaliensi) indicem observationum mearum obtuli. E. gr. n. 21. in *Regno Minerali*, de metallo ferreo, quod magnes non attrahit. No 37. de alumine sponte confecto, in montibus Lulensibus. No. 56. de arena nigra martiali in omnibus fluviis contenta. No 61. de terra conchis referta, in sylvis Helsingicis. No. 24. vinis supra mare elevatis. No. 65. de saxo, quo juga montium Lapponicorum con .t. No. 66. de saxo seminifero Lapon. Tomasii. No. 100 de 32 speciebus mineralium Lappon. No. 106. de œconomia mira Purkiijauri.

In *Regno Vegetabili*: No. 19. de 23 specibus salium, maximam par-tem incognitis. No. 24. de modo, lectum sibi commodum in sylvis ex tempore adornandi. No. 29. de gramine, omne frigus arcente. No. 40. de quadam vegetabili esca vaccarum, butyrum colore creceo im-buente. No. 44. de philtro Lapponis. No. 77. de moxa Lapponum. No. 78. de vegetabili, lac, instar casei, sine coagulatione, condensante.

In *Regno Animali*: No. 35. historia avis Carolinæ. No. 41. de pisce *Selsensogd*, hactenus non descripto. No. 54. historia insecti, pellem Rangiferi terebrantis.

u h h 2   In

In *Oeconomicis :* No. 104 de decem panis speciebus usitatis a Norlandis et Fennonibus, annona laborantibus. No. 156. de speciebus lactis Westrobotniensium. No. 205. de tempestatum prognosi, quam Fennones a cornicibus ducunt. No. 206. de Lapponum compasso triplicis generis.

A SUMMARY

A

SUMMARY VIEW

OF THE

BOTANICAL REFORMS OF LINNÆUS,

———————

PARTES Plantarum haud satis indagatæ erant; in has igitur LIN-
NÆUS sollicitius inquisivit et defectum implevit *.

Stipulæ adeo parum erant observatæ, ut nunc primum obtinerent
nomina.

Pediculus antecessorum in·duas partes diversas, in *Petiolum* et *Pedun-
culum* est divisus, quem *Scapo* separabat, ut *Frondem* a folio; ne dicam
quod *Bracteas Thyrsum, Corymbum,* aliasque partes introduxerit.

Calyx in diversas species, ut in *Perianthium, Involucrum Glumam,
Amentum, Spatham, Calytram* et *Volvam* ab *Volvam* abiit.

Organea mellea, quibus sæpissime petala instruuntur, *Nectaria* dicta,
et ambo *Corollæ* nomine insignita sunt.

Stamina, novis nominibus, in *Filamentum* et   theram distinxit.

---

* V. Amœnitat. Academ. edit. SCHREBER, vol. vi. *Erlang.* 1789, page 312, seq.

Pistillum

Pistillum in tres partes divisit, quarum superior *Stigma*, inferior *Germen*, media vero *Styli* nomen retinuit, eliminato *Tubæ* seu *Vaginæ* nomine.

Pericarpium dicebatur antiquorum fruŭus, par scilicet illa, quæ semina includit.

Distinŭionem determinavit inter *Siliquam*, *Legumen*, *Pomum*, *Baccam* et *Drupam*, quæ antea fruŭtu carnoso aut succulento innotuerant.

In semine sæpe observavit tegumentum quoddam speciale, quod *Arillus* dicebatur.

Veterum Placenta vel basis floris compositi nomen *Receptaculi communis* sibi nunc vindicavit, quod in *Umbellam* aliarum et in Cymam aliarum divisum est.

II.

Termini Artis apud Auŭores partim insufficientes, partim promiscue sumti erant; itaque eos, qui decrant, addere, et omnes ita definire e re erat, ne huc illucque varie distraherentur. Ad hunc finem obtinendum, primas lineas *Systematis foliorum* in *Horto Cliffertiano* duxit in *Philosophia Botanica* (cap. 3. et 4.) auxit, et *in System. Natur.* adhuc completiores reddidit, ubi termini etiam ad alias partes plantarum extendebantur *.

III.

Sexus Plantarum æque pulchre a VAILLANTIO determinatus, ac misere fuit a *Pontedera* impugnatus, hic etiam accuratius expendebatur, velut nucleus totius floris, cui etiam *Systema Sexuale* fuit superstruŭum.

---

* Nova Auŭoris vocabul· erant *Neŭarium*, *Stigma*, *Germen*, *Drupa*, *Braŭea*, *Scapus*, *Arillus*, *Cyma*, *Stipula*. usitata *Filamentum*, *Anthera*, *Stylus*, *Pericarpium*, *Perianthium*, *Spatha*. Distinŭa vero antea synonyma *Petiolus et Pedunculus Soliqua et Legumen*.

Hoc vero opus fuit infiniti fere laboris; nam non tantum *Genera* singula, verum etiam singulæ *Species* erant examinandæ ad *Stamina* et *Pistilla*, antea adeo contemta et nihili æstimata, ut pro partibus excrementitiis haberentur. Hoc facinus utut varii primum nimiam subtilitatem sapere judicabant, nec naturam in his minutissimis partibus conformem et constantem augurabantur, attamen nunc nullus exstat Botanicus, qui unius quidem generis charaßerem certum formare potest, nisi tam accuratam habuerit staminum et pistillorum ideam, quam unquam frußus aut corollæ.

IV.

Charaßeres Generici antea ita erant construßi, ut vix generibus cognitis dignoscendis sufficerent, quam ob causam, deteßo novo quodam genere, mutandi erant vicinorum generum charaßeres, præterquam quod in qualibet methodo dissimiles essent. Charaßeres igitur perpetuos indagare, hoc opus erat, hic labor; et quia omnes Botanici solide eruditi, Fundamentum Frußificationis, atque adeo partem quandam frußificationis pro Fundamento agnoscere debent, e novo confeßi sunt omnes charaßeres a Numero, Figura, Situ et Proportione omnium Frußificationis partium, adeo constantes, ut omnibus methodis, vel jam adoptatis vel postmodum eligendis inservire queant.

V.

Species, non tantum generibus suis subjeßæ sunt, verum etiam ut distinguerentur a se invicem, omnibus ac singulis novæ adjeßæ *Differentiæ,* antecessorum nominibus specificis omnibus rejeßis. Nam id agebatur, ut adsumtis in diffentiam notis ssimis, a congeribus

species

species quæstionis, ea qua fieri posset brevitate, sed sufficienter tamen, dignosceretur, ne ad quamvis speciem, Auctorum descriptiones et figuræ, non raro insufficientes, evolvere opus esset.

VI.

Varietates idem jus cum suis speciebus quondam possederant, a quibus solum proprietatibus accidentalibus differebant ; nunc igitur proscriptæ speciebus adjectæ sunt, unde numerus specierum dimidio factus minor.

VII.

Loca Natalia, de quibus altum fuit silentium apud plerosque, nisi in nomine specifice plantarum adjecta, diligentius investigari cœpere et speciebus subjici. Hisce dein Fundamentum Culturæ plantarum inædificabatur, præter illud commodum, quod planta quælibet quæsita, per semen aut specimen, e loco natali facile obtineretur.

VIII.

Descriptiones Plantarum hujusque stilo oratorio, vel pomposis verbis confectæ, totas paginas implebant ; jam vero ulta substantiva ex nominibus partium, et adjectiva ex vocabulis terminorum, se extendere prohibentur, omnibus verbis inanibus exclusis, ut *quot verba, tot pondera,* evaderent.

IX.

Nomina Trivialia tandem 1755 primum accesserunt, quæ mirum in modum scientiam facilitabant, et hisce pistillum quasi additum est campanæ ; cognitis enim . · unaquæque planta æque commode nominari

2   potest

potest ac proponi. Antea autem, ad quamlibet plantam determinandam, recitanda erat tota differentia, maximo cum memoriæ, linguæ et pennæ negotio.

X.

Ordines Naturales depromebantur, eisque sua adsignabantur genera, quotquot obtineri poterant, etsi multa forte secula requirantur, priusquam perfecta naturalis methodus eruatur. Interim hi ordines, tanquam speculum omnium methodorum in affinitatibus et ut lapis lydius in viribus plantarum dijudicandis, adhiberi possunt.

XI.

In *Usum* Plantarum, tam *Oeconomium* quam *Medicum* curatius cœptum est inquiri. Ad Œconomicum *Rajus* fere solus inter Botanicos attenderat, jam vero observationibus et itineribus LINNÆI multum crevit. Medicina autem, seu *Materia Medica* clariori nunc splendere cœpit lumine, fundamentis firmis superstructa, dum *Sapor* et *Odor*, una cum *Ordinibus Naturalibus*, in fundamentum assumta sunt.

XII.

Tandem ad *Proprietates Plantarum* est perventum, quæ subjecta sunt penitiori disquisitioni. Exempla in *Gemmationes, Metamorphosin, Prolepsin, Sponsalia, Somnum et Vernationem Plantarum, Calendaria et Horologia Floræ* nos ducunt, passimque in *Oeconomiam* et *Politiam Naturæ*, ubi *Pan* et *Pandora* per viridantia Floræ prata pecora sua agunt et pascunt; quamvis hæc quasi ostia reserata videntur, per quæ in posterum Botanici ad immensa Naturæ Theatra irent, dum præsens

ætas

ætas adhuc in litteris et elementis Botanicis hæret. Primum enim est, sibi tam familiares reddere plantas, ut nomine, omnibus perspicuo, speciem quamcunque primo intuitu dignoscere queamus, et profecto, in tanta confusione et mixturo rerum naturalium, primo intuitu quamcunque plantam oblatam, licet antea non visam, nomine, per totum orbem intelligibili, nominare, naturamque ejus ex Fructificatione cognoscere, res non levis censenda est, quam certe veterum nullus possibilem judicasset.

NOTES

REFERENCES

AND

EXPLANATORY NOTES.

————

WITH the following farther elucidations and illustrations of certain passages of this biography the author has been favoured, by several persons of literary eminence, who contributed to this work. Though he obtained them at a time when the printing had for the most part been completed, yet the valuableness of their contents induces him to communicate them verbatim to the reader.

The first part of these notes come from Dr. SCHREBER of *Erlangen*, President of the Imperial Academy of Naturalists at *Vienna*.

————

N. B.—*To each note is prefixed the number of the page to which it relates.*

PAGE 7.

THE father of LINNÆUS took the resolution of binding his son an apprentice to a shoemaker, at the persuasion of those persons, who for want of penetration, gave it as their opinion that the latter was not endowed with such parts as would ever qualify him for any learned

profession.

profession. They grounded this judgment upon the little progress which young LINNÆUS had then made in Latin. His proficiency in this language was certainly far from being considerable ; and it so happened merely because he felt no inclination of learning it from those books, which were assigned to him for that purpose. No sooner, however, had ROTHMANN directed him to read PLINY, than his progress became most rapid ; because the contents of that author corresponded entirely with his own natural propensity. To this circumstance may be ascribed his predilection for PLINY, and likewise the laconism of his style.

P ‹ 2.›

Of the first volume of OL. RUDBECK's *Campi Elysii,* no more than three copies were preserved, one of which is at *Oxford* and two in *Sweden.* Several copies of the second volume were extricated from the flames ; but they are become a rarity. Those of the wood-cuts of the first volume and some others which were saved, have since been reprinted by the care of Dr. J. E. SMITH.

PAGE 24.

When LINNÆUS gave lectures for OL. RUDBECK, he composed a catalogue of the plants which he saw in the Swedish gardens, especially in those of *Upland.* This work is entituled : CAROLI LINNÆI, M. B. et Z. C. ? R. Hortus *Uplandicus,* sive enumeratio stirpium, quæ in variis hortis Uplandiæ, imprimis autem in horto botanico publico Upsaliensi coluntur, nec non quæ in agris feruntur; Methodo propria. in classes distributa. *Upsal,* M.DCC.XXX. seventy-four pages in octavo, besides a ‹plan› of garden of the palace at *Upsal,* a preface in Swedish, and an index. This catalogue has never been printed,

printed, notwithstanding its having been originally intended for publication. On the back of the title of the manuscript is a dedication to . RUDBECK the patron of LINNÆUS. He says in the preface, that he wrote the work, by the desire of his audience, to save them the trouble of writing down the names of plants, perhaps erroneously, during his demonstrations. He also speaks in it with praise of his father's garden at *Stenbrohull*, on account of the great number of rare plants contained in it. LINNÆUS had, therefore, already laid the foundation to his system, at least in 1729. But the system according to which he wrote his *Hortus Uplandicus*, is only a rough sketch, widely different from the subsequent arrangement, as well in the lasses of which he counts twenty-one, and in their names. He refers on this account to his *Nuptiæ Plantarum*, and apologizes for not having given any *Differentiæ Specificæ* of the plants, which he promises to do in the second edition. I have this work in my possession in the author's own manuscript.

Thus it appears, that the said Nuptiæ Plantarum were written before the year 1730. I have also a copy of it in the author's own handwriting, which has been written at a later period. It is entituled CAROLI LINNÆI Alumni Wrediani Extraord. M. C. Nuptiæ Plantarum, in quibus Systema Vegetabilium Universale a *Staminibus* et *Pistillis*, sive *sexu*, desumtum, secundum classes, sectiones, et nomina generica brevissime proponitur. *Stockholmiæ*, 1733, one sheet, in octavo. (Compare this with the note, page 319 and 320). That this latter work does not contain the first plan, but is full of alterations, appears from its great concordance, with the first edition of the *System* of *Nature*, in which the table exhibiting the animal reign, agrees with the le pamphlet, except a few trifling passages. The system itself has or wenty-three classes..

I received.

I received both manuscripts of the late professor Lange at *Halle*, who was a special friend and correspondent of Linnæus, and formerly my own teacher.

PAGE 56.

Conrad Gesner himself died without issue, but at his death there remained alive of Andrew Gesner, his father's brother, *one hundred and thirty-five* descendants in children, grand-children, and great-grand-children. From the latter are decended the present family of the Gesner's, one of whom as a poet, is universally known by his *Death* of *Abel* and his beautiful pastorals. See Simleri Oratio de Vita C. Gesneri. *Tigur.* 1566, quarto.

PAGE 57.

The Egyptian Herbarium of Prosper Alpinus is in the library of the University of *Leyden.* It consists of four volumes in folio, classed after the Linnæan method, and described with the Linnæan names.

PAGE 58.

The voyage of Don Hernandez has not yet appeared completely. It consisted of ten, others say of twelve, and others of fifteen complete volumes in manuscript, which are still in the library of the *Escurial.* That part of the work which has been published, consists only of extracts, and many notes are added to it by the publisher.

PAGE 62.

The preface of Linnæus to his *Bibliotheca Botanica* is dated by him as early as August 8. 1735.

PAGE 63.

BELON, RAUWOLF and others, had already travelled through the other parts of the world, and CLUSIUS also obtained from *North America* many of the natural curiosities collected by Sir FRANCIS DRAKE in his voyage round the world. The garden at *Kew* was first arranged by order of the Princess Dowager of WALES, the aunt mother of his MAJESTY, now reigning.

PAGE 65.

LINNÆUS, as he frequently told his pupils, never ceased to esteem RAY, as one of the most penetrating observers of the natural affinity of plants.

PAGE 69.

TOURNEFORT found an opponent long before VAILLANT his pupil, in PETER MAGNOL, of *Montpellier*, formerly his professor, whose *Character Plantarum* was not printed till 1720.

PAGE 86.

LINNÆUS was the four hundredth and sixty-fourth member of the Imperial Academy of Naturalists. He was received on the third of October, 1736, by the name of DIOSCORIDES II. Dr. ANDREW CLEYER born at *Cassel*, afterwards first physician at *Batavia*, and a member of the great council there, received the honourable title of DIOSCORIDES I. of that learned body, and professor JOHN BURRMANN at *Amsterdam*, was chosen in 1740, by the appellation of DIOSCORIDES III.

342 NOTES.

PAGE 97.

EHRET was a Palatine by birth. When he first began to draw for
LINNÆUS he gave himself no trouble about the number of stamina
and pistilla; but the instructions which were given him afterwards pros-
pered so well in his productions, that he could anatomize the plants in a
very short time, and in the finest and most delicate manner.

PAGE 116.

The principal cause of the indifference which Baron HALLER testified
with regard to LINNÆUS, is to be found in all kinds of tell-tale reports
of acts or words of LINNÆUS, by which he was stated to have expressed
how little esteem he had for HALLER. But these reports were frequently
the work of misconstruction, wilful malice, or fiction. By such scandal
how often have not the learned been exasperated and embittered against
one another? Perhaps more than one enemy of the good LINNÆUS
had recourse to those vile arts of prejudicing him in the mind of the
Baron, who was not always strongly enough upon his guard, to treat
such insinuations with the contempt which they so justly merited. One
of these enemies waited once upon Baron HALLER about the time when
this coolness first began to manifest itself between him and LINNÆUS,
and intimated to the Baron, that LINNÆUS made it his business to tra-
duce him (HALLER); and to make good his assertion, the base slan-
derer added, that LINNÆUS had assigned a disgraceful place to the
portrait of HALLER, almost behind the door of the hall where he kept
the portraits of the botanists. The insinuations of this calumniator are
said to have operate most forcibly upon the mind of the Baron to the
prejudice of LINNÆUS.

That

That the hall of the latter contained the portraits of many botanists in different forms and sizes, is a fact which cannot be denied. But they were not fitted up according to their rank and pre-eminence, but placed so, as to produce the best effect upon the eye. For instance, the portraits of RUDBECK and GMELIN, painted in oil, and of a very large size, were facing the principal entry ; LINNÆUS's portrait, also large, and executed in the same manner, was suspended sidewards to the left, near a door, &c. Had even HALLER's portrait been exposed near the principal door, its position ought solely to have been attributed to its size, to symmetry, or to some other circumstances of a similar description. Thus operated the most insignificant trifles ;—thus was LINNÆUS calumniated, and HALLER deceived!

PAGE 119.

The younger Baron HALLER had been ensnared to write against LINNÆUS. He assured the latter afterwards, *that he was sorry to have written against him.* What a fine triumph of truth and justice for LINNÆUS! But this was not the only one; even SIEGESBECK, his first and most inveterate enemy, likewise intreated him in a letter " *to forgive the injury he had done him, and to exert his interest to procure* " *him the place of keeper of the botanical garden at Upsal.*"

The latter part of his request could not, for many reasons, be granted, although SIEGESBECK well understood the cultivation of plants.

PAGE 137.

The *Heisteria* of L   æus (afterwards *Polyga Heisteria)* is a bush with spiny leaves, but otherwise not of an unpleasant appearance.

K k k   The

The *Siegesbeckia Orientalis* is quite a beautiful plant, The *Adansonia digitata* is one of the finest and tallest trees, with an elegant flower. The *Pontederiæ* are also neat looking plants, with handsome flowers.

PAGE 181.

KALM made likewise an extensive tour in *Russia*, at his own expence. These travels have not yet completely appeared, though the author is dead. A Swedish literatus at *Abo* has been charged with publishing in an abridgement that part which remains unprinted. But he has, not yet performed the task assigned to him.

PAGE 195.

The doctrine of LINNÆUS, respecting the bastard-species in the vegetable reign, has enabled the celebrated M. KOELREUTER at *St. Petersburgh*, to produce a vast number of bastard-plants, and even to change one species into another, by means of an artificial fructification. See *Nova Acta Academiæ Petropolitanæ.*

PAGE 208.

It is a matter of the highest regret, that the *Icones Specierum Plantarum* CAROL LINNÆI, of which the Margravine CAROLINA LOUISA of *Baden* projected a publication, has never appeared. The Princess did not like execution of the work, which was interrupted by the return of the French artists, whom she employed, to their country. No more than one hundred and thirty-eight plates were finished, and even these never presented to the public. LINNÆU. . . oured the memory of the Margravine by the genus of the CARO. . LA. The first species

z   or or *Carolinea Princeps* has been inserted by Aublet, in his *Histoire des Plantes de la Guianne Francaise*, plate 291 and 292, and the second species, or *Carolinea* insignis, in the *Monadelphæ* of Cavanilles, tab. 154.

FINIS.

in

p 113

137
123
25
24

I

www.ingramcontent.com/pod-product-compliance
Lightning Source LLC
Chambersburg PA
CBHW052342110726
47901CB00005B/1326